CHAPTER 2

A couple of days after the storm, while he was in town for groceries, Gable went a little out of his way to drive past the house with white columns, half hoping to catch sight of the girl who talked to angels.

More than the other local characters Jennifer had mentioned, the girl intrigued him. He wasn't sure why. Might there be a possibility of using Dareena as the basis for a fictional character? He'd had a girlfriend once who'd berated him for thinking of everything in terms of a story, but he had to. He'd always wanted to be a writer. As a child, he'd had a habit of writing captions to the pictures in his coloring books to make his own stories, even when his mother had to spell the words for him. His imagination carried him along. His mind toyed with the events around him, manipulating them into patterns of understanding.

Writing was his way of coping with the world, with the confusion and the stress. It had seen him through many unhappy times. It was an escape, but it was also something more. Sometimes he thought it was a curse, because it impelled him to search for reason where none seemed to exist.

The world was not just black and white. Sifting through the gray was a burden.

Set back off the street, the old white house had an eerie look. Some ominous presence seemed to hang over it.

As he eased his car past, Gable searched the windows for a glimpse of the girl or some sign of the grandmother peering through the curtains. He found neither, and wondered where they were.

The house might even have been empty, but it remained immaculate. The lawn was neatly landscaped—the St. Augustine grass a green carpet across the ground—and flowers were beginning to bloom in some beds that bordered the front porch.

On the porch itself there were rocking chairs, and there were also chairs on the terrace-porch on the second floor, providing a vantage point for the women to watch cars passing, or perhaps to view the decay of the neighborhood. Across from the house were some crumbling warehouses and down the street, the shells of failed businesses.

The upper porch was smaller, railed with ornate woodwork. There wasn't anyone up there now. There were no shadows at the upstairs windows, no flutter of curtains.

Nowhere was there any sign of the occupants of the house. It was as if they were in hiding, somehow aware a spy was attempting to penetrate their privacy. Feeling like a motorist rubbernecking at a traffic accident, Gable drove on along the street.

He had to travel several more blocks before he moved into the area benefiting from the downtown renewal effort.

There were a couple of blocks with new boutiques displaying the latest fashions and other businesses with fancy lettering on the doors. Awnings of brightly colored cloth hung out over the sidewalks. On one corner the tower of a

new hotel sparkled like the spire of a castle overlooking the countryside.

Cruising past it, Gable spotted the cathedral up ahead of him.

It was still a few more blocks down, a faded building showing signs of age, but still somehow elegant. Scaffolds had been constructed on one side, where some repairs were being made. Gable found a parking place a short distance away and walked back up to the vaulted entranceway.

Gable was Protestant, a Methodist. He wasn't sure why he felt drawn to the building. He'd attended Catholic services but had never felt any affinity for the worship.

Later he wondered if it was fate, or just coincidence that led him into the building, and finally decided it was the latter. He was thinking about religious icons associated with Dareena, and the church happened to be nearby.

Pulling the heavy wooden door open, he strolled into the dimly lit interior of the sanctuary.

The air was cool, and the sunlight that streamed in through the stained glass windows had a violet tint. It brought a peaceful feeling. He looked up at one of the windows, into the eyes of a crucified Christ. There was a sad look in the eyes, a mourning for lost souls.

He stopped just a few steps inside the door to look up at the carvings that decorated the ceiling. Colors were reflected against them, producing ornate shadows.

Near the front of the room stood statues. Another depiction of a suffering Christ, this one of polished white stone, hung in front of a rose window, bathed in the sad colors.

Off in one corner stood a winged angel. Gable wasn't sure if it represented a particular angel or not. He didn't know much about angels.

23

He wondered if it was the one the girl talked to. The place wasn't that far from her home. It was possible she had visited, and the statue had planted the seed of her delusion.

The hand fell on his shoulder without warning. The priest must have approached from the confessional, but there had been no sound of footfalls. It was as if he'd come from nowhere. Gable saw the sign on the door now, displaying the hours confessions were heard. He'd strolled in in the middle of the period, but there were no sinners seeking redemption today.

"I'm sorry," the priest said. "I didn't mean to frighten you."

Gable drew a breath slowly, to regulate his breathing again. "It was just so quiet," he said. "And empty churches are sort of frightening anyway."

"Yes," the priest said, looking around. "I suppose they are. Awesome, eh?"

Gable smiled. "Yes."

The priest was a younger man than Gable might have expected to find here, perhaps somewhere in his late thirties. He had dark hair and a mustache, and his features were sharp, almost elflike.

"I was going to ask if there was something I could do for you, Mr. . . . ?" he said.

"Gable Tyler," Gable said, and shrugged. "I just wandered in, Father. I'm not a Catholic."

"My name is Joseph Conzenza. Your faith shouldn't be a barrier. Do you have some need?"

"Not spiritual."

"But something brought you in."

It was the kind of question salesmen used when they were trying to keep you in their stores, but Gable lifted his hands and let them fall to his sides. Priests were used to listening to confessions.

"I'm a writer," he said. "In search of a story." He drew a quick breath. "I heard about a young woman in town who talks to angels. That attracted my curiosity, and while I was driving around thinking about it, I happened on the church."

"Looking for angels?"

Gable laughed. "Not real ones. I think I was looking for meaning. Motivation is important in stories."

The priest looked at Gable, considering the answer. His eyes were dark and piercing. Folding his arms, he reached up to his chin with one hand.

"As it happens, you wandered right into her path."

"She comes here?"

"She's been here. To tell me about the angel, to see what I thought."

"And?"

"Well, I didn't really speak to her in confidence, so I suppose I could tell you. You won't use my name in this story? No one would come to confession if that were to occur." He smiled.

"I'm not even sure I'll write a story."

Putting his hand on Gable's shoulder, Conzenza led him through a side door that opened onto a corridor.

The office was at the end of the hall, a narrow room lined with book shelves. A large mahogany desk was positioned to one side with some chairs facing it.

Gable sat down in one of the dark leather chairs, glancing across the book titles—they were varied, many of Catholic origin but others were from presses of different denominations. Titles by Malcolm Muggeridge and Francis Shaffer shared the space. A C. S. Lewis paperback rested on the priest's desk, its spine cracked from use. On top of it was a new Andrew M. Greeley paperback.

Quietly the priest settled into his desk chair, and sat with his palms pressed together in front of his face. "Her name is Dareena Winston," he said. "She's a lovely young woman."

Gable must have given him a funny look, because he chuckled. "Priests are allowed to make those observations," Conzenza said.

Gently he drummed his fingers together, his brow wrinkling as he searched his memory.

"She calls the angel she speaks to Azarius," he said.

"Is there a biblical reference to such an angel?"

"Not specifically. It's from what you'd know as the Apocrypha, the Book of Tobit. But it's not the name of an actual angel. It's a guise that the archangel Raphael assumes in order to help a man. He guides him and eventually leads to the binding of an evil spirit. Some scholars believe it was a demon."

"So what does that mean?"

The priest shook his head. "It means she picked up the name somewhere, I suppose. Her grandmother, I believe, is very devout with a wide range of beliefs. That may have something to do with it. She may have heard mention of the name and somehow incorporated it into her imagination."

"You believe it's her imagination?"

"Perhaps so. Perhaps an hallucination. I haven't spoken with her extensively, but I don't sense her to be out of touch with reality."

"She's not really talking to an angel? I mean, in your church aren't there documented cases of visions or something?"

"I don't believe her case is one of those," Conzenza said. "Writers invoke the muses. Ever talked to them?"

"No."

26

"I don't think angels are there for us to talk to. The cases you're referring to, I assume, are about Our Lady of Fatima, and that's not the same as what this girl has experienced. The Fatima vision came to a group of shepherd children. Recently visions have occurred in Medjugorje, Yugoslavia. If I did believe this girl was having actual visions, I would have the Vatican send an investigator. These things have to be documented." There was just a touch of sarcasm in his voice, indicating a wry humor.

"What sort of things does the angel tell her?"

"I'm not sure. Probably a combination of whatever her grandmother has picked up from the Bible and supermarket tabloids. You'd be surprised at how many people's faith comes from that sort of thing, an amalgamation. I can't offhand recall specifics about Dareena, however. I tend to dismiss what she says."

"Is she in need of help?"

"I've tried suggesting it. She declines. I will say there are people less sane than she is walking the streets."

"I find it intriguing. I don't suppose it's unique?"

"No. People often think they're in contact with angels. There's a story of a doctor who's summoned to help a woman by a little girl. He assumes it's her daughter and goes to her side, ultimately saving her life. But when she asks how he knew she was ill, and he reports that her daughter summoned him, the woman says her daughter has been dead for over a year. Many say the girl is an angel assuming human form."

"Like Azarius, or Raphael?"

"To a degree. But that story is what you'd call an urban legend. It could also be considered a ghost story, depending on the perspective. Dareena's angel isn't quite like that. It's more of a personal mentor, almost like a child's imaginary friend. Have you heard of spirit guides?"

27

"From what? Meditation?"

"Yes. Some people believe those aren't products of the imagination, but are guardian angels."

"I guess people are all looking for security."

"Perhaps they are looking for God. Are you a religious man?"

"I believe in God."

"But not angels."

"I've never thought about it that much."

"Well, there's not a great deal mentioned about angels."

Gable looked at his watch. The afternoon was creeping away.

"I guess I'd better be going," he said.

Conzenza rose and showed Gable to the door.

"It's been nice talking to you," he said. "So often I'm hearing problems. This was rather refreshing."

"It was informative," Gable said. "Azarius?"

"Yes. It has a ring to it, doesn't it?"

Gable made his way back down the corridor and through the sanctuary. The colored rays of sunlight spilled across his face. He paused a moment to look again at the statues.

The angel was female. It must not have been the one the girl talked to.

Turning, he found the door and went back to the car.

The eyes followed Gable's departure before glancing back to the church. The priest was there, unsuspecting.

He would be easy to kill, a quick strike when he could be captured alone. His resistance would be futile. He was not a strong man and would not be inclined to fight back. He had been taught peace and submission all his life. It had been drilled into him in the seminary. Yes, it would be easy to kill a priest.

Then it would be time for Jennifer. She would not be difficult either.

Lightning split the sky like silver cracks opening the blackness, and the wind swept sheets of rain through the air like waves on a restless sea.

Jennifer watched, clutched in the depths of darkness. It was not real, she sensed it was not real, and yet she could not escape it.

The darkness strangled her. She was struggling for each breath, gasping when the seconds of light provided by the lightning filled her consciousness. When it flashed, she drew in deep breaths. It was like being underwater and bobbing to the surface only every few seconds.

It was only a dream, yet it was painfully real. The same fear and agony she experienced during a storm was with her.

When had that fear begun?

She was suddenly aware that this was more than a dream. She was remembering. It was something long ago, something just outside the reach of her conscious mind, yet it was real. There was something about the rain that reminded her of a time of pain and fear.

She fought to find the reality hidden in the surrealistic shadows, but it was impossible. Something was holding it back. Some part of her brain knew that the terror would be too much for her to handle.

Still she struggled to grasp the memory. It was hidden there somewhere in the darkness.

As the lightning flickered, she searched for clues. She was not sure of where she was in this dream, but there was a nagging sensation of déjà vu.

When had she been here? How long ago? She had had the dream before, many times, but she could not recall when it had first come to her.

Had it been in college? She could remember her fear of the storms in those days, and in high school. Childhood was too far back.

Another flash of lightning illuminated the dreamdarkness and she saw the dust-covered planks of a rotting floor.

The image had no meaning for her. She gasped, more from frustration now than from the feeling of suffocation.

Another flicker of lightning revealed little else. There was nothing to give her any real clues. She was in a room that she had been in once before, a room where something bad had happened, but she couldn't figure out where it was.

It was an old house, obviously, but she had never gone into old houses.

The roar of thunder made her jump, just as it would have if it had been real.

That raised a new question. How did the storm tie into it all? Was it a part of the bad thing or did it simply serve to intensify the fear?

She swallowed and thrashed about, trying to pull herself out of the sleep that imprisoned her. There were no answers here, only anguish.

She remained in the darkness. Just wanting to wake up was not enough. It had never been enough. Somehow she sensed that there had been a time before when she had wanted to leave this place without being able.

Lightning again.

She tried to take in more of the room. She saw shadows, reflections of the rain splattering against a window somewhere over her head.

She gasped again. It was still hard to breathe. Something was making it hard, something besides the fear.

"Somebody help me," she called out. The words died in her throat from lack of breath to carry them, and it became impossible to form other sounds.

That seemed to increase her fear. Her heart was thundering in her chest and the muscles were tense and filled with pain.

Sweat drenched her. She was soaking wet.

More lightning. It made no difference. Her head was reeling. She couldn't make out anything else in the room. It was shrouded by clouds of time that had settled over her memory.

She began to sob, and she felt herself sinking deeper into darkness, a thick and enveloping darkness.

Its touch was like an embrace.

It was a lulling darkness. She fought it. As it pulled her downward she struggled against its soothing effects.

She did not want solace now. She wanted knowledge. There had to be an answer to the fear, and there had to be a way to conquer it.

She still could not breathe properly, but as more darkness spilled down over her, breathing did not seem to matter as much.

A part of her brain wanted her to accept the darkness so that memory would not assault her. The darkness wanted to insulate her against the harshness.

She tried to scream as she was pulled even farther into the endless abyss. Her voice was inaudible. She forced her lungs to labor, drawing inward.

It was not enough. She kept sinking, going nowhere into a nothingness as vast as a thousand nightmares.

She could hear herself screaming when she sat up in the chair. The cries were very real now, made louder because she had worked so hard to create them.

Sunlight burned in through the front window, and someone on television was trying to win a car as Bob Barker spoke words of encouragement.

Jennifer got out of her chair and hurried over to the window to make sure the sun was real, that this was not the imagination.

Only when she touched the windowpane did she allow the sigh of relief. The smooth, cool surface, hard against her fingertips, was tangible and solid. She drew several long, deep breaths and toppled back into the chair, tugging off her T-shirt because it was soaked and clammy.

No one was after her. There was no darkness, and no shadow figure.

She laughed. There was nothing to be afraid of. The phone call had come from some teenager. Someone whose thrill came from making telephone calls, not from carrying out threats.

Someone else would get the call tonight. Someone else would have to lose sleep worrying about the threat. For her it was over. She wasn't going to worry any longer.

She got up again, headed for the bathroom for a shower. She had to get to work on her paper.

Something stirred in her memory, but now she forced it aside. She didn't want to recall it any longer. It was bad, and she had too many other things to think about. The shadows would have to wait.

CHAPTER 3

The sins filtered through the mesh window in the confessional like a voice over a radio, and Conzenza had to force himself to keep his attention on the words of the teenage girl in the adjoining booth.

She was a pretty girl, blond with blue eyes. Conzenza remembered seeing her sitting on the pew with her parents when she attended Mass. She always seemed vibrant, clean, and dressed in the latest fashions. She was involved in all the right clubs at school, but now her words were low and frightened as she spoke of her boyfriend and the things they had done.

She recounted the usual events of young people, the struggles with desire and experimentation. Groping in the backseats of cars was the weakness of every generation. How many times had he heard children spilling the same beans?

Conzenza nodded occasionally even though he wasn't sure if she detected the movement through the screen.

He wanted to do more than prescribe penance, offer some kind of comfort, but he found no other words as he dismissed her, and he remained within the booth as her footsteps echoed away through the sanctuary. He waited, but the curtain in the next booth did not open again. There wasn't anyone else waiting to be heard.

The empty sound of the girl's footsteps seemed to echo also into the emptiness he felt in his soul. Clasping his hands beneath his chin, he tried for a moment to pray yet was again unable to find the proper words, or the thing for which he should ask.

Perhaps there were other things he should be doing, things he should accomplish. He was not a good priest, had never felt confident of himself, even in the early days.

His faith was with him still. He was only wondering if he should seek some other form of service, find some new way to help people and work for God. While he maintained his smile and his wit for the parishioners, his days were filled with turmoil.

Slowly he rose to his feet and pulled back the curtain, stepping from the booth to walk over to the statue of Christ.

The anguished look on the figure's face seemed to mirror the feelings within Conzenza's own soul. He felt as if he were sacrificing himself, or at least a piece of himself, yet sacrificing for no reason. He never felt totally successful in anything he approached.

Christ had died for redemption, but the priest shook his head. Was he serving any purpose himself? Was he giving the people who came to him any satisfaction? What of the girl who had just left? What had she taken away with her? Any instruction or suggestions? Or just some murmurings to chant until the next time she was with her boyfriend.

Not that he blamed the church or the practices. It was his failing, a manifestation of his own inadequacy.

Perhaps he had chosen the wrong path. Perhaps he had misunderstood what he had believed to be the will of God.

Turning, he looked up at the angel. Was that what he

needed? To thrust his mind into some other realm in order to make contact with other beings?

His shoulders sank. No. He did not seek that sort of consolation. It would represent a lack of faith to ask God for some sign. He left the statue and strolled back across the floor to the corridor, checking his watch as he moved toward his office. It was almost time to start thinking about dinner. He liked to have his meal before the evening Mass. Since there was no line at the confessional, he could fix himself something. There was still a half hour before people would start showing up for the service.

The thought of dinner almost made him laugh. Dinner would probably be a frozen platter again, followed by an evening of reading in the rectory once he had gone through the motions of Mass.

He remembered his evening meals as a child, the meals his mother fixed for the family when his father came home from work. Those days were long gone, yet he recalled the comfort of having the family together. Tragedy had visited his family more than once, taking the lives of both parents and its toll on other family members, but memories were always pleasant. For his ability to recall the good things, Conzenza was thankful.

For his confusion with his life, he held less gratitude. What would it be like to have a wife to go home to? He laughed. He had never had to struggle with the vow of celibacy the way some in the priesthood did.

Conzenza would not be one of those who left the church because of sex, but there were other considerations that plagued him.

The thought of a companion often loomed over him as a temptation. How nice it would be to have someone to share things with, someone who could listen to the inner complexities of his soul and relate her complexities back to him

35

as well, someone to become a part of him and take away the loneliness he felt.

He stepped into his office and picked up a magazine from his desk, a copy of *Time* with photographs of a plane crash on the cover.

It had come in the mail on Tuesday, and he'd already read the book reviews and the news items that interested him, but there was a section on religion this week. Perhaps there would be something of interest.

He switched off the light and started to walk toward the exit that led to the rectory, but a sound stopped him.

Had someone come in? The doors of the sanctuary remained open. Perhaps someone else had entered to light a candle, or for the confessional.

Conzenza was alone today, and if someone sought attention he would have to be the one to help.

Tucking the magazine under his arm, he strolled back to the church, where he found only empty space. There was no one in sight.

He looked all around the room without detecting any sign of life, yet he sensed someone's presence. Someone must have come in.

"Hello?" he called.

The word carried across the vacant space, producing no answer.

Taking a few steps forward, Conzenza called out again, beginning to feel apprehensive.

He scanned the area before him, even peering into the shadows, but there was nothing he was overlooking.

If someone had entered, they might have moved on into the confessional. Although the confession period was over, Conzenza always tried to accommodate those who wished to be heard before Mass. He walked over to the booth slowly, stopping in front of the first curtain.

"Is someone there?" he asked. "Do you need to be heard?"

No answer. Perhaps they were frightened. He moved over to his curtain. If someone was present, he would speak through the screen, hear the confession.

Reaching up, he pulled the curtain aside.

The knife ripped open his shoulder. He staggered backward, raising the magazine like a shield. The muscles of his shoulder felt as if they had been set on fire. Messages of agony shot up to his brain. He closed his eyes and drew a quick breath through his mouth, biting his lower lip because of the pain.

The second blow from the blade flayed open the back of his left hand. The flesh split open in a broad gash which exposed the bone of his middle finger. The magazine fluttered to the floor, and the priest's blood splattered down onto the cover.

He tried to move backward again, hoping to stumble to the front door. It wouldn't be dark yet, not this time of year. Maybe he could find help. On the street he could call out, possibly stop a passing car.

He half turned before the blade struck again, this time sinking into his chest, just above the heart. The sound of suction reached Conzenza's ears as the blade was drawn from his body. It reminded him of the sound a stick made when it was poked into soft mud and then pulled out again.

The pain was like the fire of hell. It flared through his body, and he found it impossible to maintain his balance. His legs seemed to twist around each other.

He fell, grasping the chest wound with his uninjured hand. He could feel the hot blood spill through his fingers, coursing with each throb of his heart.

His thoughts were beginning to cloud. The room seemed

37

to be growing very dim. Even though he had his eye opened wide, it was like looking through half-closed lids.

He raised his injured arm, fingers wide in an attempt to ward off the next thrust of the blade. It was a futile gesture.

The weapon crashed down through flesh and bone. Conzenza let his head fall back on the hard floor. His skull cracked against the stone, his eyes rolling around until they focused on the statue of Christ. From his position it appeared to be upside down. He peered up into its eyes as he began to pray.

He didn't feel the final thrust of the blade or look at the shadow figure. He closed his eyes, waiting for distant shores.

The laugh echoed through the caverns of the room, off the stained glass and the high ceiling.

The task had been simple, and it was almost finished. The priest's body lay still, unmoving.

Easing forward, the figure dipped a finger into the blood on Conzenza's chest, then moved back to the wall near the confessional to scrawl in blood letters a single word—Azarius.

CHAPTER 4

Dareena got home just before dark, her arms filled with library books. She dropped her key into the pocket of her dress, placed the books on a hall table, and hurried through the front room to the dining area off the kitchen. The hardwood floors of the old house creaked under each step.

"You're late," her grandmother said.

The silver-haired woman sat at the table, an array of carefully prepared food displayed before her on the mahogany table like a set piece in a museum. Ornate silver and crystal were in place.

She might have been a mannequin placed in the room to complement the setting. She wore a dark violet dress with a high collar, a cameo broach pinned to the front of it. Her hair was pulled back in a bun, her face covered with makeup in an attempt to hide the deep wrinkles, her lips painted too bright a shade of red.

The rich smell of the roast pheasant and the trimmings gently touched Dareena's nostrils. The meal was perfect. She closed her eyes for a moment to savor the experience.

Then she smiled. "Sorry. I got caught up looking around at the library."

"You spend too much time reading books," the grandmother said. She always said that. It was her favorite accusation, "I was about to start without you."

"I'm just a minute or two late," Dareena protested.

She sat down at her end of the table and placed a cloth napkin across her lap to protect her dress before the old woman began to pass food to her.

"It's not good for me to be alone for long periods," the old woman countered, her hands trembling with the weight of the dishes. "I'm not in good health. You'll be sorry one day, Dareena."

"Yes, Grandmama." She didn't let her gaze meet the old woman's harsh stare.

She dished vegetables out and held her plate up for the grandmother to place a few slices of meat on it.

Then Dareena bowed her head and brushed her long black hair away from her face as the grandmother said a quick prayer.

The girl didn't look up again as they began eating. It wasn't a good day for the older woman, and Dareena didn't want to antagonize her. Anything she said would be turned against her.

She chewed her food slowly so that she wouldn't be admonished for eating too fast, and thought about the books. An endless hour or more would pass before she could get to them. Dinner was at an appointed time, a time with which nothing could be allowed to interfere. In her grandmother's mind, a deviation from schedule could be justified only by the Apocalypse.

The books would have to wait until after dinner, after the kitchen was cleaned and her grandmother had settled down in front of the television to watch and complain about the programming. Anything that came on after *Wheel of Fortune* was unsuitable.

Dareena was resigned to that, to the constant complaining and grumbling. Her grandmother had a good heart. She had to be tolerated for what she was.

At least when she was complaining about the television programs, she was leaving Dareena alone.

Dareena had never cared much for television. It had always been her grandmother's domain, its principal benefit to Dareena in its ability to distract.

Dareena was thirty-one and had lived with her grandmother since she'd been a teenager. She'd moved into the old white house when her father died of a heart attack, a death that came only two years after her mother's death from cancer.

The maternal grandmother had been kind to take her in, but the old woman had lived alone for many years and was rigid in her life-style and inflexible in dealing with Dareena.

At sixteen Dareena had been a shy girl, tall and uncomfortable with her height. That, combined with her grandmother's rules, served to alienate her from her peers. Even when her beauty blossomed at seventeen, she failed to fit in.

She was different from the other girls, and that was cause enough for them not to accept her into their groups.

A few boys asked her out, but soon word got around that her grandmother was stern and strict. She got only one kiss in high school, and that from a funny-looking boy with horn-rimmed glasses. She'd gone out with him only because he was a nephew of one of Grandmother's friends from church.

The night of the senior prom she and Grandmother had watched *Petticoat Junction*.

After high school her grandmother discouraged college even though there was money available—insurance from both parents plus the money the old woman's husband had left her, which was substantial. He'd owned property that had sold for top dollar, and he'd channeled the money into stocks.

But the old woman had grown accustomed to her granddaughter's company. She didn't want to give her up or even allow her to take a job. She perceived she would need the care as she got older.

She had been only in her late fifties then, but already she'd begun to stay close to the house.

Now, as she approached seventy, she was still alert and mobile, but chose to stay in most of the time, her only effort centering on the elaborate meals she prepared.

Dareena did the shopping and the housekeeping and read novels. She had no friends and met no men.

Yet she was an attractive young woman with her long dark hair and slender body. Her face was lean with high cheekbones, and her complexion dark, hinting at a trace of Indian blood somewhere in the lineage. There was a slight pout to her full lips, a pert curve to her nose.

Her clothes were always elegant. The grandmother allowed her indulgences in wardrobe. In Dareena's closet were outfits many girls would have envied, both casual and formal wear. On Saturdays and Sundays they dressed for dinner. It presented a sense of occasion.

In earlier days they had attended church on Sundays, but now Grandmother chose to watch the Baptist minister from Lafayette on television. She said he preached so well that none of the ministers in town would be able to compare, and she liked the singing on the television church as well.

Besides, if she stayed home she could catch Oral Roberts, too, and if she felt like it, Jimmy Swaggart. Sometimes he had a good message, too, although he was a stern-faced man.

Dareena accepted it without argument, but she watched

only the Baptist service before returning to her room until lunch was served at one P.M.

She read romances. She'd been through just about every used bookstore in town, and the library. Her room was piled with paperbacks of Barbara Cartland, much to Grandmother's discontentment. She didn't like to see money wasted on someone else's imaginings. She berated Dareena for spending the few dollars she was allowed on novels. "I don't know where we're going to put all those," she said every time Dareena brought in a new set of books.

It felt good to escape into those fantasies, though. The deserts or the palaces where the dashing young men lived. There was a glamour in those worlds that filled the emptiness in Dareena's life.

She often thought of waltzing with some handsome young man, a tall blond-haired general or a dashing aristocrat, but she hated the sadness that such indulgences inevitably conjured, the sadness that came when she reminded herself it was all unreal. Like the person in the old song, she worried that she was dreaming her life away. Yet what more was there for her besides fantasy?

Sometimes the angel appeared in a manner that resembled the novels, like some dashing commander, but even that was not the same as reality. Not quite.

After supper she cleaned the dishes as quickly as possible, let the cat out and back in, and then took the books up to her room.

Hurriedly she slipped off her dress and put on jeans and a pullover. Then, taking her glasses from her night table, she started to sit down on the bed.

Before she could pick up one of the books, however, she

43

noticed the flickering image in the mirror that hung over the dresser.

She had first encountered Azarius during one of her fantasies. Caught up in the events of the imaginary story she was weaving in her mind, she had at first thought Azarius was just a part of her imagination, something from her subconscious that had slipped into the fantasy.

After years of practice, daydreams for Dareena were as vivid if not as surreal as sleeping dreams.

But Azarius had emerged from the figures of fantasy to introduce himself, explaining he was a friend.

She had been picturing herself in a setting from one of the books she had read. It had almost been like standing among a group at a Victorian party. The people in their immaculate clothes, mingling, dozens of young men in the room, all of them handsome. Azarius, breaking away from the crowd to come toward her. It was as if a piece of her imagination were suddenly out of control. She didn't recognize him as someone she had conjured within her thoughts. He walked up smiling.

She was standing at the edge of the ballroom, her hair perfectly set, her gown elegant. Music, a combination of violins, filled the room.

"We know you're lonely," Azarius had said. "I've come to help." Then, in her thoughts, he had taken her hand and led her out onto the dance floor to sweep her along with the music.

That had been a few years before, and she had been in contact with him ever since. In the early days he would often emerge from the clouds of her thoughts, but as time progressed he appeared not as another person but as an image of himself.

She could see him in reflections or shadows, not clearly,

but as if through a haze, the way an image looked when photographed with a camera lens covered with gauze.

Now he was visible in the mirror, two-dimensional and transparent, but noticeably handsome. His face was youthful, his hair long—if it was hair. He was like the man she'd first seen in her imagination, yet she suspected that this was not really his appearance, that he had simply adopted an image she could understand and appreciate. In the first fantasy he had been an amalgamation of the people she pictured from her books. He had drawn on her ideas to reach her, because his real form was less tangible to her earthly mind.

In the reflection he seemed to be framed by light, as if some glowing entity hovered beyond his shoulders.

"Hello, Dareena," he said. His voice was deep and the words formed strangely, as if they were coming through a muffled speaker.

Before he checked the time on his Rolex, Hamilton Terry trailed the path of the blond-haired waitress with his gaze, admiring the gentle sway of her hips until she disappeared through the lounge doorway with a tray of mixed drinks for the Clairmont Hotel restaurant, the Riverland. It was almost seven-thirty.

His father, Doren, was late. They were going to have dinner together in the Riverland. It was appropriate, because they helped put together the deals that got the place built as a downtown luxury hotel instead of a retirement home or an office building as some had wanted. It seemed like a better idea to develop something that would attract tourism, so they had devised the Clairmont. It was a replica of a historic hotel that had been a focal point of Aimsley society in the thirties and forties.

The original hotel had been abandoned and eventually torn down, but on a trip to St. Louis Doren had learned of a hotel called the Breckenridge that had been rebuilt to preserve its grandeur.

The idea of recreating the Clairmont's glory had seemed like a good idea, especially since it would allow him to work with his son.

They were Terry and Terry, business partners in real estate and now development.

Contracting the hotel project had been something new, and Hamilton was aware his father was pleased with that. But then, he'd always been pleased with Hamilton.

Hamilton sipped his margarita, the salt around the glass rim stinging his tongue slightly. The drink had been prepared with a mix and had a nasty edge to its taste. He needed to talk to someone about that. The Clairmont had to have a reputation for quality.

Leaning forward, Hamilton rested his elbows on the bar. He was a thin man, almost lanky, with his dark hair parted in the middle and brushed neatly into place. He wore dark dress slacks and a bright blue shirt open at the collar. Some days, if he was just doing office work, he preferred to dress casually. He could get by without a tie and coat. His father, being of the more conservative generation, drew the line at jeans.

Hamilton wasn't quite good-looking enough to be considered handsome. He relied on charm and position to make up for any deficiencies in his appearance.

At twenty-six Hamilton was one of the up and coming young businessmen of Aimsley, upwardly mobile and on his way to becoming a fine southern gentleman, rooted in the South but educated in the North. It was all part of the image his father wanted to create, an image his father had never attained himself, but the American dream was, after all, to create a better life for one's children. While Doren Terry had been a workingman most of his life, he wanted his son to become a community leader and erase the new-money stigma that sometimes seemed to linger with Doren. Hamilton had been groomed since his early years to fulfill his father's image.

He ran his finger through the water ring his glass had formed on the bar and thought about the past. He'd gone to private school until he was ready to enter high school. At that point his father had decided it would be more to his benefit to attend public school. He was able to meet more people that way. Networking was not a word his father would recognize, yet it was a concept he grasped.

After high school Hamilton had studied business at Princeton, which also pleased his father. Princeton was Ivy League. Doren had never completed college. He had taken only a few courses at an extended campus of the state university, so it was also a matter of pride that he'd been able to send Hamilton wherever he chose for schooling.

Hamilton couldn't argue. He'd picked up a great deal at school, and living near New York had allowed him to tour the museums and catch the Broadway shows when he wanted.

His father liked to hear him talk in front of the local people about paintings in the Guggenheim.

He laughed. Prestige was such a game. Many of those his father liked to impress had no real affinity for culture at all. They could not tell one artist from another.

Hamilton checked his watch again, then looked around the room once more. Still no sign of his father, but the waitress was back, a tall girl dressed in a sleek lavender uniform that caressed the gentle curves of her body. Her hair was soft, falling in a cascade to her shoulders. She couldn't have been more than nineteen or twenty, and there was a delicate look about her. He'd seen her here before but had never made a play for her, never even spoken to her.

Being connected with the ownership couldn't hurt, he thought. It might impress her, but then again, it might frighten her. He could work around that. He'd heard it said that waitresses suffered from low self-esteem. That was knowledge he could exploit. Often, waitresses found it flattering to have someone like him pay attention to them. He began turning over opening lines in his mind.

He was engaged. Julia was making plans for the wedding, but the knot wasn't tied yet. He still had time for a few misadventures before he threw away his freedom. He wasn't against marriage, but the thought of giving up his freedom, even to Julia, was frightening. Sometimes she became very possessive.

There were other considerations that sometimes made him hesitate. His father's choice of a wife had not been a good one. Thinking of his mother brought a bad taste to his mouth. She had been a heavy drinker, a subject that for many years had remained one of the family's dark secrets. For a long time it had been concealed from Hamilton. Unfortunately it was not the kind of thing that could remain concealed forever. The weakness had made her deteriorate slowly, disgustingly. He never wanted to be in the position in which his father had found himself, saddled with a ruined woman.

Still, he was in love with Julia. She wasn't like his mother. Julia was beautiful, tall, and dark-haired with a pleasing sturdiness, an arrogance. It was that arrogance that Southern girls of breeding and the blue-blooded northern girls have in common. Hamilton had learned that from experiences in college. For those who could bear up to it, it was a pleasing quality. She was comforting to him. With Julia he would not find the embarrassment his father had experienced. She was attractive, and there was an elegance about her. They would make a good couple. She would fit in well in the circles of Aimsley society. If he decided to run for the city board at any time, having her on his arm would be a major boost, possessed as she was of that proper breeding.

But the waitress had a paradoxical innocence and wildness about her that attracted him. Her hair was soft, her eyes warm, yet there was too much eye makeup which looked just slightly cheap and enticing.

He should be able to make time for her somewhere. Julia wouldn't have to know.

Turning on his barstool, he began to watch the waitress move among the tables. She tossed her head every now and then to bounce her hair out of her face, causing the light to caress her curls. Beneath the dress he could tell her breasts were full and rounded, her hips perfectly shaped. She had slender legs, enhanced in their appearance by the dark stockings she wore with her uniform.

Before he could make a move, however, his father turned up and piled onto the stool beside him, mopping his brow with a handkerchief.

"How's it going?" Hamilton asked.

The older man sighed. He was heavyset, with thinning hair, and his dark suit was rumpled, slightly ill fitting. Perspiration shone on his forehead, and a shadow had spread across his chin, while the knot of his tie had been tugged away from his throat, leaving it twisted out of place.

"Always a lot of paperwork," Doren said, and flagged down the bartender for a shot of Jack Daniel's.

After he'd been given his drink he took a swallow and sighed. "It takes a lot to keep this town going," he said.

But he smiled and looked around the room. Hamilton followed his gaze. Rebuilding the original Clairmont had been a wonderful idea. The ceiling was high and there was an ornate look to the walls. A thick carpet of a deep maroon matched the draperies. Even the dim lighting had a violet tint which was designed to add to the relaxing mood of the room. It was to be more than just a hotel bar. Bars could be had anywhere, but this was the Clairmont. Doren wanted people to leave here with a special feeling. Right now Aimsley's chief hotel trade was from businessmen, but everyone was working to attract the tourism dollars from around the state. Dollars coming into the area would help everybody. In a couple of years, when more stores opened and a few more restaurants, Aimsley would be a major draw for conventions.

"I guess it's worth it," Doren said. "Once we get some conventions in here and get people talking."

Hamilton nodded. "It's going to fly."

"The whole town. You know Maywood's is remodeling. If we start getting the stores to stay open at night, get a couple of more restaurants in here." He slapped the bar. "Hell, Aimsley is going to rival New Orleans."

Hamilton couldn't stifle a laugh. Sometimes his father's enthusiasm got ahead of actual progress. Economic conditions were rough. Fluctuations in gas and oil prices hit Louisiana hard. There was a lot of hanging on to do before the city bloomed.

"You're going to have to give that a couple of years," he said, resting a hand against his father's shoulder.

Doren tilted his hand from side to side, symbolizing an unstable boat on stormy seas. "I guess we can't rush it, but then again, we want to stay on top of things." He drummed his fingers on the counter with nervous anticipation.

"What were you working on?" Hamilton asked.

"I had to talk to Phil Nelson about some papers." Nelson, Jennifer's father, was also involved in the Clairmont's redevelopment. "Then this, that, and the other came up," Doren said. He swallowed another shot of his drink. "Hell, you name it. Forget that and let's get some supper; you can't get a town lined up on an empty stomach." He placed an arm around his son's shoulders as they left the bar.

Hamilton dropped a bill on the bar and slid off his stool to follow his father into the restaurant. He glanced back fleetingly at the waitress, then shrugged. She'd be around.

CHAPTER 5

Gable shrugged off his sport coat when he got back to his house, and after he'd dumped some table scraps in a bowl for the dog, he poured himself some white grape juice and settled down at the typewriter.

Rolling a sheet of paper into the machine, he stared forward at its blank face and tried to think of a way to make key tracks that would have some meaning.

After he'd talked to the priest he'd driven back along the street in front of Dareena's house one last time, and it had proven worthwhile.

He'd caught sight of her. She was walking along the sidewalk with a bag of groceries in her arms.

He was struck by sadness at the sight, for it was a universal moment: Like everyone else, the mysterious Dareena had to do her grocery shopping.

Until that sighting she'd been just an image, some weird girl people talked about, but from that second onward she had become real to him—a person.

It reminded him of one of the first car wrecks he'd covered as a general assignment man. It had been on a hot

Sunday afternoon, and he and a photographer had driven out to the stretch of highway where the crash had occurred.

When they'd arrived, they'd found some firemen cutting a kid out of the mangled wreckage of a Monte Carlo. He'd fallen asleep at the wheel and collided with a Ford pickup.

As Gable watched, they pried the kid out of the front seat. He screamed at the pain, and blood from a cut on his forehead ran down his face like crimson tears, but the thing Gable noticed was his tennis shoes, common everyday tennis shoes, the same as Gable wore himself.

The kid had to tie his shoes just like Gable did. That made him more than a name on an accident report, and when he'd died two days later, it made him more than an obituary. Gable had not wept, but he had remembered.

Dareena was more than just a local character. She was just like everybody else, Gable realized, buying groceries and trying to find the way to live that hurt the least.

Her task was more difficult, however. She faced alienation and loneliness, empty feelings. The sort of feelings that would lead to the creation of imaginary angels as friends.

He'd expected her to look as if she belonged in the 1950s—out-of-date clothes, harlequin glasses, and lipstick smeared across her lips, perhaps a sweater she wore buttoned wrong. Surprisingly that wasn't the case.

She'd been wearing a stylish dress that flattered her figure. She was graceful, attractive, and he was willing to wager she was intelligent as well.

By nine he'd piled up another stack of crumpled pages, and he began to pace the floor to work out the knots of frustration. He ran his hands through his hair and stood at the window, looking out at the darkness. As much as he hated the idea, as much as he wanted to get away from prying into people's lives, the fact remained. If he was going to write about Dareena, he was going to have to talk to her first. He needed her words, her explanation of her life, her tears.

At the moment there was no other story he wanted to tell. None that fired a spark the way this one did.

Leaving the window, he stumbled over the dog, recovered his balance, and settled into an armchair with an Erle Stanley Gardner mystery, hoping for distraction.

He was still reading Perry Mason when Jennifer came over. She looked tired when he let her into the living room. He fixed her a cup of coffee.

"What's going on?" she asked.

Gable held up the paperback. *"The Case of the Motheaten Mink."*

"You weren't working?"

"I punted for the evening. The only thing harder than writing is getting ready to write."

She nodded, but she looked like she was thinking about something else. Her gaze seemed to be into oblivion. The dog was licking her hand, but she didn't notice.

"Is something wrong?" Gable asked.

He detected the discomfort in her eyes when she looked back at him.

"There's something I didn't tell you," she said. "It may be nothing, but I got this call. Before I came over. Someone said they were going to kill me."

"Maybe it was a joke."

"But the voice sounded so horrible. Like a monster."

"Have you left any boyfriends with broken hearts?"

"Not anyone really bitter."

"No one you can think of who'd want to hurt you? No reason?"

"Not that I can think of."

He frowned.

"I started thinking of all the nuts in town. I guess that's why I told you about them last night, but I can't imagine why any of them would have a reason to call me."

"Do nuts need reasons?"

She shook her head.

"What exactly did the caller say? Did he say 'I'm going to kill you'?"

She told him what the caller had said about the priest. "I talked to a priest today," he said. "Small world."

"Who was it?"

"A Father Conzenza."

"Why'd you go to him?"

"I was looking for your girl who talks to angels and I stopped in at his church."

"Was he all right?"

"Fine."

"He's my priest. Sort of. I haven't been to church in a long time, but until I started college I used to go and talk to him. He heard my confessions. You know how embarrassing it is confessing to someone who knows you?"

"It would depend on the sin."

"Use your imagination."

Gable laughed, and it prompted Jennifer to giggle as well.

"I guess I feel better," she said.

"I'm sure it was just a crank call." Gable checked his watch. "You want to watch the news? It's a habit of mine."

"What ever happens in Aimsley?"

"We'll find out," he said.

He switched on the set, and the black and white image

55

flickered into focus just as the news lead-in began, proclaiming the virtues of Eyewitness Six.

After a few seconds they cut to the solemn face of an anchorman. He looked like he'd had an enema for lunch.

"Good evening, I'm William Reynolds, and we have a shocking story tonight. The body of a priest has been discovered at the St. Joseph Cathedral. While details are sketchy, police have said that the body is that of Father Joseph Conzenza."

"My God," Gable said.

Jennifer had turned white. Her arms had drawn up against her chest, and she sat staring at the television screen.

"Just a few minutes ago this was the scene at the church," the announcer said, and a bouncing videotape image appeared in his place.

It was dark and hard to make out, but it was possible to see police cars and a number of people milling about in front of the cathedral.

Gable looked back at Jennifer, who had begun to shudder.

"You all right?"

She began to whimper, her lips trembling. He moved to her, gripping her shoulders to shake her, but her awareness was lost.

She gasped for breath and began to push away from him. Then her gaze fell upon his face and she tore herself away, scrambling from her chair and moving across the room to put some furniture between them.

"You were with him today?"

"What?"

"When did you leave him?"

"I don't know the time."

"Who are you?"

"We've made our introductions."

"What have I been doing? You're a stranger, and I've come to you afraid. I haven't been thinking. It could have been you making those calls."

He was shaking his head all the time she was speaking. He tried to reach out to her.

She found the wall and pressed her back against it. Her features were twisted, her eyes about to burst from their sockets.

Gable stood in the center of the room with his hands raised to show her he meant no harm.

"What would my reason for this be?"

She shook her head.

"I don't know. Do you need a reason?"

"If I'd done it, would I have taken a chance of seeing it on the news? Why not just kill you while you weren't expecting it?"

"Maybe it's a game."

Gable clenched his teeth. "Look, I'm as surprised as you are. But if you want to run, run. Before you do, think it over. Your call's taking on a new meaning. Somebody was serious."

She looked around the room, then through the doorway at the darkness.

"You'd let me walk out of here?"

"Try it."

Slowly she took a step away from the wall, almost losing her balance because her muscles were trembling. When he didn't try to stop her, she moved again, making her way quickly to the door. She stopped at the screen, spinning to look back at him.

"Can I trust you?"

"It's up to you."

She hesitated.

Gable motioned her to a chair. When she was seated, he

advanced toward her slowly, kneeling at her side and placing his hand gently on her arm. He realized he was trembling himself.

He swallowed. His mouth had become very dry. Her reaction had distracted his thoughts, but slowly the reality of the situation sank in.

"We need to call the police," he said. "You could be in danger. Real Boris-Karloff-in-the-kitchen danger."

She bowed her head, placing her face in her hands. He could hear the choked sound of weeping in her throat.

"It's going to be all right," he said. "I'll get the phone. If you want me to, I'll make the call."

"Yes. Please."

He walked over to the table and picked up the phone, stretching the cord with him to the couch, where he sat down and dialed 911. The number connected him with the sheriff's office, but they would be able to refer him to the city police.

Gable was visible through the screen door. The girl was with him, all right. Wonderful. Just wonderful. He was going to be a problem.

The girl could have been taken care of tonight if it weren't for him. Perhaps giving her a warning had been a mistake.

That wouldn't happen again.

CHAPTER 6

Fisher hated the flash of the blue lights on the top of the patrol car as much as he hated being called out at night. If he had to look at it long enough, the blue light made him sick to his stomach. Sometimes he forgot to avert his eyes, realizing only when the juices in his gut started churning that he'd been overexposed.

The blue lights spilled across the church lawn, making the area look unstable, as if it were underwater.

A couple of uniformed officers were moving about, stretching a band of yellow tape around some trees to establish a police line. They looked like seamen trying to reel in a sail. They were finally getting the tape up now with the words Police Line Do Not Cross printed on it, now that the television people with their lights and microphones were gone. Typical. There was nobody left to keep out so they were getting the place sealed off. Where had the patrol cars been when the murderer had been about? People would be asking that in the morning, reminding everyone that there is never a policeman around when you need one.

Fisher stood on the sidewalk, watching the paramedics carry the priest's body out in a black bag. It wasn't a person anymore, just an empty vessel to be carted away. There were crimson stains on the stretcher where the blood had dripped off the corpse as they bagged it. Fisher averted his eyes, cursing under his breath. He still hated the sight of blood. After all the murder scenes he'd worked, spilled blood still did something to him. It wasn't as bad as the lights, just a sort of queasy feeling.

Why did lunatics have to pull this kind of shit? Why couldn't people just leave each other alone? While he wasn't a particularly thoughtful man, Fisher often wondered why people wanted to hurt one another. It wasn't just anger or emotion. Sometimes those were reasons, but other times there was just no way of understanding killers and their motivations.

All of it made his head swim. Reaching into his pocket, he found the bottle of Titralac and popped a couple of the mint-flavored pills onto his tongue. With any luck they'd keep the bile out of his throat and help keep his stomach settled. He let a long, slow breath slip through his lips.

He was a big man, and he looked like a police detective. He was wearing an old gray raincoat and a hat pushed back on his head to reveal the thinning blond hair that crept back from his forehead. Beneath the coat his bulky form was clad in a dark brown suit that had been nice when it was new. It hadn't been new for a good while.

If he'd known someone was going to mess up a priest, he wouldn't have let his wife fix meatballs for supper. The seasoning gave him heartburn anyway, but he should have known when he'd drawn duty. Weird things always happened when he was the detective on call for night duty, especially when there was something good on HBO. When his phone had rung just as a Clint Eastwood movie was starting, Lieutenant Fisher had known he wouldn't be seeing the end of the picture.

As he stood with his hands in his pockets, trying not to let the flash of the blue light catch his eyes, one of the uniformed officers came out of the church and moved over to stand facing him. The officer wore a solemn expression, the look in his eyes stern. He was too neat and his face was too smooth. He had short black hair brushed perfectly into place and treated with hair spray. He was one of those who took everything too seriously, the type who called everybody sir.

"I want you to take a look at something, sir," the kid said. His name was Richmond. He looked as if he should still be in high school. He hadn't really learned what the job was all about yet. He still thought there was something he could do about the world. Fisher had thought that once, maybe a hundred years before. Remembering made him feel even more weary. "What is it?" he asked.

"It's in here, sir."

The young cop led Fisher back into the sanctuary where there were still lab technicians at work. The detective tried not to look at the blood splattered across the floor until he realized it was blood the kid wanted him to look at.

He tugged his notebook from his pocket and scribbled down the markings on the wall when Richmond pointed them out. They were almost hidden, scrawled on the wall near the floor where the shadows fell.

"What does that mean?" Fisher asked. "It doesn't sound familiar."

"Azarius," the uniformed man said. "It's not anything I know of."

"You Catholic?" Fisher asked.

Richmond shook his head. "Baptist."

Fisher turned around. "Anybody here Catholic?"

Tressler, one of the lab boys, waved his hand. He was near the confessional, where he'd been using a hand-unit vacuum to pick up anything that might be worthwhile. He had wiry red hair and wore glasses with thick lenses.

Fisher motioned him over to the wall and pointed toward the lettering.

"What's this?" he asked.

The technician ran a hand through his hair, then pushed his glasses back up the bridge of his nose. "I'm not sure," he said.

He shook his head. "I've never heard it before."

"Could it be like mythology or something?" Richmond asked.

"It's kind of like that," the technician said, "but I've never heard this specific name before."

Fisher turned away. It was sickening to think the word was written in someone's blood. He should be used to sick things, but he wasn't. Some things, as the saying went, you never get used to. He'd seen worse, whole walls covered with blood. There was a lot of blood in the human body. When someone was mutilated the blood came out, dark and crimson, not bright red like in the movies. Being dark, it seemed more ominous.

There was not as much blood here as on the worst cases Fisher had worked, yet it seemed more horrible, in part because it was the blood of a priest, a holy man, and in part because he sensed a sickness in the method. Someone had dipped a finger into the man's blood and written a word with it. That was more than murder. It was primitive, barbaric. He hated the other thought that came to mind, but it was true: This was ritualistic. That was unsettling.

The magazine they'd bagged for evidence had made the meatballs roll over in his gut. It was in a clear plastic bag. The sight of the blood on the pages was bad, but it was not a deliberate thing. Blood had to splatter somewhere. That was understandable.

Other things defied understanding, and he was worried on top of all the disturbing sights.

To be truthful, the word scared the hell out of him. It was like something you'd hear about in California or somewhere—some kind of Zodiac killer. He may be dealing with a cult. That sort of thing was happening everywhere. It was a crazy world.

He belched and rubbed his throat with his fingers. He tasted his wife's cooking, and it hadn't been that good the first time.

He sighed. If there was a cult, or even if it was just one killer, the fact that he was writing crazy words could mean only one thing. There would be more. He wouldn't stop at just one, not someone who'd left a message. A message was the sign of a serial killer, a sign of someone who liked what he was doing.

Fisher left the sanctuary and walked back out onto the lawn, stuffing his hands into his pockets. The world suddenly felt very heavy on his shoulders. He walked with his head slightly bowed. He had his work cut out for him. There was no question about it.

That kind of killer had a statement he was trying to make. He wouldn't stop until he was through or until he'd been caught. Like the potato chip ad, he couldn't kill just one.

The blue lights caught Fisher's eyes again as he walked past the patrol car to his own vehicle, a white Chevy with black sidewalls. The kind of car only an idiot wouldn't be able to spot as a public vehicle.

Climbing behind the wheel, he tossed his hat onto the seat beside him, breathing out heavily through his mouth. He'd have to go back to the station now. The lady who'd found the body would be there. She was some poor old soul on her way to Mass. Fisher didn't envy her her discovery.

He hoped they'd have her calmed down enough to make a statement. He needed her information. On this job he was going to need all the help he could get.

Jennifer had never been to the police station before, and she didn't like the feel of the place from the moment they walked in through the glass doors.

The entryway was tile and marble and it seemed cold, like stepping into an icy cavern.

There was also a smell she didn't like. She couldn't place it exactly. It was just a damp smell, perhaps the odor of too many bodies all mixed together. It hung in the room, a presence.

The cop behind the desk didn't help her impression of the place, either. He was worse than the odor, a foul presence of another kind.

He looked like he was melting. Skin hung in folds about his face, and his features seemed to sag. He reminded her of the sloth man in the last *Star Wars* movie. He was like a desk sergeant on television, looking up with tired brown eyes as he rubbed his neck. He had a thin mustache sprinkled with gray.

His expression didn't do her nerves any good. The cop wasn't glad to see them, but Gable had said it would be better to go down to the station. They couldn't be dismissed as easily in person as on the phone. Someone would have to deal with them and listen to their story.

"Can I help you?" the cop asked, his voice rising up in a slow grumble.

Gable moved up to the counter. "My friend may have

some information that's connected with the murder of the priest.''

The sergeant frowned.

"We saw it on television,'' Gable explained. He rested his arms on the counter and leaned toward the man.

"They're still out on that,'' the cop said.

Gable nodded. There was no effective way to deal with cops. You just had to play it by ear, bother them until they decided to do something to make you let them alone.

"I'm sure they are,'' Gable said, "but this could be important. And she could be in danger.'' His voice rose a little with exasperation. "She's been threatened.''

That made the sergeant sit up a little, adjusting his bulk in the small swivel chair. He picked up a complaint pad and looked over at Jennifer.

"What's your name?'' he asked. His voice remained gruff, but he wasn't as bad as she'd thought. She moved forward to the counter slowly and glanced at Gable, who nodded for her to go ahead.

A half hour later they were ushered across the street to the detective division, where they were pushed into an interrogation room, a drab and smelly cubicle with green walls. There was a large plastic table, the surface designed to resemble wood. It was dotted with cigarette burns. The floor had a dingy look that matched the brown stains on the tiled ceiling.

Jennifer sat in one of the dented metal chairs, but Gable began to pace. She listened to the tread of his tennis shoes against the floor. He seemed impatient, but she was glad he was with her. It was better than going through this all alone.

She still wasn't sure what to make of the cop. Although he leaned a little on the weird side, he seemed decent.

The detective who eventually showed up was another story.

He almost filled the doorway with his bulky form when he entered the room. He was carrying a paper coffee cup and a notebook. He needed a shave and a new suit. And a new disposition.

Sitting down he focused on her with narrow little eyes.

"I'm Lieutenant Dan Fisher," he said, and glanced at his notes. "Who called you, Miss Nelson?"

"I don't know."

He sighed heavily and impatiently and sipped from his coffee. His stubby fingers looked more like a paw wrapped around the cup.

"When was it?"

"The other night. Really early in the morning."

"Was it a man or woman?"

"I don't know."

He ran his hand over his face, his features twisting as he made another sound with his breath.

"Did you know Father Conzenza?"

"Yes, but I hadn't seen him in a couple of years."

"Why would someone want to kill him?"

"I don't know."

"Any reason someone would want to kill you?"

"No. I mean, none that I can think of." She pulled her hair back with her hands, letting it fall through her fingers slowly.

Gable was standing against the wall with his hands in his hip pockets, keeping his eyes on the cop.

"What's your connection with the priest?"

"He was my pastor," Jennifer said. "I talked to him quite a bit when I was younger."

"Anything else?"

"No. It's been a while since I've been to church."

Fisher sucked his teeth, making a whistling sound.

"He was no more than a pastor to you?"

"What do you mean?"

"You're an attractive young lady. Men are men."

"No." She raised her voice. "There was never anything like that."

"Come on."

"It's the truth."

"Never? I mean, I could see a boyfriend scorned being a little jealous of a priest."

She shook her head from side to side, hair bouncing about wildly. She could feel tears welling up behind her eyes, but she fought them back, swallowing. She hadn't felt stable when she'd come in here, and she wasn't up to a confrontation. Her father had always fought her battles. Sometimes she wondered if she'd ever be able to deal with things for herself.

"That's enough," Gable said. He didn't move from the wall, didn't raise his voice, but his tone was firm.

"Who are you?" Fisher asked.

"Someone who knows his rights," Gable said. "Don't put her on trial to make your job easier."

"Just trying to cover all the angles."

Gable didn't speak. He didn't seem tough, and he was much smaller than the detective, but he remained calm.

The cop expelled a breath slowly through his lips.

"Okay," he said. "You, Mr. Tyler. You talked to the priest today?"

"Yes."

"Why? Are you Catholic?"

"No. I'm a writer. I asked him some questions about theology. Angels."

"You writing about angels?"

"Not directly."

67

"Have anything against priests?"

Gable shook his head. He didn't like the cop. It was evident in his expression, but it was also evident he was making an effort not to be bullied.

"All right," Fisher said. "One other thing. The word Azarius mean anything to you? Either of you?"

"The priest mentioned it," Gable said without hesitation.

"What the hell is it?"

"A name. It's a name a girl uses for an angel she talks to."

The detective studied Gable's features.

"What girl?"

Gable paused a moment. "Dareena Winston."

"She talks to angels."

"So I'm told."

"You think the angels told her to kill a priest?"

"I don't know. I saw her walking to her house today. She didn't look like a killer."

"Nobody does." Fisher looked at Jennifer. "Do you know the girl he's talking about?"

"I know who she is. I've never met her. But a lot of people talk about her."

"Any reason she'd have to threaten you?"

"I doubt she even knows who I am."

Fisher grumbled something under his breath and pulled a package of cigarettes out of his shirt.

"Let me think about this," he said. "I'm going to have to talk to her, but we've got to make sure you're safe." He looked at Gable. "We do try to do our jobs."

"Who said anything?" Gable asked.

"I know your type. Always looking for something wrong."

"Only if it's there. Cops always treated me with such

courtesy when I was a reporter that I've never had anything but respect for those in the profession.''

''Sure. After a while, I'm going to want statements from both of you.''

The detective got up and moved from the room, his heavy shoes thudding across the floor as he moved.

''Don't take any wooden nickels,'' Gable muttered under his breath.

Gable got up from his chair and moved around the room again. There were some pens on the table. He picked up one and began to roll it between his fingers playfully. ''Open channel D,'' he said, lifting it to his lips. ''Where are you, Number Six? You've got to get out of the village.''

The lines from old television shows were lost on Jennifer.

''He was so harsh,'' Jennifer said.

''He was seeing if you were honest. It's hard to keep a story straight if someone is putting pressure on you.''

She pulled her hair back into a ponytail again, holding it with one hand, a nervous gesture she'd developed in school. Whenever she had tough test questions she always pulled her hair back.

Slowly she closed her eyes, resting her forehead against her free hand.

She felt Gable's hand on her shoulder. Without looking up, she let her head rest against his arm.

''Where did he go?''

''More coffee. He's giving us some time to talk. In a minute he'll come back in and make us repeat everything, to see if we tell things the same way.''

It was good that he seemed to know what was going on. He'd been exposed to a lot of things as a reporter, things Jennifer had never thought very much about.

''What's going to come of all this?'' she asked.

69

"You can never tell. They may find the killer in a couple of hours huddled behind a tree with a communion chalice."

"Or?"

"Or they may have to look for a while."

Jennifer folded her hands in front of her on the table. Somehow she knew it wouldn't be over quickly. She sensed something evil, something malevolent. It made her feel cold inside.

The story of the murder made the front page of the paper, the *Aimsley Daily Clarion,* but there weren't many details— only a picture of the body being carried out on a stretcher.

Doren put the page on his desk and stared at it throughout the morning, rubbing his brow from time to time as if his fingertips could massage away the anxiety. The article was still there, glaring at him, when Philip Nelson showed up for lunch.

Nelson took one look at the story and shook his head as he sat down. The same anxiety Doren was feeling was evident in the lawyer's eyes. His iron-gray hair was neatly combed, his suit impeccable as always, yet there seemed to be worry floating just beneath his surface calm.

"Hope they catch that fellow quick," he said, adjusting his tie.

Doren nodded and took his handkerchief from his pocket to touch it to his brow. It wasn't particularly warm in the office, but he perspired easily, always had. In school it had made him the subject of jokes when it was combined with his weight, which had also been a problem most of his life. Physical education classes had been the worst. He'd had to struggle through the obstacles, fumbling in sports and drawing ridicule for his lack of physical prowess.

He'd never had a problem with his brains, though. That's

what he'd always relied on. He'd always been a reader, a pastime that made him seem brilliant to the other students in his classes.

Still, it was mathematics and not English that had been his strong point in school, a strength he'd developed and used in his favor. His mathematical knowledge had been invaluable in developing his business and in its continuing management, but that wasn't all. He knew how to get things done. Half of the development of the Clairmont was due to his perseverance and determination, and people respected that. Now he had the respect he'd always longed for as a child. He was a somebody in the community, and he liked that, liked having his opinion sought out at chamber of commerce meetings and shaking hands at the Rotary and Kiwanis with people who'd once looked down on him. They didn't anymore. They knew he had bested most of them and equaled all the others. He might not be polished or suave, not handsome or exciting, but he was worth something. He mattered, and his name was going to be carried on.

"You think this is going to be a business problem?" Nelson asked, tapping his finger against the newspaper's headline about the murder.

"I've been thinking about it all morning," Doren said. "I don't know. The paper said it was a bizarre case. That's the word they used."

"It could scare people away."

"Unless they catch somebody quick. Of course, people forget things pretty fast."

"True."

"Besides, we know how dangerous big cities can be. A guy took my watch the last time I was in the French Quarter."

"Yeah," Nelson said. "Tommy Dells from our office had

his wallet stolen while he and his wife were in New York. They were about to have a buggy ride and some kid held him up."

"Danger doesn't stop people from going to those places. Things happen. Everywhere. People know that. I'm thinking, on the other hand, that if this turns into some kind of sensational event, it might even let more people know about us here. I hate to think about us benefiting from this guy's death, but the media can do a whole lot. It might even become a drawing card. People might come here to see what it was all about."

"I vote we don't worry about it," Nelson said. "The Clairmont is in good shape. We've got a good property and it's going to fly. Our children are going to be in good shape when we're gone."

Doren looked over at the artist's conception of the remodeled hotel. It hung on the wall over the couch, framed and displayed like a piece of art. Once it had seemed like a dream, but now it was open, and a big chunk of it was his and his son's.

Doren's father had been a logger in north Louisiana, dying with only a few dollars tucked away in a sock. Doren had had to take the ball and run with it on his own from there, and it hadn't been easy getting his real estate company off the ground. But for his son there was something better.

Doren had created a better world for his son. Hamilton had received a good education, and he would have a firm business to take over when the time came. Doren had done well for a country boy who'd had to climb up from nowhere. He ran the handkerchief across his brow and smiled.

"You about ready to eat?" he asked Nelson.

"Sure, let's head on. Is Hamilton joining us?"

"He's going to meet us."

"How is he settling in?"

"Doing good."

On the way out Doren checked his watch. He enjoyed lunches with his friend and his son, but he had a meeting after lunch he didn't want to miss.

Gable slept only a couple of hours on the living room couch before he dragged himself out of a restless sleep and took a quick shower. The hot water eased some of the ache that had developed in his muscles.

It had been four A.M. when everything had finally finished up at the police station. He'd let Jennifer have his bedroom because she was still too frightened to go back to her house.

The dog had opted to follow her into the room and sleep at the foot of the bed, a friend to the finish.

Gable read the news story while he sat on the porch sipping coffee. It was sketchy. He didn't envy the guy who'd had to put the thing together the night before, probably fighting a deadline. He'd had no easy job if it had involved talking to Fisher.

When he'd been a reporter, Gable had hated talking to cops. It usually meant confrontations, because cops didn't care much for journalists, and Gable didn't like clashing with them. Some of them could be the nicest people in the world, but most were tough and often sarcastic, hardened by their work. More than once he'd run into cops who were mean.

While Fisher wasn't mean, Gable didn't like him at all, and he didn't really trust the man's competency, which concerned him. If Jennifer was in danger, it meant he was going to fall heir to taking care of her. To a degree he already had. It had been an inadvertent thing on his part, a matter of courtesy to help her a couple of times. Now he didn't see a way out.

That wasn't how he planned on spending the summer, and since his funds were limited, his time was limited. He needed his days free to work.

But on the other hand, the events surrounding the murder could turn into a story he could use.

The easy thing would be to ship her back to her parents, but he couldn't do that. If he did that he'd feel like a heel, and he'd felt like that enough over the last few years, every time an editor had forced him to do a story he didn't feel right about or call somebody at a bad time, like in the middle of the night.

Turning her out would be like a continuation of all that.

He'd grown cynical of late. Maybe doing something unselfish, something with no real hope of gain, would restore him some. Somebody had to be a good guy. Besides, if she did turn out to be connected with the case, if she was a target of an angel communicator, he'd have an exclusive on his doorstep. For a hot story that could pay off he was willing to live with being a journalist awhile longer. In the long run it could pay off.

"Are you going to tell your father?" he asked later when Jennifer came out onto the porch.

"I'll have to," she said. "But I'm not ready right now. I know I can't keep imposing on you, but when he finds out, he'll make me come home. I'll be back under my parents' thumb again. I have to depend on them for money now, but I'll be giving up any freedom I have if I go home."

"Is it that bad?"

She was sitting on the edge of the porch, wearing a black sweatshirt he'd loaned her. It looked good on her. Leaning

74

forward, she hugged her knees, gazing down at her toes as she thought for a moment. "They mean well, but they don't understand. I'm twenty-three. The last time I stayed at home, they didn't want me to go over to this guy's house because his parents weren't home. I don't need a damned chaperone. You know?" She was pouting slightly. It gave her a girlish look that Gable liked.

He smiled. "My parents are that way, too. My mom, anyway." He reached over and took her hand.

"I know you don't know me very well," he said. "So you've been a little afraid. Don't be. I'll try to help any way I can."

"If I stay at my place I'll wind up running over here and waking you up in the middle of the night because I hear the wind."

"I can go back to sleep." He thought about offering to let her stay at his place but had second thoughts. The couch was not very comfortable, and that was the only arrangement that would be workable.

"I still have to tell my daddy," she said. "It'll be in the paper tomorrow, won't it? I mean about me."

"Maybe not. It depends on what Fisher releases. Or whoever talks to the media for the cops."

"What do you think they'll do?"

Gable paused.

"The truth," she said.

"They'll spill their guts. I have a feeling Fisher's going to try to let you draw the killer out. It'll make his work easier."

"This is a hell of a choice. I either go home to my daddy's regime or stay here and let a killer stalk me."

"Maybe your parents have changed," Gable suggested.

"Don't count on it. They're good people, don't get me wrong, but I'm their only daughter. You can imagine."

"I'm an only son."

"Then you know what it's like."

"Precisely."

"Why would anybody want to kill me?"

"I don't know. I can't see why someone would have a reason to kill a priest. He seemed like a decent guy."

"Maybe that girl is crazy, though. Maybe she thought he was the Antichrist."

"You'd never heard the name of her angel before?"

She shook her head.

"I'm wondering," Gable said, "if someone wants it to look like she did it. It would be an easy frame. People think she's crazy anyway."

"I hadn't considered that."

"It's just a thought. I'm a writer. My mind works that way."

He stretched his arms. The sunlight was warm on his shoulders, and it danced across Jennifer's hair, bringing out a reddish tint he hadn't noticed before. Her skin was very light, almost pale. That made it look very soft and delicate. Her eyes were swollen just slightly from sleep. She still looked striking. He had to admit, there were considerations besides story ideas.

The eyes peered across the street at Jennifer.

Things had to be done. There were things that needed protecting.

Except now it was beginning to look more difficult. Perhaps the warning had been a mistake. She was sticking close to the writer now. Too close.

He wasn't that big a guy. Not a tough guy by a long shot, but he had a hard edge to him. It showed. It was in his eyes maybe.

Killing him wouldn't be as easy as killing a woman or a man of God.

76

Yet that only made him a challenge. It didn't make him impossible. Anything that meant a danger, a threat to the flow of things, had to be eliminated. If the writer stepped into the picture, destroying him would just be one more necessity.

Dareena had just come in from her morning walk, which she always took after finishing the breakfast dishes, and sat down to read a John Jakes novel when the knock came at the front door.

Just when she had time to read for a while. Her grandmother was finally settled down in front of the television, where she would be watching game shows until time for the noon news.

"Would you get that?" Grandmother asked. "I'm watching Bob Barker."

"Yes, ma'am," Dareena called. She put a slip of paper in the book and moved to the front door.

The man standing on the porch was like a bear with an asthmatic condition. He was wearing a rumpled blue suit and a hat, standing with his hands in his pockets. He offered a forced smile, and with a massive hand raised a badge in front of her.

"I'm Lieutenant Fisher, ma'am. I need to talk to you. Can I come in?"

She hesitated, frightened. Her eyes grew large, and she was aware of her fingers digging into the wood of the door.

"Is something wrong?"

"I need to ask you a few questions."

She pulled the door a little wider to let him into the narrow sitting room. The noise of the game show drifted in from the living room.

"I don't want to disturb my grandmother," she said.

"All right."

They sat down facing each other. She adjusted the hem of her dress, a spring dress with flowing sleeves and a floral print.

"Where were you last night?" Fisher asked.

"Here."

"Around seven?"

"Right around that time. I got some groceries, stayed awhile at the library, but I was home before dark."

"You didn't go back out?"

"No."

"Did you know Father Joseph Conzenza?"

"I've talked to him. He's sort of a friend." She froze. Her eyes grew wide. "You spoke of him in the past tense."

"He's been murdered."

She felt the blood rush out of her face. For a moment she thought she might faint from the shock. Her hands gripped the arms of her chair. The priest lived so close. She suddenly remembered every time she'd seen him, remembered his face, his expressions. All of it ran before her in a rush of memory.

"He's dead?"

"Yes, he is, Miss Winston. He was killed last night."

She rested her forehead against her hands. She did not cry, but she felt a tightness in her throat.

"Miss Winston, I need to ask you some questions."

"I hadn't seen him in a few weeks."

"But you knew him. I need to know a few things."

"Yes."

He drew a slow breath which rasped across his teeth. Then, from his coat, he took a notebook, and crossing his legs, rested the tablet on one knee.

"You talk to angels," he said.

She turned her eyes from him, her face coloring with the embarrassment of the accusation. It was hard to explain her experiences, especially to someone who was skeptical, someone who didn't understand.

Often, she wished she had never told anyone of them. But she had mentioned them from time to time, so the few people she came into contact with knew about them and spread the stories until they were embellished and spoken of throughout the community.

She had talked of them to the priest, but he had been one of the few to listen without a smirk on his face. They had not agreed on many things, and often she sensed that he did not believe her experiences were true outside of her imagination, but he at least was patient and understanding. There were things in his religion similar to what she spoke of—visitations, visions. She had found some comfort in talking to him, especially in the early days of her experiences, when she had feared she was losing her mind. He'd at least been consoling, letting her know there were things outside the realm of regular experience.

But father was dead, and this policeman didn't seem sympathetic to such matters. He thought she was crazy. She could detect it in the way he looked at her.

"You've heard things about me," she said. "Stories aren't always what they seem."

"So what's the truth?"

She folded her hands together, wringing them.

"I have experiences. I don't know how to describe them exactly, but I am in contact with an angel," she said.

The policeman scribbled on the crumpled notebook.

"Would the name of this angel be Azarius?"

He pronounced it badly, but she nodded. A frown furrowed her brow.

"How do you know that?"

"People talk." He tugged his tie loose from his collar and

unbuttoned the top button, tilting his head to stretch the muscles of his throat.

"That's the angel's name."

"How long has this gone on?"

"Several years."

"You told the priest about this?"

"Yes."

"What did he say about it?"

"He was understanding. We didn't agree on things, but we were friends. I haven't seen him in a while."

"This angel. It talks to you?"

"Yes."

"What does it say?"

"That's hard to describe. Sometimes, when it appears, we go on journeys together. It's like walking through meadows. He tells me things about myself, things I haven't realized."

She wet her lips. Her voice was trembling. She looked at her hands lying in her lap. They were limp. She raised one hand and began to run it through her hair, twisting strands around her index finger.

"Does he tell you what to do?"

"There are some suggestions."

"He ever suggest you kill a priest?"

She jumped at his words.

"Never," she said.

"You said you disagreed with Conzenza. Maybe the angel felt the priest needed to be stopped from spreading inaccurate information."

"No. I liked Father Conzenza. I had no reason to want to hurt him. He was kind to me."

"Do you have any boyfriends?"

He changed subjects so quickly it was surprising. She shook her head.

80

"You're a nice-looking lady. That's kind of strange."

"I have to take care of my grandmother."

"Hmm. That must get, uh, kind of lonely."

She swept her hair back out of her face and forced herself to meet his gaze, staring back at his stark eyes. "It does," she said.

"Ever think a priest might get that way, too?"

"I suppose that would be true."

"Ever go to him? Tell him you were lonely?"

"I never really spoke to him about that sort of thing. We talked about theology."

"He was a nice-looking man, though. Wouldn't you say?"

"What are you getting at?"

"You're lonely. Maybe you figured he was, too. You thought he might stray a little from the faith. Maybe you went to him, made a few suggestions. Instead of giving in, he rejected you, and how does that phrase go? You rose up against him and slew him."

She was on her feet before she knew it. Her actions surprised her. Anger was an emotion she seldom experienced.

"You don't know what you're talking about." Her hands clenched at her sides, and she felt the blood rushing to her face. Her voice was a screech which she couldn't control. "You don't have any reason to come in here and say that."

"I'm trying to solve a murder, Miss Winston. I have to look at all sides."

"Well, I haven't killed anyone. I couldn't."

"I'm sure Cain said the same thing once." He was making fun of her beliefs.

"Mr. Fisher, I don't appreciate this. If you don't have any further questions, I suggest you leave."

He smiled and tipped his hat. "I'll go. We don't want to disturb your grandmother." He winked. "Just remember.

81

I may come back, seeing these fits of temper you're prone to."

He lifted his bulk slowly out of the chair and showed himself to the door.

Dareena sank back to the couch, dropping down and bowing her head. She hadn't expected the assault, and on top of the notice of Father's death it had been almost devastating. She began to weep, the tears dripping down off her face onto her dress.

She felt the shock of the murder, but she also sensed something. She was not in constant contact with the angel. Experiences happened only on occasion, yet now somehow she was aware of the angel, sensitive to it, and Azarius seemed disturbed, perhaps frightened of something.

Dareena couldn't understand.

CHAPTER 7

Jennifer had wanted to go alone to speak to her father, so Gable sat by himself in his living room reading the Bible as the morning passed.

It was an old volume that had been a gift from his grandmother one Christmas, and on the cover his name was engraved, although the lettering had faded.

Flipping through the brittle pages, he saw phrases he'd underlined in the past. It had been a long time since he'd picked the book up, and he couldn't remember why he'd marked some of the passages. It must have been for some Sunday school lesson or church retreat or some phrase he hoped to use as a title for a short story at one time or other.

The edition was a standard King James version with the words of Christ in red but not much other annotation.

Since it did not contain the Apocrypha, it didn't contain the story the priest had told about Raphael. Gable had learned there were some differences between the Bibles used by Catholics and the Bibles used by Protestants. He had to scan the pages to find references to angels. They were there but weren't easy to locate. After he'd searched both Testaments for a while, gleaning a few facts here and there, he put the Bible aside.

He still didn't know much about angels when he was finished, but he'd gathered enough from the biblical references to make him a little more familiar with the topic, and he'd made a few notes.

Gable wondered how much of Dareena's angel had come out of imagination and how much she had incorporated from the Bible. He had no way of knowing how much scripture had been drilled into her over the years.

If her ideas had grown strictly out of religious tradition, her angel might be visualized. That would be important. In writing about it, he could describe what she saw. That would be more tangible than a distant voice. He was beginning to think in terms of a story. Maybe even a book.

Whether she was guilty or innocent of the murder, her link to a killing was fascinating. In a way, he hated to think of tackling the project, but he was right here on top of it, in a position to put it together.

He didn't want to abandon the summer's work on his novel, but he was beginning to think it might be a good idea to look into this matter from a journalistic perspective.

He leaned back in his chair and rubbed the dog's head. For a book sale he could postpone his escape from journalism for a while. Besides, writing down what really happened was a good deal easier than trying to make everything up.

Besides, he had not failed to learn from his work in journalism. He knew how to dig for things. Stories were a matter of putting all the pieces together.

The first thing he needed to do was find somebody who knew a lot about theology, someone who might make some kind of diagnosis about Dareena's visions. Background was always important.

Jennifer had to wait for her father when she got to his office because he was late getting back from lunch. She sat in the waiting area, a dark room with thick carpeting, and watched the receptionist—a slender black girl, very matter-of-fact. It wasn't easy to talk to her, so Jennifer wound up thumbing through old issues of *U.S. News and World Report* while she waited.

Waiting was bad, because it gave her time to anticipate her father's reaction when she told him what was going on. He was going to panic.

He always reacted badly. In high school she'd always suffered when a new boy asked her out. It meant a grueling process. First, her father interrogated her about him. His courtroom procedure shone through, and she felt as if she were on the witness stand. He wasn't a criminal lawyer, but he'd handled enough contract disputes to make him good at dragging out information. When the time came for him to meet the boy, there'd be further interrogation, albeit a bit more discreet. At least Philip Nelson did exercise some tact in his cross-examination of Jennifer's dates.

Still, he was a difficult obstacle for young men to face.

More than once he'd caused her to lose guys she liked because they didn't want to put up with him. Several of her dates had informed her they never looked forward to the conversations with her father in the living room which always preceded an outing.

She was thinking about that when he finally showed up, Doren Terry and Hamilton Terry in tow.

That was a surprise. She knew he was involved in the business surrounding the Clairmont, but she wasn't expect-

85

ing to see Mr. Terry and especially not Hamilton. The last time she'd run into him had been one summer while they were still in college. She'd been home from LSU, and he'd been home from Princeton. Things had been awkward then, because once upon a time they'd dated.

He looked good, she decided. He was wearing a dark suit that fit flawlessly, and he didn't have the harried look his father had. He looked immaculate, Ivy League.

But still it felt a little funny running into him. He seemed distant when she spoke to him, and he made no effort at conversation, as if he felt equally awkward.

Nelson smiled.

"There's my literature expert," he said, hugging her. "I wish you'd been by in time for lunch. You remember Doren, and I bet it's been a long time since you and Hamilton got together."

"A while," she said.

Hamilton nodded.

"Too bad. We used to think you two would be married."

"Wishful thinking," Doren said. He looked at both of them and smiled. "You could both do a good deal worse." He laughed. "But Hamilton's engaged now, and we wouldn't want anything to mess that up. Julia gets jealous easy."

"Daddy, I need to talk to you," Jennifer said.

"What's up?" Nelson asked.

"It needs to be in private."

He frowned.

"Sure." He turned back to his guests. "Doren, if it's all right, I'll call you this afternoon and we'll talk. Jenny's so independent now, it's a rare occasion when she wants to sit down with me. I'd hate to pass it up."

"I understand," Doren said. He winked at Jennifer. "See you, babe. Maybe you and Hamilton will get together for a drink sometime. We can explain it to Julia."

Jennifer forced a smile, and Hamilton gave a brief nod, but he didn't waste any time making for the door.

When the two were gone, Jennifer followed her father down the hall, past the other offices of the firm.

His office was a large room with paneling of a dark, rich color. In one corner a rubber plant was set in a brass pot, and there were a couple of framed paintings on the walls.

One wall was lined with bookshelves containing the heavy and important-looking law library, and near the window the desk, massive in size, was positioned to face a couch and a couple of chairs.

Every time she came in here to talk to her father, Jennifer felt she was entering a throne room for an audience.

She sat down in one of the armchairs and crossed her legs, letting her purse drop to her side.

She'd put on a dress and taken some care with her hair before coming here, and she tried to create an air of composure as she spoke. Evidently no one from the police had talked to her father yet, so she broached the subject delicately.

Nelson sat with his hands on his desk, listening and nodding his head as she spoke. He didn't show any burst of emotion, but when she had finished speaking he was out of his chair quickly.

He stood looking out the window.

"You need to move back home," he said.

"I knew you were going to say that. Are you going to force me?"

He turned, a bit surprised.

"You're in danger."

"It could be just a crank."

"Not if Father Conzenza is dead. Your mother and I were shocked when we read about it this morning, but if we'd had any idea you'd been threatened . . ."

"If I was. It could have been a joke, a coincidence. I'm telling you about it because you'll hear it from the police. I didn't want you to be shocked. I'd like to stay at my place. I'd just be in Mother's way back at home, and I do have things I have to take care of. I don't have forever to finish my thesis."

"Your safety comes first. It's ridiculous that you should even think of staying alone."

"I'll be fine. I'll keep my doors locked. Daddy, I'm grown. If I didn't have you I'd have to handle this by myself. You can't keep me sheltered. Suppose I was away from home and this came up? Would you make me move all the way back from Baton Rouge or somewhere?"

He lowered his eyes.

"I just want what's best for you." The old cliché, the old excuse.

She moved to him, touching his arm.

"I know you do," she said. "I appreciate that. I came here to talk to you about it because I care about you, too. And because I want to make you understand I have to have some independence."

He put his arm around her, gently raising his hand to her hair.

"I understand what you're saying," he said. "I just don't think it's wise."

"Maybe it's not. I won't say I'm not scared. But I'm scared, too, of being back at home. Once you get me there, this will all blow over, and then you'll want to keep me there. Mother will say as long as I'm home there's no need to go through all the trouble of moving out again. I know it. I'm asking you to try to understand."

Nelson patted her back gently. She could see in his eyes he would not use strong-arm methods on her. The comfort

88

of having her under his roof wouldn't compensate for her animosity, which would be inevitable.

He walked back over to his chair and sat down. It was almost as if he were sulking, expecting her to break down without being forced. It was the way he had always been, pretending to give her a choice while making his wishes clear at the outset.

"Your mother is going to be very worried," he said. "It will be hard on her."

"She's always worried about me." Jennifer could remember seeing the bedroom curtain flick open when she returned from dates. As soon as the tires of her date's car touched the driveway, her mother was out of bed, checking to make sure it wasn't the state patrol coming to tell of an accident.

"I can't help the way Mother feels. Every time I set foot out of her sight she worries. I won't let you make me feel guilty."

Nelson placed his palms flat on his desk and looked down at the lines on the back of his hands.

"All right," he said finally. "I'll explain it to her."

"Thank you."

He raised a finger. "I'm also going to talk to some people. Make sure the police keep an eye on you. What was the name of the detective?"

"Fisher."

His features wrinkled, and he groaned.

"Something wrong?"

"How'd he get assigned?"

"I don't know. He was just on duty, I guess."

"That's just wonderful. He's an idiot." He picked up the phone. "Madelyn. Get me the D.A.'s office." He cupped his hand over the receiver. "I'm going to make sure the D.A. puts someone with some sense on this."

Jennifer nodded. She'd won. He was going to pull strings to look after her, but that was better than having him shackle her and drag her home.

The thought of going back to her place was frightening, but she could cope with it. Gable would be close by. She hoped she could trust him.

She also hoped the police would catch the killer quickly. With any luck, the matter would be over soon.

She breezed past the receptionist, forcing the fear from her mind. It was a pretty day, not a day to be afraid of clouds or of darkness.

But she was watched as she left the office building and moved along the sidewalk. It wasn't time for her to die yet. The first trail had to get cold, and she would have to let her guard down again. There were precautions to be taken. There was no reason her death couldn't be enjoyed, but enjoyment couldn't take precedence over purpose.

The eyes trailed her path down the street, past shop windows, where she paused briefly to look at displays. She was a delicate creature.

Yes, her death could be enjoyed.

Walker Vincent entered the office and closed the door before he shrugged off his sport coat and moved toward his cubicle.

He was just inches from his chair before one of the secretaries flagged him down with a little pink message slip.

He muttered under his breath but forced a smile as she drew near. It was Jessica. She was a short girl, always well dressed. Her blond hair bounced against her shoulders as she walked toward him.

"The big man wants to see you," she said.

"I do something wrong?"

"You never do anything wrong." She flashed a smile

90

before turning away from him. He watched the twitch of her form beneath her skirt as she returned to her desk.

Walker was nice looking. Most of the women in the office, the ones who weren't too shy, flirted with him. He had straight black hair that had a sheen to it, a glow offset by the gleam in his blue eyes. He was only five nine, but women didn't seem to mind. He'd exercised until his shoulders were broad and his form lean.

Three times a week, unless he had a heavy court date, he worked out with weights at a local health club. He managed to find time to go jogging every morning. He had to keep his body in shape to match his intellect. Vincent had plans, and he didn't want anything to interfere.

He did make time for some important indulgences, however. He'd never hesitated to take advantage of the allure he seemed to hold to women, although the majority of his dates weren't with girls in the office.

He concentrated his conquests on those he didn't have to work with and face later. Shattered relationships could be awkward, and Vincent didn't want friction in the workplace. He didn't want anything that might interfere with his career. He had priorities. Sooner or later he would need a wife, but that was not something to rush into. There were other moves he needed to make first.

At thirty, and rising through the ranks, he was in a good position as an assistant D.A., and he was well aware that he was a good deal smarter than some of the people in higher positions in the office. In addition to his other gifts, he had a legal mind he liked to think of as razor sharp. He'd studied at Tulane and graduated at the top of his class, done some work for a New Orleans firm right out of school, and then moved back to Aimsley, where he worked briefly for a local attorney.

When the offer of assistant D.A. had come along, he'd

91

jumped at it. While arrogant about most aspects of his career, Vincent didn't deny he was lucky, damned lucky, as he put it, to be where he was at such a young age.

Tossing his jacket on his chair, Vincent moved down the hall toward Norman Jackson's office. Jackson had been district attorney for almost a year now, and he was making inroads into the drug trafficking in the area. Prosecutions on possession with intent to distribute impressed the public. Now and then Jackson liked to drop the message that a third of the cocaine entering the United States came in through Louisiana, and there were also crack and angel dust on the street to damage young minds. That got everybody shaking.

If Jackson could just learn to talk to the media properly instead of letting his fat PR boy do it, he might be in for a decent term of office, and if Jackson was secure, Walker was secure. That would do until he was ready to be D.A. himself.

He knocked on Jackson's door and walked inside. The D.A. was sitting at his desk, sleeves rolled up to his elbows and his gray hair out of place because he'd run his hands through it. He'd unbuttoned his vest. It was the look they'd photographed for his campaign. Today he hadn't had to cultivate the image.

A paper coffee cup sat in front of him, and a cigarette smoldered among a pile of butts in his ashtray.

Beside him stood a tall black man in a pinstripe suit. The black man, Isaac Arbor, looked much better preserved than did Jackson.

"Where the hell have you been?" Jackson asked. "I've got something I need you to take care of."

From the way Jackson looked, Walker had a feeling he wasn't going to like it. It had to be something touchy, something that could be held against him if it fell apart, whether it was his fault or not.

The fact that Arbor was here didn't soothe his feelings any. Arbor was Jackson's favorite investigator. He was good, no doubt about it, but if he was being called in for this special case, it was going to be the queen mother of bitch assignments.

"What's up?" Vincent asked, trying to sound energetic, the way he described himself in his résumés.

"We've got a lulu," Jackson said. "You heard about the priest killing."

"Yeah? Have we got someone already?"

"I wish the fuck we did," Jackson said. "We don't, and Fisher is on it. He was on duty last night when it came in, and he's holding on to it. The problem is his method is sluggish, and we need to kick ass." Jackson leaned back in his chair, touching his rounded stomach. He winced for a moment. "Dogged persistence is good, but I want somebody on the chopping block quick."

"The latest," Jackson went on, "is that some nut has threatened Phil Nelson's daughter. He gave me a call a while ago. His support is important at election time, and I don't need to remind you how important my reelection is."

"Yes sir."

"So we're going to do something a little different. We aren't going to worry about building a case. We're going to bust our asses trying to find out who did it. Before he kills Jennifer Nelson, too. I have a feeling that would piss Phil off real bad."

"Yes sir."

"That's what I want you and Arbor to do. Fisher will complain, but he'll get over it. On top of everything, this will look good in the media, like we're task-forcing it. The city police will have other people contributing to the investigation, so image-wise it's going to look positive all around."

93

Shit. Walker had known it was going to be bad, but this was worse than he'd thought. He was looking at a real mess, and if they couldn't find the killer, he was going to be holding the bag. This was the sort of thing his future opponents would love to have on him when his own election time rolled around.

If he didn't break this, he'd never have his shot at the top office, which meant he'd be stuck as an assistant from now on unless he wanted to set up his own office, and he didn't give a damn about being a defense attorney. He was a prosecutor; that was his talent. He was skilled at making other people look bad.

He definitely wasn't a manhunter to track down maniacs. Some days it didn't even pay to get out of bed and get your first cup of coffee, he thought.

He sank down in a chair, still trying to maintain his look of enthusiasm. He turned to Arbor, who stood about six nine, it seemed. He was as tall as an oak.

"What have we got?"

"It's a strange one. Fisher's got one lead. There's a girl who talked to angels. Her favorite angel's name was written on the chapel wall in the priest's blood."

Vincent's spirits lifted. "Then it is a matter of building a case."

"I don't know," Arbor said. "The guy was cut up pretty bad. That's not something women normally do."

"She's psychotic," Walker suggested.

"Still, there were some pretty strong blows, according to the coroner's prelim. We'll know more when we get the forensic report from Shreveport, but this may not have been a job for a woman's strength."

"Have you seen her?"

"Fisher interviewed her. She's thin."

Walker pursed his lips and rubbed his chin with his thumb.

"Crazy people surprise you with their strength."

Arbor still shook his head. "I think we need to keep looking. We can keep an eye on her, but I don't want us to let our guard down. If we're watching her too closely and the killer is somebody else, that leaves too much freedom for another strike."

Vincent nodded. It would be embarrassing to make a show of having the killer, only to see another murder occur. Vincent had no desire to railroad the wrong person, just to put an end to the matter.

The way it looked, he had a great deal of sweating to do for the next few days. Why did these things have to get handed to him? He didn't ask for easy cases, was willing to tackle the worst of them and work long hours, but weird ones, touchy ones, were another story.

Besides, he had no doubt that Jackson would throw him to the wolves if necessary.

This wasn't going to be fun. He looked forward to it being over as he walked back to his cubicle. The sooner things were back to business as usual, the happier he'd be.

CHAPTER 8

Gable made some phone calls and wound up contacting a theology professor at a small school called Pine College located in a town ten miles from Aimsley, Penn's Ferry.

The man was named Leonard Seaview, and his voice had a slow southern drawl that made him sound easygoing and jovial.

"Angels?" he said. "I know a little bit about angels. What do you need to know?"

Gable couldn't help but laugh at his tone. "I'm doing some research for a possible article," Gable said. "I was wondering if I might talk to you."

"You plannin' to quote me?"

"Only in print."

That brought a chuckle over the line. "I guess I can clear some space for you. The only thing I'm involved in right now is trying to get my notes ready for summer school." There was a pause, and Gable imagined the man winking. "Don't tell the dean that, though. He thinks I'm working on a paper. It's a publish-or-perish world."

"I'll keep that in mind," Gable said.

"So tell me. What is it you need to know about angels?"

What are you up to? Isn't there some girl over there in Aimsley that talks to angels?

"Word travels."

"This is the South, son. It's too damned hot to do anything but talk." The man laughed. "Yeah, I've heard of her."

"She may be involved in a murder. A good defense attorney could build quite a case. Even if she doesn't get into trouble, there could be an interesting story here. I need to know something about the traditional beliefs about angels, and I guess the possibilities of psychosis."

"Come on over here tomorrow then, son. We'll talk. I'll tell you all I know. It's not a whole lot."

Gable wrote down the directions.

Seaview hung up the phone and leaned back in his chair. He was a thin man in his fifties, his brown hair receding slightly at the temples, where it was also beginning to turn gray. His face was lined, showing age earlier than it should. Wrinkles circled his eyes.

He had smiled while he talked to the young man. Once off the line, his smile faded. He had feelings of apprehension, and he wasn't sure why. It wasn't about being quoted. He'd experienced that before, even been misquoted a time or two. He'd grown used to seeing people from the *Clarion*.

He couldn't imagine what else would be troubling him, unless it was the sound of youth in the caller's voice.

There was something more in the young man's voice—an openness. The young man was prepared to have an open mind, whatever he was told. He didn't sound like the type to swallow everything that was dished up to him, but he wouldn't turn his nose up at something without trying it either.

97

That somehow reminded Seaview of himself when he'd left rural Mississippi to study theology and become a preacher.

He missed that wide-eyed, open-minded version of himself, the scholar destined to become a visionary. In school he'd been fascinated by the whole process of scholarship, the studying, the research. Unlike many students, he loved the hours he spent in libraries, haunting back shelves, digging up old volumes and making notes.

While in seminary, he'd worked at small churches, but it became apparent during that period that he would be a teacher and not a pastor, because there was so much he wanted to do, so much he had wanted to study and write. There were things he had to tell.

He missed those early days. Back then he'd still had faith, a strong faith that transcended the intellectual understanding of principles. He could feel it deep within himself when he prayed.

Sometimes he wondered when he'd lost it, where it had gone. He'd taught in some important seminaries after receiving his doctorate, had lectured at Harvard and attended conferences with some of the major theologians, the thinkers of the day.

Gradually he'd sought more quiet surroundings, however. He'd been at Pine now for five years, teaching basic philosophy courses and sitting in on discussions of medical and scientific ethics.

He was supposed to be here because it afforded him time to devote to his research. He was expected to come up with some major treatise, some great statement of truth.

That wasn't happening. He knew the truth and sometimes even confronted it. The truth was he liked the quiet, liked the lack of challenge. He was safe here, safe in his quiet little office, safe at this quiet little college, a quiet little world.

Part of him dreaded seeing the young man, feared what news the young man would bring. It might be something that would thrust him back into the mainstream. He might have to contemplate some real question of truth, something harder to grapple with than the morality of recombinant DNA.

Another part of him looked forward to it. There was a certain excitement in the thought of confronting something unknown—a girl with some psychosis related to religious beliefs. That was something tangible, something he might be able to make legitimate comments about.

He got out of his chair and began to tug books from his shelf. The young man's primary interest was in the nature of angels in the Judaeo-Christian tradition. That would be a good starting point, probably the point where the girl's disorder had begun. Whatever religious training she'd had about angels had probably planted the seed in her brain. What could produce a psychological disorder based on those teachings, well-meant teachings by parents or churchmen?

Leonard felt a shiver dance down his spine. It was strange, something he hadn't felt since watching frightening movies as a child. For a moment he hesitated, unsure of what he was feeling. When the sensation did not return, he turned his thoughts back to his library.

Jennifer got home by three. She saw Gable's car in his driveway and felt relieved that he was there. She thought about going over and saying hello, but she stopped herself.

She didn't want to have to rely on Gable. That would be just switching her dependence from her father to someone else. That defeated the purpose.

Gable was there in case of an emergency. That was all he should be, a neighbor. Not someone to lean on, just someone to turn to when there was no other alternative.

If something developed between them, she didn't want it to grow out of an uneven relationship. Starting things off on the wrong foot would only cause problems later on. She didn't want to become a little girl to Gable. She wanted to be his equal.

Besides, he had things of his own to take care of, just as she did. He wasn't there to be her guardian.

She unlocked her door, went into her house, and climbed the stairs to her bedroom.

There, she sat down on the bed and pulled the covers around her, using them like a security blanket.

She felt like a child again, seeking security in warmth and quiet. As a little girl her room had always been her favorite place when she was afraid.

This room was not as bright or as cozy as her childhood refuge had been, but it did have that calming effect of familiarity.

With the sunlight streaming through the windows she felt happy and safe. Storms and darkness and intangible memories were not a threat here.

This was a place where nothing bad could happen. She told herself that over and over so she could believe it. There had to be a good place to go to. Everybody needed one.

She'd found something akin to an anchor. Now that she'd stood up to her father she was committed to sticking out the situation she was facing.

Another dark stormy night might be a challenge, though.

Dareena didn't tell her grandmother about the policeman's visit. The old woman never asked who had been at the door.

She had probably forgotten, and that was best, much easier than trying to make her understand. This way she wouldn't worry or become upset.

The girl spent the afternoon in her room while Grandmother watched *Another World* and *Santa Barbara*.

For a while she read one of the new books, eventually putting it aside because it was too difficult to concentrate. The policeman kept drifting back to her thoughts—the big, harsh man. He was frightening. What if he really believed she'd had something to do with Father Conzenza's death?

The idea was absurd, yet the detective had been menacing, and what if he did pursue the matter, building a case against her? It was possible. She had known the priest. How would she be able to prove her innocence if they came up with some kind of circumstantial evidence?

She envisioned the complications, maybe even a trial. A nervous knot of tension began to grow in her stomach. She had no one to turn to; her grandmother wouldn't be able to help, and they hadn't had a lawyer in ages, not since her custody arrangement had been worked out. She had no idea how to go about finding an appropriate attorney now.

Rising, she moved across the room to the dresser, switching off the lights on the way because they cast a glare against the mirror.

The curtains were already drawn, so the room was dim, full of shadows with only the slight luminance of the sun through the curtains keeping away total darkness.

Opening a drawer in the dresser, she removed a red candle and a small holder. With a package of paper matches she touched flame to the wick.

In the darkened room the glow was eerie. It reflected against the mirror, casting a white-orange light without eliminating the shadows. The glow danced around the walls, shimmering.

Dareena closed the drawer and stepped over to the door, making sure it was locked before she returned to her place in front of the mirror. She opened the next drawer and looked up into the glass.

The shadow figure was there now, not facing her exactly, it wasn't as if it were within the mirror. The image seemed to hover inside the reflection, but she knew if she looked behind her there would be only shadow.

The dry, humming sound pierced the room, slowly gaining volume.

"You are frightened," the shadow figure said, the voice so deep it seemed to be turned inward upon itself.

She nodded.

"They think I killed a priest. Your name was written by his body in his blood."

"I know."

"How?"

There was a laugh. She'd come to know there wouldn't be any further answer after that. Azarius was penurious with information. It had always been that way, always a degree of ambiguity.

He sometimes spoke in riddles. Other times he was free in giving what he wanted her to know.

He spoke of the realms beyond the reality she perceived, the realms to which he would someday take her, the worlds of light and color. He tried to explain what the remote colors were like, those colors that couldn't be seen within the earthly spectrum.

They must be very beautiful, and she looked forward to the day of seeing them, the day when she had progressed enough in her understanding and wisdom to follow or travel with Azarius into those realms of which he spoke.

He wanted to take her, but it wasn't yet the time. She

wasn't ready to make the crossover. Her soul was not liberated and pure enough.

She was impatient, but Azarius was reassuring. The time would come, he told her. There would be a moment when she would be prepared. Her awareness would be ready to expand, to allow her to travel through the dimensions across the misty bands of division.

Azarius was patient, always reassuring. He loved her. She could feel that love in his words and in the presence amid the shadows. That wasn't his true form. At times she found the seemingly more accurate image of him within her imagination, but she knew that wasn't really his appearance either. As long as she was grounded in reality, or the perceived reality of the world around her, the natural world, she knew she wouldn't have the true impression of him, just as she would not have a true perception of the remote colors until she was able to see them.

She was waiting for the time when she could really be with him, the time when the gulf between the realms did not divide them. They would be able to find a bonding unlike that of human lovers, something far superior.

What would it be like to be held by him? Not like being in someone's arms, she knew. Yet certainly it would be something more wonderful than the embraces in the novels she read, embraces of unimagined warmth.

While she waited, she had to settle for the comfort Azarius could offer through his descriptions. The words were like coarse discord transferring into this realm, yet they became a melody, a sweet whisper.

Closing her eyes, she searched her imagination for the image, the portrait of Azarius, the sunlight flame.

Her hands crept over her body slowly, down her sides, and then back up along her thighs and across her abdomen. At her throat her slender fingers trembled as she began

103

to unfasten the collar of her dress. The backs of her fingers moved across the skin of her throat as she pulled the cloth away.

Her caresses continued, still slow, but her movements coincided with the voice. Slipping away her dress and her undergarments, she sank to her knees on the carpet and eased backward on to the floor, letting her hair spill back behind her.

The carpet was soft beneath her skin. She kept her eyes closed, fingers still moving, down across her breasts and abdomen and over her thighs—soft, delicate touches that coupled with the voice to trail her back into oblivion.

Fisher bulldozed into the conference room with his jacket over one arm and a happy-face mug of coffee in his free hand. He stalked over to one of the metal chairs near the table, turning it around to straddle it.

Vincent could tell the big bear wasn't happy about having to share the case.

"Evening, Fisher."

Fisher took a swig of the coffee and nodded his greeting before he began to drum his thick fingers on the tabletop.

"What gives?" Fisher asked.

"The killing of a priest is a touchy subject. It has to have special attention. This way, we have a task force."

"I hear it's political. The little cunt that got threatened has a daddy who's connected."

Vincent shrugged.

"Yeah," Fisher said. "I bet you don't know. We pull this one off, you won't be far from making D.A. when the time comes. If the public forgets, you'll get the PR people to remind them at election time."

"Look, Fisher, we've got a job to do. Save your hostility for the reporters."

"This is my cheerful side. You haven't seen hostile."

Vincent attempted to touch the detective's arm, but the big man moved out of his reach with a jerk of his arm.

Vincent tried to force a smile. "Fisher, there is no need for you to react this badly."

Fisher nodded his head, his face taking on an expression of disgust.

"You're stealin' my fuckin' case. What am I supposed to do? Tap-dance and kiss your shoes? Or is that what your partner does, your buddy, the gentleman of color."

"That's enough, Fisher. Isaac is a good investigator. Before this is all said and done, you're going to need all the help you can get."

"Yeah, but before you showed up my help was going to be from another policeman the way it's supposed to be. Now I've got the damned Miami Vice boys. How much did you pay for that suit, Walker?"

Vincent felt his face flush, and he pushed himself up out of his chair. He didn't want to discuss the dark three-piece he'd had tailored. It would only aggravate Fisher further.

"Listen, Fisher. We're going to work together, and we're going to crack this case. If we don't do it quick, we've all got a lot to lose."

Fisher chuckled and sipped his coffee without looking at Vincent. The big jerk knew how to be irritating. Vincent sank back into his chair, straightening his tie.

They didn't speak again until Arbor showed up about ten minutes later. He sat down at the end of the table opposite Fisher, but as the two glared at each other it was apparent the black man was giving no quarter.

Eventually he turned his gaze to Vincent.

"You want to lead?"

"I've already given Fisher a little pep talk. I guess the next thing is to figure out our plan of action." He looked at Fisher. "Anything from the lab yet?"

"Nothing that points a finger anywhere. He was stabbed eight times. He was dead before it was all over."

"Weapon?" Arbor asked.

"Knife. Large blade, probably a kitchen utensil."

"That's something the girl would have had easy access to, then."

"Yeah." Fisher pursed his lips, taking his time about making another statement. "There's one problem," he said.

"What?" Vincent asked.

"This isn't saying she's not the one," Fisher said. "Just that one of the blows was pretty deep. Deeper than you'd expect a woman's strength to land one. Like I say, that doesn't rule her out. She could have been lucky. Besides, they say she's a looney. Crazy people can be real strong even if they don't look it."

That was the second time that issue had come up. Vincent didn't like the sound of it. "You talked to her," he said. "Could she have done it?"

"Anybody could have. I won't rule her out."

"Can she account for her whereabouts?"

"No, but she lives just with her grandmother. If she had an iron-clad alibi, I'd be inclined to wonder."

"What about the business with the angel?"

Fisher shrugged. "Beats me."

"How crazy is she?"

"She didn't seem nuts," Fisher said. "I've picked up some real head cases, and she wasn't like any of them. Religion is a funny thing."

"What was her relationship with the priest?"

"Just an acquaintance. I've done a little checking. I don't think there was anything going on there."

Vincent got up from his chair and walked along the room with his hands in his pockets. This wasn't going to be open and shut. If she was guilty, it was going to be hard to prove. With no witness they were going to have to establish circumstantial evidence. The name written in blood gave a connection, but he didn't feel it would be enough for a conviction.

They'd have to produce the weapon, maybe even hint at a motive, and when it got to trial they were going to have a heavy insanity defense to go up against. Not to mention the fact that two experienced investigators had questions about the girl's ability to inflict the fatal wounds.

This was a mess, no doubt about it.

"Is there somebody watching Jennifer Nelson?" Vincent asked. "I don't want her hacked up, too, in the course of this."

"The patrol in the area is going to keep an eye on her place," Fisher said. "We've got an unmarked car out there, too. Watching. There's some writer she's hanging out with. He brought her in last night. He needs to be checked out."

"What's the possibility on him?" Vincent wondered.

"I don't know. He's a little bit weird. Kind of long hair. Says strange things."

"You got info on him?"

"Yeah, we got it all last night."

"Issac, you want to check him out?"

"Yeah. It's as good a start as any."

"We need to know some more about the priest," Vincent said. "His friends. Enemies. That sort of thing."

"That's what I was gonna do next anyway," Fisher said. "I guess Ike will be helping me now."

"I'll do what I can," Arbor said solemnly.

Vincent ran his hand across his hair, letting it slide through his fingers.

107

"That leaves Dareena. I'll do some more checking on her."

"Are we going to have any more help on this?" Arbor asked.

"The chief is juggling some schedules to free some people," Fisher said.

"There's always the chance the killer will go after the girl," Vincent said.

He turned to Arbor. "Get something quick on this writer. If she's hanging around with him, he could behead her while the patrols think they're in her living room watching television."

"He shouldn't be too hard to trace," Fisher said. "Just do some sniffing, Ike."

Arbor ignored him.

"Let's roll," Vincent said. "Let's get this thing cleared."

Fisher got up out of his chair slowly, eyeing Vincent with contempt. The lawyer had to clench his teeth to keep from lashing out at the guy again. The arrogant bastard. Vincent hated having to depend on him, but he didn't have any choice.

Vincent cursed the whole situation under his breath. He wasn't supposed to be involved in the investigation. That wasn't how the game was played. His whole career was riding on this.

He prayed Arbor would come through. Or maybe he could turn something up himself. He knew he wasn't going to be able to rest until he got this out of the way and got back to his regular work.

The warm rays of the sun glistened off the blue water of the pool as Julia eased across the water in a backstroke, her long legs kicking gently until she reached the edge of the pool.

made enemies just like anyone else, but she could think of no concrete link between herself and a priest.

She was Catholic, but so were lots of people, many of them more devout than she was. During college and then her master's work, she had gradually slipped away from the church except for attending an occasional Mass.

The caller must have been trying to dream up some bizarre statement just to frighten her, something that would sound sinister in the middle of the night.

At any rate, she wasn't going to let it get to her.

She was visible in the front room when the curtains visible than in any other room in the house. Som required stealth to catch a glimpse of her, but room, a perch across the street was

There was a cold look window, as if th

as a reporter and he seemed to like talking about them. As he'd talked, she'd watched him. He had a tendency to look around while he spoke, surveying, his gray eyes darting over to meet her gaze only on occasion.

He was fairly nice looking, too. Not a Robert Redford, but he had rugged features, and the long hair made him look radical, maybe like an anarchist. She wondered if he was cultivating that look because he was trying to be a ʳriter.

⋯entually, he had fallen asleep in his chair, and she'd ⋯⋯p watching early morning television with the dog ⋯r lap.

⋯ in her own armchair with sunlight spilling ⋯ her fears of the dark and the thunder ⋯ugh she had always been frightened ⋯anting her freedom, that ⋯ from her parents:

In a quick pivot she changed position in the water and headed back down the pool in a graceful breaststroke.

At the far end of the pool she lifted herself from the water and walked over to the grass where she had spread her towel. She liked swimming at this time of day. There was more privacy. Most of the people in her apartment complex were at work.

This was about the only time of day she had free. She was so busy, planning her wedding to Hamilton.

Picking up her suntan lotion, she quickly massaged some onto her skin before leaning back on the towel to let the sun caress her already tanned skin.

She was a lean girl with long dark hair. The black one-piece suit she wore clung to the firm curves of her body. She wondered if anyone was looking at her. Hamilton promised her she was beautiful, praising especially her gray-green eyes.

She liked him to tell her she was beautiful. She had come to love him very deeply in the past few months. In private, he was a quiet man, his touch gentle. They were good for each other, good on the social scene and in their relationship. They belonged together, for they were a part of each other. Closing her eyes, Julia pictured their future, an unfolding mural of promise.

Hamilton had seemed worried on the phone today. She smiled. When they were together they wouldn't talk about the worries of the Clairmont. They would talk only about each other.

Jennifer invited Gable over for dinner partly because she was interested in him and partly because she didn't want to spend the evening alone.

She needed to prepare herself for the night, and company was the best method she could come up with.

A twofold project, she decided. She liked Gable. It had been a while since she'd found someone remotely intriguing. There were always men around, but there were few who didn't prove to be jerks in a short time.

She hadn't dated much in college, not since she'd had an unhappy fling with a graduate student during her sophomore year, her first real time-out from under her father's thumb.

Before that she hadn't gone out very much. At least, she hadn't dated many boys seriously. Her lack of circulation, as she sometimes called it, wasn't totally due to her father and his tendency to drive boys away, however. For some reason, she didn't fit into the game very well; perhaps didn't know the rules.

She didn't like to play sexual games, didn't like guys putting their hands into her bra on the second date or groping her. Physical relationships just weren't that casual to her. That attitude didn't make for popularity among college boys, but she didn't want to change it.

As for the affair with the graduate student, a guy who was 26 and studying English literature, that had not gone well from the very beginning. She hadn't been able to commit herself. It was hard to open up, to share things. He'd been a nice guy, friendly and kind, yet she'd alienated him, building a wall, until he finally got discouraged and moved on.

She wasn't sure why she'd been that way. It had just happened. She'd felt it before, as if she had a barrier that went up whenever she began to get serious or draw close to someone.

So far things hadn't been that way with Gable, probably

because things had been so strange, their meeting, then the business with the police.

She hadn't had time to build a barrier with Gable. Even that first night in the rain she'd found it easy to talk to him.

And he'd remained casual. Some guys would have taken a knock on the door in the middle of the night as only one kind of indication, but Gable hadn't made that assumption.

She wasn't sure what he liked, so she wound up fixing fried chicken, figuring she couldn't go wrong that way. He was a southern boy, bound to like chicken, while an exotic dish could easily turn out to be something he didn't care for.

She spent a short time getting it ready. This was a simple meal, not something to spend the whole afternoon on. If he expected too much, he could forget it.

She laughed. She was making him out to be pushy and macho. He was coming by invitation. He'd probably be happy with whatever she prepared.

Jennifer's efforts were visible through the kitchen window. She would have company tonight. Probably the guy from next door.

Patience was needed now. Let it suffice to think of the girl's death. If it went well, she would die slowly. Her death was a necessity, but there were things that could make her death very interesting.

Gable went next door at six, the dog trotting at his heels. The aroma of the chicken touched his nostrils as soon as Jennifer let him through the door, and the dog barked behind him to confirm mutual delight.

It had been a long time since he'd had fried chicken that didn't have the thick fast-food batter. He didn't spend much

111

time with the meals he cooked. Had he known how to go about frying a chicken, it was still something he wouldn't have undertaken because of the time it consumed.

Jennifer looked excellent. She'd curled her hair so it spilled around her face, framing her features with soft curls that caught the light with a gentle shine. She wore a dark blue blouse with a red sash, jeans, and boots that stretched just above her ankles.

Her eyes, he decided, were the color Raymond Chandler would have called cobalt blue. She smiled as she ushered him into the living room.

The curtains were drawn over the picture window, and an old-style floral lamp cast a warm glow over the room.

Gable noticed a bookcase across the room. It was a habit of his to survey the titles in people's libraries. The shelves here were lined mostly with textbooks and literary commentaries, although here and there there were a couple of wrinkled paperbacks by Sidney Sheldon and Fern Michaels. He scanned the shelves while Jennifer put the finishing touches on dinner.

She led him into the kitchen a few minutes later and seated him at a small round table covered by a red and white checked tablecloth.

The dog dropped to a seat at his side, practicing a sad-eyed look.

The setting was like a photograph from a cookbook. The plate of golden chicken the centerpiece, bordered by the mashed potatoes and vegetables.

Some fresh tomatoes decorated the salad bowl.

She opened a couple of cherry Cokes before she sat down across from him.

He relaxed. He'd been a little nervous about coming when she'd called. It took Gable a while to get comfortable with new people. Now he found Jennifer's smile comforting. At the moment he wasn't looking for anything serious, hoping instead to concentrate on his work, but she was a pretty girl. She seemed sensitive. It couldn't hurt to get to know her.

"I found someone to talk to about angels," he said as they began to eat.

"Really?"

"Over at Pine College. In Penn's Ferry?"

"Oh, yeah. I went there my freshman year before I transferred to LSU. My parents had to build up to letting me go away from home. It's not a long drive over to Pine, so they had me stay at home and take basic courses until they were able to deal with me living away from home."

"How did things go, talking to your father?"

"I'm here. I'm not locked in my bedroom. He's probably going to have half the police force swarming the neighborhood before he's through pulling strings, though."

Gable laughed. "My dad's like that, too. Parents mean well."

"I guess." She handed him the plate of chicken to change the subject. "But so, you're going to talk to this guy?"

"I may be wasting my time. I'm looking into a possible story about Dareena, *the girl who talked to angels.*"

"Could be interesting. If she comes over and stabs me to death, you'll have an exclusive on my last days." She sighed. "Guess I shouldn't be negative."

"You have a right to be frightened."

"I suppose." She waved her hand in a motion of dismissal. "Forget it. How's the chicken?"

"Crispy."

"Been a while since you've had a home-cooked meal?"

"Too long. I function, but I'm no gourmet cook."

One corner of her mouth turned up in a wry expression. "Are you lonely, Mr. Tyler?"

"I've got the dog." He folded his arms. "To be honest,

113

I guess I'm not at the moment. All my broken hearts have healed, and I've learned I can get by.'' He wasn't sure if that was going to scare her off or not. It didn't mean he wanted to be a hermit, but he was being honest.

"I guess I still have some mending,'' she said.

"Bad experience?''

"Not bad exactly. Just something that didn't work out. It's been awhile now. I've been concentrating more on school. I don't fall in love very easily. Sometimes I wonder if I'll ever fall in love.''

"Sometimes it feels a lot easier not to have a relationship. No struggles, no aggravations. No one lying to you.''

She laughed. "It's true. It's safer that way.''

They laughed during dinner, finding humor in each other's words. Afterwards, they stacked the plates in the sink and moved back into the living room.

She put a Billy Joel tape on the stereo and lit some candles.

"Can I ask you something kind of personal?'' she asked.

"I've never been convicted of any felonies.''

"No. Not like that. It's your name.''

"What about it?''

She bit her lower lip to keep from giggling. "It's a little different, don't you think?''

"Not really, I've had it for years.''

She laughed and picked up a pillow from the sofa, tossing it at him. He blocked it with his arm.

"No, my mom gave it to me,'' he said. "Her favorite book was *Gone with the Wind*.''

"So?''

"She couldn't really see naming me Rhett or Ashley, and I was a boy, so that ruled out Scarlett or Melanie. Clark was too much like Clark Kent, so Gable was the alternative.''

"Good name really. Dynamic."

"I suppose. I don't really match it."

She wrinkled her nose. "You're not so bad."

"I'm no Rhett Butler."

"And you don't give a damn?" She raised her eyebrows.

"Not really. That's my life story, what about yours?"

"No, no. It's still my turn. I wanted to ask you why you want to be a writer."

"It's just what I've always wanted to do."

Jennifer lifted her thumb to her lips, gently biting the tip. "So what do you want to know about me?"

"You going to be a teacher, or what?"

"I think I'm going to try to get my doctorate. Then teach, maybe tie my hair in a bun and get some glasses and spend my days at some quiet little college. I like literature. I'm not a writer like you, though. I don't think I could ever make up stories."

"It's easy."

"Not for me. When I was in high school I wrote poetry. This boyfriend found it and laughed and it crushed me."

"What do men know? As a rule, we can be real jerks."

"Some of you are all right."

"Wait till you get to know me. I have my bad points. They just don't show right away."

Gable was sitting on the floor, and she slipped off the couch to drop beside him. It was an abrupt move, but she kissed him gently on the cheek, then sidled back a few inches to look into his eyes. The candlelight cast a warm glow across his features. She could see the reflection of the flames in his eyes.

He smiled, easing his arm around her, letting her rest her head against his shoulder. It wasn't the time for anything heavy, just a moment of closeness.

He liked the way she felt, nestled beside him. Her hair

was soft against his face, her breath warm and moist against his neck.

Her arms around him, she gripped him tightly as if she didn't want to let go. On the stereo Billy sang a song about loneliness.

"I need you right now," Jennifer whispered, "but I don't want to become dependent on you."

"It's all right," he said. "I'm here. Sometimes we all need a shoulder."

They stayed there silently, not moving, and she drifted slowly off to sleep.

He looked down at her face in the faint light that crept through the shadows. Her features were angelic and placid, for a moment free from the tenseness of her life.

CHAPTER 9

Hamilton left Julia's place at ten and made it to the Clairmont by 10:30. The blond was on duty and he made conversation with her whenever she passed his table.

She knew who he was. He was sure of that. She smiled at him a time or two, displaying even, perfect teeth.

He watched her ass. The silky dress clung nicely, and beneath it he could make out the shape of her breasts.

He'd taken care in arranging his hair, fixing it the way the stylist had shown him so that the thin spot on top wasn't so noticeable, and he had on a stylish gray shirt and slacks with a light gray jacket. His shoes were shiny with sharp toes. He spent a bundle on casual clothes, taking care to make sure the items were tasteful. He didn't want to be some jerk in a John Travolta outfit.

For jewelry he wore only his Rolex, his college class ring, and a gold wrist chain.

He looked around the room. There was not a big crowd since it was a weeknight.

There were various businessmen, probably in town to make calls on their customers. A few local people had also drifted in and were clustered at the bar and around tables throughout the room. A few people had moved onto the dance floor to sway with the music of the small band.

Hamilton watched the musicians for a few moments, drumming his fingers on his table until the waitress came back into view. She was named Kim Ellington. He'd done some checking. She'd been hired just before the hotel opened. Prior to that she'd been working in a club across town. This was definitely a step up for her, but she didn't look like she belonged in a club at all. She didn't have that hardened look.

Her features were fresh and there was no sign of harshness in her eyes. Absent was that look women got when they were used to being hit on by men all the time.

She had to get a lot of attention, yet it hadn't made her hostile. She was friendly when she came around Hamilton's table, and he began to notice she was making a point of drifting by.

That was a good sign.

He sipped his margarita and traced her movements. She was beautiful. He liked the way she moved.

Any luck, and he'd be able to have a drink with her when she got off. Not here, but up in the Magnolia Suite. It wasn't rented tonight, and he could get access to it if he wanted.

It was one of the finest suites in the place, nestled up on the eighth floor, decorated in Victorian style.

He'd taken Julia up there one time before the place had officially opened. There were some privileges he exercised. Their visit there had been interesting. Julia had liked the Jacuzzi. She was a health nut, and she said the bubbles were good for the circulation.

After she dropped off a cocktail for a fat businessman across the room, the blond girl weaved back through the tables to stand beside Hamilton's chair.

"Can I get you anything else, Mr. Terry?" So she did know him. Hamilton was pleased.

"Call me Hamilton," he said, lifting his drink toward her in a salute.

"All right." She smiled.

"What's your name?" he asked, playing the game. He didn't want her to know he'd been checking on her.

"Kim Ellington."

"What time do you get off?"

She smiled. "Midnight."

"Maybe we could get together for a little while. Have a drink."

She made an awkward movement but coupled it with a smile. "Okay. That would be fun. I've seen you around here a lot."

"The place is nice for a lot of reasons. I see you in here a lot, too."

He lifted his glass again. "If I'm not here when you get off, I'll wait for you in the lobby."

"Fine. I'll look forward to it."

He watched her weave back through the tables. He'd felt a little nervous asking her, but it had been easy. She was sweet and more sexy than Julia. She wasn't a substitute for Julia, but she'd make a nice supplement, he thought as he leaned back over his table.

Julia had a tendency to whine if he didn't do things her way. He couldn't fault her much, though. She was good to him. She took care of him.

Kim was different. In a way she was a softer girl. She reminded him of his mother, in some ways at least. In the good ways. It had been a long time since he'd seen his mother, and he sometimes couldn't remember what she looked like. At times that was a blessing.

He remembered the times he'd cried about her being

gone. His father had always tried to comfort him, then wound up losing patience when the sobs didn't stop.

Doren's eventual solution had been to take him to talk it out with the parish priest. Religion was supposed to solve everything. Just ask God and it'll be taken care of.

The priest had been pleasant, had tried to help, but he couldn't explain where Hamilton's mother had gone, and he had no answer to Hamilton's big question: If she really cared about him, why didn't she come to see him every now and then or at least write or call? That had mattered then. Now it was a blessing that he didn't have to set eyes on her.

He finished off his drink. The past was the past. The hell with it. The evening looked promising.

When she got a break, Kim went to one of the pay phones in the lobby and called her sister, who was taking care of her little boy.

"I'm going to be late tonight," she said.

"Anything wrong?"

"Not at all. If you will, put Tommy to bed and I'll come by with some things for him in the morning before he has to get on the bus."

"What's going on?"

"You know the one I told you about? Hamilton?"

"The rich one?"

"Yes. He asked me out tonight."

"Is he cute?"

She had explained all about Hamilton, but her sister had a tendency not to listen. "Quite cute," Kim said.

"Nice?"

"Seems to be. I'm not expecting a proposal, but you never know. Maybe he's lonely. Rich and lonely with no one to spend his money on."

"Don't get your hopes up."

"I'm fine. Don't worry. I've gotta go. Kiss Tommy good night."

Kim hung up the phone. She hated leaving Tommy that way, but her sister lived in a trailer right next to Kim's so it wasn't like he was that far from home, and besides, she hated to juggle him around in the middle of the night when she came home from dates or from her shift. It was better to let him get a good night's rest.

It was hard on him when she had to work the late shift. At least she didn't have that many dates. That was not particularly pleasant for her on one level, but it did usually mean more time to spend with her son.

In a way it was a cycle. Even though she was pretty, a lot of men got turned off when they found out she had a kid. She knew of several women with children who'd remarried. It just never seemed to happen for her.

She was twenty-five and Tommy was six. His father had stayed married to her only a few months before he took off in his pickup truck for higher ground.

She hadn't bothered to look for the guy, feeling she was really better off without him. She had time.

Fortunately she looked nice enough and was able to fix up well enough to land pretty decent work. At least she didn't have to dance at the sleazy clubs. Her last job had been better than the one before it, and this job was the best yet.

The Clairmont was a classy place. The uniforms were nice and the clientele was sophisticated. Sometimes they made remarks, but most of the men refrained from pinching her. She didn't have to put up with rednecks in baseball caps the way she had at her last job.

And she'd finished high school and a little college. There was no reason she couldn't hit it off with Hamilton. Things

121

might go well. She might be able to move out of the lounge and get better work if she was nice to him. There might be even better things than that ahead with him.

She said a little prayer to that effect before she went back to work.

Before meeting Hamilton, she would pay a quick visit to the rest room to fix her hair and freshen her makeup. She wanted to make a good impression.

Vincent sat in his car across the street from Dareena's house. He'd driven by it a thousand times without giving it a thought, never expecting to be staking it out. He'd never expected to be staking anything out. He hated departures from normal procedure. An unorthodox investigation was supposed to impress the public, but how effective was it going to be? He cursed under his breath as he looked at the front of the house.

It was dark now, and he could see the girl sitting by a window at the front of the house. She was reading. On the windowsill her cat sat as if watching the darkness.

Earlier, before nightfall, she'd been sitting on the upstairs porch, the evening breeze gently caressing her hair. She was more attractive than Vincent had expected.

Women were his weakness, he had to admit, and she was a striking girl. She was innocent looking. That was always a temptation.

Innocent girls, the quiet ones with pent-up desires, were usually easy prey for Vincent's good looks and charm.

It had been that way in high school, and things hadn't really changed, except that he didn't have a big problem with guilt anymore. This was a modern world. If you weren't using someone, someone was using you. When he'd been younger he'd wrestled with regrets about women, until he got into college anyway. Times changed. He became an agnostic, and with the absence of rigid religious guidelines, a good deal of the strictures for relationships had deteriorated.

He looked up at the window again. How timid was the girl? How easy would it be to corrupt her innocence and lure her into the fulfillment of her desires?

He shook his head. This wasn't the time for that kind of thing. She was a suspect, not someone with whom he could afford to get involved. That was the stuff of which scandals were made.

He'd decided not to try to interview Dareena tonight. There would be time for that later. She didn't seem as if she were going out to kill anyone at the moment, so he preferred just making some observations. If he caught sight of her performing rituals in her backyard or something, he'd reason she was capable of killing a priest. That was all he needed to know. He drummed his fingers on the dashboard. The evening crept by.

At 11:30 she put her book aside and moved away from the window. A second later the cat hopped down from the sill and disappeared into the house.

Quietly Vincent got of his car. The street was deserted, just an empty and silent void.

He tried to stay in the shadows as he moved into Dareena's front yard. There were some streetlamps, but the pools of light were separated enough to provide some cover, and there were heavy trees with drooping branches shrouding the area near the house.

Placing his steps carefully, Vincent moved up to the front of the building. He felt like a teenager creeping about, but he had a job to do and his whole career was riding on it. He kept coming back to that. Each time he did, it made him feel worse. He had to solve the murder or make sure it got solved quickly.

Along the edge of the house there was a rose trellis. It had been a part of the building for a long time. There were only dry, twisted stalks of rose plants remaining, but the structure seemed secure and it stretched up past the second floor porch.

Shrugging off his sport coat and loosening his tie, Vincent tested the trellis with his weight. It rattled a little, but it held. He was no acrobat, but he was in good enough shape to scale it with relative ease.

He made his way upward slowly to avoid making too much noise. The climb over onto the porch strained his muscles. He felt something pull in his left leg and knew it was going to be sore in the morning.

Ignoring the pain, he managed to loop that leg over the porch railing. He tried not to look down. It wasn't very far to fall, but he knew dropping wouldn't do him any good, and there was always the danger of falling wrong and breaking his back. No one would elect a D.A. in a wheelchair.

Pushing the thoughts from his mind, he let go of the trellis and swung the rest of his body over to the porch.

He got over the railing without a problem, planting his feet on the porch floor and crouching in the darkness for a moment. When he felt certain his efforts had not been detected, he crept over to the window. He moved slowly across the planks, making sure none of them creaked before he put his full weight on them.

Before peering through the partially open curtains, he cast a glance back to the street. It was still deserted—no observers to spot the assistant D.A. acting as a Peeping Tom. That was a relief. He wasn't used to intrigue.

Bending, he looked through the glass. The bedroom was small, looking oddly Victorian with its furnishings. The reading lamp beside the girl's chair cast shadows across the carpet, flickering slivers of light through the glass prisms that dangled from its shade.

Across the room a door opened into a bathroom. The girl stepped through it, back into the bedroom, wearing a long white nightgown and a pale housecoat over it. It was a conservative outfit, yet it revealed the outline of her body. Vincent felt an inner stirring as he watched the outline of her legs through the folds of the nightgown.

With a brush in her hand she moved to the mirror on the dresser near the bed and sat down.

The light gave her hair a glossy sheen as she began to run the brush through it, tilting her head first to one side and then to the other.

Her hair had a soft look, slipping through her fingers, cascading down around her features.

It was evident she wasn't doing anything out of the ordinary, yet Vincent found himself captivated by her slender form and the grace of her movements. Keeping to one side of the window to remain partially hidden, he kept watching her, picturing her legs beneath the cloth of her nightgown, even admiring her bare feet.

When he felt the jerk at his pants leg, his heart nearly burst up through his throat. Someone had approached behind him and he hadn't noticed. His attention had been locked on the girl. He saw his career melting away. All these thoughts came in a quick rush.

He spun around, pressing his back against the wall in preparation for whatever was about to strike.

The relief made him light-headed. The cat sat in front of him, eyeing him casually with clear blue orbs. It was a white cat, large and calm the way only felines can be.

It tilted its head to one side and meowed a few times. In

a way, its eyes seemed to be glowing, more even than a cat's eyes might usually be expected to glow.

Vincent swooped the cat into his arms and stroked its ears gently. It gave no resistance.

He waited in the shadows until the lights within the room were turned off. He peered in one last time, just in time to see Dareena slip beneath the covers.

Then he waited awhile longer before he released the cat and climbed back down the trellis.

The faint whisper of Muzak drifted through the speaker on the elevator.

Kim stood beside Hamilton, watching the lighted numbers flash on and off as the car climbed up to the eighth floor.

She'd been shown the suites on a tour of the place given to new employees, but she'd never expected to be visiting anyone in them. They rented for almost $200 a night.

She was a little afraid of going up there, but Hamilton's father did own part of the place. She'd learned that the first time she'd seen Hamilton looking at her.

If he said it was all right for them to go up there for a nightcap and to watch the television, which had satellite access, it must be all right.

He'd picked up a bottle of white wine and garnered a couple of glasses from the kitchen.

She wasn't naive. She knew he probably had more on his mind than television. That sort of thing was what she'd had to live with since she'd been in high school. It was something all girls had to put up with. She was pretty, almost beautiful, definitely desirable. She'd learned to expect advances and she'd learned how to deal with them. On dates her boyfriends always tried things. She had learned how to stop them when she wanted to.

She'd decided she would let Hamilton hold her and make out for a while, but she wouldn't sleep with him tonight. If that was all he wanted, he was out of luck. If he was interested in her, really interested, he'd be patient. Kissing would hold him for a while. Going slowly would allow her more time to win him over. If she let him have it all tonight, he might just discard her. He might toss her aside if he didn't get it, also, but if all he wanted was an easy lay, it didn't matter anyway. There were plenty of people out there like that. She could do without it.

He seemed decent enough. He wouldn't threaten her with losing her job if she didn't give in to him.

She knew it was a long shot that he had anything lasting on his mind. He was rich and she was a waitress, but you never knew. Kings had stepped down for love. She liked romantic things like that.

She smiled at him when the elevator sighed to a stop, and they got off and walked arm in arm down the carpeted hallway to the burnished-wood door of the suite.

She leaned against the wall as Hamilton inserted the key into the lock and shoved the door open with a sweeping motion of his hand.

Then she moved into the living room slowly, her arms folded. She was still a little nervous.

Switching on the light, Hamilton moved into the room and set the glasses on the coffee table.

He popped the cork and poured the white wine into the glasses.

Kim sipped lightly as she strolled around the room, looking it over. It had a classical appearance. What was it like to be able to afford this elegance just for one night's lodging? On the rare occasions she and her sister traveled, they stayed in a Motel 6. There they had a key to turn on the television in case you wanted to save money by not using it.

Here everything was geared toward luxury. The decorators had done a good job. The lights were soft and sparkled, casting their glow over the plush furnishings.

The wallpaper had a floral design of soft colors that contrasted with the color of the carpet and the draperies.

This would be a nice place to live, she thought. She moved to the window and looked out into the darkness. The area beyond the hotel was attractive at night, landscaped with spheres of light marking walkways through the fountain areas, where water spilled over into lighted pools.

"They did a good job on this place," she said.

"Beautiful," Hamilton said, but she could feel his eyes on her rather than on the furniture.

When she turned back from the window, she saw he was reclining on the couch. He'd kicked his shoes off, and he raised his glass in a new salute.

He was expecting her to come over and sit beside him.

Hesitating a moment, she settled down beside him, careful not to touch him. She didn't want him to misinterpret her actions. She crossed her legs and folded one arm across her body, keeping her glass in front of her as well.

Hamilton turned toward her, eyes still raking over her. She felt the gaze, almost as if it were a touch, but she avoided his eyes.

She was beginning to feel uncomfortable. It had been silly to assume that he was bringing her up here for anything other than one thing. The thing. He wanted her, not to marry, not for a relationship. He just wanted to make love to her—one time. That would be enough. One time and then he could tell his friends back at his club about it.

She felt her stomach knot just slightly. It wasn't going to be easy to get out of there gracefully, but she'd have to manage.

Her plan to give only a little was unrealistic. Anything he got would only encourage him further. The realization came to her quickly. Or perhaps the truth had been with her all along and she'd just been unwilling to admit it, preferring to maintain a fantasy.

He inched closer to her on the couch, setting his glass on the table. She didn't move her arms, made no effort to make it any easier, but he kissed her cheek gently.

"You're very pretty," he said. He took her glass and set it on the table. Then he moved closer to her, easing one arm around her as he craned his neck to find her mouth with his.

She didn't part her lips, still didn't uncross her legs. The resistance and reluctance she displayed did nothing to discourage him, however.

Coming here with him was taken as a sign of total acceptance. She was a waitress in a bar. She was supposed to be that kind of girl.

He slowly began to move his hands over her body, first down her sides and along her legs. She kept her legs tightly together as his fingers brushed across her knees.

Then one hand found its way up to cup her left breast, gently kneading the flesh through her dress and undergarments.

Still, she didn't pull away, frightened of offending him. She didn't want to insult him even if he was being lecherous. She didn't need to lose her job. Working here was better than in the other clubs.

His fingers moved to the collar of her dress, and he began to ease the buttons open, running his fingertips along her neck, down her throat, and along the valley between her breasts.

As the fingers began to creep beneath the fabric of her bra she could contain herself no longer.

Pulling away, she moved across the room, clutching her collar closed in front of her.

"What's wrong?" Hamilton demanded. His voice wasn't understanding at all. It was coarse, almost ragged. He was growing angry.

She felt the first of the tears spill hot along her cheeks.

"I can't," she said hesitantly. "It's happening too fast. Please, Mr. Terry."

He got up and moved across the room to stand facing her.

"What do you mean? Why'd you come up here?"

"I thought we'd watch television. You seemed nice. I thought maybe we'd talk."

She didn't like the look in his eye.

Concentrating on his expression, she didn't see him raise his hand, so the blow was a surprise, crashing across her cheek and jerking her head to one side.

The force of it caused her to crumple to the floor. The tears fell faster now as she tried to push herself up on her hands.

There wasn't time. He grabbed her arm and pulled her around to face him, then, with his foot against one of her shoulders, forced her down onto her back.

"What did you want to do? Play a game?" he demanded. He called her a bitch, then a string of other filthy names. She wanted to strike back, but she could only whimper.

His hands grabbed at the collar of her dress again and tore it open. Kneeling beside her, he pressed his face against her neck, slobbering on her as he moved his lips across her skin.

The stubble of his beard scratched, tearing at her.

Her eyes closed tightly. Continuing to resist as much as she could, she prayed this would end. She felt the belt of her dress being yanked away, but was too frightened to open her eyes.

Hamilton pressed her hands together as he used the belt to bind her hands in front of her.

He struck her again, this time quite hard across her face, dazing her. She lay still on the floor as he moved across the room.

He returned a moment later with a coat hanger, a wooden one, which he raked across her ribs and abdomen. The pain sank deeply into her. She tried to cry out, but her breath was short. She couldn't make any sound but a choking rattle.

She could feel the heat of Hamilton's breath on her face as his hands moved along her body once more.

She wanted to faint but couldn't. Nor could she find her voice to scream no matter how she tried. And who was there to hear her? The suites weren't rented. That's why they were able to be here. There was no one in this room or in any of the others on the floor.

Hamilton looked down at her with contempt. They were all alike—like his mother. There was no way to count on them. Julia was the only one he could trust. It was foolish of him to think about anyone else. The immediate thrill just wasn't worth the anguish.

They were weak. Bitches all. He had known that about this girl all along. He just hadn't been willing to admit it. She had seemed nice, but she was a whore just like all the others. He told her so through clenched teeth.

It was true. She knew what she was. She could only

131

whimper and submit to him. He brought the back of his hand across her cheek, leaving a bright red welt on her pale skin.

Leaving her there in the center of the floor, he moved into the bathroom.

He turned on the hot water in the sink and the shower, letting the temperature rise until shimmering quivers of condensation rose in the bath stall. Vapor filled the air like smoke. Hotel water was always scalding.

CHAPTER 10

Sunlight cast a golden glow over the day and spilled through the branches of the trees of the front yard as Gable prepared for his trip to Penn's Ferry.

As he dressed, he watched the dog dart on the lawn playing with butterflies.

There was something about the spring that seemed to calm Gable. He stood at the window and watched the morning breeze move through the treetops and gently tilt the blades of grass and the wildflowers back and forth. There was the metaphor he was so lacking, the soft side of the world unmarred by the complications of men and their devices.

Before he went out to his car, he moved across the lawn to knock on Jennifer's door.

She looked rested, far less haggard than the first time he'd seen her. Her curls framed her face in a neat semicircle with the sunlight dancing among them. She wore a sweatshirt with cut-off sleeves and a tattered pair of cut-off jeans. Her glasses slipped down the bridge of her nose as she looked out.

Gable stood across the threshold surveying her for a moment, feeling a few stirrings at the sight of her. This was the first time he realized, in a simple way, how beautiful she was. With the glasses and the faded clothes, she had a fresh look, perhaps uncomplicated was the word.

The directions she gave were exact but simple—which highway to take and even a shortcut around the outer grounds of the Penn's Ferry Regional Mental Institution, the small town's one point of notoriety.

He left the dog with her even though she insisted she was all right and didn't mind staying alone. She was trying so hard to be tough, to overcome the vulnerability she acquired growing up under a protective shell.

That was something he had to admire. The easy thing to do would be to succumb to total reliance on her parents, to run back home and hide under her father's wing.

As he cruised along the highway, he dialed the radio to an easy-listening station and settled back into his seat.

He was going on an interview, but there was no deadline and no pressure to produce copy.

If this turned out to be a hopeless quest, something he couldn't turn into a salable article, it wouldn't matter. It was just something he was interested in, a story of his choice rather than an editor's demand. Somehow it felt better that way. It would do, especially since he had no ideas for a novel yet. Sometimes he wondered if he ever would. Gable often wondered what he was really meant to do in life.

It was perhaps the religious angle to this matter that intrigued Gable the most. While he didn't consider himself a particularly religious person, he did have an interest in religion and its various facets.

He'd left the church several years before after watching

134

a bitter political struggle among factions of the congregation. That had left him with a disenchantment, not for God, but for the practitioners of the politics of church management. He was tired of organized religion and doctrines that seemed to take precedence over the religious principles they had been established to uphold.

As he tooled along the road to Penn's Ferry, it occurred to him he might be looking for something more than just a story. Maybe he was looking for some kind of faith, some guidance. Even, perhaps, hoping that angels were real. Hoping also, he guessed, that the priest's death had an explanation, something tangible. He was looking for another kind of metaphor, a reflection of the material world that would make everything clear. Along with that there was an edge of fear lurking amid his emotions.

He didn't want to find out that angels killed people.

She was alone, and the writer was away.

The neighborhood was quiet. A placid place; it was as if it were sleeping. Almost no cars traveled down the street. It was just the kind of isolation needed. She could scream, but no one would hear. She would die and no one would know the reason, just as they would never know the reason the priest had died.

It would always be a mystery. Something people would remember and talk about—something they would recall with fear, wondering if it was over. They would never find a reason.

Kim made it back to her trailer alone. She left her child with her sister. She didn't want to pick him up yet, wasn't ready to face him right now.

First she had to pull herself together. It was hard to accept

135

how stupid she'd been, how wide-eyed and innocent, following Hamilton like a lamb.

She should have known what he had wanted, what all men wanted or, at least, had always wanted from her.

She shrugged off her coat when she entered the narrow living room of the mobile home, then moved into the bedroom to slip off the dress. She would have to mend its ripped seams.

From the hook in the bathroom she picked up her white terry-cloth bathrobe and pulled it on. It was soft and warm, and donning it was comforting because it was so familiar.

She didn't want to look at herself, but she entered the bathroom and faced the image in the mirror.

She grimaced at what she saw, but actually it wasn't as bad as she'd feared. There was a bruise around the cheekbone on the right side of her face. It had that ugly violet tint, but some rouge and Pan-Cake makeup would cover it enough to let her excuse it as a bump from a cabinet or something when people asked. She'd laugh a little and say how clumsy she was and that would take care of it.

The other bruises wouldn't be a problem. They could be covered with her clothes, from sight if not from memory.

She chose not to look at them again. She'd surveyed them once already while still in the hotel bathroom. Bruises from his hands marked her breasts, and her nipples had the dark discoloration of the blood beneath the skin drawn up by his teeth and lips, passion marks like teenage girls left on their boyfriends' necks.

Her body was like a roadmap of expended desire. There were streaks down her back and thighs from the fiery needles of the shower, teeth marks, and scratches.

A shower would have been nice, except she feared it would bring back the memories of the night and the scalding water running down over her body.

Closing her eyes, she sank back into a corner of the room, shivering and fighting to chase the images of the ordeal out of her brain. She had to compose herself so that no one would know.

She couldn't leave her job, and she certainly couldn't confront the Terrys. Her word would never stand against theirs. She could only forget and try to move on.

The professor's office was in a Gothic-looking building near the center of the campus—a huge old structure with broad, steep steps that led up through thick columns to the vaulted doorways.

It was awesome, like walking into a shrine. There could have been a pharaoh buried here, and it gave Gable a jitter, the same as looking at the towering concrete walls and wrought iron gates around the mental institution he'd passed.

Both places would have fit well into something by Bram Stoker, he thought.

Inside, the college building was all polished tile and fluorescent light, antiseptic looking. It reminded Gable of a hospital.

He found Leonard Seaview's office at the end of a hallway on the fourth floor. A secretary who looked to be about 19, with fuzzy hair that bounced about her face showed Gable through the door.

Like the offices of all teachers, this one was lined with bookshelves, each filled with textbooks and works on all varieties of religious thought. A copy of *The Golden Bough* shared space with books by Saul Bellow and Albert Camus.

Leonard was sitting behind his small wooden desk, leaning back in his chair so that he could look over his shoulder and out the window.

When Gable entered, the man pulled himself out of his chair and shook hands.

"Good morning," he said in a drawl that seemed to curl from his lips.

He was older than Gable had expected. At least he looked older. He was dressed in dark slacks and a brown corduroy jacket with patches at the elbows. A pipe would have completed the scholarly image, but Gable didn't spot one.

"What did you say your name was again?" Leonard asked.

"Gable Tyler."

"And you're a reporter?"

"Sort of. I'm a journalist, at least."

"Working on a story about a girl who talks to angels?"

"It gives me something to do," Gable said with a smile.

"I suppose so. You used to work for a newspaper?"

Gable nodded. "Now I'm trying to decide what I want to be when I grow up." It was a line he used often, but people understood it only some of the time.

"Sometimes I think that's true of me, too," Leonard said. He was back in his seat now, looking out the window again. Patches of blue sky were visible through the pine branches, and the professor's eyes seemed drawn into infinity.

"Angels," the professor said. "What do you want to know about them?"

"I don't know. Ever talked to one?"

"Not that I know of, but then, one never knows. We sometimes entertain angels unawares according to the Bible. In Tobit, Azarius is a man through most of the book. Tobias turns to him repeatedly and refers to him and says, 'Azarius, my friend.' "

"But it's Raphael?"

"The archangel, not the one from the Italian Renaissance." He chuckled. "In the apocryphal story Tobias, the

138

son of Tobit, is destined to marry. The young woman has been pledged to seven men before, and each of them has died, slain by an evil spirit, a fallen angel that waits in her bedchamber if memory serves.

"Raphael, disguised as Azarius, journeys with Tobias to meet the girl. Along the way he prepares him to defeat the evil spirit so that he can eventually wed the girl."

"Do you think there's some significance to that story where Dareena is concerned?"

"She's lonely. She could perceive Azarius as an angel who will bring her Prince Charming to her."

"So what are the chances that any of this is real and not just some delusion from a lonely girl's imagination? Do you really think Raphael pays her visits?"

"Let's think it over. Angels, in the Judaeo-Christian tradition, do have the ability to come into the realm of our world, the material world, if you will, as compared to the spiritual. According to biblical references, angels can do whatever people can do. Traditionally they have a superiority to humans, though. There are things angels can do that men can't."

He leaned forward, placing his hands on his desk, palms flat, as he peered over at Gable.

"Are you a religious man, Mr. Tyler?"

There was an intensity in the question that was unsettling. Questions about personal beliefs always made Gable uncomfortable.

"I believe in God," he said.

"Are you a Christian?"

"I was raised in the church. I guess I am."

"But all this still sounds rather bizarre to you, doesn't it?"

"It's not something I've encountered in church."

"We don't tend to think about angels that much. There

are actually a number of things about them in the Bible that when looked at collectively tell us quite a bit about them. That is the sort of thing you're looking for, isn't it?"

"Well, whatever tradition could have influenced the girl's delusion. I'm assuming it's from her church background."

"It's possible," Leonard said. "That doesn't necessarily mean her image is going to conform to tradition, however. Her imagination could twist in all sorts of directions."

"I believe I need to know the basis she started from."

Leonard got up and pulled a heavy leather-bound King James Version off the bookshelf and flipped it open in front of him on his desk. He remained standing and leaned over the book, flipping through the pages and running his finger across the verses.

"We have references here to angels doing all sorts of things," he said. "Raphael, the one who assumed the name Azarius, is, as you know, an archangel, what you might call a leader of angels. In the regular scriptures there are references to other archangels. Gabriel I'm sure you've heard of. Michael is called a prince and is mentioned in the Book of Daniel as a ruler of Israel.

"Besides the archangel, there are also the traditional angels who supposedly perform the various tasks like protecting men and performing works for God."

"They ever order people to kill priests?" Gable asked. "I mean, would there be a traditional basis of that? Something this girl might have picked up on that would have encouraged her to do that sort of thing?"

"As you can witness by the various television ministers and cult leaders of the world, there are many ways to interpret the Bible. You can even write supplements, so who's to say she didn't come upon something that suggested that to her?"

"I wouldn't think biblically that would be supported."

Leonard chuckled. "Perhaps not. No, that's not the motivation of angels according to the writings in the Old or New Testaments."

"Let's suppose there was a real angel talking to her," Gable said. "I'm not trying to sound like a fanatic or anything, just assuming that anything's possible."

Leonard nodded. "There are more things in heaven and earth than are dreamed of in your philosophy. . . ."

"Exactly. So suppose there *is* an external influence?"

"If there were a real angel, would it tell her to kill a priest?"

"Right."

"It doesn't sound like something Raphael would go in for. If you want to play *National Enquirer,* suppose there's an alien intelligence, a space being, who's only convinced her he's an angel. Actually he's a malevolent being playing games."

"That's further outside the realm of reality than I'm prepared to speculate," Gable said, "but I do know there are things that go on that are hard to understand. I don't want to overlook something significant because I have a closed mind."

"And I haven't been that informative yet. Let me see, angels." Leonard paused, lost in thought. "What else do I know about them?

"I mentioned they have bodies. I'd say also they're capable of emotion. But they are spiritual, highly intelligent."

"Superior to men?" Gable asked.

"Yes. By their very nature. And powerful." He put his fingertips against his forehead. "There's a verse in Thessalonians about that." Turning, he pulled a small green book from his shelf, a Greek-language Bible.

First he flipped through the leather Bible on his desk, then opened the smaller book.

" 'And to you who are troubled rest with us, when the Lord Jesus shall be revealed from heaven with his mighty angels . . .' Now, *mighty* in English is translated from the Greek word *dunamis,* which refers to a great and inherent power."

"Then angels are formidable."

"According to what's been written," Leonard said, closing the book.

"They have bodies. They are powerful."

"The angels of the Judaeo-Christian tradition would be able to come into contact with people," the professor said.

"They could stab priests to death?"

"If they exist as the tradition states, except that I wouldn't *expect* an angel to do that sort of thing. A demon maybe."

"What about demons?" Gable asked.

"Ah, the fallen angels. Now we're getting into the nitty-gritty. Let me remind you that the tradition holds that angels, fallen or not, are created beings. They are powerful, but they're not infinitely powerful. They're under the command of God. Biblically they're under the authority of men through the power of God also."

"Psychologists speculate on the reality of demon possession, I've read."

"True, it's not limited to the scribblings of old priests. Instances are awfully difficult to document, however. And exorcisms are often conducted in secret on dark nights. Even the church has turned away in part from that sort of superstition even though it's the Catholic Church that developed the rites of exorcism. There's no step-by-step blueprint in the Bible for getting rid of demons."

"Do demons have the same powers as angels?"

"I should point out, Mr. Tyler, that the Bible refers to them mostly as fallen angels, although there are a number of other terms used."

142

"Such as?"

"The 'sons of God' mentioned in Genesis, for example. The ones who took the daughters of men as wives. That might be something a lonely young woman could relate to. Perhaps her angel is an imaginary lover whom she's defied in effect."

"The possibilities are infinite, aren't they?"

Leonard nodded. "All depending upon which verse she's decided to twist around in her brain, or which reference she's pulled out of context. If that's the case. We are really just speculating."

"Have you ever known of this sort of thing happening? This kind of delusion?"

"I'm not a psychologist, so I haven't dealt with individual cases, but there are all sorts of things that come up related to people's belief structures. Maybe you should go and talk to the girl and get a specific idea of what her delusion is. I'll be glad to talk to you more after you've learned what the situation is. You may find out she's a young woman in need of help. Perhaps we can help her find it. I have to admit I'm as intrigued by all this as you are."

"So even if I don't track down a story, something good may come of this?"

Leonard smiled. "We can always hope."

Gable got up and shook the professor's hand again.

"Pleasure to meet you. Appreciate your time."

"Certainly. Get back to me."

"I'll do that."

The discussion had been brief. Gable walked out past the receptionist, feeling confused and more than a little troubled.

* * *

Leonard sat back in his chair, again looking out the window. The session hadn't gone as he'd expected. He felt that he'd cast more doubt over the young man's research than anything. He'd taken an approach of skepticism and disbelief, and intellectual and analytical approach.

There had been so many things he'd intended to tell Gable that he'd never gotten around to, or had held back on. He had a terrible sinking feeling that he'd failed in some way, as if he should have prepared Gable for something.

The feeling was unlike anything he'd experienced before. The sunlight was comforting. It chased away the shadows. In the sunlight nothing bad could happen. He'd always felt that as a child, and he felt it now.

The sunlight was a haven, but from what? Why did he have this terrible feeling that something was hovering, that something evil, truly and inherently evil, was nearby and was about to take some action?

Gable drove slowly along the outside of the mental institution's fence. The stones were thick and old, crumbling in places, but they looked impenetrable, the spiked iron around the top a sinister barrier to any escape.

He thought of the young woman he'd seen walking home with her groceries. She'd looked so innocent, not wanting to harm anyone, just minding her business, lonely perhaps, but not dangerous.

What if the girl were innocent, and he bumbled in and drew attention to her? Would that draw the coroner down on her to commit her to this institution, sealing her away behind the gray walls, where she would be restrained and studied?

It was happening again. He was back to prying into people's lives. Journalists jumped into people's lives, meddled

really, in order to put together stories for people to read—
stories that weren't any of the people's business.

So much of journalism was in telling people not what they
needed to know but what they wanted to know, what they
were curious or nosy about.

What was Dareena's story if it wasn't a curiosity piece,
a journey into the unusual?

Or was there something he could do that would be worthwhile in all of this? Perhaps he could help the girl, draw her
out of her loneliness.

Sometimes Gable wondered if there was any peace for
him. He had the knot in his stomach now that he always
got when he started on a rough story.

As he drove along, almost lost in those thoughts, he spotted a lake that bordered the highway. Easing the car off onto
the gravel parking apron, he walked down to the boat
launch.

The water was silver in the glistening sunlight, like a sheet
of crystal. It was calm, with only a few birds hanging on
the wind currents.

His hands in his pockets, he began to walk around the
water's edge.

There was no hurry to get home.

He moved slowly, thinking of Jennifer, pushing unpleasant memories out of his thoughts, faces that danced in his
mind's eye which he didn't want to recall. Jennifer was
pleasant to think about.

In a tree above him, birds darted among the branches,
playing. It was spring.

Perhaps that was what he felt now—spring fever. Mixed
in with all the other confusions of his life, he was beginning
to feel a twinge of emotion for Jennifer, a sadness of wanting that was not like sadness at all.

If all of this served no other purpose, at least he had met

her. Maybe something could develop. If it didn't, it wouldn't be too bad, but he half hoped for a surprise, a sudden love.

He picked up some pebbles and tossed them out into the lake, watching the stones' kisses send ripples across the water's surface.

Stepping back from the water, he thought about the positive things, about Jennifer and his novel, but suddenly he felt a chill wind sweep around him. It seemed to come from nowhere and just as suddenly it was gone, yet he could not shake the uneasy feeling it left with him. It bit deeply into his spine, like the kiss of an icy serpent.

CHAPTER 11

Jennifer's typewriter was set up in an unused bedroom on the second floor.

It was a good office, and the desk was beside a window that overlooked the side lawn, where there were flower beds and some small trees.

Whenever she got writer's block, she could look out and daydream for a while.

This time of year there were always birds darting around. Resting her chin in the palm of her hand, she surveyed the ground. Bees were buzzing over the blossoms of the wildflowers. She watched them go about their activities as the dog curled around her bare feet and grumbled slightly in his sleep.

She turned back to her desk. It was littered with note cards and stacks of Faulkner paperbacks. Plodding through his complex prose in search of meaning was a formidable task, sometimes appearing almost hopeless.

She was rolling a fresh sheet of paper around the cylinder when the dog sat up, his ears perked.

"What is it, boy?" she asked, suddenly glad she was dog-sitting.

The dog didn't turn to her voice, but deep down in his chest there was a faint rumble of anger. He pulled himself to his feet, his tail alert and pointed straight up as he moved over to the door which was only partially closed.

Jennifer felt her heart leap into her throat. If it was Gable coming back, the dog wouldn't react this way.

What had he heard? There hadn't been any sound that she'd noticed. She moved over to the doorway and gripped the frame as she peered out into the hallway.

It was empty, but the dog trotted on down the corridor to the top of the stairs, where he barked again before moving on down.

She listened again, but there was still no sound. Quickly she scurried along to the banister and peered down into the front room.

The dog was there now, sniffing around, the hackles stiff on his back. He moved from the base of the stairs over to the front door and began to run his nose along the floor where someone entering the house would have had to step.

The door was closed now, but that didn't mean someone couldn't already have entered and closed it again. She couldn't remember if she'd locked it when Gable had left. She hadn't been frightened at all then; the day was so bright with sunshine.

She hurried back down the hallway, away from the sight of the first floor. Her thoughts suddenly felt jumbled, as if her head were swimming. Closing her eyes, she forced her thoughts to clear, but still an image of a darkened room with approaching footsteps wouldn't leave her. She pictured herself huddled in a room, in darkness, hiding.

That made the fear feel worse. She moved into her bedroom and closed the door. Then she dragged the chest from the foot of her bed across the room to the door. It was heavy but it slid easily on the carpet, and with it she was able to brace the entrance.

With that done, she held her breath, listening. Still no sound. Her gaze began to dart around the room in search of some kind of weapon.

The only thing she saw was her pillow. Drawn to it, she lifted it into her arms, clutching it to her body as if it were a person.

Her eyes closed tightly, she sat on the edge of the bed, watching the door, half expecting the handle to turn. And the thoughts came back. A dark room—the sound of a thunderstorm rattling the window—harsh wind—and footsteps coming down the hallway. She remembered something, being unable to breathe, and the feeling of coarse hands moving over her body.

She had to shake her head to clear that away. The phone voice moved in to replace it. She remembered the harsh tone. That horrible, rasping sound.

The phone. Of course. She had been so nervous she'd forgotten about it. She reached over to the nightstand and grabbed the receiver.

There was no sound when she pressed the receiver to her ear. The line was dead.

She slid off the bed and moved to the window. The day was still so bright, but now the ground looked far away. It was a long drop, and there was no cushion down there.

If she tried escaping that way, she might injure her ankles, and then she'd be unable to run—an easy victim.

She heard the dog begin to bark then, a vicious bark. Someone was definitely downstairs.

A second later she head a pained howl issue from the dog. Someone had struck him or done something worse.

"Oh, God," she murmured. "I should have gone home."

With the pillow still clutched to her, she moved over to

the window and tried to pull it open. It wouldn't budge. Her fingers were trembling, making it hard to undo the latch. She fumbled with it until she managed to turn the mechanism, but once it was undone, the window still wouldn't move upward.

The place had been repainted when she'd rented, and the paint must have caused the window to stick. It wasn't an avenue of escape at all. Even if she broke the glass, it was sectioned with wooden cross pieces that would be impossible for her to break.

She turned back to the doorway. There was no sign of movement, but her heart was pounding and her breath was labored. She was almost smothering.

She tried swallowing but couldn't as tears began to splash down her cheeks.

Straining her ears, she listened. She could hear footsteps on the carpeted hallway; they were dragging along the corridor.

For a moment she froze. There was someone in the hallway. No question of it now.

"Gable?" she called out.

No answer, and now there was movement at the doorway. The doorknob began to twist from side to side.

Images flashed through her mind. Footsteps down a long hallway. Smothering.

"Who's there?" she demanded.

Only a rasping breath came in reply.

As the knob continued to twist, she heard a weight begin to press against the door.

The chest held for the moment, but it was easy to slide. It would give in time.

She heard the weight strike the door again, and this time the chest moved slightly, allowing the door to open a crack.

The thin fingers of a black-gloved hand crept around the

edge of the door, gripping it in an attempt to force it forward.

"No," she screamed, and ran across the room, crashing into the chest with her own weight, using it to force the door closed.

The fingers struggled, but Jennifer had struck with surprise and momentarily had better leverage.

Barefoot, she dug her toes into the carpet to force the chest forward until the door eased back into its facing.

The fingers were withdrawn just before the door snapped closed.

Jennifer was drenched with sweat now, her hair wet and clinging to her face. The sweatshirt did not absorb the moisture from her body, so she felt the icy droplets beneath it force back against her skin, causing her to shudder.

The weight outside the door crashed against it again, rattling the chest. With her weight against the chest it didn't move as much, but she wondered how long she could hold out.

The job had not turned out to be as easy as anticipated. The dog had alerted the girl too early, given her time to barricade herself.

The gloved hand slipped beneath the jacket and extracted the blade. If the doorway gave, she would pay for the resistance. There were all sorts of things that could happen to her, horrible things she would think unimaginable. And she couldn't keep the door closed forever.

If she escaped now, there was always later, perhaps even at a time that would allow hours for the task to be performed. Long and sinister hours.

When the idea came to her, Jennifer could have kicked herself for not thinking of it earlier. Scrambling away from the door, she grabbed the phone from the stand and yanked the cord free from the wall.

Then she scurried across the bed and used the phone to crash out two of the windowpanes. She began to scream for help through the jagged openings.

Her voice carried into the hall. Most of the people who lived nearby were not at home. Chances were there was no one close by to hear her, but someone might be walking by, a mailman perhaps.

With an angry slash the gloved hand slammed the blade into the door, dragging the blade downward, splintering some of the wood and scraping away paint, leaving a jagged warning. Seeing the slash in the wood could give her an idea of what the blade could do to flesh.

That was all there was time for. Someone would be coming soon.

Jennifer was sitting in the living room when Gable returned, the dog cradled in her lap. It wasn't seriously hurt but had received a blow or a kick that had left it trembling.

Still holding the dog, she ran to Gable and put one arm around him, gripping the back of his neck as she pressed her face against his shoulder.

"What happened?"

"Someone was here. Whoever it was who called. It wasn't a crank, Gable."

"Did you get a look at who it was?"

She shook her head.

"I had to hide. I started screaming for help and whoever it was got scared off. The dog must have gotten kicked."

152

Gable took the dog and stroked its head gently as Jennifer moved back to the couch to sit down.

"I was so scared. There was a knife. It left a big gash in the bedroom door."

Putting the dog on the floor, Gable moved over to Jennifer's side, and she reached up to embrace him. She looked like a different person now, her hair a wild mass of tangles and her clothes disheveled. A doll lay at the end of the couch. She had evidently been clutching it as well as the dog.

He stroked her hair as she pressed her face against his shoulder.

Across the street the viewer stared through the front window. The sun was in a better position now, no longer striking the window.

So she thought the writer could help her. She felt comforted with him close by.

She would see. Everyone was vulnerable. She had been lucky, but weakness and mistakes would occur, and she would be open. Open and helpless.

Vincent lay in bed long after the alarm went off, not wanting to exert the effort required to lift himself from beneath the covers. The strained muscles ached, and there promised to be stiffness in the limbs now that the adrenaline had seeped out of them.

Slowly he ran his hand over his face, finding his skin gritty with sleep and stubble. He felt worse than he should have, as if there were no ambition left in him.

He thought of the woman. She was beautiful in her way, lithe and slender—a delicate sight. His memory conjured the silhouette of her outlined in the narrow window, and he recalled the way the light had danced off her hair, so smooth and soft looking. He longed to run his hands along the hair, tracing the silky feeling.

Vincent had dated some of the most beautiful women in town, luring them back to his apartment or letting them draw him back to theirs, but never had a feeling of longing struck him quite the way this image of Dareena had.

He couldn't understand it. He couldn't get the girl off his mind.

When he got the chance, he was going to go by to see her again. Not to talk, just to watch her, catch a glimpse of her.

Isaac Arbor spent the morning in the offices of the *Daily Ledger* talking to Gable's old editor, Alex Denson, who didn't speak badly of his former employee but didn't have a high opinion of his performance either.

The investigator also went through the files of yellowing news clippings the paper's librarian had quickly compiled for him.

It was hard to tell much about someone by reading newspaper stories he'd written. News stories didn't reveal much about their author, but in a couple he picked up a few hints.

The guy had written a few times about people in need— a young man and wife with a very ill baby, a woman with a lost child. Those stories were longer than some of his others, and they looked like he'd taken more care with them.

He put the papers back together, returned them to the folder, and replaced it on the library desk.

He relied on instinct a lot, and he had the feeling Gable wasn't involved in the killings.

Good enough. It hadn't taken long to get that out of the way. Now there was just a matter of finding the real killer.

His next order of business was to check into the priest's life a little more closely. Maybe there was some clue that could be turned up. He headed back to his car. He had to hit the road, back through Alexandria and down to Aimsley again.

He wanted to get this over with as much as anybody did. The longer a case remained open, the more likely it was never to be solved.

That wouldn't be good for anyone in this case—not with the victim being a priest and a prominent citizen's daughter being threatened. It could be used against the D.A. and everyone else, including Arbor.

As long as he was doing a good job he had people's respect, but he knew there were those who would turn against him if he ever slipped up—the D.A. included. Jackson would turn on anyone to save his own hide, and Walker Vincent was the same way.

Arbor intended to prevent that from happening, and the only way to do it properly was to find the killer.

He wished he knew how he was going to do that.

Fisher stood in the hallway, running his fingertips across the jagged line the knife had torn in the door.

"Did the attacker say anything?" he asked.

Standing beside Gable near the wall, Jennifer shook her head. She had put on a sweater over her clothes, unable to shake her chill even though it was a warm day.

Fisher took a deep breath as he turned to look at Gable.

"And no one was in sight when you got here?"

Gable shook his head. He still didn't like the big detective, but he was trying to cooperate. "I didn't see anything."

Fisher sighed. "No unusual cars?"

"None."

A uniformed policeman moved up behind them, his

thumbs hooked over the front of his belt. He had red hair and a mustache, and a cocky expression.

"The phone line was cut, all right, sir," said the young officer. "Hacked in two. Could have been done with the blade used on that door."

"Footprints?" Fisher asked.

"Not a sign. The ground's pretty dry and solid out there."

"The perfect crime," Fisher muttered. "Aren't you journalists supposed to be trained observers?"

"When there's something to observe," Gable said. "It was all over when I got here."

"How long after it happened did he show up?" Fisher asked.

"Only a few minutes," Jennifer said.

"How many are a few? Twenty? Thirty."

"Less than twenty."

When Fisher expelled his next breath it sounded like a growl. He shook his head.

"I'm afraid we don't have much to go on. All you saw was some fingers?"

"Yes, sir."

"Could it have been a girl?"

"I suppose. I don't really know. There were gloves. Whoever it was tried to force the door. I managed to stop them, but they seemed pretty strong."

Fisher turned that over in his brain for a while, running his hand across his craggy chin.

"We're going to step up patrols in your neighborhood here. We'll get this together. I don't know what's going on here, but I'm going to find out."

He pushed past Gable and followed the uniformed man down the stairs.

Jennifer raised a hand to her face, shaking her head.

"How can they find anybody? It seems impossible. There's nothing to go on."

"Cops have their ways."

It was her turn to sigh, her shoulders sagging as she expelled her breath.

"I felt so helpless. You never think of how vulnerable you really are, but even if it was a girl, what would I have done against a knife?"

Gable could find no words of reassurance. He didn't know what he could do in such a situation.

"Maybe I should go home," she said. "But how much safer would I be there? My daddy's not a big man. And if my mother had been here with me, she'd have panicked worse than I did. I'd probably wind up getting them hurt, too."

Gable put his hands in his pockets. "Sorry I wasn't here."

"It's not your fault. You have a life."

She wasn't his responsibility, but that didn't make him feel any better. He wasn't coming off as a very good knight in shining armor.

As much as he hated it, he was involved now. He was starting to care for her. He followed her down the stairs into the living room.

The dog was up and moving around now, sniffing the carpet. There were all sorts of conflicting scents for him to investigate.

The cops had moved back outside for further inspection of the lawn and the street.

Gable sat down and watched Jennifer move over to the stereo, where she put on a Neil Diamond tape.

"I need to get some kind of protection," she said.

"A gun?"

"Not something someone could take away from me and use on me. Maybe some Mace, or whatever that spray is."

157

"That should help," Gable said. If the attacker was a human. Hadn't Leonard Seaview said that angels had physical bodies?

It sounded farfetched, but Gable was beginning to wonder. What if something strange was taking place? Something out of the ordinary.

Even if this sort of thing had happened before, it would have been dismissed as an unexplained phenomenon. It happened all the time. People looked at things in literal ways, based on the material world, but more and more evidence was pointing to a realm beyond everyday reality.

What if there were beings out there different from humans? Would they necessarily be good beings the way all the movies were starting to assume? Was it inconceivable that malevolent forces existed?

Gable shuddered. He suddenly wished he had a sweater as well. It was chilly.

He folded his arms in front of him. If there was an Azarius, who or what was he and what did he want?

CHAPTER 12

Fisher and Arbor met in the conference room they'd used before. Arbor sat in a chair at the end of the table with his feet propped up on another chair, a cup of coffee in front of him, and eyed Fisher as the big man entered the room.

"Somebody tried to kill the girl," Fisher said. "Came damned close before she started screaming and scared him off."

"Any leads?" Arbor wondered.

"Nothing really. Her boyfriend showed up right after it happened."

"I don't think it was him," Arbor said. "Call it a hunch."

Fisher hated to agree with Arbor, but he was right. The kid had had plenty of time to bump the girl off before the first patrol car had arrived. He'd checked that out.

"I stepped up the patrols in her area," Fisher said. "If we catch whoever it is on the next attempt, we'll be in good shape."

"That's the only way we're going to be in good shape," Arbor said. "We don't have anything to go on. No prints in the church, no witnesses."

"Just this crazy girl. Has Vincent turned anything up on her?"

"He said he hadn't, but he looked pretty screwed up when I saw him. He hadn't shaved and they said he was in late this morning."

"Shit. Our task force is spinning its wheels. Gable Tyler went up to Penn's Ferry this morning and talked to some professor there about angels."

"Our writer got a head start on us, then. Maybe I'll have a talk with him."

"I don't know if knowing about angels is going to help. We could use the help of some angels, though."

Arbor smiled.

"If Azarius is the name of a real angel, this girl Dareena doesn't have a corner on the market. Maybe somebody else has delusions of angels."

"Maybe it's some new cult like that bunch of hippies we caught slaughtering cattle a couple years ago."

"I've got a call in to the priest's brother. He doesn't live too far away. I'm looking around for friends of his."

"Can't hurt. Did he have any lovers?"

"No indication of anything like that yet."

"I hope it's not some fag thing."

"I don't think that's the case."

Fisher belched. "Well, let's plot the plan of action. We're going to keep watch on Jennifer Nelson. You're going to check on the priest's background."

"And Vincent is looking after Dareena."

Fisher nodded. "That leaves the girl's background. Maybe there's some boy she broke up with because the priest told her to."

"Maybe there's somebody who lusts after her and wants to put a stop to it."

"When you get into religious stuff, you get into all kinds

of questions, don't you? No tellin' what kind of fanatic we got on our hands.''

Arbor lifted his coffee cup to his lips. "We'll find him. Or her. Or them.''

"Sure we will.''

With a sigh Fisher turned and ambled out of the conference room. He'd have to talk to the girl's father. Just what he wanted to do, have a conversation with a rich lawyer.

Arbor stayed in his seat and nursed his coffee. Station coffee was lousy, but he wanted to think for a while. He wanted a cigarette badly. There was a machine outside where he could get a pack of Salems, but he was trying to quit. At least it was nice and quiet here.

He needed to think. More of this case was resting on his shoulders than he wanted. Fisher wasn't a total screw-up, but this was a little bigger than the average murder investigation. It wasn't a couple of rednecks shooting each other over a few bags of pot, and it wasn't some neurotic teenager murdering his girlfriend.

That left one of two things. It was either a psychotic or whatever the word for them was nowadays, or it was some calculating bastard who'd planned a puzzle for them for some reason or other.

Either way, it was going to take more than the typical investigation and interviews to solve. Some way the killer would have to be smoked out.

No problem. Arbor had done the impossible before. He'd manage. As long as it was a real killer, he could handle it.

He chuckled. If it was an angel, it might be hard to put the cuffs on him.

* * *

In late afternoon Dareena sat on the second floor porch, reading, while across the street Vincent, again huddled in his car, sat watching her, fantasizing about her.

Her hair was parted in the middle today and brushed back away from her forehead. She wore a beige dress and sandals without stockings. Every now and then the breeze toyed with the hem, revealing a portion of her bare, slender legs.

He wanted her. There was no other way around it. He wanted to take her into bed and unleash her passions. She'd been alone all this time; there had to be desires simmering inside her body.

He ran his hand back through his hair, not worrying whether it stayed in place or not. He hadn't washed or blow-dried it today. He wasn't worried about impressing the girls in the office or his boss. Being the perfect young lawyer wasn't concerning him right now. There were other things in the world at the moment, other interests.

Maybe he would talk to her after all. It couldn't hurt to break the ice. Charming her shouldn't be a big problem. It wasn't as though she got that many offers, right?

Flipping the rearview around, he did a little work on his hair. Now he wished he had taken the usual care that morning, but he hadn't planned on approaching her today.

He got out of the car and walked slowly across her lawn with his hands in his pockets.

She didn't see him until he was standing near the house, looking up at the balcony.

"Can I help you?" she asked, moving over to the railing.

"Walker Vincent. D.A.'s office. I need to talk to you some more about Father Conzenza, but don't worry"—he smiled—"it's just a few questions. Maybe you can help us solve this thing."

A few moments later she appeared at the door to let him in, her reading glasses dangling from one hand.

Her eyes were beautiful—warm brown eyes. She motioned him into the front room a little awkwardly. As he walked past her he caught a whiff of the fragrance of her perfume, a smell like wildflowers.

The sound of *Wheel of Fortune* drifted in from the television set in the other room, so she closed the door before she sat down across from Vincent.

"How can I help you?" she asked.

"Did the priest ever talk of anyone who didn't like him?"

Her brow wrinkled. "No. Never. I didn't know him terribly well."

Vincent searched his brain. He wasn't an investigator. He was used to asking his questions of witnesses on the stand, where the goal was to present information, to get the witness to tell the jury something the attorney already knew, or in cross-examination to find a hole in their testimony. In an investigation you had to ask questions that would draw out information.

And he hadn't really come here in search of information about the case. He wanted to look at her, to get to know her.

"How long did you know him?" he asked.

"It's hard to say. The church isn't that far away, so quite a while really."

He struggled to find words. He felt like a schoolboy. He'd never had this kind of trouble talking to a woman. Maybe this hadn't been a good idea.

What was wrong with him? He looked back at her, raking his eyes over her, tracing the lines of her body, imagining what was beneath the folds of her dress.

"Are you all right, Mr. Vincent?"

He rubbed his eyes.

"It's a tough case," he said.

"Could I get you a glass of water?"

"Yes. Please."

She slid from her seat and moved across the room, disappearing through another doorway.

He waited a few seconds and then followed.

The kitchen was small, and she stood at the sink, letting the water run.

He glided across the soft flooring and slipped his arms around her waist. She hadn't heard his approach, and her muscles jerked when she felt his touch.

He encircled her with his arms and brushed his face gently through her hair to touch her neck with his lips.

She began to twist, struggling to pull free of him, but he tightened his arms around her, pinning her arms to her sides as he let his hands move up her body.

His left hand found one of her breasts, fingers closing gently to cup the flesh through her dress. it was small but firm and rounded and he squeezed gently, moving his thumb about until he felt her nipple harden through the fabric.

"No," she muttered, jerking about suddenly.

Vincent was taken by surprise and she was able to pull free. The glass went clattering into the sink, shattering when it struck the drain.

Dareena scrambled over into the corner of the room, where there was a small knife rack. Clawing at it, she tugged free a narrow, stainless-steel blade and clutched it in front of her.

The look in her eyes was one of terror. She extended the blade forward at arm's length. Her fingers and her lips trembled.

Vincent stumbled back against the cabinet, raising his hands to his face. His head was swimming, and his stomach felt twisted and sick.

164

He felt as if he were someone else. He couldn't have let this happen. She was a shy girl, she'd probably never been touched by a man. A subtle approach to her would be required.

She was probably frigid from the seclusion of her life and her religion. He'd violated her.

Closing his eyes, he shook his head.

"I'm sorry," he muttered, but it was hard to form words because his throat was suddenly very dry.

She didn't lower the knife.

"I don't know what happened to me," he said. "Really. I was out of line."

"You'd better leave."

"But I didn't mean it."

"Mr. Vincent, my grandmother didn't hear anything. Leave before she finds out and I have to do a lot of explaining. I'll forget about it. Just go."

He swallowed. His palms were sweating and his legs were tingling, as if tiny pins were being driven into his blood vessels. The blood was also hot beneath the flesh of his face.

Turning, he moved out of the kitchen and found his way to the front door. He started across the lawn, slowly moving toward his car, but he didn't make it very far before the nausea swept up through him, causing him to double over and throw up. He retched until his stomach was empty. His body seemed to be trying to turn itself inside out.

He gasped, fighting the reaction until he was able to control his stomach again. Then he knelt there in the grass, drawing quick breaths of the night air.

His hair was wet around the edges with perspiration, plastered to his face. He pulled it away with his fingers and prepared to struggle to his feet when he saw the cat sitting on the ground nearby in the shadows, its eyes glowing bright green in the light from the nearby streetlamps.

Dareena hurried to her room, her arms folded around her. She was still trembling and frightened.

She dropped onto the bed and pulled the cover around her, fighting a chill.

His touch lingered over her. Nothing like this had ever happened before. She felt like crying, but she struggled against the tears, trying to let her emotions settle down.

She shut her eyes. The first time she'd ever been touched by a man besides her father, which she could not remember, and it had been almost like an attack.

Slowly she sat up on the edge of the bed, gazing toward the mirror.

"Frightened?" the voice in the mirror and in her mind asked.

She wet her lips with her tongue and nodded.

Azarius laughed, and she saw the image in the mirror, faceless, just an outline surrounded by a glowing light. It was golden, almost bright enough to hurt her eyes, yet it was warm.

Dareena slid from the bed and took her steps slowly to stand in front of the mirror.

"What did he want?" she asked.

"You are beautiful."

"But it was wrong."

"How did it feel?"

"Wasn't it wrong?"

"His touch?"

She could see her own image in the glass, as if the being's face were superimposed over it.

"I didn't want to be forced."

166

"But you've dreamed about that sort of thing. It's in the books."

"Are you saying it was all right?"

There was no answer. She swallowed. Still trembling. Her fingers twisted around each other until she let the bedspread slide off her shoulders.

Her skin suddenly felt hot, tingling, and damp with perspiration. Her fingers moved to the neck of her dress, undoing the buttons slowly, pushing the garment back from her shoulders, letting it fall to hang from the belt at her waist.

Beneath it she wore a camisole which she also shrugged from her shoulders, staring forward into the mirror as she opened the clasp of her bra, peeling it back.

"How did it feel?"

She cupped her breasts, moving her fingers across their full pink crests gently at first and then harder, caressing the flesh.

"He wasn't supposed to touch me that way. It's a sin to let a man do that."

"How did it feel?"

"It was wrong."

Her fingers continued kneading the flesh.

"How does it feel?"

She began to feel tears on her cheeks.

"I don't understand," she wept.

"How does it feel?"

"It feels good," she said. "It feels so good."

Azarius was silent.

Leonard Seaview sat in his office going through old volumes, the much dog-eared and underlined paperbacks of his seminary days.

It seemed an eternity had passed since he'd gone through some of these books, avidly reading and underlining important segments with his Paper-Mate. He felt old and tired thinking back on that vigor set forth by a young ministerial student with a starched collar and a crew cut.

He was far removed from that person now and did not lament much of what he had lost. He had no desire to stand in a pulpit and shout at the top of his voice.

Still, he missed the energy he'd felt then. Now he was weary. If only he could recapture part of what he had once been, recapture faith without the other trappings.

Perhaps he had read too many books and papers and speculated on too many occasions.

"What if there are angels?" the young man today had wondered.

What if there were? If there were angels, then was there a God? Didn't that stand to reason?

Seaview shook his head. If God existed, where was He? In these books? In the sermons he had preached in his youth?

Was God the gray-haired old man Seaview had pictured as a boy? Or was He all things the way some prophets described Him?

Pulling himself up out of his chair, Seaview gazed out the window. It was dark now, the streetlights pooling on the sidewalks of the ground below.

No matter. He was in no rush to get home. He tugged another group of books off the shelves and began to look through them.

He wasn't sure what he was searching for, but he hoped to come up with something to tell Gable the next time he called. Somewhere in the world's religions there had to be an answer to all things, if the world was not a random place brought together by chance.

If, in fact, there were angels and Supreme Beings.

The office was dark when Arbor stopped in to pick up some papers, but he sensed someone's presence.

An instinct had developed in him over the years. During the time he'd been a cop, he'd had to depend on it a couple of times to keep him alive.

There seemed to be a new edge to the feeling tonight as he eased into the room. He felt the hair on his neck rise in a way he hadn't experienced since watching horror movies in the balcony of the Strand Theater as a child.

Slowly he reached beneath his coat and tugged his gun from the holster, the .38. He never liked the feel of it, and even in tense situations it didn't bring comfort, but he had it ready as he reached over for the light switch.

The white light seared away the darkness with the suddenness of lightning, revealing Vincent sitting at the receptionist's desk.

The sight startled Arbor even though he'd been braced for something out of the ordinary. For a brief second Vincent had a wild, almost inhuman look on his face.

Arbor jerked the gun around, leveling the barrel at the lawyer's chest. He lowered it in an instant when he realized who he was seeing.

"You drunk?" Arbor asked.

Vincent looked up at him, a bland expression crossing his features, replacing the twisted grimace that had been there before.

"What are you doing here?"

"I work here," Arbor mumbled. "I might ask you the same thing."

"I was looking for someplace quiet to think."

"It's a rough case, but we'll break it."

"We'd better do it quick. The papers are going to pick up on it if we don't clear it in the next few days."

"I'm bustin' ass, buddy."

"Yeah? So am I. The pressure's pretty bad, isn't it?"

"What are you worried about? You can pass the buck."

"Nope. It's my baby. I don't think it was the girl either."

"We're getting a good feel for who it wasn't."

Arbor frowned. The lawyer had slumped down in his chair now and was studying the backs of his hands.

"She's beautiful, that girl is. So beautiful."

He began to mumble. Arbor spoke again, but Vincent didn't seem to hear him.

"Walker," the investigator said.

The mumbling continued. He must be drunk, worried so much about his career.

Arbor moved past him and picked up the folder he wanted.

Just what he needed. Perfect. Vincent was going to pieces.

This case really was Arbor's baby. It was going to be up to him to clear it. Just what he needed to make his life complete.

The headlight beams from Doren's car swept across the cluttered ground of the alley and bounced along the rear wall as he parked at the mouth of the passage and climbed from behind his steering wheel.

Looking over his shoulder, he made sure the street behind him was empty before he walked farther down between the two crumbling buildings. Both had been ruled unsafe and were marked for demolition to make way for the downtown growth.

This truly was one of the seedy areas even though it was only a few blocks away from the Clairmont. Doren didn't feel safe here, but then, he never felt safe when he was meeting with Salem.

He put his hands into the pockets of his coat, checking to make sure the envelope was still in place before he continued to the rear wall. Crumpled papers and broken bottles crunched under his shoes. He didn't look down because his eyes were busy searching the shadows.

Finally he reached the end and stood, checking his watch. It was 10:30. The bastard should be here by now.

With a sigh he scanned the alley once more. Moonlight streamed down through the opening between the two buildings, glistening off the forgotten wine bottles and bringing just enough luminescence to create an eerie look.

Why was Salem always late? It must be a game with the bastard. He liked to make Doren squirm.

Even seeing the guy made Doren's skin crawl, but he didn't exactly have a choice. Circumstances had a way of dictating the course of destiny.

Doren checked his watch again, pulled his jacket around him a little tighter, and began to pace.

The figure appeared as a silhouette in the mouth of the alley a few minutes later. Doren turned and waited as the lean form moved toward him, stopping only a few paces in front of him.

Salem stood in a narrow slash of moonlight, his thin lips pulled back over his teeth in a grin that made Doren cringe.

"Lovely evening, ain't it, mate," Salem said, mocking an English accent.

"Perfect," Doren said. He eyed Salem with disgust.

The fellow was just over six feet tall, and his body looked thin, but Doren knew that was deceptive. Salem wasn't someone to antagonize. If the guy's brain had been a computer,

Doren would have said there were a couple of chips missing. That wasn't faulting his intelligence. He had the cunning of the proverbial serpent, but there was something missing. It showed in his eyes, which were bleak and gray. Most men knew some kind of restraint, but Doren always sensed that Salem was lacking in that area. That made him dangerous.

Tonight Salem needed a shave, which made him seem even sleazier than usual. With his oily blond hair falling to his shoulders, he reminded Doren of the characters in old horror movies—the men who supplied cadavers for English doctors.

Grave robbing would have been a part of Salem's repertoire if there were any money to be made at it. He toyed with the lobe of his left ear, which was decorated with a little golden stud.

"I haven't talked to you in a while," Salem said. "I've missed you, Doren. How's your motel?"

"It's a hotel," Doren said, unable to keep the contempt out of his voice. "And it's not mine. It belongs to several people."

A mocking look of dismay crossed Salem's face.

"Excuse me. I'm just a low-class lad who pulled himself out of the gutter by sheer willpower."

Doren ignored the remarks as he pulled the envelope out of his pocket.

"To business?" Salem said.

"Let's get this over with."

Salem took out the stack of bills and riffled the edges.

"I'll take your word it's all there," he said.

"It is."

"Good."

"Where's your part of the deal?"

"I'm afraid I may have left it in me other pants."

"What?"

172

He giggled and threw up his hands.

"Just jokin', mate. It's right here."

He pulled out a small white envelope and handed it over to Doren, who ripped the flap back without hesitation.

There was a negative in there, a single frame from a strip of thirty-five-millimeter film.

"How many more are there?"

"A few," Salem said. "We'll just have to see."

"Why can't we simply get this over with?"

"If I sold you all the negatives right now, that'd just be one fixed amount of money. I need a steady income. We should take care of the whole film roll by the end of the year. I've got to make a livin', you know."

"You're giving me an ulcer."

"Come on. This is just a business deal. You thrive on business."

"This isn't the same."

"Just think of it as an investment in your son's future, then, like that money you poured into Princeton."

Doren stuffed the negative into his pocket. He would burn it later, as he had burned all the rest.

He'd almost thrown up when Salem had shown him the prints the first time—a series of color glossies of Hamilton and a girl of about fourteen.

Salem, of course, had set up the meeting between the two. She was one of Salem's girlfriends, in fact, but her past wouldn't make that much difference if the pictures came out.

For the last four months Salem had been selling the negatives to Doren a frame at a time. He wouldn't say how big a roll he had. It was a real fear for Doren, because he wanted it to be over. At best, he was going to have to put up with it for a year. Salem kept hinting that he had a roll of twelve exposures.

Doren feared he might have a thirty-six, though, and dreaded dragging things out that long.

The girl in the picture was pretty. It was possible Hamilton hadn't known her age. He didn't expect his son to be perfect, but he did want to protect him. He wasn't going to let someone like Salem cost the boy his future. Doren had worked too hard to build things up for him.

"Is that all?" he asked Salem.

"Until I call again. You know how it is. Sometimes I get lonely and want someone to talk to. I was going to suggest we have a drink, but I guess you're in a hurry."

Doren didn't reply.

"See you later," Salem said, stuffing his cash into the pocket of his old army jacket. "Pleasure doing business with you."

"I'll be glad when it's over," Doren said.

"What makes you think our arrangement will terminate?" Salem asked. "Your son's a busy lad, don't you know?"

"What do you mean?"

"Nothing."

Doren took a step toward him.

"What do you mean?"

"Don't make such a big deal out of it."

Doren grabbed him by the collar, anger searing through his brain.

"What else have you gotten him involved in?"

Salem's own anger flared, and his arms streaked forward, tearing Doren's hands away from him.

"Don't fucking touch me like that, you old shithead. Don't ever do that, or I'll mail you pieces of your son special delivery. Then you'll have to have pictures to remember what he looked like when he had ears." His eyes were fiery, orbs of madness glowing in the shadowed alley.

Doren moved out of his immediate reach, taking slow steps, keeping his hands in front of him to block an assault.

"But what were you talking about? Are there more pictures?"

"Ask him where he went the other night."

"Which night?"

"Does it matter?"

Doren watched Salem turn and move down the alley, dancing a little jig before he reached the street and disappeared into the darkness.

CHAPTER 13

Gable and Jennifer drank coffee while sitting on Gable's front porch the next day. It was a fresh, clear dawn of bright sunlight. Only a few cotton-white wisps of clouds dappled the morning sky.

While she had spent the night at her own house, Jennifer had risen early, waiting to see a light come on in Gable's window before she ventured over.

Actually, she had slept all right until another of the dreams had come, taking her again into the realm of nightmare with stormy darkness and shadowy figures.

None of the images had faces. They remained anonymous specters, personifications of the attacker from yesterday perhaps.

"You're going to stick it out?" Gable asked.

She realized she'd been silent for quite some time now, and he must have been sitting and watching her.

She flashed an awkward smile. "I made it one night. I feel like I'm in AA."

Gable nodded.

"Maybe I should get a gun."

"I'm not much on that sort of thing. Guns scare me," he said.

"They scare me, too," she agreed. "But I've got a problem here."

"Houston, we've got a problem," Gable said, mimicking a microphone with his hand.

"If the killer comes back, I want to be ready. I did see the police cruiser several times this morning, early."

"But you want a little more reassurance."

"Exactly."

"I'd be afraid someone would take a gun away from me and use it on me."

She laughed. "It's possible, I suppose. The knife the killer brought along was pretty scary, though. No need to steal a weapon if you've got your own."

"True."

"Am I imposing on you?"

He shook his head.

"There's not much you can impose on."

"If you meet a girl or anything—" She hesitated. "I realize it would be awkward with me here all the time."

"Don't worry about it."

"I don't know how to talk about it without being blunt. You've been very kind, but I'm not going to sleep with you."

He was silent, but his expression didn't change. She'd been afraid he was going to expect something if she kept hanging around, so she'd had to get the topic out in the open.

Shielding her eyes, she shook her head. "I didn't mean it to sound so abrupt."

"I know," he said, and smiled.

"Don't take that the wrong way. I'm not ready to go to bed with anybody right now. I just didn't want you to be thinking I was trying to lead up to that or anything. A broken heart makes you cautious.''

''Yeah.''

Their gazes met, and she looked deeply into his soft, gray eyes. They held a look of gentleness. He wasn't trying to put any kind of pressure on her. She'd been worried about how he would react, but it wasn't a problem.

It felt good to find someone who would be a friend without rushing or making demands.

That relieved a little of the tension she'd been feeling, because she'd wondered what he was thinking about her.

Now there was just the matter of the killer.

They were sitting there on the porch, so perfect and so sweet. A picture of innocence. She'd been a problem, more of a problem than had been expected, but that wasn't any big deal. She could still be taken care of.

The circumstances just called for a more careful approach. A random attack wouldn't do. It would have to be something special, something unexpected.

Nelson sat at his desk watching Fisher move into the room. The big detective waddled in and plopped down in a chair, uttering a heavy sigh as his weight produced a moan from the Naugahyde cushion.

Fisher slipped his hat off and balanced it on one knee.

''I need to talk to you about your daughter. Maybe we can turn up something that will lead us to whoever's been threatening her.''

''I see.'' Nelson pressed his fingertips together. ''You have no leads on this matter yet?''

The detective bowed his head slightly, apparently embarrassed.

"No sir," he confessed.

Nelson nodded. He was not surprised. Fisher did not impress him. He'd known the man for several years, and it often amazed him that Fisher ever broke a case.

"What is it you need to know about Jennifer?" he asked.

With his thick fingers Fisher tugged a small notebook from the pocket of his faded gray sports coat. It seemed to take him forever to get the pages turned to a blank sheet and then to get his pen ready.

He leaned back in his chair and rested the pen against the pad, anchoring one elbow on the chair arm. He wasn't one to exert any needless effort.

"I've talked to her. There may be things she's forgotten. Things you'll have a different perspective on."

"Yes."

"Boyfriends."

Nelson nodded and paused for a moment, thinking back. It had been hard for him to accept Jennifer's dating. He hadn't allowed it until she was sixteen even though there were coed parties among her classmates several years before that.

When she'd entered the tenth grade, however, he'd become aware of the fact that he could hold her back no longer, had realized she was growing up—a fact he had no choice but to accept.

Her first date had been to a back-to-school dance. It wasn't a formal dance, and somehow he found that a little easier to accept. She wore jeans and a sweater instead of an evening gown. That wasn't as bad. It didn't make it seem as if she was growing up so fast.

He worried, but he managed, and the permission had made her exuberant. She'd gone with some young man he couldn't remember now, except that he had been polite and nervous sitting in the living room.

Nelson had never been comfortable having Jennifer date boys he didn't know. Aimsley was a growing town. More and more there were new families. That made it harder to learn the backgrounds of some of her dates.

When he could, Nelson encouraged her to date the sons of men he knew and worked with.

He considered himself fortunate in some respects. She'd never tried to date people he didn't approve of just to spite him. He'd always been able to count on her not bringing home a Hell's Angel. Most of her dates had been decent young men.

Sometimes he worried about what had happened to her when she went away to school. He knew she'd had some unhappy experiences, but she never talked about them. That was one problem with Jennifer. She kept things to herself, buried them inside her. As much as he loved her, Nelson found it impossible to be close to his daughter. Often he feared that was his own fault. His work had kept him busy in her younger days, but he also feared his protectiveness had made her resent him.

Fisher breathed heavily, making Nelson realize he'd been staring at his desk, almost lost in thought.

"Can I get you a drink, Mr. Fisher?"

Fisher nodded.

He hadn't expected the detective to drink on duty, but he got up and moved over to a narrow table near the window, where a decanter of Rémy Martin was set up.

He poured a few splashes into a pair of glasses and carried one over to Fisher, who gulped a large swallow.

"I'm worried about my daughter," Nelson said.

"We're trying to keep a close watch on her. Especially since yesterday."

Nelson was on his way back to his seat behind his desk, but he stopped and wheeled around.

180

"What happened yesterday?"

"I thought she would have told you."

"She's keeping things from me, trying to be independent."

It took a long time for Fisher to draw and exhale his next breath. It was apparent he was doing his best to bridle impatience.

"Someone tried to get into her house. She screamed for help and it scared him off. Could have been anyone. Maybe someone who thought her house was empty for the day. We have a lot of burglaries."

The detective looked away from Nelson, searching for something out the window. Nelson felt his stomach quiver. He sensed Fisher was abbreviating what had happened, perhaps to keep down the worry.

Slowly Nelson returned to his seat. He couldn't help but worry. She was his only child, now in danger but refusing any help from him. He was paying the price for sheltering her too much. Now, when she really needed his assistance, she wouldn't accept it.

"Is she all right?" Nelson asked. He felt like kicking himself for not calling, but he was trying to give her space, let her know he was trying to let her be free.

"She's fine," Fisher said. "That writer was with her."

She'd gone to the writer instead of to her father, Nelson thought. She was scared to tell him what happened. Breaking away was more important than safety.

Across the desk Fisher finished his drink.

"I really need to get on with this," he said.

"Yes. I've been lost in thought. Go ahead."

"Has she dated much, Mr. Nelson?"

"She's had a number of boyfriends over the years. None were very serious. She's cautious in relationships. I've noticed that in her."

"She break some hearts?"

"Probably. All young girls do, I suppose. I think she had her heart broken a few times as well. She's an introverted girl, often solemn. Contemplative, if you will. That's not something that's easy to deal with. Young men often gave up on her."

"I see."

"I, of course, tried to keep a watch on things. Thinking back, perhaps I was too strict with her."

"What's her religion?"

"We're Catholic. She was raised in the church, although she doesn't attend Mass very regularly any longer. That's something that's disturbed her mother quite a bit."

"What was her relationship with the priest?"

"Father Conzenza was the parish priest when she was a teenager. She liked him, enjoyed talking to him, I think. I hope you're not implying anything beyond that."

"Just fishing. Trying to find some kind of connection. We can't determine why someone would want to kill Conzenza and her also."

Nelson shook his head. "I can't imagine. The only connection is that he was her priest."

"That doesn't give us much to go on."

"I see what you mean. That's not a very singular connection. He was the priest for a number of people," Nelson agreed.

"You can't think of anything else?"

"I'm afraid not. It's upsetting to her mother, but I don't think Jennifer has even been to confession in several years."

He looked across the desk at Fisher, who was scribbling on his notepad.

"I wish there were something more I could tell you," he said.

Fisher shrugged. "It's a weird case. Weird cases are a little harder."

"I wish we could get her to come home."

"How long has she been away from home?"

"Almost six years now. She's been in school. College, then she began work on her master's."

"And she's only been back in town how long?"

"A few months. She's completed her course work toward her degree."

"Has she gone out with any of her old boyfriends?"

"I don't think so. I don't think there are any romances she wanted to rekindle."

"Can you think of any of the boys that she used to date that are still in town?"

"Several I'm sure." He paused, thinking. "There's a kid named Benjie Roth who's still around. She went out with him only a couple of times, and that was years ago. One young man who's a teacher now, Brian Price. Hamilton Terry, of course, who's the son of my business partner. I always hoped they'd hit it off, but it never worked out for them. I think she dated him a few times just to humor me, but she didn't have any real interest in him."

"Any of these people have any connection with the priest?"

"She knew some of them from church, yes."

"That still wouldn't explain why someone would want to kill her and the priest. That's a loose tie."

"How much of a motive would a crazy person need?"

"Maybe not a tangible motive, but some kind of link probably exists in the killer's mind. It may be a motive we'd never dream of. Twisted minds dream up weird things. Could be your daughter and the priest just reminded some guy of two people he didn't like."

That thought settled onto Nelson like a weight. If the

motive was that obscure, it meant it would be very hard for them to find the killer, making Jennifer's danger even greater.

Slowly he got up from his chair. With his hands in the pockets of his pants, he walked to the window and looked out, then poured himself another drink. He didn't offer Fisher more.

"Mr. Fisher, you have a difficult job."

"Yes sir."

He turned toward the detective.

"I know it's not usually done, but I'd like to offer you an incentive. I know also that's not allowed, but it will be just between us. I have to make sure my daughter is safe if she insists on this independence."

"I couldn't—"

He raised his hand, halting Fisher's words.

"Five thousand dollars, Fisher. Find the killer and I'll pay it to you in cash."

Fisher's eyes locked on him, studying him, his lips parted slightly.

"I can't."

"Yes you can. You will."

"I have to find the killer anyway."

"So be it. If you work hard anyway, then you have a windfall. If this offer will make you work harder, well, that's fine, too. It will make me feel better."

"I'll catch the killer. Then we'll talk."

"Yes."

Fisher put his notebook in his pocket, returned his hat to his head, and gave Nelson a nod before he moved from the room.

When the door closed, Nelson returned to the window to look out at the sunlight. Perhaps the offer would do no good in the case, but it let him feel as if he were doing something

184

more than just standing by, waiting for harm to befall his daughter. There wasn't much she would allow him to do, but there were some things she didn't have to know about.

Gable had always been nervous about conducting interviews. There were times in his newspaper work when he had put off assignments until his editor started threatening him with physical violence.

He hated calling people he didn't know on the telephone. Even worse, he hated going up to people he didn't know and trying to strike up conversations.

He didn't expect Dareena to react with hostility, but he still felt awkward about approaching her, or at least apprehensive. It was no fun invading people's lives.

Yet he knew he needed to talk to her, needed to know more about Azarius if he was going to come up with anything worthwhile.

Even if she wasn't a killer, there was still a fragment here, perhaps something he could deal with fictionally if nothing else panned out. Deep down he had a feeling that there was something important about her, although he wasn't sure what gave him the feeling.

He drove by the house a couple of times as the morning crept away, watching the porch and the front of the residence, hoping Dareena would appear.

A couple of times he noticed someone else, not at her house or even in the yard, but across the street and later on a corner.

It was a young man, a man in his early thirties perhaps, definitely not a vagrant. He wore nice clothes although they had an unkempt look, and his hair was in tangles even though it was cut short. He apparently hadn't shaved in several days.

185

Dark-haired, of medium build, nice looking except for his disheveled look—Gable tried to memorize the features. He could be important. If he was hanging around Dareena, he might be connected with the killing in some way.

After a while he returned to thinking about Dareena. One way or another, he was going to have to meet her.

When she showed up working on the front lawn, he knew there wouldn't be any better opportunity. Cruising past in the car, he parked against the curb a short distance away and walked back.

The dark-haired man was not in sight any longer.

With his hands in his pockets Gable strolled up the street in front of Dareena's house, stopping at the edge of the lawn.

She was wearing a red blouse and tan shorts, kneeling on the grass in front of the flower bed that bordered the house. She used a small hand tool to till the impacted earth. On a newspaper beside her were spread an array of bulbs, small buds which would grow into flowering plants when buried.

"Tulips?" Gable asked, moving up the sidewalk.

The girl turned to his voice, frowning, but her features melted into a more pleasant expression when she saw his smile—a part of the Gable-Tyler-interviewing-the-man-on-the-street package.

"Surprise lilies," she said. "They bloom bright red."

"I've seen them," he said. "Very pretty."

She stood and brushed the dust and dirt particles from her knees. Her legs were slender, firm, and trim, just managing not to be too thin.

"Are you a touring horticulturist?" she asked.

He hadn't expected wry comments from her. The image he'd developed had her an an introvert, shy and withdrawn.

He laughed. "Just interested."

She picked up one of the bulbs. "I'm getting these planted

a little late, but I just happened to find them in a garden shop.'' She let the bulb roll off her fingers to drop beside the others on the paper.

"Are you from the D.A.'s office or the police or where?''

He didn't speak for a second because he would have fumbled his words. He just looked at her and shrugged slightly. "Just one more guy invading your privacy,'' he confessed when he found his voice.

"I didn't kill the priest.'' She looked him over. "I don't do that sort of thing.''

"I'm not an investigator.''

Her eyes searched his face. "What does that leave?''

"I'm a writer.'' He told her his name.

"From the paper?''

"No.''

"What's left?''

"I'm not sure yet. You going to tell me to go to hell?''

"Do a lot of people?''

"They used to. When I was playing reporter.''

"You don't seem too bad. I'm just learning I should be careful about talking to strangers.''

"Has anyone threatened you?''

"Not with murder. Why?''

"I'm a friend of Jennifer Nelson.''

"Oh, yes. I read the papers. So you have a personal interest in this.''

"I'd like to understand it all.''

"So would I.''

"I may write a story about it. Maybe a book.''

"Will I be in it?''

"If I say yes, are you going to quit talking to me?''

She shook her head. "Make fun of me if you like. I've developed an immunity. You've heard people talk about me. I don't care anymore.''

"It must be difficult sometimes."

"It hurts. It's lonely. It's always been that way. Even before I became the girl who talks to angels."

"Which brings us to Azarius, I guess. Is he a real angel?"

"As opposed to what?"

Gable had to shrug.

"I don't always understand it myself," she said. "I can try to explain it."

"Sounds good."

"Mainly because it's good to have someone to talk to. Use what I tell you however you want."

"I'm not out to hurt you."

She nodded. "Let's take a walk. It's a pretty day."

She put her hand on Gable's arm and urged him over toward the edge of the lawn. Together they walked along the sidewalk, meandering through the downtown streets past deserted buildings and occasionally past new shops.

"What is this?" Gable asked.

"I'm seeing if you're embarrassed to be seen with me."

"I don't have any reputation. Nothing to lose."

"We've something in common. Neither do I."

"So back to your angel."

"You're wondering, 'Is he traditional?' An angel in the same way we all think of angels."

"Right."

"He's an angel. It's difficult to explain to you how he manifests himself."

"Not physically?"

"No. He's more of a spirit, more ethereal. I don't see him in a tangible form. He appears to me, an image. We talk. At times in my mind, I'm able to visualize things he tells me. It's like taking a journey, but he tells me I haven't

188

reached a point yet where I can achieve the total release I need to understand him."

"What's his purpose?"

"He wants me to understand love and infinity. There are so many things beyond this world, Mr. Tyler. You may not believe that. Are you a religious man?"

"People keep asking me that." He looked up toward the sky. "It's a big world. It had to come from somewhere."

"And it's so vast. There are realms outside our perception."

"That's where Azarius lives?"

"Where all the angels live. Watching this world, waiting for us to find them. Their job is to help us, lead us, and bring understanding. They want to unlock the other realms for us."

"How come they don't talk to everybody?"

"They do. When the individual is ready to open his mind to them."

"What if someone doesn't get ready?"

"It's evil within the person that prevents it. If he doesn't purge that evil, then he suffers the pain of separation from God and the angels. That's where so much of the pain in the world comes from."

"Azarius told you that?"

"Yes. He's teaching me. There will be a point when I'm ready to cross over into his realm, to join him. My understanding is still too limited right now. Sometimes I even get confused. I question him. It takes work."

"Where did you first get in touch with Azarius?"

"In a dream. Of sorts. More like a daydream. I read a great deal, and I was lost in thought, you might say."

Gable glanced over at her. She seemed to be hedging around that question. He didn't press.

189

Finally they reached the end of the street at the edge of the sloping rise of the levee that bordered the river.

She started up it, so Gable followed her to the top, where it leveled off to a plateau for a few paces before sloping down to the water's edge.

The river was wide and brown, and the breeze that played across its surface was cool and moist.

Gable watched the ripples in the body draw varied patterns as the water rolled past.

"This is a nice place," Dareena said. "I come here to think. The other realm is something like this, only not in a way I can explain it to you. It's a different form."

"Astral?"

"Does that have any meaning?"

"Sounded good."

"I don't know what you'd call it. I haven't been able to cross over to it completely, like I said, but it's placid. So peaceful and bright."

Gable turned to look at her as she gazed out across the river. The sunlight danced off her hair and outlined her features. She was soft and delicate-looking, her eyes intense but warm. There was a sadness about her that seemed to lurk just beneath the surface of her being, the sadness of her alienation, the sadness that grew out of having only an angel as a friend.

"Sometimes Azarius explains things to me that I don't understand," she said.

"What do you mean?"

"Just things he tells. It takes work to get ready, to understand."

"Is that all?"

"Some things are different than I expected. You have to change your way of thinking in some ways, because this is a material world. And also because some of the teachings that have been handed down have been confused and distorted."

"Azarius conflicts with some ideas?"

"Not conflicts exactly. Interprets differently."

She was being vague. Gable turned back from her to look at the water again. He wasn't sure what to make of the girl. She spoke with such candor, with conviction. Her discussion didn't sound like ramblings. She spoke rationally and with intelligence.

Yet he was somehow uncomfortable with what she was saying and sensed she was as well, at least in part.

There were more things he could have asked, but he held his further questions as they turned and walked back toward her house.

He glanced at her from time to time out of the corner of his eye, studying her features and expression.

She turned and looked back at Gable.

"Have you found some of your answers?" she asked. Her tone had grown solemn.

"A few. I'm still curious."

"Maybe your angel will find you."

She put her hand on the doorknob.

"Can I talk to you again?" he asked.

She hesitated, as if frightened.

"I guess it would be all right," she said. Then she shoved the door inward and disappeared into the house.

For a moment Gable stood looking at the grain of the wood as the door shut. Then he turned and walked back toward his car.

Dareena returned trembling to her bedroom. She had felt the quivering feeling in her stomach from the time she began to speak to Gable, and it was something she couldn't understand.

She hadn't been frightened of him despite the encounter with Walker Vincent. Gable had seemed kind, a pleasant man, friendly, in fact.

She'd even managed to come up with a clever line for him. It had been easy to talk to him, yet she had felt an underlying sense of paranoia.

The whole time she'd fought it off. From the beginning she had sensed he wouldn't openly scoff at what she said, and she needed someone to talk to, just someone who would listen.

It was difficult keeping everything to herself. She'd been nervous about the killing and the investigation, but in a way, having the policemen come around and ask questions had been interesting, a diversion. Until the man had tried to attack her.

She hadn't been as disturbed by that event as she might have expected. It had been frightening, but it had happened so quickly, seeming almost unreal.

And Azarius had ultimately been comforting, although he had begun their contact with ambiguity. That was always the angel's way, to remain vague, speaking sometimes in riddles, which forced her to search for his meanings.

It was helpful; the searching gave her a greater understanding when she did find answers.

Sitting on the edge of her bed, she sensed his presence. Perhaps he was the source behind the nervous feeling she'd had.

She slid off the bed and drew the curtain to shut out the sunlight that might obscure the mirror and burn away the shadows.

"What's wrong?" she asked.

She could see the image in the mirror now, flickering as much inside her mind as before her eyes.

"You seem frightened."

"Not frightened. But I feel disturbed."

"The man you were talking to."

"His name was Gable."

"I know his name. I wanted to draw you away from him. He may be a danger to you."

"Him? He was so nice."

"You did not expect anything from the other man either."

"But he was different. It was easy to talk to Gable."

She felt a nervous twinge inside her, mingled with a growing confusion and unrest.

"You can not tell where the evil will come from."

"Why is he dangerous?"

"He is a threat."

"Why?"

"Why must you question?"

She swallowed. "Because I don't understand you."

"He could be the killer. The one who killed the priest."

She frowned. "Why? Why would he do that?"

"Evil has many reasons."

"Azarius, please. I must understand."

"The time for you to come with me is drawing near. There could be forces that would attempt to prevent that."

"The man who attacked me?"

"Perhaps. And perhaps this other man is a threat in other ways. He could attempt to entice you away."

"He didn't do anything like that. He just listened. He questioned. That's all. What's wrong with questions."

"They can lead to confusion."

"Questions can't harm truth, can they? You use questions."

193

"The wrong questions can mislead. What if they caused you to doubt me. It could set back your preparation."

"You're afraid of him."

"I am afraid of nothing. He is a man. A mortal."

"But you are afraid of him."

"Afraid he might harm you."

"He doesn't seem to be the type. You didn't make that sort of indication about the other man. You only convinced me to submit to your ecstasy."

"To keep you from feeling scars from his attack. He was a different danger."

She put her face in her hands, shaking her head as tears began to well in her eyes. "I'm confused. It's all such a jumble. He's just a writer."

"It's not what he is," Azarius said. "It's what he might become."

"What do you mean?"

"He could be manipulated or serve some purpose unwittingly."

"You're not making sense."

"Then you are at fault. You must search for meaning as always, until you understand. And keep away from that man. I command it."

CHAPTER 14

The priest's brother, Archie, lived at the end of a long dirt road that stretched past a series of fields and then wound back through a stand of oak and pine trees.

Arbor guided the car through the turns and twists of the road with a little more speed than was safe, stirring up a heavy cloud of red dust as the tires swirled through the gravel. He squinted against the hot afternoon sun.

He'd had to stop for directions at a little grocery store, where he'd drawn suspicious stares from the locals. Gray-haired old men with baseball caps had eyed him as if they expected him to rape the women.

The town was called Bristol Springs, located about twenty miles south of Aimsley, no more than a gap in the highway with offshoot trails.

A fat woman with curly black hair who sat on a stool behind the counter of the grocery store reading a paperback romance had been able to direct him.

The house was a small white frame building with a porch shielded by sagging screens. There were chickens pecking about on the small front lawn, and they scattered when Arbor pulled his car to a stop beside the pickup truck parked in the driveway.

He got out of the car slowly and put his hands into his pockets. He had spoken to the man on the phone, but he was being careful after his experience at the store. This was the kind of place where they used shotguns to question strangers, and black strangers were the worst kind you could have as far as many were concerned.

He walked up the steps and knocked on the door. A brown and white bird dog that was sleeping by the welcome mat looked up but didn't bark.

A moment later the door swung inward, and a young woman looked out. She was thin, her blond hair pulled back into a bun. Wisps of hair escaped, twisting around her face in odd patterns. She wore a faded print dress that didn't fit well. It might have belonged to someone else once.

"You must be the detective," she said.

"I am," Arbor answered, finding nothing else to say.

She pushed the door back and let him enter. The front room was a small area with hardwood floors, and the light was bad. Arbor moved in slowly, the floor creaking with his weight. He looked over at the man sitting across from the doorway.

He was young and there were still some signs of muscular shoulders. He was wearing jeans and a plaid work shirt. The clothes hung loosely on his frame.

His wheelchair hummed as he guided it over to the edge of the room, where he managed to lift a trembling hand toward the detective.

"Hello," he said.

Arbor gripped his hand gently.

"I'm sorry to have to come to you at a time like this," Arbor said.

"No. I understand," the man said. "You have to find

out who killed him.'' He tilted his head back, shaking his shoulder-length hair out of his face. The skin of his face was stretched tightly so that it seemed to outline his skull.

From one of the parishioners, Arbor had learned of the brother. For some reason it had come as a surprise. No one had mentioned it to him from the priest's records. It seemed priests weren't supposed to have any family since they didn't have wives.

The brother had been crippled by a fall from an off shore oil rig where he'd been working to make extra money to support his small farm.

A baby began to cry in the next room as Arbor settled onto the couch and took out his notebook. The woman moved through a doorway, wiping her hands on her apron.

These were people Erskine Caldwell might have created, Arbor thought.

"Your brother visited here often?'' he asked.

"He came down pretty regular, yeah. He was busy, but he'd slip down for supper every now and then, bring some groceries.'' The man's clear blue eyes wandered over toward the door, as if he expected his brother to walk in once again.

"Did he mention people to you very much? The people he came into contact with?''

Archie shook his head. "Not really.''

"What about friends?''

"He was kind of solitary. When we were young he was always reading. He started getting ready for the priesthood when he was about fourteen.'' The man rubbed his eyes gently, "My brother never seemed very happy.''

"He ever mentioned a girl who talked to angels?''

"Not to me.''

Arbor tapped his finger against his notebook.

"Why would someone want to kill him?''

"I don't know." His voice was strained. "I can't think of why anyone would want that." He moved his head back slightly. It was not easy for him to do that, because the paralysis seemed to creep at least partially into his neck. When he moved, his eyes seemed to float around in his head.

"He never mentioned anyone in his congregation?" Arbor asked. "Someone who might have been angry with him."

"No. He was well liked."

"Why was he unhappy?"

"He just wasn't meant to be a priest. He was thinking of leaving the priesthood. He talked about that the last time he was here."

Arbor had been looking at his notebook, but he lifted his head quickly.

"Why?"

"He told me there were other ways he wanted to serve God. I don't know what he was going to do. It wasn't an easy decision for him."

"A woman?"

"No. Not that. Not that at all." The man's arms were limp, but there was a movement in his fingers. If he'd been able to, he would have clenched his fists.

"I'm trying to find out who killed him," Arbor said. "I have to look at all the angles."

"He wasn't having an affair. He was true to his vows. He was a good man."

"I understand. But anything could be a clue that tells who killed him and why. I have to dig."

"I know. I'm telling you the truth. Why would somebody want to kill someone just because he was leaving the priesthood?"

"Maybe somebody felt let down."

Betrayed. Arbor wrote a note to himself in his notebook. "Who would have known he was thinking about this?"

"He'd talked to me about it. He may have discussed it with a few others. Word travels about that sort of thing. He hadn't made it definite or anything."

"Secret knowledge, in other words."

"Yeah, I guess so."

"That gives me something new to look for. Who would have known?"

"Could be anybody."

"That's not even necessarily the reason. But it's a possibility."

"Anything's possible."

"Yes," Arbor agreed. "Anything's possible."

Gable had been home for a half hour when someone knocked on his front door. He was in the kitchen working on some supper, cutting up bell peppers from Jennifer's garden. Putting the things aside, he walked through the living room with the dog trotting along in front of him.

He recognized the man looking through his screen door. It was the guy who'd been hanging around outside Dareena's house.

Curling his fingers around the door, Gable prepared to shove it forward if he needed to, because the man had a wild look about him. His eyes were distant, glazed as if with madness.

"Can I help you?" Gable asked.

The man tilted his face toward the sound of Gable's voice like a blind man. Gable had the feeling the man wasn't actually seeing him.

"My name is Vincent. I need to talk to you about the girl." His voice was raspy.

Gable frowned.

"Which girl?"

"Dareena."

"I just met her. I don't know much about her."

"Please. It's very important."

Gable hesitated a moment but finally reached forward and unlatched the screen.

"Who are you?" he asked.

"I'm investigating."

"I've already talked to the police."

The man walked in slowly, and, turning, pushed the door shut. He paused then with his back to Gable, palms flat against the front door.

"Is something wrong?" Gable asked.

The man whirled around quickly, arms shooting forward, hands clutching Gable's collar. Before Gable could react, he felt himself being half lifted into the air. His feet dragged along the floor as the man shoved him backward, banging him finally against the room's rear wall.

The impact sent a shudder of pain through his shoulders. He tried to struggle.

"Stay away from her," the voice croaked.

"Who the hell are you?" Gable demanded.

The man jerked his arms violently to the side, releasing his grip and sending Gable flying across the room. He landed hard on his shoulder and rolled to one side seconds before Vincent rushed forward to pounce on him.

The man landed with a thud beside Gable but didn't remain disoriented. He spun around and began to claw at Gable's throat.

Bringing his knee forward between them, Gable managed to keep the attacker at bay as he scrambled backward.

As he got to his feet, he picked up a chair and swung it around, striking Vincent on one arm, near the shoulder.

The chair splintered, but the impact didn't faze the dark-haired man. He continued to pull himself to his feet and scramble after Gable.

The dog had moved over behind the couch, growling but also trembling. The hair along his spine bristled as he hunched down, peering around the edge of the couch. His eyes were filled with a look of terror.

Gable had only a second to look at him before Vincent was upon him again. He didn't manage to get out of his way this time. The hands closed around his arms, and he felt himself being lifted upward again.

The guy was short yet powerful. Struggling against the grip, Gable realized he was going to be thrown again and there was nothing he could do about it.

He tried to brace himself, but needles of pain jabbed into him as he crashed against the wall a second time. When he hit, he sank slowly to the floor, throwing up his arms to ward off the blow that he saw coming.

Vincent smashed his forearm against Gable, then grabbed his collar and brought a closed fist across his face.

Gable crumpled, unable to resist as the next blow struck him in the face. It wasn't very hard, but it jerked his head to one side. He groaned slightly.

Vincent followed the blow with a kick to Gable's midsection that sent the air out of his lungs in a single rush.

Gable lay still, his eyes half closed as he looked up at the man.

"Stay away from her," Vincent repeated.

He turned slowly and walked back to the door, letting himself out.

The guy had been gone five minutes before the dog would move from behind the couch. He came creeping out at about the same time Gable felt like moving again.

"You're great protection, killer," he said. He patted the dog's head. "I guess I got what you got yesterday."

The dog made a soft sound in its throat.

"You were scared of him? Is he the one? The one who came in yesterday?"

The dog nestled close to Gable's side and put his nose against Gable's chest.

"Wish you could talk. As soon as I can move again there are things I need to do."

He had to get up slowly. The pain was severe as he moved. There were going to be some aches for several days.

Pulling himself to his knees, he eased over to the coffee table to use it as support to lift himself to his feet.

Then he made his way to the telephone, lifted the received, and hit 911.

The line rang twice before a sheriff's deputy picked up on the other end.

"I need the police department," Gable said.

"I can call them for you, sir."

"I'll do it. Just get me the number."

"You all right, sir?"

"I've felt better."

He scribbled down the number as the officer read it off.

"Thanks," he mumbled, and hung up the receiver. Then he tapped out the police number. He got a sergeant.

"I need to talk to Fisher," Gable said.

"Mr. Fisher has gone home."

"You got anybody else there working the priest killing?"

"Why?"

"Because I need to talk to them."

"I'll check."

There was a pause of several seconds before another voice came on the line.

202

"Can I help you? This is Arbor. I'm with the D.A.'s office, but I'm working the case, too."

"My name is Gable Tyler. I talked to Fisher the other night."

"Yes, I know about you. We ran a check on you, Mr. Tyler."

"Great. Look, some guy just attacked me. He may have been the one who attacked Jennifer Nelson."

"Where are you, Mr. Tyler?"

"My house."

"I'll be right there."

Gable was resting on the couch when the investigator showed up. He didn't budge; he just yelled when Arbor knocked, prompting him to walk on into the living room.

"You okay?" Arbor asked.

"Considering I've been bounced around the room a few times. I feel like James Garner."

Arbor sat down on a chair beside the couch.

"What'd your attacker look like?"

"He was a short guy, but he was pretty tough. Dark hair, needed a shave worse than I do."

"Ever seen him before."

"Once. This afternoon."

Gable told him about going over to Dareena's.

"He was just hanging around there?"

"Yeah." Gable groaned slightly. "He must have been watching her, because he told me to stay away from her."

Turning his head slightly, Gable looked at the investigator. The man was staring at his notes with a puzzled look on his face.

"He didn't say why?"

"No reason. Just gave me the warning. And his voice was dry, rough. Jennifer said that first call she got had this really harsh voice."

Arbor nodded.

"Oh, he said his name was Vincent."

Vincent walked along the street with his hands in the pockets of his sport coat. It was just after dark, and he tried to stay in the shadows, avoiding the light from the streetlamps. His head was throbbing, and his stomach seemed to be preparing to turn itself inside out again. The darkness was serving as a refuge.

What had he done? What the hell was going on with him? First the girl and now the writer. He'd followed the guy, but why?

He stopped walking and put one hand against the wall of a building to steady himself. The events of the past two days were a jumble; there were things he couldn't remember, things he couldn't understand.

Slowly he lowered himself into a crouching position. Once again he felt as if he were going to be sick, but the feeling subsided.

The memory of the contact with Dareena slipped through his mind, touching off a turmoil. What had he done to her? And the attack on the young guy, what had that been about? Was this the pressure of it all?

He felt something brushing against his leg, and the movement startled him. He jumped and lost balance, then twisted around to see the green cat eyes staring at him.

The creature moved slowly out the shadows and peered up at him without making a sound. Somehow, it seemed to understand him. He reached out and cradled it in his arms.

Fisher banged on Brian Price's door at seven-thirty, and the little guy answered quickly, a book in his hand and wire-rimmed glasses sliding down his nose.

"Can I help you?"

Fisher took his badge wallet from his pocket and flashed the shield in front of the young man's eyes.

The kid swallowed and took a step backward.

"Is there something wrong? Is my mother all right?"

"Far as I know. I'm just here to ask you a few questions about a case I'm working on." Fisher sighed. He hated explaining these things. People always went to pieces when a cop approached them.

"Can I come in?" Fisher asked.

"Yes."

Fisher followed the young man into his small living room and sat down with his hands on his knees as the kid returned to his armchair, putting his book aside.

The room was small with little in the way of furnishing. The carpet was worn looking, and the curtains were dusty.

Price seemed to match the room. He wore faded jeans and a red plaid shirt that was wrinkled. His hair was straight but neatly trimmed, and his skin was smooth, making him look younger than he really was. He could have gone to school as a student instead of a teacher and fit right in.

In his way he was nice looking, but his appearance didn't seem to be of that much importance to him. He didn't look like a match for the Nelson girl, Fisher guessed.

He put his hand on his chin and surveyed the kid carefully. Price probably didn't impress women very much. He was the introverted type.

That made Fisher wonder. Could this kid be bearing a grudge against Jennifer Nelson? Had she hurt him, left him feeling inadequate? And if that linked Price to her, what was his link to the priest?

"You used to date Jennifer Nelson," Fisher said.

Price nodded, using his index finger to adjust the position of his glasses. "What's this about?"

"You heard about the priest who was killed?"

"I read it in the paper."

"She may be in danger from the same killer. We're checking all the angles. When did you date her?"

"We were juniors in high school. She was really the first girl I'd ever gone out with. I was kind of shy."

Fisher didn't grin, but he felt a little rush. He could still peg them.

Price swallowed and shifted in his chair.

"We didn't go out very long; I guess just a few weeks. We had a biology class together and I sat close to her. She sort of had a problem with it, you know. It just wasn't her thing, and I could sort of help her. It impressed her."

"She liked you?"

"Yeah." He smiled. "I didn't know how to ask a girl out or anything. She helped, let me know she'd go if I asked, so we went to the homecoming dance."

"Why'd you quit seeing her?"

"I guess I bored her. The stuff she liked about me didn't do much for her in large doses. She got tired hearing me talk. We were just teenagers. It hurt, but I got over it. I teach biology and chemistry now at Brenner High."

"I know. I checked you out. You haven't seen much of Jennifer lately?"

"Not in years. It's not a big town, but you just don't run into people that much."

"Did you know the priest?"

Price shook his head. He was still moving around in his chair, uncomfortable.

"What else can you tell me about Jennifer, then? Was she popular?"

"She was pretty. That makes you popular in high school, but she didn't date many people. Really she was quiet. She stayed at home a long time. Eventually she started dating a guy, I guess it was while we were seniors."

"Remember a name?"

"It's hard to say."

Fisher flipped back in his notebook. "Benjamin Roth?"

"She went out with him, but he's not the one I was thinking about. That was probably only a couple of times. There was this rich kid she went out with for a while."

"Hamilton Terry."

"That's him. I never really knew him, just knew who he was. A polished guy, dressed nice."

"So she dated him a long time?"

"Well," Price said, "everything feels like a long time when you're in school. I used to see them in the halls. Sometimes at school events, you know."

"She like him?"

"It's been a long time."

"She was your old girlfriend," Fisher coaxed. "You kept an eye on her, didn't you? It's human nature."

Price leaned forward in his chair. "Am I a suspect? Look, I haven't even thought about her in years."

"I'm just looking for information. If you haven't bothered her, you're in the clear."

Price seemed to relax just slightly. He settled back into his chair. "I saw them. I'd kind of glance at them. You know, in school, a lot of times people date because it's secure. You get a steady and you don't have to worry about having a date. And it takes some of the pressure off. So they hung around together, but a lot of the time I used to think she was bored with him. She had that look on her face that girls get. Tired, indifferent.''

"She would have been happier if she'd stuck with you?''

"Look, I won't deny I thought that, but it really was a long time ago. I want you to know that.''

Bullying the kid seemed to keep him talking. "Fine,'' Fisher said. "So what happened? You never got her back. Why not?''

"I never tried. I don't know. I had a couple of other dates. She was just busy. When she broke up with what's-his-name, Hamilton, she didn't act like she wanted anybody else.''

"She broke up with him?''

"Yeah. Toward the end of the year. I don't know why. I never heard, but it just seemed like one day they weren't hanging around together anymore.''

"When was this?''

"The spring of the year. I remember I thought about asking her to the prom, but I never got up the courage again.''

"You never heard why she and Terry broke up?''

"I didn't know him, like I said. Nobody else ever talked about it. It wasn't really my business.''

"Did Terry seem upset when it was all over?''

"He was really nice looking, and he was part of the big crowd, the cool people. He always had girls, cheerleaders and everything. He never stayed with girls long.''

"What'd she do after that?''

"I guess she went out with other people.''

"You didn't resent all that? Didn't resent Hamilton Terry?''

"No. By then I was over her.''

"You dating anybody now?''

"There's a girl who teaches with me. We go to the movies sometimes."

Price seemed to want to get angry, but he wasn't quite brave enough to stand up to a cop, somebody who could put him in jail.

Fisher studied his face and his eyes. They were soft, reflective. He was probably clean. Badgering him wasn't going to accomplish anything. Maybe what he'd talked about would be useful and maybe not.

At any rate, there were other things to check on. Pulling his hat down a little tighter over his head, Fisher got up and made his way to the door.

CHAPTER 15

After he was finished talking to Gable, Arbor went back to the office to type up his report about his conversation with Archie Conzenza.

He needed to get the information down so he and Fisher could compare notes, and the best way to do that was by typing. His handwritten notes couldn't be deciphered by anyone but himself.

The best place to get the work done was the office. He had a decent electric typewriter at home, but they had newer models at the office which allowed easier corrections. Besides, he didn't trust himself to get to the work if he went home. His easy chair and his new Clavell novel would be a temptation.

As he rolled the paper around the cylinder of the electronic machine, he thought about Vincent.

Arbor was upset about the attack on Tyler. He wanted to take immediate action.

It wasn't a good feeling. The pressure must have cracked the guy. Tomorrow, if Vincent didn't show up, he'd have to warn people to look out for him.

Only the loyalty to fellow workers that had been drilled

into him as a policeman kept him from filing an immediate report on Vincent's actions. Cops didn't tell on cops without checking things out first. They covered for each other. As much as he hated that credo at times, he felt it applied with Vincent as well.

It was hard to understand why he'd wigged out so early. Things hadn't even been that tough yet on the case. Perhaps it was best. Better to find out now that the guy couldn't handle pressure than to learn at some crucial moment during prosecution, or even worse have him fold sometime down the road while in the D.A.'s chair.

Arbor shook his head. It was a shame. He was going to have to do something with the guy, but he wanted to talk to him before he went to Jackson about it.

He didn't want to think about the other things he'd discussed with Gable. It was absurd that there was anything to the business of angels or the supernatural. There was a very real explanation for all this, a real killer who'd knifed Conzenza to death and placed those phone calls to Jennifer Nelson.

Yet he did sense something else was happening. When he'd entered Gable Tyler's apartment, the hair on the back of his neck had stood on end, and he'd seen the dog, still cowering behind the couch.

Could that mean something? He tried to push the thoughts from his mind and began to type his notes.

The office was empty and quiet, not the time to think about eerie things. There were too many shadows. Those were the kinds of things to turn over in the mind during daylight hours, when there were lots of people around.

He hammered away at the keys for a while before the sound of the main door opening caught his attention.

Flipping off the typewriter, he pushed his chair away from the desk and slipped his gun from the holster.

211

Easing his way back to the wall, he pressed his back against the paneling beside the door, straining his ears to pick up the sounds from the entryway.

He could hear footsteps, heavy, clomping steps. Someone seemed to be stomping around the front room with no real direction, just moving back and forth.

With his shoulder Arbor flipped the switch to throw his office into darkness. Then the fingers of his free hand curled around the knob, and he twisted it slowly, freeing the catch to allow the door to pull slowly inward.

He peered around through the doorway before he stepped into the hallway and moved quickly down its length.

At the mouth of the corridor he paused again, pressing his back to the wall as he looked out into the entrance room.

Vincent was there, still wandering from one side of the room to the other. He looked like an unmade bed—his clothes were rumpled, his hair tangled, and his face scraggly with stubble.

Arbor didn't holster the gun, but he let his arm hang to his side so that the pistol wasn't readily noticeable.

Stepping into the room, he planted his feet and cleared his throat. The sound caught Vincent's attention and he turned from the wall and looked over at the investigator.

"Arbor."

"What's wrong with you?"

Vincent ran his hands over his face and jerked his head from side to side.

"Walker, you jumped on that kid tonight. What was that all about? Have you lost your mind, man?"

Vincent took a step forward.

"I don't know what I was doing. He was over talking to the girl. I really can't remember much of it."

"You knocked him all over his apartment. It's a good thing he's young and healthy. You could have hurt him, and that would have really caused a mess. You're lucky. He doesn't want to press charges."

Hiding his face in his hands, Vincent walked over to the couch. He groaned and mumbled as he lowered himself onto the cushions.

Arbor slipped his weapon back into its holder on his right hip before he walked toward the lawyer.

When he reached the couch, Arbor knelt on one knee at Vincent's side, placing his hand gently on the younger man's shoulder.

"We can work this out. We can put this case together."

"I don't know what's happening."

"Do you need some help? We can do it discreetly. It won't hurt your career."

"I've got to get straight."

Vincent's hands fell way from his face. He let them rest on his legs.

"You need some rest," Arbor said. He looked away from Vincent at the front door which remained open. A cat had just strolled into the room.

It crept across the floor and crouched near the center of the room, peering over at Arbor with its pale green eyes.

Arbor would have to get it out of here later. Once he took care of Vincent. He at least wanted to get the lawyer home. He didn't want to take responsibility for Vincent, but he also didn't want to see this case crumble and the department face a scandal.

Jackson didn't need one of his top people going on the psycho list. It would look like he didn't know how to pick a staff, which would make life harder for everyone, especially with the priest killing wide open.

"You want some water?" he asked Vincent.

"That would be good."

Arbor went down the hall to the small bathroom. He got

a paper cup and filled it from the lavatory and carried it back into the waiting room.

Vincent still had his head bowed. Arbor walked over to him and offered the cup as he watched the lawyer's hand extend. Arbor thought Vincent was reaching for the water, so the blow took him by surprise.

The force of the fist Vincent jabbed into his face was more than Arbor expected, even as he saw it coming. Hard knuckles dug into the investigator's face on the side, near his ear, and he went reeling back across the room.

His head began to spin from the impact, and he staggered, unable to keep his balance.

When he hit the floor, one arm was beneath him and he felt it twist into an angle it shouldn't have. Some muscles gave, enough to let him know he wasn't going to be doing much with that arm for a few days at least.

The pain of it shot up through his shoulder, and he was attempting to get his weight off the limb by rolling over when Vincent moved in on him.

Reaching down, the lawyer grabbed Arbor's lapels and lifted him to his feet, then shoved him backward, at the same time slamming a fist into the lean muscles of Arbor's stomach.

The wind rushed out of his lungs and Arbor doubled over. He clutched his stomach with his damaged right arm and started to scramble across the room to get out of Vincent's way. Gable had been right. The guy's strength was remarkable.

Before Arbor could move more than a few steps, Vincent came forward, wrapping his fingers around the black man's throat.

The touch was icy. Arbor gasped for air as the lawyer forced him back to the wall, pinning him against the paneling.

He tried to get a knee up into the short man's groin, but Vincent blocked the motion with his own leg and then drove his knee straight up into Arbor's stomach.

Again the investigator gasped and bent forward. He almost vomited but choked back the bile in his throat.

With his hands still around Arbor's neck, Vincent tossed his weight to one side, then lunged forward, hurling Arbor back toward the center of the room.

Arbor crashed onto the floor again, rolling this time into what was almost the fetal position. He wasn't faring as well as Tyler had. The pain was complete. His nerves were throbbing, his neck twisted.

He was going to have to do something. The pistol wasn't easily accessible to his left arm, and he wasn't that good at aiming with that hand, but he had to give it a try. It was his only hope.

He slung his weight over, rolling onto his left side and jerking his left hand over to pull the pistol free of the leather binder.

Bringing himself up onto one knee, he leveled the pistol in Vincent's direction.

"Hold it, Walker. Don't make me hurt you."

Vincent paused, arms stretched out at his sides. He smiled just slightly.

"What the hell's the matter with you?" Arbor demanded as he pulled himself to his feet. "You could have killed me."

He stood, eyeing Vincent, trying to read something in the attorney's eyes, but there was nothing there, no expression and no explanation.

Flexing his fingers around the grip of the gun, Arbor started to step forward.

It was a mistake.

Vincent moved quickly, leaning forward suddenly, rushing the distance between them.

Arbor hesitated just a second, his finger twitching at the trigger, then he began to squeeze. There was enough space between them to let him drop Vincent before he could reach him.

Then new needles of pain suddenly cut into his arm. When he fired, the bullet thudded into the wall.

The cat was wrapped around his forearm, claws knifing through the fabric of his coat and shirt. He could feel skin tearing and the first warmth of his blood spilling.

He began to thrash his arm about, attempting to shake the cat away, but it held fast, claws clutching into him as it opened its mouth to dig long needlelike teeth into the back of his hand.

The blood began to spurt out even worse. He shook his arm more wildly until the cat let go and sailed halfway across the room before bouncing to the floor. It screamed, but landed on its feet.

Arbor tried to level the gun again at Vincent, but the lawyer was upon him now.

Another blow slammed into Arbor's face. He went down hard, onto his back, head plopping down onto the carpet.

He looked up at Vincent standing over him, but it felt as if he were at the bottom of a dark pool looking up through murky water.

He felt Vincent tug at his hand, felt the gun slip from his grasp, but he could not resist or even react.

He just lay there, sinking back into the blackness.

CHAPTER 16

Fisher found Hamilton Terry and Julia having dinner at the Clairmont. The meal arranged on their table, complete with appetizers and a fine wine, would have cost Fisher a month's pay, he wagered.

He walked across the room slowly with his hands in his pockets, and when he reached the edge of their table, he took off his hat and cracked his face with a broad grin that didn't match his mood. He was tired, and he wanted to go home. There was a certain thrill in working a case, but every time he got into the middle of one, all he could think about was getting home. Then, when he was home with his wife, all he could think about was getting back to the case. Today, however, had been a long day and he was ready for it to be over. He wanted to sleep. Nothing gave him much problem in that area. When he got ready, he slept well.

He hadn't spent very long talking to Benjamin Roth. He'd waked the guy up. As it turned out, Roth was not gainfully employed and worked at odd jobs to support himself. He had been out of town for most of the past week doing some work for a local man, something about delivering a stamp collection. It could be verified, and it suited Fisher.

217

Roth had dated Jennifer only once or twice. He didn't know as much about her as Price had, and he hadn't seen her in years.

As Fisher approached the table, the lady looked up at him, surprised. She was pretty in a severe sort of way. Her dark hair was pulled tightly back from her face and the collar of her blouse seemed to choke her. Her high cheekbones gave her face a hardened look, yet she was elegant and athletic, her skin well tanned.

"Hello," he said. "My name is Fisher. I need to talk to you, Mr. Terry."

The kid picked his napkin up out of his lap and gripped it with both hands as he looked up into Fisher's face.

"What about?"

"Routine stuff. It's about an old friend of yours, Jennifer Nelson. You know she's been threatened."

"Yes. It's terrible."

Fisher smiled over at Julia, giving her a cordial bow.

"If you'd excuse us, ma'am."

He took Hamilton's arm and led him easily across the room to a corner near some plants.

"What do you want with me?" Hamilton protested.

"Just to talk."

"I haven't had anything to do with Jennifer in years."

Fisher patted his shoulder. "I know. You dated her a long time ago. You just never know about these things. You may be able to help. Maybe somebody she was connected with in the old days has come back after her for some reason."

"I really don't see how I can help you."

Fisher didn't take his eyes off Hamilton as he reached into his pocket for his notebook. He had just a slight snarl on his face.

"You never know."

Hamilton nodded and stepped a little closer to the wall, apparently trying to keep out of sight.

That was another thing Fisher had noticed. People were embarrassed when they had to talk to cops.

"How long did you date her?" Fisher asked.

Hamilton shrugged. "It was when we were in high school. We went out. We hung around. I don't know how long really. We just didn't hit it off."

"Why'd you break up?"

"We were kids," Hamilton said. "It's hard to say, but you know how it is. You just get tired of people. They get tired of you."

"What went on between you two?"

"Not much. There was no chemistry. We went out mainly because our parents thought it was a good idea. At least, her father was in favor of it and my father went along. We were never very happy together."

Fisher looked into Hamilton's eyes.

"Did she break your heart?"

"No. It wasn't that serious. I had other girlfriends after her. I don't think she missed me much either."

"No regrets?"

"None."

"Cute girl you've got with you."

"We're going to be married. In June."

"Not much reason for you to even look back then, is there?"

"None at all. I hope you're not trying to imply that I've had anything to do with Jennifer getting calls or anything."

"I'm just asking questions," Fisher said, scribbling a note to himself on his pad. "Just doing my job."

"Well, you're awfully abrupt."

"That's just my nature. Somebody has it in for the girl.

Old boyfriends just naturally come into question. Even nice guys like you.''

Hamilton stared back at him hard, his fists curling into tight little balls at his sides. "I don't care for your tone."

Fisher expelled a deep breath. "I'm sorry, Mr. Terry, but I don't really care. A priest is dead and a girl's in danger and I've got to find out who's responsible. If you can't understand, I'm sorry."

Hamilton's expression melted just slightly, and he nodded. "I overreact. I'm sorry myself."

"Now then, can you think of anybody else who might have a grudge against Jennifer and the priest? We can't seem to figure out what the connection between them was. We've ruled out an affair between them. Everybody agrees that wasn't the situation."

"Definitely not." Hamilton rubbed his hands together, a bit uncomfortable. "He was my priest. Hers, too. I guess she went to him pretty regular in high school. I did, too. More than now. Some things lose their importance for you."

"But confession is good for the soul."

"Perhaps it is."

The hard stare, a defiant stare, returned to Hamilton's eyes. He set his jaw and did not look away from Fisher.

Fisher did the same, almost snarling again as he pocketed his notebook and headed for the door.

Vincent shoved the pistol into the waistband of his slacks and pulled his coat over it, buttoning the garment as he walked along the street, the cat trailing at his side.

A car rounded a corner and cruised along the street past him, but he didn't adjust his brisk walking pace. He moved on with confidence.

At the corner he crossed the street and moved on along

the sidewalk which stretched off from the downtown area, winding back up into the neighborhood where Dareena lived.

Eventually he stood in front of her house, looking up at the lighted window of her room.

When the cat began to brush against his leg, he bent down and lifted the creature into his arms. Gently he stroked the soft gray fur, producing a mellow purr from the cat's throat.

Vincent looked down. The cat turned its face upward, green eyes wide and bright in the darkness.

Vincent laughed, the sound bubbling up from deep in his throat.

"She's up there," he said. "She's beautiful. Such a beautiful girl."

He looked back toward the window. He would go to her soon. She wouldn't expect it, but when the moment came he would make her accept him.

He would hold her, touch her, and bring her to himself, and she would not resist. She would not be able to.

Dareena sat up in bed, thumbing through a copy of *Vanity Fair*. She wasn't concentrating on the magazine, however. Closing it, she laid it on the nightstand and pushed the bedcovers back.

She walked barefoot across the room and sat down at the small dressing table to look at herself in the mirror. This was not a summoning of Azarius.

She had other things on her mind. Slowly she ran her hands through her hair, letting the strands slip gently through her fingers. She had always liked the way her hair felt. It was soft and smooth, shiny in the light.

Among the few compliments she had received, most had

been about her hair. The few guys who had noticed her in school had liked it.

Leaning a little closer to the mirror, she examined her features. She was pretty, attractive, at least, if not beautiful.

She hadn't garnered dates in school because she was introverted, because people had always talked about her and her strangeness. That sort of thing had a way of overriding anything else. Weird girls didn't get to go out much, not even if they were nice looking.

The alienation had carried over from school. She'd known a few people she would have liked to go out with, but they never asked.

Occasionally she ran into people at the library, but the ones who talked to her weren't particularly interesting, the ones with drab sweaters and glasses that had out-of-style frames—men who couldn't impress other women but tried for her because they figured she was desperate.

She sidestepped their advances. Once, one of them had made obscene phone calls to her. She believed she knew which one, a skinny guy, but wasn't certain. After she'd hung up on him a few times he'd given up.

Thinking back over it all, she continued to study herself in the mirror. She was still youthful looking for her age, still appeared to be in her mid-twenties.

That still made her older than Gable Tyler, but how much did age really matter?

Not at all, she decided. He wasn't interested in her, not romantically. She knew that, and there was no point in pretending otherwise.

He was polite, soft spoken with her, but to him she was a curio, another subject to write about the way he had probably written about a thousand others.

She got up from the stand and walked back across the

room. Switching off the bedside light, she moved to the window, intending to look out at the darkness.

She was startled when she looked across the lawn and saw the man standing there, maybe even the one who had attacked her. She couldn't be sure.

He stood in the shadows near the edge of the lawn, his hands in the pockets of his jacket, and he seemed to be staring at her window.

She felt a rush of fear. Quickly she drew the curtain closed, folding her arms around herself and turning from the window.

He was watching her. It could be just for the investigation, but she feared there was more to it than that.

After what had happened the other night, he might be the threat to her.

She moved back to the mirror, sitting down quickly without putting on any lights.

Her eyes gazed into her reflection, what there was of it visible in the dimly lit room, and she concentrated, searching the shadows for the angel.

"Azarius?" she called in a light whisper. "Azarius?"

There was no response. The usual stirring of her thoughts, that slow detachment that usually carried her into the realm where she found the angel, did not come about.

She was afraid, really afraid, and her guardian was nowhere to be found.

The lamp on Leonard's desk cast a small white pool around the books that lay open in front of him and the notepad where he'd been scribbling.

He eased back in his chair and rubbed his hands across his face before glancing at his watch. The minute hand was creeping past nine. That meant he'd been in the office almost twelve hours except for a few trips downstairs to the faculty lounge for coffee and the few minutes he'd taken to get a sandwich for lunch.

He'd felt compelled to stick with what he was doing. He wasn't sure why exactly, but he'd stayed at it. He kept telling himself he might be able to put together a paper or article, although he knew he wasn't persisting because he really had any enthusiasm for publishing.

He just couldn't quit thinking about the topics that had come up while he was talking with Gable Tyler, and he had started going though books and papers, researching with a different perspective, looking for evidence in the ancient Hebrew writings that would give some sort of idea about what an angel would do in the life of a human as well as for some answer that might explain somehow what an angel really was.

He pulled out an Anglican Bible, which he hadn't thumbed in years, to read the story of Tobias and his encounter with Raphael once again.

It didn't seem to parallel the rumors he'd heard about Dareena's encounters. It simply told of Raphael helping Tobias and eventually defeating an evil spirit.

He continued to search through the Old and New Testaments, making notes from various annotations.

Also, he pulled a few modern books from his shelves, looking at perspectives on angels offered by other philosophies. Spirit guides were described in some eastern philosophies, and he'd attended seminars in which they were described as guardian angels, usually to incorporate eastern ideas into something with which westerners were familiar.

Yet now Seaview was wondering if there might be some measure of meaning to it all.

Perhaps the angels were beings sent by some greater Being to minister to mankind, to serve as guides and soldiers.

Might they not be inclined to hide themselves to avoid misunderstanding, establishing contact only if they were sought out, because, in seeking, an individual was preparing for acceptance?

That might explain the girl's experiences. She was lonely, and loneliness often led to introspection. It was possible that somehow she might have stumbled upon her guardian angel, her spirit guide.

He made a few notes, this time from his own thinking rather than from any other scholar, then began to flip through the New Testament, skimming briefly through the Gospels before running his fingers across the writings of Paul.

He was still reading, moving into the first epistle of John when he heard the sounds coming from the outer office.

He called out, wondering if it was one of the student workers wandering in to catch up on some typing.

No one answered.

Pushing his chair away from his desk, he stepped over to the doorway. The front room was empty, but an odd sensation struck him.

"Is anyone here?" he called out. No answer. The ceiling lights were on, so the room was bathed in a white, fluorescent glow.

There was nowhere for anyone to hide. He took another step into the room, slipping his hands into the pockets of his jacket.

Beyond the reception desk he could see through the front window into the hallway.

It also was lighted, and a look down it revealed it was clearly vacant. He was alone in the building unless the security guard was lurking somewhere.

He slowly began to turn back toward his office, still scan-

225

ning the surroundings as he prepared to head back to his work. He flipped the light off by the door.

The blow struck him like a boxing glove just as he reached the doorway to his office. He was in midstep, so his balance was not steady, and he tumbled over against the bookshelf, grabbing for it to keep from falling.

Adjusting his stance when he was on his feet again, he spun around, searching for whoever was there.

There was no one. He flicked on the ceiling light which chased away all the shadows, and the room was still empty.

He lifted a hand to massage his eyes. Perhaps he had just misplaced a step, imagined the noise and the touch. He had been working all day. He was hungry, and his mind was on the supernatural.

He started toward his desk again.

The onslaught struck him like a high wind, throwing him back through the doorway into the wall of the corridor. He was slammed hard against the tile.

He staggered to one side and slumped to the floor, dazed.

He felt a stinging in his face, then something like a slash from a straight razor streaked along his cheek, and he felt his flesh parting.

Lifting his fingertips to his face, he felt the warm moisture of blood flowing through the cut.

His mouth sagged open as he moved the fingers down to look at them, at the bright crimson stain. It was impossible.

He was shaking his head to clear his thoughts when the crash came from his office, actually a series of crashes.

Hurrying back to the doorway, he stood looking at the books spilling from the shelves or flying through the air. On his desk his notes fluttered about and pages flipped wildly. It was as if a wind were sweeping through the room, a whirling and brisk wind, but the window was closed. There was not even a crack, no way for any wind to enter.

Seaview started to move toward his desk when a blow that was like a cannonball struck him on his left shoulder. It was such a hard strike that it sent him hurling forward, crashing into the front of his desk.

He grabbed on to it, holding tight as the wind swept around his head. He was preparing to get up when he felt two more blows—one on his back and another on the upper portion of his left arm.

He screamed with the pain of the strikes, realizing again that something had cut into him. He reached over to his arm, feeling the torn cloth of his jacket and shirt, and beneath them the torn flesh. His arm had been ripped open, leaving jagged tears of muscle.

The blood coursed freely as he gripped the wound, trying to keep pressure on the gash. He looked at his reflection in the window. The blood from the cut on his face had already run down his cheek, covering the side of his face with a shiny scarlet half mask. He was reminded of the Phantom of the Opera.

His appearance terrified him.

"No," he cried, because he knew he had another wound just like it where he'd felt the pressure on his back.

Scrambling to his feet, he pulled himself out of the whirling wind and bolted through the doorway into the outer office, where he pushed open the entrance door.

Something else struck him just as he cleared the room. This time it was on his upper thigh. Again his clothing was torn and the wound went deep into his flesh. It caused him to stumble. He dropped to the floor.

Forcing himself to keep moving, he scrambled over to the wall to press his back against the tile.

Looking down, he could see the wound on his leg. The others had not been in a position in which he could observe them carefully, but this one was right in front of him. As blood oozed out of the opening, he could see the torn muscle and fatty tissue, but it was not like a knife wound as he had expected.

He swallowed back a scream.

It was a bite. He couldn't believe it, but, dammit that's what it was, a bite.

His leg had been torn open by teeth, the flesh gouged the way teeth clamped down on it would have done. A piece of his leg had been ripped out, leaving not a cut but a hole with a jagged outline.

He had been attacked, as if by some beast, yet the building was still empty. There was nothing here. He pulled himself to his feet once again and yanked his handkerchief from his slacks, pressing it against the leg as he hobbled down the hallway toward the stairs.

He was at the top of the stairway when he was hit again. He tumbled down to the first landing, feeling more blood.

He stopped there, head resting against the banister. He couldn't run anymore. He just had to sit. His clothing was soaked with blood, his shirt was plastered to his back, clinging to the wounds, and spurts of liquid bubbled from the leg wound with each pulse of his heart. He felt more tears and tasted bile in his throat. The fear made his heart beat faster and expel more blood through his wounds. He felt as if he were bathing in his own lifeblood.

He waited for something else to happen.

There was silence. Nothing but silence.

He strained his ears, trying to detect something.

Nothing. His eyes darted from side to side. No sign of anything, but then, there never had been.

On his knees he pulled himself over to the next flight of stairs. He managed to get on his feet again as he continued his descent.

He thought he was going to make it to the ground when

a blow took his legs out from under him, slashing across the backs of both his calves.

He grabbed onto the banister to steady himself. It didn't hold. The wood was shattered in a sudden explosion, torn apart into a thousand splinters by some other unseen blow. Some of the slivers dug into his body.

He went headlong down the steps, but it was only a few feet to the floor.

He crashed against the hard tile and rolled, using his battered legs to push himself along. He didn't know where he was going, but he knew he had to keep moving.

His blood, so thick and red, left a trail like the path of a tortured slug. He made a long, sickening strips across the white floor.

He made it to the front doorway quickly. With an effort he lifted his hands toward the latch bar. On the first try he missed, and his hands slid back down the glass, leaving muddy-looking handprints. With an effort he lifted himself, throwing his weight forward. His hands fell upon the bar this time, and the door gave.

He spilled out onto the sidewalk in front of the building. He heard the wind behind him, still somewhere inside the building. Somewhere he heard something more, something worse. It was laughter, deep and inhuman laughter.

"Help," he screamed. "Somebody help me."

No one.

The laughter seemed to grow, as if it were feeding on his fear.

He started along the sidewalk, still forced to drag himself. At the corner of the building there was a telephone module, a little bubble on a post with a pay phone.

It was all he could do to make his legs function, kicking like a swimmer in a stormy sea trying to get to shore. The last tear had opened a slit that was spilling blood down into his socks. Now his pants legs, too, were soaked and sticking to him, and the wind seemed to be coming from in front of him. He had to fight against it.

But the phone was ahead. He could see it in the wash of light from the streetlamp.

He was within ten feet of it when he felt the hands close on his shoulders.

Doubling his fist, he tried to swing around, get a piece of his captor, but it was no use.

He crumpled into the heavy arms, almost weeping. There was nothing more he could do now except submit to whatever this attacker was. His mind could find no explanation for it, but that no longer mattered. He closed his eyes and sank to the ground, preparing for whatever terror he was facing.

The voice didn't register on him for several seconds.

"Dr. Seaview? Dr. Seaview."

Dear God, it was familiar. He looked up into the wrinkled face of Dennison, the security guard, the man he'd had coffee with so many late nights. Dennison had found him somehow. Thank God.

Lifting his hand, he grasped the guard's sleeve, staining without meaning to.

Seaview opened his fingers to reveal the quarter on his palm.

"Nine one one," he pleaded. "Get me a doctor."

CHAPTER 17

Gable and Jennifer took a walk the next morning. It had the signs of being a peaceful day. Some blue jays fluttered about the pine trees, squawking and fighting one another while the smaller birds gave them room for their battles and conquests.

Again there were no signs of clouds, at least not any threatening clouds. The sky was dark blue against the sun's morning glow, and the droplets of dew were like pearls in the rays that streamed down across the lawns along the block.

Jennifer wore cut-off jeans and white tennis shoes and a red and white pullover, her tanned skin creating a certain glow of its own, Gable thought.

She had slept well, she said, and this morning she laughed often and smiled. It almost seemed as if she had forgotten about the terrors for a while. Gable resolved not to rekindle them and did not bring up any topic to remind her of the threats or her bad memories. Eventually she led the conversation into that vein herself.

She had not purchased a gun, she said. Told at the discount store she had visited that there was a waiting period for a handgun, she reconsidered.

"I guess the waiting requirement served its purpose, then," Gable said.

Jennifer kicked a pebble with the toe of her shoe and watched it bounce along into the street. "I guess it did. I slept well last night anyway."

"How?"

"I just didn't let myself think about it. I put on a Billy Joel tape and listened to it until I fell asleep. And I held my dolly close, too," she said, laughing.

"Quite a combination."

"I started to add wine, but I managed without it."

"I guess natural is best."

"It prevents addiction."

They stopped near the grass that bordered the sidewalk. The smell carried Gable's mind back to walks he remembered taking with his father on spring mornings and to games he had played as a child. He remembered Easter vacations and the trips he had taken with his imagination as his magic carpet.

They knelt to watch a small black bug scurrying about the concrete. Plucking a blade of grass, Jennifer touched the bug, causing him to roll himself into a protective ball.

"A roly-poly," she said. "I haven't seen one in years. Do these have scientific names?"

"Rolius polius insecti," Gable said in an exact tone.

"Really?"

He threw up his hands.

She swatted him. "I was going to believe you."

"The imagination of the writer."

The bug unrolled, finding itself on its back. Unable to right itself, it kicked it's legs about until Jennifer gave it the blade to grab on to.

232

As the bug clung to the blade, she gently placed it back on the grass.

"Amazing, the variety of life forms," she said. "It makes you think about how vast creation is."

Gable nodded, looking over at some little yellow wildflowers that had climbed up out of the grass.

As the breeze shifted, the smell of the concrete, some of it damp from dew accumulations, touched his nostrils.

Jennifer froze suddenly. The expression on her face was suddenly sullen, her eyes mirroring fright.

"What's wrong?" Gable asked.

She was silent for a moment, then shook her head, another smile crossing her features.

"I could smell moisture. I don't know what was wrong. It triggered something for a moment, but then it was gone."

"Moisture?"

"It made me think of rain, of wet clothes. I don't know why or what that means."

"Rain. Your fear of storms?"

"I can't put it together." She shook her head. "I don't want to think about it. It's too pretty a day."

Gable didn't press. Something was trying to break through. He just hoped it would come in time to let them know what was going on, before it was too late.

The phone was ringing when they got back to Tyler's apartment for coffee. The dog scurried in, barking, and Gable had to dodge him to keep from falling.

It was Arbor on the line.

"You all right, Gable?" he asked.

"Fine. What's up?"

"I've been trying to call you for a while. Watch out for Vincent if he comes around again. He may have a gun."

"Damn. What's going on?"

"He's flipped his fucking lid. He jumped me and tore

233

me to pieces last night. He's tougher than I expected, and you had a walk in the spring rain compared to what he dished out for me."

"You told anybody about it?"

"I talked to my boss when he found me lying on the floor this morning in front of the receptionist's desk. We're looking for him, but we're doing it discreetly. They're watching your neighborhood closely."

"So I'm in danger now, too?"

"This is the worst mess I think I've ever encountered," Arbor said. "It's twisting all over the place. It's weird."

"Any closer to solving any of it?"

"I'm meeting with Fisher in a while to compare notes. We may be able to put something together. Don't hold your breath."

"I won't. I'll just keep my fingers crossed."

"Good idea. Look, when are you going to talk to Seaview?"

"I haven't called him yet, but I'll set something up."

Arbor gave him a number where he could be reached.

"Anything can happen," Arbor said. "I'm trying to keep my mind on the investigation, but it keeps slipping back to Vincent."

"Could whatever has happened to him be tied to the killing?"

"He wasn't going nuts before this all started. At least, not visibly, but you never know. Maybe Seaview can help on that count, too."

"Maybe."

"I have to go. Look out kid, okay?"

"I'll keep my head down."

Gable hung up. He felt funny. Vincent could be dangerous. He was beginning to understand what Jennifer had been going through these past few days. It was no fun, this

234

being in danger after you'd been minding your own business.

The eyes had trailed Gable and Jennifer's movements all morning, had traced the path of their walk and now watched the front window of Gable's house for some sign of movement.

Time was passing.

She had been alone the night before, but it hadn't been a viable time to strike. There had been other matters to attend to, some more pressing business.

Jennifer Nelson wasn't the only one on earth, but her time was drawing close. There would be a moment when she was alone, when there was no one there to help her.

Arbor had to wait twenty minutes for Fisher to show up for their meeting at the detective division.

It was embarrassing hanging around, pouring down coffee, waiting for the big slob to show.

Fisher'd been working hard, but it was stunts like this that made him look like an asshole.

Arbor wasn't feeling particularly patient anyway. Most of his muscles were throbbing. He was lucky everything was holding together after the encounter with Vincent. The bad thing about it was the pain wasn't as severe as it was going to get. The soreness was just beginning to be noticeable. Once all the adrenaline had worked its way out of his limbs, the ache was going to be almost unbearable.

Sitting at a table, Arbor listened to the conversations of the other cops, ignoring their laughter when he sensed they were making jokes about him and Fisher.

Arbor shut out the conversations and sipped his coffee

until Fisher stomped into the room with his hat pushed back from his forehead.

He already had his tie loosened and there were perspiration stains on his shirt.

"You ready, bub?" he asked.

Arbor got out of his chair. "I've been ready."

He didn't mask the discontent in his voice.

"Sorry. I had some delays."

Arbor just followed him down the hall to the conference room. He didn't ask any questions about the delays. For Fisher a delay was a big breakfast with a second helping of eggs.

"What's going on with your friend Vincent?" Fisher asked when they got into the room and shut the door. "He been taking nose candy from some of those lawyers?"

Arbor ran his hand over his face. There were bruises and he had a Band-Aid over one eyebrow.

"I don't know what his problem is. The pressure's too much for him, I guess."

"It ain't doin' any of us no whole lot of good," Fisher said. "We've got a trail that's getting colder by the minute." He took out his notebook and fluttered through the pages.

Quickly he rambled over most of what he'd picked up during his interviews.

Arbor made a few notes of his own, then relayed what he'd learned, then handed Fisher a copy of the report he'd finished this morning after he'd had his bruises checked over.

Naturally Fisher didn't have his notes typed up.

"That's not helping things," Arbor said. He had more ire in his voice than he intended, but he felt rotten. He was running on the caffeine alone. He knew Fisher was used to working things his way, but he didn't need the big guy flipping past something that could be important, something that might cause the whole thing to fall into place.

He had a feeling Fisher was prone to hold things back, but he didn't express that. He listened to Fisher grumble for a while, letting his own temper cool in the process.

"Okay," he said eventually. "Let's look at the fact that Conzenza was thinking of leaving the priesthood. Does that mean anything?"

"Not to me."

"He wasn't leaving it for Jennifer Nelson, was he?"

"We've been over all that twenty times. I haven't found anything to indicate that he was after any women, including Jennifer Nelson. She's had a few boyfriends, but that hasn't really yielded anything big." He flipped through his notes.

"You got any more follow-ups?"

"Couple of things. I'll let you know if I turn up anything."

"You think we need to get somebody else on this?"

"Everybody's got a pile up already. What about the paper today? Have you had a chance to look at it?"

Arbor nodded. "Not much. It may be dying down. They had a statement from Jackson and your fearless leader, but they didn't drag us through it."

"Who's writing it up?"

"Philip Walden."

"Phil's all right. He knows what we're up against. Long as his editors don't ride him and one of those young kids over there don't get ahold of it. They hate cops."

"Funny how people hold grudges against cops just because they act like a bunch of assholes," Arbor said.

He knew how some of the uniformed officers treated the reporters. He'd seen it at crime scenes.

There were some really good guys in uniform.

The ones who were bastards made it hard on the rest of

them, taking their problems and the frustrations of their jobs out on the public, not giving a damn about anybody else. Arbor had been there, but he could look at both sides of the street. Sometimes he couldn't blame the world for hating cops.

Fisher flashed him a nasty look but refrained from comment. "I guess we'd better roll on this."

"Yeah."

Arbor went in to get another cup of coffee before he left the building. He still felt lousy.

He needed some rest, but he had too much to do. He had to check out Vincent and then try to turn up something on the killing.

And hope Fisher wasn't fumbling the ball on the home team's ten-yard line.

"Great week I'm having," he mumbled to himself. "I need a guardian angel."

He wished he believed in something like that, but the supernatural wasn't something Arbor could accept. Lawmen's business was in facts.

Arbor was in agreement with that. He didn't like things that couldn't be classified in terms of traditional reality. That's why he liked history and historical novels. It all made sense, tied together. The supernatural was just imagination and delusion.

He steered away from horror movies and Stephen King novels.

Horror wasn't his idea of a strawberry delight with whipped cream.

The girl at the ticket booth fumbled with the buttons on her console as she punched up Salem's ticket while he stood beyond the glass, peering at her.

His gaze was rattling her; amusing, but he didn't crack a smile. He kept his face almost devoid of emotion. He'd found that was what frightened people most of all. Without some expression to read, they couldn't tell what was going on inside his head. For most people, wondering was worse than any threat he could make. Even a malevolent look would be better than not knowing at all. Giving them nothing kept them confused.

Reaching through the opening in the ticket booth, Salem picked up the little square of paper and finally did let his lips curl into a grin, something he'd practiced until it conveyed his most sinister quality. Slowly he let his eyes rake over the girl without trying to be discreet. She was slender, about nineteen. Her hair was soft and brown and there were freckles sprinkled across her cheeks. Dressed in her red and blue uniform, she looked like a little soldier, and the way she nervously fumbled with her hands let him know she felt naked under his gaze.

Finally he walked on into the theater, knowing she would be sighing with relief as soon as he was out of sight. Everything became a game for Salem.

He was going to a horror movie. Salem loved them—the zombie pictures, the slasher films. As a kid he'd wanted to be a vampire. After all, it was a chance to live forever if you didn't get some bloke with a stake after you.

When the show was over, he was going to have to see Doren Terry again. Doren was always interesting.

After Doren he had other business here and there.

He settled back to watch a couple of hours of torture.

Doren sat in his car in the alley behind the cinema, checking his watch every few seconds. He'd seen a crowd of people flow past the mouth of the alley an eternity earlier, but there was still no sign of Salem. The bastard was supposed to have been out right after the movie, but he loved to keep Doren waiting.

With a sigh Doren sank deeper into his seat and gazed around the area. It was decorated only with trash Dumpsters that overflowed with paper cups and popcorn boxes.

He thought he noticed a rat wandering around among them, but he wasn't sure. While it wasn't dark yet, the sign of vermin made him tremble. In a way, this area between buildings was like a tomb.

He was thinking that, searching the debris in the Dumpster with his eyes, when the passenger door popped open. The sound made him jump, and he twisted around to look at Salem's face leaning into the car.

"What's up, mate?" he asked, flashing a grin.

"You scared the shit out of me."

"Kind of fun, ain't it? Little vicarious thrills. Just watched a movie that done that."

He settled into the car, pushing the fedora he was wearing down over his eyes.

"What was so important that you had to see me?"

"Just something you might find interesting."

"You want more money?"

Salem laughed. "I always want more money, but, hey, I work for my daily bread. Let's talk about what I can do for you."

CHAPTER 18

The elevator sighed open on the third floor of Penn's Ferry General Hospital and Gable and Arbor stepped off together to move down the carpeted hallway. The place had been built in the forties, just after the war, but had been renovated and modernized recently so there was a mixture of futuristic plastic ornamentation and the ivory and tile look of postwar days.

Little plaques hung beside the doors displaying the room numbers.

They had to search along the hallways for the proper room. Downstairs in the lobby a blond-haired girl—who'd rubbed them both the wrong way—had at first denied there was any Leonard Seaview in the place, until Arbor had finally flashed his identification and told her she'd better check again. She finally found the listing in a memo that had been sent in while she was on her coffee break.

Gable had learned through the school that Seaview had been hospitalized following an accident that had occurred the night before.

He hadn't been able over the phone to find out the nature

of the accident, but for some reason he had a disconcerting feeling about it.

Slowly he pushed the door open and they filed into the room. It was small, with only enough room for the essentials, the bed, a basin, and one chair.

Against the wall stood a table that could be wheeled over to the bed for meals. It was not a Catholic hospital, but there was a Crucifix over the bed, an elaborately carved ornament depicting a suffering Christ.

The bed had been elevated to give Seaview a sitting position. His head was tilted back, but he rolled it to the side when he heard movement.

"Hello," he said, his voice strong even though his color was chalky. An IV had been jabbed into his left arm, and a bag of colorless liquid hung at his side, dripping slowly into his vein.

"Kind of makes you think of Chinese water torture, doesn't it," Seaview said. "I go crazy watching for the next drop to fall."

Gable had to smile, and even one corner of Arbor's mouth twitched upward for a second.

"One of you have a seat," Seaview said. "The other one can skateboard on the food table."

Arbor gave a nod for Gable to take the chair. With his hands in his pockets, the investigator stood at the foot of the bed.

"This is Isaac Arbor," Gable said. "He's an investigator with the district attorney's office."

"You think I attempted suicide or something?"

Arbor did smile this time. "I'd like to know what the hell is going on," he said.

Seaview flashed a smile of his own. It lasted only a second. Beyond it, Gable could see there was a look of anxiety in his eyes.

"I wish I could tell you," Seaview said. He folded his hands together.

"What happened to you?" Gable asked.

"Ever hear of biting poltergeists?"

"Sounds like a movie."

"I wish it were."

He adjusted his weight, easing over onto one side. The hospital gown was split up the back, and where the cloth parted near his shoulder blades, there was a bandage.

"Mr Tyler, if you would peel that aside," Seaview instructed.

Carefully Gable reached over and eased the bandage free on one side, peeling it back to reveal a pattern of stitches.

The scar on the professor's back was circular, about five inches in circumference and composed of a series of ridges. The kind of marks made by teeth, except this was too large to have been made by a human, yet not the mark of an animal's teeth either, at least none of which Gable was aware.

He looked over at Arbor. The detective shook his head, his expression explaining he had no answer.

"What'd the doctor say about this?" Gable asked.

"He didn't have an answer," Seaview said, settling back into place. "But he didn't argue when I asked for that." He pointed up to the Crucifix.

"So what happened?"

Seaview massaged his eyes for a moment, then let his head ease back against his pillow. His hair was in tangles and his face drawn with fatigue.

He recounted the events from the previous night in a slow monotone.

"Were you on the verge of some discovery?" Arbor asked.

"Not a discovery. Maybe a rediscovery."

"What's that?"

243

Seaview had to think a moment, formulating his thoughts before presenting them. "That evil exists in a tangible form," he said. "That there are things out there that operate beyond the realm of what we usually perceive as evil."

"Poltergeists?" Gable asked.

"That's just a word," Seaview said, "something men have come up with to explain phenomena they can't explain."

"What are you getting at, then?"

"Malevolent spirits of some kind. Beings that bring destruction."

"What has that got to do with all of what's going on?"

"I don't know yet. I've got an idea, but I need to do some more reading. And some more thinking. I'll need you to pick up some of my books, Gable."

"Sure."

"Is this tied to the murder of the priest in some way?" Arbor asked.

"Maybe and maybe not. The murder of the priest may not be related, except that it might have served to touch something off," Seaview said. "That's speculation. Maybe a little intuition, but I can't tell you anything for certain, except that there is something evil happening."

"I can't arrest a ghost," Arbor said.

"Not ghosts," Seaview said. "Beings of some kind. You've heard mention of them. Reference in many religions."

"I'm trying to find out what's wrong with a lawyer and solve a murder, not deal in some speculation about boogeymen," Arbor said.

Seaview turned to Gable with an inquisitive look. Gable quickly told him about Vincent.

"Another question," Seaview said. "I don't have many answers, but maybe I can find them. I'm afraid all of us may be in danger until we arrive at some conclusion and do something. Things like this don't happen very often."

"It's not the kind of thing you read about in *Time*," Arbor noted.

"Still, there aren't many spirit attacks, and that's what happened to me. Believe it or not. I'll help you any way I can, Mr.Arbor. If you want to be helped."

"Looks like we're all in it," Arbor said. "Whether we like it or no."

Gable studied Seaview's features. He thought he'd been ready to believe anything, but now, listening to what Seaview had been through and hearing what the professor believed had happened to him, Gable wasn't so sure.

Earlier his discussions with Seaview had revealed the man to be skeptical, looking at matters only from an intellectual standpoint. Suddenly, and perhaps understandably from Seaview's position, the ideas were different.

"You think I'm crazy?" Seaview asked.

Gable realized he'd been staring. He smiled. "I guess not."

"You had an open mind the other day. You're going to need to keep it open."

"This just never came up very often in Sunday school."

"I wouldn't think so. The church doesn't have a tendency to dwell on this sort of thing. It scares people."

"Fundamentalist churches dwell on it," Gable said.

"Not as much as you'd think. There are a lot of problems in the world, and the church is turning more and more to social issues. It doesn't concentrate as much on things that go bump in the night anymore."

"A couple of days ago you had a pretty light attitude about it, too," Gable noted.

"I didn't have teeth marks all over me then either. I was researching when it happened. Look at it this way, Gable.

What if the ancient writings are true? What if there are malevolent beings out there? Beings that are evil. What would they want to do?"

"Perpetuate evil?"

"By their very nature," Seaview said. "They'd seek to corrupt. To confuse and beguile. To destroy."

"But why? What are they?"

"I've still got some thinking to do."

"Hobgoblins?" Arbor muttered. "I don't believe in spirits."

"I'd stopped, too," Seaview said. "I've changed my mind."

"Maybe there's some other explanation. Just like there's some other explanation for my murder case. And for everything else. People are going nuts. This girl talks to angels, Walker Vincent has slipped off the deep end. Some nut is killing priests and threatening girls for no apparent reason."

"The sort of things evil would delight in," Seaview pointed out.

Arbor only shook his head.

"I guess we'd better let you rest," Gable said.

"Yes. Tomorrow I need you to pick up some things for me if you will."

"Sure."

"I'll call my office in the morning and have the secretary get things together. You can pick them up around eleven?"

Gable nodded.

"Thank you."

With another nod Gable got up and followed Arbor through the doorway. They walked back down the hallway side by side.

"I don't see that this is going to help me," Arbor said.

"Don't you have to look at all the possibilities?"

246

They reached the elevator and Arbor thumbed the control button.

"The minions of evil? I can't go chasing off on something like this."

They stepped onto the elevator when the doors opened. Arbor looked up at the numbers and watched them flash along.

"I have an investigation to conduct." he said. "A rational enquiry into a murder and an attempted murder."

"I understand."

"Vincent isn't my responsibility."

"Right."

"Chasing ghosts isn't either."

"Sure."

"You can keep after it though. You're a journalist. It's a weird subject, but it could be a story."

Gable nodded.

"And if you find out anything, you might mention it to me. Just in casual conversation because we've gotten to be such good buddies."

Salem tore open a fresh package of Marlboros as he walked along the sidewalk. It was dark now, his favorite time. He liked the darkness, the shadows. It was something that many feared, but he found it exhilarating.

He'd liked the movie, a foreign-made job full of rotting corpses that roamed the night. It was a ripoff of Romero, but it was pretty good anyway. For the most part, Salem didn't care for foreign-made horror movies. Even with the dubbing they were hard to understand and often the production values were low, but when there was nothing else to choose from, he'd sit through one. Every now and then it paid off.

He turned the collar of his jacket up for effect more than

to fight the wind as he strolled up to a pay phone positioned outside an office building.

He felt a little like a spy with his hat pulled down over his eyes—a spy making a secret phone call to pass on information.

Dropping a quarter into the slot, he tapped a number he knew from memory onto the push button, whistling along with the tune.

A woman's voice answered. That made him grin. He told her what he wanted as he turned away from the phone, keeping the receiver to his ear but watching the darkness.

There was a slight chill in the air. It was early enough in the year and brisk enough to keep the insects away, but he liked the feel of the air and the very look of the darkness.

Under his breath he began to chuckle, but just slightly.

Dareena sat on the terrace, reading a paperback novel. Her chair was positioned near her bedroom window to capture the light from inside the house. It might have been easier to move inside, but the breeze was pleasant, a soft night breeze.

Vincent stood in the shadows of the warehouse across the street, out of the girl's sight.

She'd seen him standing on the street the night before. He'd seen her look out. That was fine, but he didn't want her to realize he was returning, keeping watch on her.

Eventually she closed her book and slipped off her glasses, then rose and went back into the house. The movements were so fluid, so perfect, Vincent thought.

He waited until the lights were off in her room before he emerged from the shadows. He crossed the street and stood at the edge of her lawn, considering whether he should climb to her window.

Deciding against it, he shoved his hands down into his pockets and headed off along the street.

His shoulders felt heavy, and a tiredness coiled around the muscles in the back of his neck.

He realized he couldn't remember when he slept last. Funny, he wasn't sure what was going on.

The inside of his head was a jumble. He had to get things together. There was work he needed to do on the case. Arbor was probably going nuts, having to deal with Fisher.

When he reached his apartment, Vincent climbed the stairs quickly to his door and stumbled into the room.

He also couldn't remember when he'd had a shower last.

The sight of his face greeting him when he switched on the bathroom light. The image in the mirror was tortured— face unshaven, eyes glazed, hair in tangles.

And his clothes were rumpled and baggy. Yanking off his tie, he turned on the water to let it get warm, then pulled out his shaving equipment.

Forty-five minutes later he was beginning to look human again, more like the old Walker Vincent. That was more like it. He stood in front of the mirror, examining his face and eyes. The glaze was gone from his pupils. His eyes were clear again. He gazed deeply into them, frowning.

He wanted to rest, but instead he decided he wanted to take another walk. That would be refreshing. There were places he could go.

He selected a pair of gray slacks and a fresh sport shirt. He decided against a tie but tugged on a jacket he'd bought recently. It looked good on him. Looking good was important. It always had been. Always . . .

Fisher smoked almost half a pack of cigarettes while he sat in his car. He'd quit three times since New Year's. The last time had been the longest. He'd purchased this package out of a machine at the station, and the first cigarette was the first he'd had since early March.

There was nothing to do while he sat in the car, so he smoked. Stakeouts were always murder. He hated waiting most of all.

At least it was dark now. That made things better. Sitting in a car in daylight had plenty of drawbacks. For one thing, when the sun was out it was hot as hell. The other problem was that people kept looking at him as they drifted by.

Sometimes they even walked up to the car, asking who he was. He always grumbled as he flashed his ID. He preferred the darkness. He didn't like people looking at him, just on general principles.

Finally he saw the car cruising along the street. It turned into the driveway opposite him, and Fisher got out of his car quickly.

Dropping his cigarette, he stepped on the butt and then hurried over to the driveway where Doren Terry was climbing out of his car.

"Mr. Terry?"

The man turned to him and nodded, a bit surprised. "Can I help you?" he asked.

Fisher tugged out his badge and let the man have a look at it. There was enough light from the porch bulb to let him read it clearly.

Doren looked at the badge only a second before the color drained out of his face.

"Is there something wrong?"

"I just have a few questions. You okay?"

"Fine. Policemen just don't turn up on my doorstep very often."

"Sorry. I've been waiting for you. I rang, but there was no answer, so I just watched for your car."

"Yes, my wife no longer lives with me. We've been separated for some time. Come in."

Fisher followed him into the living room, where they sat down.

"Can I get you some instant coffee?"

Fisher shook his head.

"Then what can I do for you?"

"You've read of the priest being killed?"

"Yes. Of course."

"I'm investigating that. Something you may or may not be aware of is that Jennifer Nelson has received threats, apparently in connection with the matter." He sighed. Explanations were a pain.

"I see," Doren said.

"I understand your son used to date her," Fisher said.

Doren wrinkled his brow, creating a deep furrow along his forehead. "I believe he did, ages ago. When they were youngsters."

"You remember much about the old days?"

"It's hard to say. Hamilton was a popular kid, so he saw a lot of people."

"Did he ever have any problems with Jennifer?"

"The usual things. Those are difficult years, the teenage years, but they didn't have a bad breakup that I recall."

"Can you remember anyone who might have had something against the girl? Or your son for that matter?"

"No."

"I'm asking because we don't know what the connection between the priest and the girl is. I don't want to alarm you, but your son could be in danger as well."

"I hadn't thought about that."

"Did you know Father Conzenza?"

"No, I didn't. My wife was a Catholic, but I never joined that faith."

"What about Dareena Winston?"

"I guess not."

"The girl who talks to angels?"

"Oh, yes. I've heard of her, of course. Hasn't everyone?"

"Does the name Azarius mean anything to you?"

"No. Not at all."

It was time for Fisher to expel his breath and rest his head on one hand. "Why would somebody want to hurt a nice girl like Jennifer Nelson?"

"Beats me. It all seems so senseless."

Fisher nodded. He'd had enough for now. He wasn't finding anything new.

"I guess I'll be going," he said. "Just wanted to run through a couple of things. Touching base."

"I see."

"How is your son doing these days? Any problems?"

Doren frowned. "He's fine," he said. "A good kid. He's working with me. He just got out of Princeton."

Fisher got up and headed for the door. "Thanks," he said. He wondered if he was really finding any answers.

When the policeman was gone, Doren went over to the phone and picked up the receiver, quickly tapping out Hamilton's number. There was no answer even though he let the phone ring fifteen times.

Hanging up, he moved over to the couch and sat down.

He didn't like the idea of police getting around Hamilton. There were things they didn't need to know about. Things he'd already taken care of.

The boy had his problems, but he'd turned out all right. The things Salem had set up could have happened to anyone. They were mistakes, not something a boy like Hamilton should have to pay for the rest of his life.

CHAPTER 19

While she was at work, they told Kim there was a Harry Stevens on the phone for her, but she didn't take the call. Harry was a man she'd dated a few times, a truck driver. It was 11:30, and she knew he'd want to ask her out. She didn't feel like making up an excuse. He was a nice man, nothing against him. She just didn't want to see any man at the moment.

She didn't want anyone to touch her for a while. She wanted to isolate herself.

Harry was a decent fellow, about forty and hardworking, but he would expect something if she went out with him, if not sex, at least some physical contact, because things had happened before. That they would happen again on a date was just kind of an unwritten rule.

Any deviation from the game would mean explaining to him that something was wrong, and she wasn't up to that yet.

Harry was a widower, a simple, lonely man—the kind who wore plaid shirts and a baseball cap. He assumed there was more of a commitment between them than really existed.

He'd want to exact some kind of revenge on Hamilton if he found out what had happened, which would probably cost Kim her job.

It was much easier just to avoid him. He'd probably be out of town tomorrow on a haul, and that meant she'd have a couple of days freedom before she had to see him again.

As for work, the business was fairly slow even for a week-night, for which she was thankful. The patrons were sprinkled about the lounge, talking and listening to the singer who rattled off popular tunes in a country twang.

When last call came around, the people began to drift out. The staff was able to get cleanup done pretty quickly.

From the pay phone in the hall Kim called her sister and told her she'd be coming by in about twenty minutes to pick up her child.

Then she got her purse, said good night to the other girls, and took the front entrance out to the street. Her car was parked in the second lot, which was about a block away from the hotel. Employees were required to park there so the guests had easy access to the building.

Kim was always glad the streets were well lighted. She walked along quickly, her heels clicking on the concrete as she headed toward the parking lot.

The sidewalks were empty. She walked in front of the desolate shop fronts along the street that stretched north of the hotel. They had all gone out of business over the years, and only remnants of old displays remained.

The plate glass windows bore cracks, and dust lined the doorways.

A crumpled piece of paper scraped across the sidewalk in front of Kim. It made that dry, lonely sound that lost paper always makes.

As she moved on, Kim opened her purse and started digging for her keys. She remembered it was always best to have keys ready, just in case there was some kind of trouble.

Passing the last building before the parking lot, she peered briefly through the window. It had been a café, and a rusted Coca-Cola sign still hung from the door. She remembered sipping cold drinks there on Saturday afternoons after shopping trips with her mama.

How much things changed, she thought as she stepped over the curb at the edge of the lot and started toward her car.

It was parked at the far edge of the lot. When she'd come in, the lot had been full, but now hers was one of the last cars.

She dangled her keys at her side and stepped toward it. The wind swept down in a brisk gust and caught her hair, and she raised her free hand to smooth it.

She was brushing hair from her eyes when the figure popped up from behind the black car.

She knew the car. It was a Nova from the early seventies. It belonged to Jerry Falcon from the admitting desk who'd bought it used after he wrecked his own car on a wet road.

It wasn't Jerry Falcon standing behind it now, however.

Kim had an impulse to run but found her feet would not budge. Her keys slipped from her fingers and clattered to the ground.

She couldn't find the strength to fight, not after what she'd been through. She felt mesmerized as she watched the blade rise, catching a flash of light from a streetlamp before it descended, plunging into her flesh.

It struck first near her left shoulder, cutting into the flesh and gouging through some cartilage before pulling free and plunging downward again.

It cut a streak across her cheek, a line of blood. She felt

the moisture spread down her face, but she didn't try to wipe it away.

She didn't even scream. She just waited for the next blow, which came an eternity and a split second later, opening her throat.

She crumpled to the hard concrete ground and did not move.

Arbor didn't look any happier than Fisher when they arrived at the scene at 2:30 A.M. It had taken a little over an hour for the cops at the scene to decide the killing might be related to their case, and then another forty-five minutes was needed to relay the information back to them.

"Anybody find Vincent?" Arbor asked.

"Still looking," an officer told him.

"Still out on his binge," Fisher said.

The body had not been moved. It lay in a pool of blood near the center of the lot. A white sheet had been placed over the form and had begun to absorb the blood the way the television commercials demonstrated paper towels soaking up spills.

One of the coroner's people pulled the sheet back to give Fisher and Arbor a look at the body.

"Got the jugular, from the looks of it," the guy said.

Arbor nodded, wishing he'd go ahead and drop the sheet again, but he didn't. He held it in his hand while he mentioned the other cuts on the body.

Arbor looked away. Some uniformed officers were stringing yellow tape around the lot, a banner which had Police Line. Do Not Cross printed all along its length.

That meant the lot was going to be tied up tomorrow. The parking downtown was going to be worse than ever, Arbor thought.

Fisher lit a cigarette and blew the smoke in Arbor's direction.

"Same M.O.," he said.

"No words this time," Arbor noted.

"Maybe the killer didn't have time," Fisher suggested.

Arbor looked around. "I don't know," he said. "These streets are pretty quiet at night."

"Over here," a uniformed man called. Together the investigators walked over to where he was standing near the edge of the lot. There was a rosary on the ground at his feet. It was partially concealed in a depression in the concrete where the water drained. Some leaves and pine straw had been carried there during the last rain and remained after the water had dried.

"Put it in a bag," Fisher ordered. "There's your connection," he said.

"A game," Arbor said. "We need some more people on this," he said.

Fisher didn't disagree.

Jennifer awoke bathed in sweat. Slipping out of bed, she peeled off her nightgown and moved toward the ray of light from the bathroom.

Gable's dog was asleep at the foot of her bed, but when he heard the movement, his ears perked and he lifted his head.

"It's all right," she whispered, and he seemed to accept that, putting his head back down.

She wished it really were all right. She turned on the shower, stepping under it quickly to let the warm needles of the spray wash away the sticky perspiration.

Her dream had come back, a dream of dark hallways, rainy nights, and smothering. The dark figure lurked among

257

the shadows of her nightmare, a figure she could never quite identify. It was like a memory, frustrating, lingering just below the threshold of her conscious mind.

She let the water spill over her hair. It reminded her of rain, but it didn't connect with the terror of a storm. Why was a storm so frightening? That also lingered just out of her reach, lodged somewhere in the nether region of her brain, where it was inaccessible.

Stepping from the stall, she wrapped a towel around her and then used a hand towel to absorb some of the water from her hair.

She returned to bed with the towel still wrapped around her, still damp. It felt cool against her flesh.

A shower wasn't the best thing in the world to help with sleep, but she did feel relaxed now. It was as if she had been cleansed of the terror. Reaching over, she picked up the doll and embraced it.

She felt ready to analyze the matter logically. She stared at the ceiling, turning over in her mind the fragments of the dream as if they were pieces of a puzzle—a jigsaw very difficult to assemble.

She dozed off without realizing it, and slept until morning.

Gable woke her by banging on the front door. The sound was frightening at first because she wasn't aware the night had passed. The sunlight announced that fact when she turned to the window.

She climbed out of bed, exchanging the towel for a robe before hurrying down the stairs to greet Gable.

"You all right?" he asked, his expression serious.

"Fine. No trouble at all. I had a bad dream, but I managed."

Gable moved into the living room and sat down.

"Is something wrong?"

He nodded toward a chair, which she settled into slowly.

"I just got a call from Arbor from the D.A.'s office. There was another killing last night. It's probably related to the first. The cops kept your house under surveillance all night."

"Oh my God. Who was it?"

"A waitress from the hotel downtown. That big one."

"My daddy's got part interest in that development. My God. What time is it?"

"Around seven."

"Daddy must not have heard yet."

"He will."

She rested her face in her hands. "What am I going to do, Gable? Why don't they catch someone?"

"They're trying. They're supposed to put some more investigators on the case, step things up."

"Daddy's going to make me come home. I was hoping it would all blow over before it came to that."

"They don't have any answers yet, but maybe this time there was some mistake that will give the killer away."

"Maybe it means I've been forgotten. There haven't been any more phone calls."

Gable nodded, gave a slight smile. He wanted to be optimistic.

"Do you want me to sit here with you for a while?" he asked.

"Thank you. I'll fix some breakfast. Sooner or later Daddy will call."

She got up but hesitated, then moved over to his chair and took his hand.

"I appreciate your being here. I know you have things to do, but you've really been great."

"Somebody has to be a nice guy every now and then."
She kissed his forehead. "I guess I've just been lucky."

They were just sitting down to the bacon and eggs when the phone rang. Her father had received word. She could sense that.

Jennifer lifted the receiver gently, expecting him to be raving with fear.

Instead, he was calm.

"Have you heard what happened?" he asked.

"Yes. Tyler came over to tell me. Somebody called him. Who was the girl?"

"One of the waitresses in the lounge. I didn't know her. Neither did Doren. I guess this makes you realize the danger you're in."

"Yes, Daddy." She braced herself for him to tell her she was going to have to come home.

Instead, he surprised her. "I know you don't want to come back here. I guess I have been hard on you over the years, and for that I'm sorry. I'm not going to force you. I can't see you being brave enough to hold out after what's happened, but it's a changing world."

She tried to interrupt, but he continued talking.

"I've checked around. I can hire private security for you. I can get a guard to stay in your house."

He would be pouring out more money on her behalf, she realized, creating just another form of bondage.

Yet, it would still not be the same as being back at home. Once she got moved in they'd catch the killer and her father would reason that as long as she was back in the house there wasn't any need to bother moving out again.

With a guard he'd feel better and her freedom would be safe. Besides, it would mean security. Gable next door was nice and his dog was some comfort, but it wasn't Gable's job to keep her safe.

"Maybe that's not a bad idea," she said. "I could live with it, but I hate to make you spend the money."

"It's not that much extra." He paused. "To be honest, I'd hire the firm if you were at home here also. You need protection wherever you are. I should have taken this step sooner. I don't know what I was thinking."

When she hung up, she explained to Gable what was going on.

"I guess it is a good idea," he said.

It did mean a bit of an obstacle, she realized. Things had been moving slowly between them, but the addition of another figure would interfere.

Perhaps Gable was seeing it as a wedge, a further wedge, since she'd been keeping him at arm's length because of her desire not to become dependent on him.

She studied his face for some sign, uncertain of what his feelings for her might be. She cared about Gable. There was a gentleness about him, a concern. He had things he wanted to do, but he didn't see himself as the only person on earth. He'd been very considerate of her situation.

"What are you thinking?" she asked him.

He grinned, shrugged, and pursed his lips. "Hard to say," he said. "There's so much going on. It doesn't look like Kansas anymore."

She laughed. "It gets curiouser and curiouser."

They fell silent, just looking at each other.

She eased out of her chair slowly, cautiously, and moved over to him, standing behind him and slipping her arms down around his neck.

"You're a decent guy. Did I tell you that?"

"Maybe. I forget."

She rested her face against his head. "Nicer than a lot of the guys I've encountered."

His hair was soft. She moved her hands along his shoulders, then relaxed slightly as he rose from the chair to embrace her.

Standing this close, she was surprised at how tall he was. She had to stretch to meet his lips with hers, but it was worth the effort.

They gave Fisher two of the younger detectives, smooth-faced kids with shiny hair and neat suits.

He and Arbor dragged them into a conference room and briefed them on most of what had been picked up so far on the case.

Harper, the taller of the two new men, asked a few questions, but Benchley, who had a coppery complexion and dark hair, just nodded.

"The main thing we need you two to do now is start digging up the latest victim's past," Fisher said. "Start with the people she worked with. Find out if there's any connection between her and Jennifer Nelson or the priest."

They didn't put up any argument. After the briefing they filed out of the room, leaving Arbor and Fisher behind.

"Are they going to help?" Arbor asked.

"They're decent kids." Fisher sighed. "We can get more legwork done with them, but who cares how much we get done if we don't find any answers?"

Arbor agreed. There was still the matter of Vincent concerning him as well.

A phone on the wall rang.

Fisher answered and spoke into it briefly before hanging up.

"Walden of the *Clarion* is looking for news."

"It's your ball game," Arbor said. "You know how Jackson is about his people talking to the media."

"Dump it all on me. Glad we got a D.A. who was trained in Nazi Germany."

He shoved the office door open and thundered down the hall to the outer waiting room, where Walden was waiting.

He was a dapper man of medium build, silver-haired. He walked with a cane because he'd been shot in the leg during the course of an investigative story once.

This morning he wore a fresh sport coat with display handkerchief, neatly pressed slacks, and a hat with a small red feather in the band.

Fisher gave him a nod and led him back to his office.

"I can't tell you much," Fisher said as they sat down. He spent the next fifteen minutes refusing to answer questions and talking Walden into holding back information that might hamper the investigation.

There were some things Fisher wanted to run down, but before he could get out of the office one of the uniformed girls flagged him down.

"The chief wants to talk to you."

"Does it have to be right now?"

She shrugged. Fisher grumbled under his breath as he pushed past her to thread through the hallways back to the chief's office.

Chief Edmund White was a big man, almost as heavy as Fisher. He had thick, prematurely gray hair and a face like J. Edgar Hoover.

He sat at his desk as Fisher walked into the room.

"What's up?" Fisher asked.

"You going to crack this thing?"

"I'm going to try. I told that to the paper."

"That should keep them happy about twelve hours. I've been making statements to the radio people all day. We've got a mess, Fisher. I want it wrapped up. A priest killer shouldn't get away with it."

"I'm gaining on it. I really think I am."

White didn't raise his voice, but he leaned forward to rest his elbows on his desk. His tie was tight and his white collar was buttoned at his throat, making his face seem to bulge. His pale gray eyes almost looked like they'd pop out of the sockets. He stared hard at Fisher and clenched his teeth.

"Don't screw this one up. You can be a good cop when you want to be. That's why I've let you run with this one. I could have pulled you off it, but I didn't. You fuck it up, and it's your ass. No pension, no nothing, and the civil service board won't be able to bail you out of it."

Fisher nodded without letting his expression change. He reached into his pocket and took out his cigarettes, torching one of them with a Bic lighter he'd just bought.

"Can I get back to work now?" he asked.

CHAPTER 20

Seaview was sitting on the side of his bed in a fresh pair of pajamas when Gable and Jennifer arrived. They had gone by his office as requested and picked up the books from a fuzzy-haired student assistant who was busy trying to get the ruins of his office back in order.

Looking over the shambles of the room had been disconcerting for Gable. Seaview couldn't have imagined the mess, and with the heavy shelves toppled across the floor, he realized more had been done than a man alone could have accomplished.

It looked like things he'd read about, haunted houses where poltergeists had struck, crashing furniture.

The professor was going through the Gideon Bible, but his expression showed he was glad to see what Gable was carting in. Several annotated reference Bibles were included.

Gable placed the books on the serving table and wheeled it over to the edge of the bed.

Seaview immediately took out a legal pad and a new Flair pen Gable had picked up for him in the lobby.

"You ready to tell me what this is all about?" Gable asked.

Seaview selected a heavy black leather-bound Bible and flipped it open.

"The basis of most modern Christian religion, the mainstream, stems first of all from the ancient Hebrews, Gable. You're aware of that?"

"I guess."

"Yahweh was their God at a time when there were many other gods being worshipped. They believed that they worshipped the one true God, the Creator."

"I'm familiar with that."

"From that tradition stem the teachings about the devil. Now, what we find in the Bible about the devil is limited, but there are numerous references."

"Right, Lucifer, son of the morning."

"Lucifer, who became Satan after he led the rebellion of the angels against God."

"You're rehashing Sunday-school lessons," Gable said.

"Do you believe it, Gable?"

"I believe there's evil."

"Think about it. Think about a being of pure evil, a being who turned against his Creator in an attempt to take control of the universe. He wasn't successful, not totally, but he wasn't destroyed either."

"Satan is alive and well?"

"Perhaps. Along with his minions."

"Demons?"

"That's what they have become. What we read of is fallen angels, beings who joined Lucifer in his rebellion and who were banished. One-third of the angels, the ones who 'kept not their estate.' "

"Okay. I've heard of all this."

"But think about it. Think about it intellectually. If those fallen beings existed, what would their goal be? How do you hurt someone, Gable?"

"Attack him."

"But your attack will not make your victim suffer enough, not if He is your Creator. Your powers are limited. You need some other way to make Him suffer."

"I don't understand."

"Genghis Khan once had a man whom he wanted to terrorize. The man was defiant, enduring his pains and torments with arrogance. So Khan summoned his guardsmen and they brought the man's wife and before his eyes she was raped and eventually killed. The man was filled with rage and the rage drove him insane."

Gable shook his head. "I'm still not following you."

"You hurt someone through the suffering of those he loves."

"So the devil, or whatever this being of evil is . . ."

"Strikes out at the Creator by seeking to destroy His children, by perpetuating hatred among us. At some point the fallen angels led man to the Fall, the apple, Gable. Whatever the apple was, it represents the point in which the fallen angels drew men into joining the rebellion. After the apple, men opened themselves up to joining into the rebellion of the angels."

"How?" Gable asked.

"By murdering each other, by hating, by creating wars. Sin, evil. All of that is a manifestation of evil because it perpetuates hatred. Hatred is the opposite of God, the opposite of love. Once man turned to evil, it gave the fallen angels a new dominion and they seek to lure us to them."

"Okay, great. You've reiterated the Judaeo-Christian tradition. Quite a few people have professed that belief without having poltergeists attack them."

"How often do these things happen that we don't hear about?"

"I don't know about this."

"Azarius is one of the beings, one of the fallen angels. For some reason he's frightened of me, and I believe of you also."

"Why?"

"Because we know what he is. Somehow he knew we would find out. We stand to interfere with his destruction of Dareena. Perhaps in whatever other efforts he's undertaking. We could weaken his power."

"I still don't understand what makes him frightened of me," Gable said.

"You're a good man," Seaview said.

"I thought no one was good," Jennifer said. "Isn't that in the Bible?"

"No man is good without the cleansing of God."

"I'm a decent person," Gable said. "I'm not a saint."

"No, but I think the fallen angels are afraid of what you can become. Azarius tried to have me killed because he didn't want you to find out things from me. They have a certain power over you when you are ignorant of them. If you learn what they are, you stand to defy them."

"Tried to have you killed?"

"Much of what I'm working from is my intuition, Gable. From the bits and pieces you've relayed to me from the girl, and maybe a little divine direction, I don't know. But you understand what Raphael was or is?"

"An archangel."

"Do you understand what that is?"

Gable looked at Jennifer and shrugged.

"A leader of other angels," Seaview said. "Perhaps Azarius is a parallel."

"A leader of the fallen angels?"

"Something like that. He directs their movements. Listen to this," Seaview said as he flipped open a Bible. " 'And the great dragon was cast out, that old serpent, called the Devil, and Satan, which deceiveth the whole world: he was cast out into the earth, and his angels were cast out with him.' "

"So you're saying Azarius is one of Satan's followers."

"A leader of the minions of hell. I sense that he is trying to prepare the way for others. Now the devil is the leader of the fallen angels. He's known as Diabolos, the Creator's adversary. Many of the references we have for angels liken them to military units, regiments."

"Azarius is a lieutenant," Jennifer said.

"Exactly."

"What's his purpose?"

"To corrupt. To destroy and to create whatever havoc he can. As an archangel, he is probably almost as powerful as Satan himself. He can't be two places at once, but he can send other fallen angels to do his bidding."

"Why the attachment to Dareena?"

"I don't know, except that you said she was religious. Perhaps her faith has served as a protection for her, something that Azarius feels challenged to wear away. That may prevent him from being able to totally possess her, and he's working toward that."

"What do you mean?" Jennifer asked.

"He wants to turn her belief away from God, bring that belief to himself. The corruption of the pure is more effective than the corruption of someone already following. The evil will find their way to hell. The good take some persuading. Maybe corrupting someone like Dareena gives Azarius even greater power."

"All this is traditional?" Gable asked.

"It's not something that comes up very often, but the

lore has been around. Sometimes you find it only in the volumes of obscure scholars.''

''Or fundamentalist ravers.'' Gable paced in the small area at the foot of the bed. ''I have a problem with all this,'' he said.

''Because you live in a physical world,'' Seaview said. ''You live in a world where these things seem farfetched, unreal. This is the lore of dark ages told huddled around campfires. You've heard the tales, some of them, but they've always seemed removed from the present day, perhaps symbolic in their message.''

''Okay, yes. It's wild. It's far out, if you'll excuse the expression.''

''Because the fallen angels don't want you to know they exist, or at least they don't want you to recognize them for what they are. They want their thrills, but they want it without alerting people to their purpose. Besides, I think they do have certain limitations. In the Book of Jude it says they were bound under darkness. I can't find reference to their physical presence. Something keeps them from coming into the world in physical form. They inhabit other things—people, animals . . .''

''Serpents?'' Gable supplied with a curt turn of his head and a grim smile.

''Take it as you will,'' Seaview said. ''They have to have some kind of vessel to occupy in order to experience human feelings. Obviously they can do things without physical forms, however.'' He indicated his own wounds. ''You'll probably be safer if you don't believe. But they're here. They possess and they oppress. They manipulate people into doing their bidding.''

''The devil made me do it?''

''It's written that way. Who knows what they do? They could give urges, play on existing desires. They can move in and out of people who don't have any kind of resistance. And more than one of them can live in a single person. You've heard of that verse haven't you? Jesus asked a demon in a possessed man its name, and the demon replied, 'My name is Legion, for we are many.' There are limitations, but they can do a great many things.''

''Convince people to murder priests?''

''Maybe,'' Seaview said. ''If the person had some concern about the priest, then the fallen angels might be able to act on that, urging him along without his even knowing he was acting from an outside impulse. They might even keep a person from knowing what he's done.''

Gable stood at the foot of the bed with his hands in his pockets. ''Let's get back to another subject. Do you believe I'm in danger now?''

''Since the first moment you asked a question about Azarius. You became a danger to him, a danger to his destruction of Dareena. Who knows what else?''

''You've had a bad experience,'' Gable said. ''You're shaken up, Leonard.''

''No. Reawakened perhaps. When I was fifteen years old I had a religious experience at a revival service in an old country church. It was emotional, you know the scenario. After that I set out to be a minister, preached in my home church, studied the Bible. During college and seminary I pastored. I had a couple of churches before it all wore off. I ran out of energy. I started doubting. I started thinking about religion being more a state of mind than a spiritual reality. That's the way I've spent the past fifteen years, Gable. I only halfheartedly believed in God all that time. I'd been looking at everything as symbolic. I'm not turning hard-core fundamentalist on you, I'm just pointing out I've been missing something. Some of these things that go on are real. You weren't there when I was attacked. I can't

271

expect you to understand it, but it happened. It was real. As real as anything in this physical world, as real as that table, this book. There's more than we see, more than we think about. Evil exists. When that force hit me the other night, I knew there was evil. I could feel it, and I knew then I'd been wrong. There's more than just man, more than just man's ideas. There's good and there is very real evil. They don't tell you about that anymore in the church. They get up there in their three-piece suits and squall about political matters. We've forgotten about evil, forgotten what evil can do. Our technology, our reality, they make us forget there are things we can't explain.''

"Suppose you're right," Gable said. "What are we supposed to do? Can you drive a stake through the heart of a fallen angel?''

"I'm afraid it's not that simple. The best thing to do is get ready for an assault.''

"Right.''

"Laugh, Gable. But it's coming. You can mark my words. It's coming. Azarius is angry.''

The cops in the prowl car spotted Vincent almost by accident as he rounded a corner on one of the streets in the crumbling area of town near Dareena's house.

It bothered Chet Johnson, because it was 5:10, fifty minutes from shift change, which meant he and Cruise were going to be writing reports well after quitting time—if they caught up with the guy. That meant he was going to miss *Wheel of Fortune* at 6:30 and there was no telling when he'd get supper. If they were very late getting finished, he was going to have to pick up something from one of the drive-ins instead of fixing the ground meat he'd left thawing.

He was almost tempted not to follow the guy. If Vincent

was hanging around this zone, somebody would spot him later; the be-on-the-lookout description of Vincent had been on the blotter for two days now.

Still, Johnson put a little extra pressure on the gas pedal and turned the corner, following the lawyer's trail. He was dedicated. He did everything by the book. He had to cover his back, and besides, the rules were rules for a reason. There had to be order to things.

Vincent was headed up the street at a slow amble, his hands in his pockets, head tilted back lightly. He looked like a zombie out for a stroll.

"Is that him?" Johnson asked.

Cruise waited a second until the car was a little closer so he could get a better look at the guy. "It's him," he said.

Both of them were young cops, but they'd testified in cases Vincent had handled, so they knew him on sight.

Cruise picked up the microphone and hailed the dispatcher.

"What's up, boys?" she asked in her slow drawl. Johnson could picture her. She was probably sitting in her swivel chair smoking a Virginia Slims and reading a Stephen King paperback.

"We've got Walker Vincent in sight," Cruise said. His voice, too, was slow and easy. It had an impish quality about it. It matched his personality and his appearance. He was a slim, dark-haired guy, nice looking with boyish features. "We're over on Tagle Street, and we're going to check him out."

"You want me to send another car over?"

"Naw. We'll handle it and see you in a little while. I'll let you nibble on my ear while we're filling out our reports tonight."

He wasn't supposed to be sending that kind of stuff over

the air, but Johnson didn't correct him. Somebody else would, and he'd weasel out of it with his charm.

Easing the car on past Vincent, Johnson parked against the curb a few feet farther down the street. Then they got out, jamming their nightsticks into their belts and putting their hats on as they walked back toward him. Hats were required anytime they were out of their car, and chances were good the media might show up with cameras since they'd called the station. The media always monitored scanners.

Vincent didn't look at them at first, just kept on sauntering forward as they walked toward him. He was wearing a dark suit and a black overcoat even though the weather was mild. His hair was neatly combed, his face shaven. He didn't look like he'd been out on a binge, which was what Johnson had been thinking since they'd received the BOLO on the lawyer.

When they were only a short distance from him, the officers stopped, standing shoulder to shoulder, their feet planted.

Casually Johnson rested his hand on his pistol. He was taller than Cruise but not as heavy. He tried for a pose that would command authority and convey that he was lean, not skinny.

"Excuse me, sir." *Sir* was a term many cops used, a practiced, tactful way of dealing with people. It kept them from getting too personal. It was a distancing technique that let them know everything was business.

Vincent did look up at the cops now. It was if he were confused. He didn't look like the guy Johnson remembered from the courtroom at all, at least not in manner. In court Vincent had always been poised, cocky. He was a tough courtroom presence. Now he looked dazed, maybe even a little confused.

"What do you want?" Vincent asked, taking one more step before stopping.

"We need to talk to you, sir. Some people are looking for you."

Vincent looked forward, grinning. It was the expression of a street tough. He made Johnson think of one of the characters in an old black and white version of a Dickens story.

"What have we here?" he asked. "Mr. Solemn and Mr. Smiles."

Johnson always had a serious look complete with a little wrinkle across his brow. He was twenty-nine, but he looked older, and he took his job seriously. Too seriously, some said.

Cruise, on the other hand, was only twenty-four, and he had a smart-ass look even when he wasn't trying for one.

"Mr. Vincent?" Johnson said.

Vincent didn't look toward him. He didn't look toward anything.

That's why his strike was so unexpected. His hand came around suddenly, catching Cruise on his jaw. The cop's head spun around hard, and he tumbled off balance into Johnson, who almost lost his own balance.

Steadying Cruise, he yanked his nightstick from its holder and prepared to use it on the lawyer, but he wasn't quick enough.

Before he realized it, Vincent was behind him, one arm curled around his throat while the other pinned his arm to his side.

"Going to use that on me?" Vincent asked. The voice came from somewhere deep in his throat, a coarse, guttural growl.

Johnson remained silent as he struggled to pull free. It

275

was hopeless. The grip was like being held by some kind of iron claw. He couldn't budge Vincent's arm even slightly.

For a few moments he refused to release his nightstick, but Vincent's fingers slowly tightened around the officer's wrist, closing like a vise until the pain was so great that Johnson couldn't control his hand. His fingers opened, and the stick clattered down on the sidewalk. "Thank you for dropping that, *sir*," the lawyer said. "How about if I pull your fucking head off, sir? That be all right, sir?"

Vincent half lifted the cop and hurled him into the wall of the building at their side. Johnson hit hard but tried to spin around to meet his attacker.

He wasn't fast enough. Just as he was turning, a blow hit him across his throat, gagging him. He began to cough.

The second blow tore into his solar plexus. It wasn't placed well enough to sever the things it was supposed to sever, but the punch did drive Johnson to his knees. Doubled over, he continued to cough, and saliva and blood spilled over his lips.

He was trying to pull himself up when Vincent's foot slammed into his face, slamming him backward again into the wall. His head bounced off the brick and he crumpled to the ground.

Lying on his side, he couldn't move. He was stunned, totally in pain.

He watched Vincent slowly walk back to where Cruise was crouching, holding his head. The lawyer raised his open hand slowly, deliberately, like an executioner. He brought it down in a single slashing motion across the back of Cruise's head. The young cop crashed down onto his face, and blood quickly began to pool around his features.

Vincent crouched beside him, grabbing a handful of hair to lift the face away from the concrete.

The nose had been crushed when Cruise had gone down.

276

It was flattened now, with blood seeming to gush from both nostrils, making little bubbles from his breath. He'd lost a couple of teeth, too. They were lying there in the puddle of blood on the ground. His mouth sagged open, a jagged opening to a cavern, and blood spilled out over his lips.

Satisfied, Vincent let go of the hair, and Cruise's face thudded back to the concrete.

Vincent's fingers moved on down to the belt, where he unhooked the strap over Cruise's revolver so that he could pull the weapon from its holster.

Johnson held his breath. For a moment he thought they were both dead men because he still found himself unable to move. He braced himself for the report of the weapon, but Vincent twirled the cylinder for only a second, then swung the gun around, his finger looped through the trigger guard like a gunslinger. Then he tossed it into the gutter.

Turning to Johnson, Vincent took a step forward and gave him one more hard kick in the stomach before moving off down the street.

Two things kept running through Johnson's mind as he sank into a merciful unconsciousness.

One was that he wished some other unit had spotted Walker Vincent. The other was that he should have had Cruise call for backup. Everything should be done by the book. There were always unexpected variables.

"What do you make of all that?" Jennifer asked as Gable drove past the mental institution.

"What Seaview was talking about?"

"Yes."

He shrugged. "Is it compatible with your world view?"

"We weren't taught that much about the Bible when I was growing up. That's kind of a Protestant thing. Strict

277

Bible study, I mean. Scripture memory and all. I've always heard about demons and that sort of stuff, but I don't know. It's so weird.''

A soft tune was playing on the radio. Gable didn't even glance at the crumbling walls of the mental institution this time. He didn't want to think about the tortured souls within its confines. He felt tortured himself at the moment, or at least beset with anxiety.

"Leonard's convinced of it," Gable said.

"Totally."

"Maybe I should be scared, then," Gable said.

"Maybe. It lets you know how I've been feeling."

"Yeah, but you've got a bodyguard on order."

"You think a bodyguard can stop a biting poltergeist?"

"Tell your father the guard needs a Crucifix in addition to his side arm."

She laughed. "The world can turn strange quickly, can't it?"

"Yeah, some years it just doesn't pay to adjust your life-style."

Her father was waiting when they returned to Aimsley. He was sitting in his car in her driveway along with a tall man in dark slacks and a sport coat. The two climbed out of the car as Gable drove in.

He parked in his own drive and walked with Jennifer across the lawn. Their steps disturbed the bees that were working on the yellow flowers blossoming amid the grass, another reminder of spring, Jennifer thought. This wasn't supposed to be such a tense time. The sun was still shining even though there were just a few shadowy clouds in the distance. Everything was alive. Why did there have to be so many distractions?

Why did she have to have a bodyguard? She was never going to get any work done on her thesis with a gorilla living in her spare room.

Nelson and the big man met them about halfway across the lawn.

"This is Edward Gardner," Nelson said.

When he reached over to shake Gable's hand, Edward's coat pulled away slightly to reveal a pistol nestled in a holster under his right arm. He towered over Gable, which made him well over six feet.

He had a solid frame and a face that was almost nice looking. The problem was more in the expression than in the actual shape of his features, a rugged, cruel look that seemed to emanate from the dark depths of his eyes. Jennifer decided he looked like one of the wrestlers on television who bragged about his performance and his own superiority. He smiled, but there was no humor in him. He was here on business, so he remained cold.

"This is my daughter," Nelson said. "Mr. Gardner comes highly recommended."

"Good." Jennifer forced a smile. She was glad she was going to have the protection, but again, she wasn't thrilled at having the man around and not just because of his looks or his manner. In a way it was like an extension of her father's influence over her life.

"Been in this business long, big guy?" Gable asked. That quirky side of him that surfaced every now and then had floated to the top.

Edward wrinkled his lip as if to say he'd been at his work long enough. The mustache on his upper lip seemed to accent his snarl.

"So, you broken any important bones of anybody's lately?" Gable asked.

Edward just smiled politely and shook his head.

"So you got any hobbies? Ever strong-arm a union organizer?"

Jennifer realized Gable was intimidated by Edward's presence. She hated to see that coming just when things were starting up between them. She didn't want to see Gable turn macho and start trying to prove himself. She liked him too much for that to be necessary. Even if she didn't like him, it wasn't needed.

Hopefully all of this would be over soon. Maybe the killer would come while the guard was around to take care of things. That would be acceptable. Then life could get back to normal.

A guard. Perfect. Another delay.

There was a look of pure hatred in the eyes that peered over at the group assembled on the lawn.

The girl had to die soon.

Wouldn't want the priest to die in vain after all. He'd given up his life, why should she keep hers, the bitch. There was no pity that needed to be felt for her, only contempt.

Her strength and will to survive had been surprising in the first attempt on her life. Now she had a mountain lion on her doorstep.

A roll of thunder sounded, crackling like an echo in the mid-afternoon sky. The weather had been sunny for so long, at last it was turning hostile. Thunderstorms were threatening.

A storm could be an advantage.

In a storm, approaching footsteps were muffled.

In a storm, no one could hear screams.

CHAPTER 21

Julia had a stack of things to show Hamilton when he went to her house after work, everything from the design of the wedding invitations to the china and silverware patterns.

He sat through it all, sipping the drink she fixed for him, listening and trying not to move around too much in his chair. Julia would interpret that as disinterest; she'd studied body language, and would get upset with him. She had a fragile ego, was constantly worried about their relationship, and always asked questions about the meaning of everything.

Sometimes, Hamilton tired of the introspection, but on a whole he accepted her. She was attractive, and they got along, and all of her reading wasn't limited to psychology. She'd read quite a few books, some Joy-Ofs and other variation manuals. Also important—his father approved of her. She was from a good family, too, liberally educated and trained in social etiquette. She would make a good wife, hostess, and member of the Junior League, which would fight for the proper social causes of Aimsley.

She would produce healthy children, he believed—

children that would be attractive—and all the while she would maintain her own appearance.

There were many good features about her. She wouldn't be like his mother at all, and not like so many other women, yet she was there for him to lean on. He had come to depend on her support. In a way she was like a mother in that he could turn to her. That was another aspect of marriage to which he looked forward. She would be there at home for him when he came in from work, a refuge from the worries and pains of his job. With her caress she could make all the bad things go away.

She knew when he needed her to play that role. That was another reason their relationship was so perfect. She had her insecurities about their love, but she knew deep down it was real between them. Hamilton could sense that.

"Are you daydreaming again?" she asked. Hamilton realized his thoughts had been wandering despite all his attempts to keep his mind on the things she was showing him. He smiled, confessing his guilt with the expression.

"I was thinking about you," he said.

She let the design pages slip from her fingers. "I guess that's acceptable, then." She came to him, settling onto his lap and threading her arms around his neck.

"I wouldn't want to catch you thinking about anybody else."

"Never."

"I'll bet. I know your wandering eye, but I'm creative. I'll keep you interested." Leaning toward him, she slipped her tongue into his ear and twisted it about.

"That take your mind off everything but me?" she asked.

He had to smile. "That it does."

She was wearing a sweatshirt and jeans, but removing her arms from around his neck, she slowly slipped off the shirt, revealing that beneath she wore a black camisole decorated with lace.

He moved his hands up along her shoulders. Her skin was soft and smooth, almost pale.

Gently she shook her head, tossing her hair into disarray to give it a wild look.

"Don't let your mind wander," she said, looking down at him.

"Never."

She slipped off his lap and her fingers unfastened the clasp of her jeans, letting the denim slide to the floor, revealing long, slender legs.

Her form was perfect. She did exercises to keep in shape, aerobics, some weight-lifting and whatever else it took, and she used some kind of treatment to keep the cellulite from forming on her thighs.

She was fond of telling him all this, the efforts she made to be perfect for him so he could enjoy her body. He didn't mind hearing it. The results were worthwhile.

Stepping a few feet back, she began to sway to imaginary music, striking seductive poses that accented her hips. Then, opening her mouth slightly, she ran her tongue slowly over her lips, the moisture making them shine.

Rising slowly, he took her into his arms, kissing her on her lips, then letting his mouth move down to her neck. Her flesh was warm, almost hot.

"Am I all you need?"

"Everything," he said, knowing that wasn't all she wanted to hear. She would ask in a moment for more words, more elaboration on the matter. She needed to be told she was spectacular, needed to hear him expound upon her beauty at length. Sometimes that was a problem, but he dealt with it. He kept telling himself he was going to read more Victorian love poems to give him ideas of what to say,

283

but so many other things took up his time he never got around to it.

But no matter. It was only a small idiosyncrasy on Julia's part, only a small annoyance.

As he whispered how beautiful she was into her ear, he gently lifted her into his arms and carried her past the Madonna that guarded the living room.

The Virgin's face seemed to look at him with disapproval as he moved toward the door of the bedroom, but he buried his face quickly in his lover's flesh.

Later, while Hamilton slept, Julia slid from beneath the covers and moved across the room.

Her cigarettes were on the dressing table, and, still naked, she sat down there to light one with a disposable lighter as she turned to the mirror.

Brushing her hair away from her face, she looked back over at Hamilton. He snored lightly, his features twisted in sleep.

One arm dangled over the edge of the bed, his knuckles barely touching the floor. He had been gentle tonight, his caress slow and soft. Her flesh still tingled from the touch of his lips. He loved her body and that thrilled her. In a way it was like being worshipped, knowing his desire to hold her, to kiss her breasts, to enter her body. What more could she want? She rose from the chair and returned to the edge of the bed, where she looked down at him.

He didn't appear formidable in his present position, not at all like a ruthless businessman with an Ivy League degree.

Julia expelled smoke from her lungs. That didn't matter. He was handsome enough and had the potential to provide a good life.

She knew he had weaknesses, knew there had been other women in his life, but the past didn't matter. She wasn't going to let anything from the past get in the way. She would keep his attention on nothing but her. They would have a good life—together. That was all that mattered.

Dareena awoke from her sleep suddenly, feeling sick and dizzy. The sensation reminded her of a time when she'd been sick with a fever and had drifted in that realm of pseudo-reality created by her illness combined with the medication she'd been given to cure it.

Today she had settled down only for a nap but instead had drifted off into a deep sleep in which she'd dreamed something horrible. Now she wasn't sure what it had been, but she realized it was bad because the sensation lingered like a harsh smell.

Running her hands through her hair, she realized it was soaking wet, just like her clothes. Slowly she eased her weight out of the bed.

Her first inclination was to go for a shower. That feeling faded when she looked across the room and saw the glowing presence in the mirror.

Azarius had come back. He had returned angry. Somehow she could sense that even without speaking to him. Fear, like a tense hand, gripped her. She trembled, finding it difficult to draw breath.

Most frightening of all was the fact that she could not stop herself from moving toward the mirror.

"Come to me," the voice said. It was coarse, not the familiar voice of Azarius but instead a dry, throaty sound.

"What do you want?"

There was no reply. She was in front of the mirror now. She stood looking into the glass.

The sight was not what it had once been. The face was horrible, like something from a nightmare, the countenance twisted and scarred.

"There are those who would misunderstand me," Azarius said. "Those who would use my name. All of them circle around you."

"I don't understand."

"There is danger."

"From where? That man? That lawyer."

"No. Not from him. Not from the killers. The danger is from the writer, Gable Tyler, and his friends. The writer would take you away from me, would seek to destroy me. There will be a confrontation, and if you side against me, you will be taken into the pits of damnation, banished into the abyss."

She threw her hands over her face.

"Look at me," the angel commanded, but she couldn't move her hands. "Look at me!" he repeated, his voice booming. She felt the rattle of it in the depths of her soul, and she forced herself to pry her fingers away from her face and peer into the depths of the glass.

The angel's eyes flared bright orange and red, searing into her.

"Understand, you have my promise of eternity if you come with me. If not, I will destroy you."

His image began to glow, growing in intensity, the colors burning into her eyes. She jerked her head to one side, eyes closed, her hands moving up to cover her head. The room's temperature seem to be rising, and things began to vibrate.

Items on her nightstand rattled off onto the floor, spilling and breaking.

A picture frame slid down the wall, a spiderweb of cracks spreading across the glass.

Dareena could feel her lips quivering, and the blood seemed to rush through her veins.

A sound, like a roar, began to build. She could not determine its origin, but it was like hearing a gust of wind from deep within some cave or cavern.

It grew louder, and the vibration seemed to grow worse. The room began to rattle. Even the planks of the floor were quivering. It was a show of strength like nothing she could have imagined.

She whimpered deep in her throat because she could not summon a scream. Closing her eyes, she tried to control her growing fear. Crouching to the floor, she hugged her legs against her body.

She still had her eyes closed when the movement stopped as suddenly as it had started.

Her eyelids fluttered open. What had happened?

Just as she was about to stand up, the mirror shattered, as if it were exploding. The sound was deafening.

Shards of glass burst across the room in a spray, the debris pelting down onto Dareena's shoulders or scraping along the wall.

Sharp chunks sliced into the wallpaper over the bed, and slivers ripped along the lace of the bedspread.

The pillows were ripped apart while the curtains on the windows were shredded into ragged strips.

More glass slashed across the ceiling, digging furrows in the soft material. Small pieces of the tile drifted down like snowflakes.

The smallest slivers brushed across Dareena's back, making tiny cuts in the cloth of her dress and drawing faint scratches on her skin, just enough to make her aware of the effect.

Dareena didn't look up. She huddled on the floor, facedown, as if she were in a disaster drill.

The glass continued to spray everywhere, more glass than the mirror should have contained. It filled the air like shiny silver powder, glistening and gleaming.

Still bent to the floor, she wept, unable to control the fear. As the final shards of glass fell about her, she heard the roar again. This time she was able to make it out. It was laughter.

There was no rain the next morning, but the clouds remained thick and threatening, the color of dark smoke. Spread across the sky they blotted out the sunlight and masked any trace of color.

Julia wore a jacket when she went downtown to the jeweler to pick up Hamilton's wedding ring and also visit the dress shop where her going-away outfit was being tailored.

She went alone because her mother wanted to concentrate on some of the wedding arrangements. Carolyn Harper was planning an elaborate reception.

Julia would have preferred a simple ceremony, but she didn't begrudge her mother the pleasure of the event. She was the only daughter, and her mother's own wedding had not been a terribly happy occasion.

Julia's paternal grandparents had not approved of the marriage, so the ceremony had been rushed, informal, and devoid of the romantic trappings her mother had desired.

Coming from a poor family, Carolyn had longed for an elegant wedding, but without the approval of her fiancé's parents, that wasn't possible. There had been no pageantry, just a quick legal ceremony by a minister who was gracious but lacking in compassion.

There hadn't even been an announcement of the wedding in the newspaper, a fact that was always a part of Carolyn's lament about her marriage ceremony.

All of these things Julia had learned over the years just as she learned of her mother's hopes.

She could not count the number of times her mother had told her about her image of her daughter's wedding. It had begun long before Julia was conceived, a dream for whatever daughter might have been born to Carolyn.

She always stressed the importance of marrying well, because she remembered the poor days. Carolyn's father had gone to prison, leaving the children without support. Much of the time they'd gone hungry.

She didn't want to go back to that, and she didn't want Julia making any kind of mistake that would net her that kind of life either. All the time she drilled that into Julia's head.

Julia had accepted her mother's lessons. There had never really been a temptation to date boys below her social stature. She'd never had that need to rebel and go out with boys from the wrong side of town.

In high school she'd always had boyfriends of suitable social standing, and she'd been pleased when she finally landed Hamilton.

They'd never dated in high school, but she had been aware of him, watching him but never being too forward. Now people tended to believe they were reunited sweethearts. "Did y'all used to date in high school?" her friends would ask.

Júlia always replied with her explanation, that they had known each other but they hadn't dated.

When they had started dating the summer before Hamilton's graduation, she'd told him she'd always known it was meant to be.

"You think so?" he'd asked.

"I've just been waiting for you to realize it," she answered.

That summer had been like magic, something right out of her mother's imagination, and when they had returned to school for their last semesters, they'd written reams of letters, living for the vacations when they could return to Aimsley to be together. Never had Aimsley seemed such a wonderful town.

So many people Julia knew were dying to leave Louisiana, but she was content. Married to Hamilton, she knew things would be suitable. They would reign as one of the small town's superior couples.

Why move to New Orleans or Houston when they could do so well here, welcoming the cultural events to town and volunteering for local fund-raisers?

Aimsley and Hamilton were all Julia needed. She realized much of that philosophy had been adopted from her mother, but that didn't matter. It was a good philosophy.

She was headed for a little downtown restaurant to have lunch when Salem stepped out of a little cranny between a couple of run-down buildings that were awaiting redevelopment. Sawhorses stood in front of the shadowy structures, signs warning that the buildings weren't safe.

When he appeared, Julia didn't hesitate to follow him through the doorway of an old shop into the darkened interior. She didn't want to be seen with him.

He was unshaven, dressed in black pants and a faded sport coat, a black glove with no fingers on one hand, hair glistening with too much oil.

He took a few steps back into the dusty interior of the building before spinning around to face her.

"What do you want?" she demanded.

He smiled, a broad grin which she found sickening.

"I don't have anything to say to you." She looked around

at the empty display cases and the empty shelves. The place was eerie, not so much because it was empty as because she was occupying it with Salem, alone.

"Come on," he said. "We're friends."

"You're no friend of mine."

"I hate to hear that. I was hoping I'd get to fuck the bride before the wedding night."

She set her jaw firmly and glared at him, knowing she couldn't afford to give him any ground. The crude remark was supposed to throw her off balance, but she only looked back at him defiantly.

"You're not getting anything from me." The first time she had ever set eyes on him she had thought he was a rapist coming toward her on the street. She'd tried to run, but he had cornered her to introduce himself as a friend of Hamilton's. His harassments and taunts had continued ever since, and he seemed to be able to read her fears. He knew her future with Hamilton meant everything to her, and he used the threat of losing that future to intimidate her.

"You don't know what you're missing," he giggled.

"I'll survive the wondering," she said, repulsed.

"Thought since your Hamilton plays around you'd want to do a little sampling of the other things the world has to offer yourself."

"I'm afraid of what I might catch."

"Oh. Too bad."

She continued to glare at him. She knew what he wanted. For weeks he'd been trying to set her up for blackmail. God knew who else he terrorized, but he kept hinting that there would come a time when she wouldn't want it known her husband slept around, a time she would have to pay to keep that knowledge secret.

"I'm aware Hamilton hasn't been a saint," she said.

"I've told you that before. It doesn't matter to me. Men have that kind of peer pressure."

"Not worried about where he's dipped his wick?"

She tasted something bitter in her throat, revolted by Salem's vulgarity.

"No," she said. "I'm not."

"Have you been keeping abreast of the news?"

"Not particularly."

"One of his, ah, consorts had a spot of trouble. You hear about that?"

"No."

"The little lady from the hotel? She's dead. Murdered."

Julia drew a quick breath without unclenching her teeth.

"Hamilton wouldn't kill anybody."

"You don't think?"

"You probably read the paper every morning, looking for something you can use to scare somebody. I'm not going to give you any money now, and not after I'm married. And Hamilton isn't either."

Salem placed a cigarette in his mouth and lit it with a match he struck with his thumbnail.

"We'll see," he said. "You never know. Just remember, I know things about your husband-to-be. You're right. He's no saint, love."

He took a step forward and wrapped his arm around her waist suddenly, dragging her toward him.

Before she knew it he'd pressed his lips to hers, forcing his tongue across her lips quickly. He slobbered across her lips and brushed his mouth down her face to her throat before letting her go.

As he walked from the building, she could feel the prickly burn from the touch of his beard.

"Bastard," she murmured. "Bastard."

* * *

When she saw Gable approaching, Dareena turned and tried to hurry into the house, but he caught her arm when he realized she was trying to flee him, his grip preventing her from moving up the front steps.

She'd been halfheartedly working in the front flower garden, but she looked lost. Her eyes were hollow, vacant, with dark circles staining the skin beneath them.

"What's the matter?" Gable asked.

"I can't talk to you."

"Why?"

"Azarius."

"What about him? What's wrong?"

"He said you're evil, that you'll try to harm me."

Relaxing his grip on her arm, Gable looked into her eyes.

"Do I seem evil?"

She turned her face toward the ground. For a moment she wouldn't look at him, but she couldn't maintain the defiance. Slowly she lifted her face.

"I don't think so," she said.

"How do you know Azarius is telling the truth?"

"Angels don't lie."

"How do you know he's what he says he is?"

"He's shown me so many wonderful things. There are promises he's made."

"Lies the serpent told."

Her eyes flared. "What are you saying?"

"What do you think?"

"That he's evil? That's not true. He's done so many good things. Why would he do good things if he was evil?"

"Would you have spent any time with him at all if you'd thought him to be evil?"

293

She jerked her arm away from him and started up the steps. "I don't want to hear this."

"Satan himself appears as an angel of light."

That stopped her in her tracks. It was something Seaview had told him over the phone in a conversation earlier. It was a biblical statement, something with which she was probably familiar from her early teachings.

Gable wasn't wild about playing that kind of game, but he'd had to lay a card of some kind.

"He was angry last night," she said.

"What did he say?"

"That my soul would be lost to damnation if I didn't obey him. That I should stay away from you."

Gable felt the short hairs on the back of his neck prickle. He remembered Seaview's statement, a confrontation was coming.

As if to punctuate his feeling, a faint rumble of thunder rolled through the clouds.

"What can you do?" she asked.

"I don't know, but I have a friend. He's studying this. He'll figure something out. That's why I came by. He wanted me to talk to you."

"Who is he?"

"A theology professor."

"Why didn't he come?"

"He's in the hospital. Something attacked him. Something he couldn't see. It came out of nowhere. He was studying some texts at the time, studying because of what I told him about you and about Azarius."

"I don't understand."

"Suppose your Azarius is evil? Suppose he's trying to deceive you?"

"I can't believe that."

"Even with all that's happened?"

"I'm afraid. But you can't mean Azarius had something to do with Father Conzenza's death?"

"Maybe not, but that seems to have touched off everything else that's going on. Weird things are happening. There's a lawyer who's gone nuts."

"From the D.A.'s office? He was here. He tried to rape me."

"Oh my God. He tried to attack me for talking to you. Maybe Azarius does have something to do with that."

"How?"

"I don't know, but he doesn't want me around you," Gable said.

"Why is that? I still don't understand what's going on. What are you getting at?"

"Maybe he wants to destroy you, and he thinks I'll stop him in some way."

"How do I know you're not the murderer, and Azarius wants to protect me from you?" Dareena said. "He's never seemed angry before."

"If he's a guardian angel, he should be able to stop me without any problem. He wouldn't have to warn you off. If he's evil, then I must be a threat in some way."

She nodded. "He does seem to be afraid of you."

"Now it's my turn to ask questions," Gable said. "What is it about me that frightens him? I'm nothing special. I promise you I'm not a murderer."

"I don't know. But when he spoke of you, the last time he contacted me, the mirror burst out into the room."

"Did he say what was wrong?" Gable asked.

"No. Just that I should stay away from you."

"Show me."

She seemed hesitant.

"If I was going to hurt you," Gable said quietly, "would I pick a place where your guardian angel has easy access?"

She studied his face for a moment, finally shrugging. "Come on."

He followed her into the house and they moved together up the stairs. She eased open her door slowly and let Gable step past her into the room.

The frame of the shattered mirror still stood against the wall.

At the window the curtains were drawn, so the room was heavy with shadow. The shards of glass had all been cleared away, and the empty face of the dressing table frame seemed to yawn open like the mouth of some night creature.

Gable walked toward it slowly, his hands loose at his sides. There was no vent behind it. He checked for any other outlet that might have somehow explained the breakage, but there was nothing, and around the frame there were bits of twisted metal and melted plastic from the screws that had held the glass into place, melted as if they had been exposed to some great heat.

Dareena lingered in the doorway, her arms folded nervously across her stomach.

"He appeared in the mirror?" Gable asked.

"Sort of. But in my mind also. It's hard to explain how it worked."

"And he called you?"

"Usually I had to call him."

"But this time?"

"Yes, he contacted me."

"You never felt he was—" He paused.

"What?"

"Possessing you?"

She had to think about it. Some sort of realization seemed to flare behind her eyes.

"He seemed to want to. To come into me. That's what

he said we were working toward, a day when I would be able to join him totally.''

"How was that supposed to happen?''

"It was to occur only when I was ready.''

"In what way?''

"I never understood that, but when it was to happen I was to pass into another point of existence with him, so that we could be together. Really together.''

"You were to leave this world?''

"Yes.''

"He was going to have you commit suicide,'' Gable concluded. "He was working you toward that.''

"No. He wouldn't do that. He loves me.''

"How much?''

"He wants us to be together.''

Gable frowned. "Explain.''

Their eyes met, but she quickly averted her gaze. When her words came, she spoke very softly, stammering at first before she managed to articulate her thoughts.

"He spoke to me in my mind, while I . . .''

She couldn't look at him. She couldn't go on.

"The top drawer,'' she suggested finally.

Gable turned slowly and eased the drawer open. In the shadowed room he had to look into the depths for several seconds before his eyes picked up the shapes of the instruments and the jars.

He closed the drawer without speaking, afraid the bitter taste he felt in his throat would touch off a chain reaction in his stomach. The lubricants and vibrators belonged somewhere else, not in the world of Dareena, not in the world that was supposed to be one of innocence. These were implements for seedy shops with discolored lighting.

"Do you think an angel would have you do something like that?''

She still wouldn't look at him. He moved over and grabbed her arm, spinning her around.

"He couldn't be with me any other way," she said.

"He gave you an alternative to love, in other words. A substitute for the human touch. He kept you from breaking out of here, out of your seclusion. He kept you where he could control you, where he could destroy your soul. That's why he's frightened. He's afraid of anything that might try to draw you away from him, anything that might undo his work and release you from the dependence he's created."

"No."

Tears were welling in her eyes now. She struggled to free herself from Gable's grasp, but his fingers tightened on her upper arms.

"Think about it," Gable demanded.

"I have thought about it. You're wrong. You've just been told a bunch of things you're trying to impart to me."

"No, I'm not. I'm just beginning to have my eyes opened to what's going on myself."

"You're wrong."

"Let's find out. Call him."

"What?"

"Call him. Call your angel. We'll both talk to him."

"He won't appear with you in the room."

"If he's an angel, or whatever he is, he shouldn't have to be afraid of me. I'm just a man."

"It won't work. You should be frightened of him."

Gable remained emphatic. "Call him."

He released his grip on one of her arms and led her slowly over to sit on the edge of the bed.

She closed her eyes reluctantly, beginning to rock slightly from side to side. Her expression tightened, her lips moving silently as she called the angel's name.

The feeling that settled over Gable was disturbing. Again

he felt the short hairs on his neck bristle, and a tingling sensation spread over him, even to the roots of his hair.

He felt his eyes drawn toward the empty mouth of the frame. There was nothing there. He should have been able to see directly through it to the wall, yet that now was not the case.

He blinked at first, thinking there was something wrong with his eyes. He'd had that happen before—eyestrain from too many hours at the word processor's VDT, staring at green letters.

Except he hadn't worked at one of those in months now. His eyesight should have been clear.

Yet he couldn't seem to focus on the area within the frame. It looked, he realized, like the Guardian Arch in *Star Trek*.

The space confined by the border of the frame was becoming like a swirling mass of infinity. Looking into it was like looking into a bottle filled with smoke.

He averted his gaze, turning toward Dareena. Her eyes were still tightly closed, her fists at her sides clenched into white balls. He started to speak, but held his tongue, afraid to break her concentration. Something was happening. He could feel it in the very depths of his soul.

It was not right. It was not a good thing. This he knew by the shiver that traveled along his backbone.

Looking to the mirror again, he could see the presence there. Now he could see the wall, but the smoke was there also, as if superimposed, like overlaid photo negatives.

Somehow outlined in the gray shadows Gable could see the shape of the angel. He looked back to Dareena. Her eyes were open. She slid off the bed and came to stand beside him, clutching his arm with both her hands, half hiding behind him.

She peeked around Gable's shoulder like a child hiding behind a tree in a game of hide-and-seek.

"It's different."

Without feeling the sensation in his eardrums, Gable heard the laughter. It was harsh, the sound of a coarse desert wind.

"Who are you?" he asked, voicing his words.

"Don't you know?" the voice said inside his head.

"I have an idea."

More laughter. "An idea that only accents the finite nature of your moral brain. Do you think you can combat me?"

"I'm not challenging you. I'm trying to understand."

"What do you want to know?"

"What you are."

"Dareena?" the angel asked. The words were not audible, but from her reaction Gable decided the girl must have heard them, too.

Her fingers tightened around his upper arm. He felt her nails biting through his shirt-sleeve into his skin.

"He's an angel," she said aloud.

"There's your answer," Azarius said.

"That's not an answer. You call yourself Azarius. A name from an ancient language."

"A word. Something you can understand. A means of identification."

"But it doesn't tell me anything."

"What would you have me tell you? There are things beyond your comprehension, things you are not ready to know. Dareena is learning, but she is not fully prepared. You have not even begun the journey toward the light. You are not all you perceive yourself to be. You are not a righteous man. You do not have the authority to question the process."

"Truth doesn't fear questions."

"There is nothing about you that I fear."

"Not me, but what I might learn, what I might tell. Dareena might slip from your grasp."

"Dareena knows what will happen if she turns away from the light."

"You've deluded her. You are not the light."

Dareena jerked at his arm. "Gable, please. Don't."

"Did you kill the priest?" Gable asked.

The angel continued to laugh. "Men have free will. There are many things that suit God's purpose."

Dareena cried out, her tears streaming down her face.

Gable glanced at her only briefly before turning back toward the mirror frame. His eyes were drawn there, riveted. The sensation remained the same; he was seeing the image of the angel without actually viewing it within the frame. Somehow Azarius was inside his mind, yet not there. The being hovered just within the scope of Gable's awareness.

And although the figure was really no more than an outline—an impression designed for Gable's benefit more than a depiction of the angel's true form—he found he was looking into its eyes.

They were red, narrow, hooded, almost like the eyes of a serpent or something worse. A word from a science fiction story crept into his mind to describe the eyes—saurian, more hideous than a serpent's.

They were eyes that could envelop him; he felt himself drawn into the gaze, lost within the swirling gray shadows.

It became difficult to draw breath, and he realized he was no longer conscious of the room around him. It was as if he were drifting, afloat in some surreal realm.

"Welcome, Mr. Tyler," Azarius said.

Gable saw the angel ahead of him and began to move

toward it, traveling through an expanse of blackness before he reached the figure that now seemed to be more tangible.

The angel seemed to be standing just ahead of him, its back turned. He approached slowly, the sensation of movement reminding him of a trip on a mini–roller coaster through a spook house at the fall carnival.

Yet he was not in a rail car. He simply traveled, floating through the darkness until he was just inches away from the form he perceived to be Azarius.

The figure began to turn toward him, its movement slow and fluid.

Somehow he could see the figure more clearly, make out the lines of its being, and when it turned fully toward him, he could see its face.

It was a pleasant face, a handsome face. It could have belonged to a man of about Gable's age.

Azarius smiled, and Gable found himself reaching out to touch the hand the angel was extending.

"You feared me?" Azarius said.

"No."

There had been a tension about him as he moved through the smoke, but Gable felt himself relax. This being was not the threat he had expected, nor a horror at all.

He smiled back, attempting to free his hand to let it drop to his side, but the angel did not let go.

Tugging harder, Gable struggled to pull away. It was useless effort. Azarius clung to him, the smile becoming sinister, then turning into a laugh that echoed through the walls of his brain, a deep and vacant sound.

He tried even harder to free himself, but without success. He was forced to remain face-to-face with the angel, and then the handsome, youthful face began to melt, sliding in huge globs away from the skull.

It revealed a twisted countenance of dark colors covered

in what looked like scales, and the eyes that had been blue crumbled away, again revealing saurian eyes, yellow and red in color, no more than slits.

The face had become reptilian and harsh.

The dark angel continued its hideous laughter as it began to twist about, spinning around, dragging Gable by his arm as it gained momentum.

He felt himself billowed upward by the movement, circling the angel that had become like an axis.

"Do I fear you?" the angel asked. Then he let go, sending Gable sprawling through the vast emptiness. He tumbled through the void, head over feet, and over end in an endless succession of somersaults.

Another doorway of darkness seemed to open, as if blackness were peeling away from blackness to plunge Gable even deeper into this abyss.

He sank down through something like clay, dropping through the mire without touching it.

Then suddenly his eyes were seared by the bright flash of lightning, twisted lightning that flamed blue and magenta, cutting open the darkness.

Gable continued to fall, passing through more blackness. Direction had no meaning, but he felt as if he were falling.

Then there were flames. There was no source for them; they were not like torches, they just seemed to flicker and dance from everywhere, jets of orange and blue merging into an infinity of fire.

Through the fires he could see faces, faces without features, like the faces of mannequins. They were the faces of lost souls, and he could hear the cries of their agony.

And echoing through their cries was Azarius's laughter, like accompanying music.

"You are not a righteous man," the angel said again. "Your soul could be banished here forever."

Gable tried to cry out, but his throat was suddenly dry and he could not form words. He choked, making rattling sounds in his throat.

The flames wrapped around him so that he could feel the agony of their touch. Then, rising out of them, he saw the heads of snakes, large snakes with thick red tongues. They began to flicker toward him, their mouths opening to reveal fangs that dripped with acid venom.

The sickening smell of burning sulphur filled his nostrils. He tried to close his eyes, tried to hold his breath.

It was impossible. He felt his head twisted forward. He was being forced to look at them, as if the angel had a handful of his hair.

The inbred fear of reptiles seized him. He struggled against the angel, fought without result. The snakes slithered toward him through the nothingness.

As they coiled around him he began to scream. It did no good. The cold, slimy touch gripped his whole body. They wrapped around the length of his legs and then around his waist and his arms.

They did not bite as he expected. Instead, they dragged him farther downward. Through the flames, to which they were somehow immune, they passed with him. The next chamber was like a cavern, and when the snakes uncoiled he was plunged into its depths.

It was a vast kingdom of more serpents. While the heat scorched him, he felt the fear more intensely than the pain.

There were snakes everywhere, some of them as large as those that had brought him here, others small and wicked looking. They slithered over him, moved into his nostrils and under his fingernails.

They were under his skin. He watched their slithering forms creating bulges in his flesh as they twisted here and there.

He shook and thrashed and twisted, terror making him convulse. He bent double, slobbering.

Then his stomach tensed and he began to vomit. They spilled from his throat and over his lips, hundreds of them, thousands of tiny snakes. They wriggled from his nose and out the corners of his eyes. Thousands more crawled from his ears. Then they were wriggling out of every pore, every orifice. Finally they were all free.

He began to crawl, dragging himself through the mass of coils. They crawled over his arms and legs and back as he slogged through them, but he ignored that.

When he saw the opening, he scrambled toward it. It was narrow and dark, but it was an escape from the snakes. He would do anything to get away from the scaly creatures now, anything.

He squeezed through the hole, leaving the snakes behind. Some of them coiled around his ankles, trying to hold him, but he kicked free and tumbled on into the darkness.

He soon began to fall again, sliding down through a winding tunnel. All around him he could see stars and other visions of the cosmos, but they were out of reach.

He went spilling on down through the tunnel, his speed building. The feeling of plunging became almost as horrifying as the serpents had been.

He began to roll and bounce off the walls. The pain was noticeable but not intense.

He was beginning, almost, to develop a feeling or sense of composure when he plunged into the pool.

He sank down into the liquid despite efforts to swim. There was some kind of whirlpool and it dragged him through the liquid.

He sputtered, fighting the current without success until he realized that it was not water. After a moment he could tell it was blood. It was thick and red and filled with bits of bone matter and rotting flesh.

He was sucked down through the depths of it all. The whirlpool drew him through its vortex and deposited him in another cavern.

More screams filled his ears, the screams of human agony. It was a dark place illuminated by flames. He looked up at the blazes. There were torches made from human bodies impaled on huge stakes.

The walls were splattered with blood and ripped pieces of tissue and brain matter.

He knelt on the burning stone floor and looked about. It was like a dungeon from the Dark Ages, or something dreamed up for the Inquisition. All about him was torture.

Naked people were everywhere, trapped by hooks that bit into their bodies or dangled them from chains. They were hooked to the walls or stretched over flames. They were beaten or their flesh flailed in the dark corners.

They were herded about by fat, naked men, hideously deformed. Eyes blinked from their chests, hands grew out of their shoulders, and tiny legs blossomed from their stomachs.

Others of the guards were even more hideous, their forms like nothing human at all. They dragged themselves along the floor because their bodies were so deformed they could not stand erect. Some were mere masses of jelly. Others were more like animals with tails and claws.

Gable realized most of the people were being herded through another opening. It was a black hole, and from within it the agonies of millions of souls were heard.

He felt a near madness sweep into his brain as he peered through the opening. Only the shadows of the horrors that awaited him there were visible. They were more terrible than anything he could imagine, and the creatures that waited just inside were from nightmares, dark beings with red eyes. Foul odors drifted through the crevice. He could not make out the forms inside, nor did he want to.

He looked up at the lettering scrawled in blood above the entrance. It was there as they had always said: ABANDON ALL HOPE YE WHO ENTER HERE. It was there as a joke, mocking man's attempt to explain it.

He was only in the antechamber. The place had indeed been created for the devil and his angels, but they had made well of it as a place to torture the souls they captured.

A huge bald man kicked Gable from behind and began to prod him toward the entrance.

It could not be real, yet Gable sensed danger. Somehow he knew he would have to remain here forever if he did not escape. If he went through the final passage, he would remain in the nightmare of torture forever.

The deformed guardsman was going to force him into that final cavern.

Gable fell to the ground and dug his fingers into the fiery stone. The bald man looped a chain around Gable's feet and began to drag him along. He could not avoid the demon's effort. He was going to be cast into the flames.

The screams filled his awareness, and all around him others were being prodded or dragged toward the opening.

He fought for some kind of grip to stay the bald man's progress. It was hopeless.

He heard the screams again.

Looked back at the shadows and their reflections of eternal agony.

Inch by inch the demon moved him toward that agony.

But somewhere, he heard voices—not the cries of the damned or the cackle of the angel. These were different, faraway but familiar sounds.

Someone was whispering a prayer.

He managed to look upward somehow, and he could see past the top of the cavern. Leonard was there.

The professor seemed to be looking through a doorway at him. Gable felt as if he were at the bottom of an elevator shaft looking up at Seaview, who seemed to be peering through an opening many stories above, but his hand reached downward, beckoning.

"Gable, come with me," he called.

Gable felt himself being lifted; he was being drawn toward Leonard and the echo of the other voice. It seemed to be coming from somewhere behind the professor.

He tried to struggle upward, but found he could not. All he could do was accept the circumstances, letting himself be drawn toward the opening.

The flames disappeared, and he drifted back through the lightning. It stretched out, trying to encircle him, but he broke through even though it continued to flash. It was the way Saint Elmo's fire had always been described to him.

He closed his eyes, kept them closed until the second voice rang though his consciousness.

"Gable. Gable, wake up."

He opened his eyes, and he was standing in Dareena's bedroom again. The frame was empty now. He could see the walls beyond it, and Dareena stood at his side, her hands gripping his shoulders, shaking him.

He felt as if he'd walked through a water sprinkler. His clothes clung to him. His hair hung limp around his face. Perspiration ran down his calves, so much that he first thought his bladder had collapsed.

He heaved a deep sigh of relief.

"Are you all right?" Dareena asked, still holding on to his shoulders.

"I'm fine."

"He was speaking to you?"

"It was like I was in a void at first. Then in hell itself, or maybe purgatory. Is that how your contact with him works?"

"It's like a trance, but it's never been horrible. When I'm with him it's like we're together in open fields or walking beside streams in the forest."

"He was trying to scare me."

"I don't understand it."

"He must be evil, Dareena."

She shook her head. Her eyes tightly shut.

Gable gripped her shoulders, shaking her until she looked at him. Her eyes were once again filled with tears.

"I don't want to hear any of this," she said. "I won't listen to you."

"Why not? You're the same as he is. If he isn't evil, why does he fear any questions of him?"

She twisted away from him, stopping at the wall with her back to him, her head down.

Gable's movement was checked as he started to move toward her. What felt like hands closed upon his shoulders, jerking him backward. His feet left the floor, and he traveled upward abruptly before being dropped hard onto the floor.

He tried to get up quickly, but again he was seized and hurled across the room. He crashed into the night table, crushing it with his weight. He landed in a heap among the splintered debris.

The bruises from the encounter with Vincent began to throb with new pain. He raised his arms in front of him quickly, just in time to block the small lamp that was hurtling across the room toward him.

"Gable!" the girl cried. She had turned just in time to see what was happening.

Gable ignored her, rolling quickly to one side just as a

small chair crashed into the wall above him, showering him with a new set of splinters.

There was a wind sweeping through the room now, a cold and bitter wind that tore at his face and felt as if it were going to tear his hair out by its roots. It was like an Arctic wind or the forewarning of a blizzard.

It swept over Dareena also, but without causing her to lose her footing. She looked as if she wanted to scream and couldn't as it whipped around her.

Gable scrambled forward, seizing the frame of the bed and digging his fingers in, holding fast.

The rush of air was coming from nowhere, crashing through the room, continuing to gain velocity. Gable's mother had told him of a time when she'd been in a house and a tornado had struck just down the block.

The terror of that experience as she had described it was nothing compared to this, Gable thought. This was like being in the heart of a cyclone or like being hurled into the eye of a hurricane.

"Gable!" Dareena screamed again. "What's happening?"

Gable couldn't find words. He just held fast to the bed as his weight was lifted in the wind. He billowed, like a ribbon tied to a fence post, like a wind sock.

The air continued to sweep around Dareena, sparing her the worse of the onslaught, but she was terrified. Her tears were blown from her face, her hair flowing away from her head.

The pain in Gable's fingers as he fought to maintain his grip on the bed was like fire. His nails were ground back into the cuticles as he fought to hold on, but the wind seemed to increase until he could tense his fingers no longer.

They relaxed, giving his body over to the wind that lifted him quickly to carry him back across the room.

The force with which Vincent had hurled him was nothing compared to the force with which he now struck the wall. He took most of the impact with his right shoulder, and the pain jarred through to his bones.

Pressed against the wall, he looked forward, feeling the wind crush in upon him. It was like film he'd seen of spaceflight simulations, the effects of high rates of speed. For a moment he thought his skin was going to be peeled away from his skull.

He couldn't move his arms. They were cemented against the wall by the wind pressure.

Tears began to flow from his eyes, wrapping back around his face. He tried to draw breath and found it impossible.

He could only watch as Dareena struggled away from her place against the other wall, moving toward the center of the room.

Her dress was wrapped around her, clinging as if it were soaking wet. She clasped her hands in front of her and looked toward the ceiling, her lids squinting at the wind.

"Let him alone. Whatever you are, let him alone. I'll hate you if you don't stop. Damn you, whatever you are, damn you if you hurt him. I'll know you're evil."

Abruptly the wind stopped, cut off from its nonexistent source. In a final rush all of it seemed to sweep through the wall at Gable's back, gone into nothingness.

He fell forward onto his hands and knees, coughing for breath. Every muscle in his body was exhausted.

He lay facedown until he felt Dareena's touch. She rolled him over slowly and cradled his head in her arms.

He could feel her breath on his face as she searched for some sign of life in his features.

"I'm all right," he said, but his voice was dry. He couldn't manage much more than a whisper.

"He would have killed you," she said.

"He means business," Gable said. "He wants your soul, and he doesn't want anything to stand in his way. He'll be back for you. And for me."

"What are we going to do?"

"I don't know," Gable whispered. "I'm just a man."

PART II

Jesus asked him, "What is your name?" He replied, "My name is Legion; for we are many."

—Mark 5:9

CHAPTER 22

After the priest's funeral, which had been delayed several days by the autopsy and the investigation, Arbor drove slowly back to Aimsley, his thoughts on the sad eyes of the people who had stood around the gravesite.

He had been elected as the task force member to cover the event, watching for any signs that might be useful.

He'd taken the trouble of dragging out his best suit for the trip, but he didn't find anything useful at the service. Jennifer Nelson was there with her father and mother. The women both wore black dresses.

A thick-necked legbreaker named Gardner had stood behind them. He'd looked uncomfortable in his plaid sport coat amid the sea of dark suits. Arbor knew him. He was a licensed private investigator, good at what he did without seeming particularly bright. At least he ought to be able to stop anything short of an elephant that came after Jennifer.

That thought was what really made Arbor breathe easier. If there was another murder, even if they did catch someone afterward, careers were going to be suffering irreparable damage.

That he wanted to avoid as much as the horror of another murder.

The Terrys had also been present at the funeral. Hamilton had stood beside his father. Beside the young man had stood his fiancée, clinging possessively to his arm.

Arbor had scanned the crowd for Gable Tyler, but didn't catch sight of him. The boy had not really known the priest that well, but Arbor had expected to see him there anyway. He hadn't received a call from Gable in two days, and he was beginning to worry.

He didn't know about the kid's ideas, but if they turned up something useful, Arbor wasn't going to turn the information down. He was ready to welcome anything that would get this case over with.

The funeral service had been simple with much less pageantry than Arbor had expected. The church eulogy had been brief. His Missionary Baptist upbringing hadn't prepared him for the kneeling, but the event had ended quickly.

At the cemetery the old-gray haired priest who'd given the graveside service had been calm and reflective, reassuring about eternal life through Jesus Christ and a retrospective in recalling Conzenza's youth in the church parish.

The priest's brother took all of it in without crying, but there were tears from some of the members of Conzenza's parish. Mrs. Nelson sniffled, but she didn't cry, Arbor noted. The Terrys didn't cry, but the son's girlfriend shed a few tears before resting her face against Hamilton's shoulder for comfort. Her dress was also black, a sad irony. She was probably to have stood before the priest in a white gown originally. Conzenza almost certainly would have been the one to perform their wedding ceremony, Arbor realized.

He was always amazed at how far the ripples from a murder traveled, how many lives were touched by the loss. John Donne had been right. Every man is a piece of the continent.

As he cruised back into town, Arbor watched the heavy clouds move over the city. They still threatened as they had for several days, but so far there had been no rainfall harder than a drizzle.

That wasn't a good sign. It meant a heavy storm was gathering its strength for an assault.

He parked in a reserved spot in the police parking lot and went into the building, turning up his jacket collar against the chilled breeze that drifted through the air.

He found Harper and Benchley waiting for him in a briefing room. There was no sign of Fisher, and no one knew where he'd gone.

Benchley was the only one who'd turned up something new. He sat at the end of the table, his hair parted in the middle and brushed back, the bangs held out of his eyes by the sunshades he'd pushed back over his forehead.

He wore a loose-fitting blue pullover and jeans and white tennis shoes. He looked like he ought to be studying for a final exam.

As he spoke, he referred to a notebook about the size of a credit card he took from his hip pocket.

"The rosary came from a shop in Penn's Ferry, a Christian book and tape shop that sells all sorts of religious items. They don't do a big business in rosaries, but they couldn't pinpoint its purchaser. It was probably sold about a year ago, maybe a little less than that."

"If it was purchased there, chances are it didn't belong to the priest, then," Arbor said.

"Agreed," Harper said. "I wouldn't think a priest would pick up his tools of the trade in a knickknack shop."

"You talked to the bishop?" Arbor asked.

Harper nodded. Fisher had called on the head of the diocese early in the investigation, but for only a brief discussion.

"He still has no ideas," Harper said. "I had a long discussion with him. Nothing significant. He praised Conzenza. Said he was doing well in his parish considering he had to work without much assistance. There's a shortage of priests these days. Anything at the funeral?"

Arbor gulped some coffee. It was strong and bitter and not as hot as it needed to be. He didn't want it to stay in his mouth very long.

"Nothing obvious," he said.

"We're not getting anywhere," Harper said. Arbor could see he wasn't very happy about being assigned to a case that refused to open up.

Benchley probably didn't give a damn. He looked as if he'd stepped off a television program. As a detective, he made decent money for a single man. He had good looks, and he could impress women with what he did for a living. With a little embellishment his adventures could sound really good in a bar.

Harper, on the other hand, was more severe looking. He wore an inexpensive gray suit with a pale tie that had just a touch of blue in its pattern. His hair was neat, and his fingernails clipped perfectly even.

His concern was with being a good cop. He didn't want a case he couldn't crack, not just because it would look bad on his record, but because it would nag him personally. It had been his own idea to go back and talk to the bishop. He'd been following up the smallest fragments in the case for days.

Arbor knew how he felt. A case that couldn't be broken was like a movie with the last reel missing, or an Agatha

Christie novel with the final page gone, a nagging thing gnawed away at you.

"I hope Fisher's on to something," he said.

Something was nagging Fisher, and he was irritated that he couldn't figure out what it was as he sat in his car watching the front of Doren Terry's house, waiting for everyone to show up after the funeral.

He watched the street for some sign of the car—they'd gone in Hamilton's. Then he looked at his watch, a plain little Timex with a plastic band and a white face.

Finally he turned on the car radio and fumbled with the dial, twisting it from side to side in search of something he wanted to hear, sliding the little orange needle past country and western and grinding guitar music before finally turning it off with a hard twist of the knob.

The sleazy-looking guy was standing at Doren Terry's front door when Fisher turned his attention back to the house. He hadn't noticed the guy's approach, but Fisher determined he must have driven up in a battered Duster, a black car with a white racing stripe. It was parked against the curb in front of the house.

The detective settled a little deeper into his seat as he peered over at the guy.

He looked familiar—greasy hair, dark clothes. Fisher had seen him around the station a few times in the past. Someone ought to be able to place him, he thought.

Fisher watched him carefully, memorizing details of his appearance as the guy rang the bell on Terry's front door. He waited around for several seconds before he finally gave up and headed back to his car.

As he moved, he took out a package of cigarettes and

peeled away the plastic, letting the wrapping flutter away in the breeze as he lit the cigarette.

That made Fisher want one, and he started fumbling through his pockets. He could see the brand of the guy's cigarettes from his seat, not because he had telescopic vision, but because the color of the package was pale green. Once upon a time Fisher had smoked Salems, but he couldn't decide why it seemed so appropriate that the guy he was watching smoked that brand.

He finally shrugged and lit his own cigarette with the spool from the dashboard which miraculously still worked properly.

Gable took the elevator up to Seaview's floor. When he stepped into the hallway, he moved slowly, because there weren't any muscles that didn't ache even though he didn't have any fractures.

After the encounter with Azarius, he'd gone to the emergency room of Aimsley's general hospital, but his injuries hadn't required that he be admitted. In the ER he got a checkup and some pain medicine before they dispatched him back to his home. "Treated and released" as he'd always written in news stories about accident victims.

He hadn't been able to sleep. Two days had passed now, and he was frightened to close his eyes. When he did, he only began to relive the events of the vision. His thoughts kept reminding him of the glimpse of hell.

Gable now had an idea of what Seaview had gone through when he was attacked.

As he passed, several nurses and orderlies looked at him. He wasn't sure if it was because of his appearance—he was unshaven, his hair shooting wildly away from his head—or of the look in his eyes, the look of terror he knew must be lurking there.

The hypothetical situations he had been considering were no longer a matter of speculation. All of it was suddenly very real, more real than it had seemed in all of his thinking up until this point. Azarius had used his own imagination against him, showing images of damnation. He found it hard to accept. What could have been more terrifying?

He knew it had not been a real journey to some nether realm, but that offered no solace. When he was not remembering the flames, he was recalling the dark angel's hideous, melting countenance. Even that had been drawn from Gable's own nightmares, born out of horror-movie matinees and television broadcasts of old films. Yet Azarius had served his purpose well. He had planted seeds of fear and rattled Gable's self-assurance. All of it had created sensations difficult to overcome.

Seaview was sitting in the chair beside his bed with a legal pad and some books spread across his lap.

He wore a faded terry-cloth robe over his blue and white striped pajamas, but his face seemed bright and alert.

When he looked up, however, his expression displayed his shock at Gable's appearance.

"What happened?"

Gable sat down on the bed, slowly.

"What happened?" Seaview repeated.

"I went to talk to the girl. I wound up having an encounter with Azarius."

"How?"

"It was like he got inside my mind."

A look of dismay crossed the professor's features. "You shouldn't have let that happen."

"I know."

He put his pad aside. "Gable, I know you don't believe

in this sort of thing, but if he gets access to your mind, he can possess you."

"Maybe he didn't want me, then. I thought for a while he was going to destroy me."

"Tell me about it."

Gable quickly recounted the events he had experienced, describing when he could the sensations that had accompanied his visions.

"Something must be stopping him, Gable."

"I don't see what you mean."

"Something is intervening, something that's keeping Azarius from taking the girl. The same thing protected you. The lawyer wasn't so lucky."

Gable shook his head. "But I don't see what you're talking about."

"God. The spirit of light."

"Why would God single me out?"

"Maybe He has some special purpose for you, something He wants you to do, and there's an intervention taking place. You're not an overtly religious man, but your beliefs are essentially pure." Seaview smiled. "Maybe God sees potential in you. Maybe the roots of your belief are strong enough to protect you. Faith is a more powerful force than you realize."

"Maybe."

"The same thing has kept the girl from total possession. What she's been experiencing, from what you describe, is spiritual oppression. The angel hasn't been able to penetrate her beliefs totally. He's wearing her down. He'll do the same with you if you allow it, if you don't prepare yourself."

Seaview picked up a glass of juice that was on the arm of his chair. "You're either blessed or lucky. You should never have tried to go against Azarius. If he was able to establish contact with you, you were tampering where you didn't belong. You're lucky you didn't get killed, or worse.

"Azarius is a created being; he's not as powerful as God, so that's where your salvation, if you will, came from. You may be called to a further confrontation."

"What purpose can I serve?"

"You're a writer. You can tell people what you know, save others from the assaults and beguilings of demons."

"I don't know about that. This is real, Leonard. Very real. I know you're ordained and everything, but this is outside your scope. There are experts on this sort of thing. Doesn't the Catholic Church still do exorcisms? I mean, is that real or is it just stuff that's made up in movies?"

"The Catholic Church does them, yes. So do other churches. You also have a number of professional exorcists who operate on their own, not to mention the practices some Fundamentalists undertake. It's often said the results of some of the efforts are more harmful than positive to the individuals. There was a case of a child's eye being gouged out during one of those ceremonies. And some people tried to exorcise a child with Down syndrome. Ignorance also is a weapon of evil.

"Then there are parapsychologists who supposedly approach matters from a scientific standpoint. I don't think any of those are what we need here. You can't approach the Catholic Church very easily, and you don't want some mentally misguided tent preacher. None of this is to be taken lightly. Exorcisms aren't games. Besides, possession isn't what we've got here."

"Why couldn't we find someone who really knows what he's doing? There must be somebody? If all this is real, someone has had to have dealt with it before."

"I feel it. I've prayed about it. This is for us to handle.

Not for someone else. And we can. The Lord doesn't let you be tested more than you can bear.''

''Leonard, I'm not terribly disposed to accepting your intuitions as a decree from God in this matter. It occurs to me that the uninitiated shouldn't take up the gauntlet against superior forces.''

''All men have authority over demons through the intervention of Christ. It's just a matter of claiming it.''

''I can't accept it being that cut and dried. Azarius is powerful.''

''Then start thinking about it. The time is coming. Let me try to get you ready. Azarius will come for you. He's begun his inroads. If you don't prepare yourself, when he launches his attack you'll be destroyed, and so will all of those he seeks. 'Seeking whom he may devour.' ''

Gable swallowed.

''We've got to do something, Gable. Something's going to happen. Something bad.''

Leonard spoke with the fervor of a revival preacher as he leaned forward in his chair. The veins at his temples throbbed and his cheeks were growing red, but Gable couldn't discount what he was saying, not after what had gone on.

''What do we have to do?'' he asked finally.

Salem took one last, slow drag on the joint, letting the smoke nestle in his lungs for several seconds before exhaling. Then he licked his thumb and flicked out the end of the cigarette before tucking it into the pocket of his jacket.

He swayed gently as he pulled himself to his feet. Before he could walk, he had to lean against the wall of the alley for a few moments to steady himself.

324

When his wave of dizziness passed, he straightened his clothes and moved out onto the street, walking slowly.

The sky was gray, fading quickly to darkness. With nightfall Aimsley's streets became deserted. There were a few people over near the hotel, there for the restaurant, but that was it. Moments like this made Salem wonder what he was doing in Aimsley.

He longed for crowds, for the rush of people, the excitement that crowds generated. He'd stood in Times Square before, just watching the masses jostle about, and he missed that sensation now.

Moments of emptiness sometimes plagued Salem, moments in which he did not know what to do with himself. There were times he hated to be alone, times that isolation became agony and he wanted to lash out at someone.

Thrusting his hands into his pockets, he began to walk a little faster as he started turning over in his mind places he might go—bars where he might find friends or other rendezvous points. Anywhere he might find people would be suitable. Even old Doren Terry would have been good company. Pity he'd missed Doren when he'd dropped by to see him. That would have given the old boy a nice surprise. While Terry had told him never to come to his home, Salem did not feel bound by that proclamation.

He threaded his way through the narrow downtown streets quickly, planning to head up the stretch of road that curled out of the downtown area along a strip of taverns where he might find people he could raise glasses with, women he could fondle and enjoy.

With his mind slightly fogged from the weed, he didn't hear the footsteps as they echoed along the concrete sidewalk behind him.

His mind was still spinning from his drags on the cigarette. He smiled to himself and began to sing the refrain from a song he'd learned as a youngster.

He was stepping in time with his music when he finally became aware of a figure moving up behind him.

He stopped in his tracks and whirled around, frightened at first, then grinned broadly, his mouth spreading back from his yellowed teeth.

He did a slight bow, miming a cap with a sweeping gesture of one hand.

"Well, hello there," he said. "Good to see you. I've got a bit of joint left if you're interested. It'd be a nice gesture, to show we're friends, eh?"

The knife was protruding from his stomach so suddenly that he thought it was his imagination, a delusion created by the marijuana.

The weapon became real only when he began to feel the pain and warmth of his blood coursing out over his skin. It bubbled out around the blade and spread across the front of his shirt before spilling down over his belt buckle.

He tried to speak, but he tasted the blood in his throat. Suddenly it was drooling across his lips as well. In a way he was fascinated. It was just like the movies. Just like some harlot encountering Jack the Ripper.

Except it had always been funny in the movies, enjoyable. This was different. He looked over at his attacker with a pleading look in his eyes, but he found no sympathy or compassion.

He tried to speak, but the words wouldn't form. The pain was too great. It gnawed its way up through his abdomen, triggering impulses in his brain that became overwhelming. He tumbled forward into an unconsciousness from which he would not return. He met no angels.

* * *

Having the bodyguard in the living room made Jennifer nervous, but that feeling was more acceptable than the fear she'd had to live with the past several days, and it eased the worry of imposing on Gable.

There were things he had to take care of in his own life. Now he was free to pursue his research with Leonard Seaview, and she was free to work on her paper. She hoped all of the tension would be over soon so she and Gable could let their relationship develop along a more natural course. If there was to be love, she wanted it to blossom between them, not be forced out of desperation.

Gable had called earlier to make sure everything was all right, saying he was going to be out for a while. She found herself hoping it was concern in his voice and not obligation.

Now, while Gardner watched television, Jennifer found herself in her bedroom eyeing Gable's driveway. She didn't expect him to drop over tonight, but she thought it might be nice just to catch a glimpse of him.

The night was heavy. The darkness seemed to envelop the land beyond her window. The shadows were scattered like patches of midnight, some so black that they seemed to have a density, and that made her mind wander.

Somewhere in the distance there was thunder, still threatening even though there was yet no sign of rain.

The thunder was enough. She felt a chill run down her spine and picked up an afghan from the foot of her bed to drape around her shoulders.

In her mind's eye she could picture again that long, dark hallway that came in her dreams whenever there was a storm, a hallway that seemed to stretch toward eternity as she felt her way along it, running because she knew someone was in pursuit, not moving fast but coming along behind her at a slow, steady pace.

And she could not seem to get anywhere along the hall-way no matter how hard she tried.

She looked back and could see the figure coming after her, but she couldn't make out a face. There was just the outline and something familiar.

Turning, she continued to run along the hallway. Her breath was labored now, her lungs aching, and there was a pain in her side—the pain that always came when she ran too hard. It dug into her abdomen like a knife.

Then she saw it—a doorway. Hurrying to it, she rattled the knob and, miraculously, it opened. She went stumbling inside, into darkness.

It was a small room, dusty with cobwebs. Old magazines littered the floor and a small bed sagged in the corner. Just above the bed there was a tiny window, and through it she could see the rain. The lightening flashed in like a strobe.

Something had happened here—something horrible. Suddenly she wanted very badly to leave this memory, step back out of the dream, but she could not. She forced herself to remain, trying to prolong the scenario in hopes of finding answers.

In her mind Jennifer studied the images of the room, so vivid that they seemed real—the splintering plank floor, the musty odor of the mattress and the cobwebs, the flicker of light across the faded pages of the magazines, then suddenly the sound of footsteps in the hallway outside.

Air rushed into her lungs as she spun around toward the doorway, and fear paralyzed her as she saw a figure standing before her. She almost screamed but stifled the sound in her throat as she realized there was a mirror beside the door. It was just her own reflection.

But the footsteps were real. She stopped just outside the rickety door and slowly the knob began to rattle again.

The creak of the hinges coincided with a loud belch of

thunder as the door pushed inward and light from the hall-way spilled through the room.

She was blinded, unable to make out the features of the figure outlined in the doorway. Her arms were raised in front of her, trying to block the advance. It was futile. Her fear tensed her muscles, leaving her unable to struggle.

Hands closed around her upper arms, lifting her from her feet and tossing her back onto the lumpy mattress of the old bed.

Clouds of dust curled up into the air when her weight struck the bed. She began to choke, coughing as she tried to scream. She was unable to find her voice.

And the hands moved over her, gripping the neckline of her blouse, ripping it away, briefly caressing her bared flesh, then moving to her jeans, tearing them open. She kicked and swung her arms forward with her fists clenched, but her strength wasn't great enough.

The hands touched her, violating her body. She tried again to scream, but her bra was ripped away from her breasts and stuffed into her mouth. She could only tilt her head backward, could see only the rain against the narrow panes of the window and the lightning, could hear only the thunder.

"Jennifer."

Gardner's words made her jump. She opened her eyes and stood up from the edge of the bed.

"Is everything okay?"

She was out of breath, and a thin sheen of perspiration had spread across her brow.

"You looked like you were having a bad dream," he said.

"Not exactly," she said. "Just a bad memory." She raised her hand to her brow to mop away some of the moisture. "It was pretty vivid," she said.

"Maybe you should try to rest," he said.

"Yes. I think I'll go to bed."

He smiled and nodded and left the doorway.

Jennifer shrugged the afghan away from her shoulders and moved to the window.

Gable's car had still not appeared in the driveway. There was no use waiting any longer. It was silly to sit up like this.

Silly, too, to subject herself to nightmares. Or were they memories? Were they real? Her hands were still trembling as she reached up and drew the curtains closed.

The eyes watched through the window. The time was near. The body-guard would not be an insurmountable obstacle. Nothing would when the moment arrived.

And that moment would be soon. Everything had to be completed soon, all of the situations corrected.

Any possible obstacles had to be removed.

Fisher's raincoat was making him sweat, but he knew if he left it in the car there'd be a flood, so he just wore it open, letting in as much air as he could as he ducked under the yellow ribbon that marked the cordon of the police line around the murder scene. The small area beside the road-way was crowded with people who scurried about like ants— lab people, the police photographer, and God knew who else.

The television crews and the news people were hanging around on the fringes, stalking the perimeter like vultures after carrion, Fisher thought, and cursed them under his breath. If it rained on them, that might make it all worth-while.

That thought of hardship coming to people he didn't like made it all a little easier for him to accept the rumble of the distant thunder and the gloomy gray look in the clouds. A storm had been threatening for days now without delivering a single punch. When it broke, Fisher was afraid there was going to be a heavy rain, and most of Aimsley was a low-lying area.

When he reached the body, a coroner's investigator pulled back the bloodstained sheet to give him a look at the face.

Fisher gave the investigator a nod, and the man let the sheet slide through his fingers to fall back into place.

The face belonged to the man Fisher had seen at Doren Terry's house, all right. He had no doubt even though the features were considerably paler now.

The identity of this victim confirmed for Fisher that there was a connection between this stabbing and other aspects of his case.

The big detective turned away as he saw the deputy coroner open his kit and take out a long needle that would be plunged into the corpse's heart.

Harper, in a blue suit that fit him almost too perfectly to be true, was standing over to one side of the murder scene, questioning the elderly black man who'd found the body while on his way to work.

He was a small man, his face dappled with fuzzy gray stubble. His chin jutted out too far, the way chins did when their owners had lost their teeth. He wore a faded sweater and a baseball cap, and his pants looked like he could have accommodated two other people in there with him comfortably.

Harper said the man's name was Nicky.

Fisher gave him a nod. "What time you'd find him, Nicky?"

He spoke from deep in his chest, his voice a hollow sound.

331

"About five-thirty, I guess. I has to be at the store by six and it takes about a half hour to walk there from my house."

Fisher ran his finger under his nose to quell an itch.

"What's his name?"

He expected the answer from Harper, but it was the old man who answered.

"They call him Salem," the old man said. "He was a mean one."

"Did you see anybody around here when you found him?"

"Nobody."

"So you think he had a lot of enemies?"

"Lots of people disliked him."

"You heard of anybody who'd want to kill him?"

"I don't know that anybody disliked him that much."

Fisher handed the old man his card.

"Give me a call if you think of anything."

"I will."

Turning, the old man moved away, but stopped to mingle with the crowd and watch the action. Finding the body had been the highlight of his week. It probably wouldn't take the news people long to latch on to him.

Fisher wheeled around to look at Harper.

"What's the word?" Fisher asked. "Cause of death?"

"Knife wound. This could definitely be related to our case."

"Could be." Fisher nodded, a sarcastic look on his face. "I saw this guy yesterday, and I wondered what somebody like him would be doing in Doren Terry's neighborhood. I find that kind of interesting. Don't you, Harper?"

"Yes sir."

"They find anything on the body?" Fisher asked.

"Street drugs. He had a wallet. It had a prophylactic in it, an expired driver's license. Few other things."

"At least he won't die of AIDS now. Anything about Doren Terry?"

"There was a paper with some phone numbers. We haven't had a chance to run them down yet."

"Raise me on the radio when you do. I want to know who he's been in contact with. Find out if he was a Catholic. Find out if he knew Father Conzenza."

"Yes sir."

"And where the hell's Arbor anyway?"

"I don't know, sir."

"Find his ass, too. I'm going to talk to Doren Terry."

CHAPTER 23

Arbor found Gable sitting in the porch swing with a worn-looking Bible and a stack of other materials spread across his lap. It was ten A.M., and the kid looked tired, as if he'd been poring over the books for a long time.

"Thinking of going into the seminary?" Arbor asked. He wondered when Gable had slept last.

Gable sighed. "Seaview has me going through all of this."

"Why?"

Gable shifted his weight around in the swing. "It's kind of hard to say."

"What are you? The Exorcist? You two going demon-hunting?"

"We think the demon may come to us."

Arbor had to laugh. "I don't know about that," he said. "It's weird. You haven't heard from Vincent again?"

"No. Some other things have happened." He paused. "Weird things."

Arbor studied the writer's eyes. There was a deep look of anxiety. What he had mistaken for weariness was more a vestige of fear.

"What happened?"

"Let's just say I'm beginning to believe more and more."

"Well, look. There's been another murder. Same type as far as method. A street thug was the victim."

"Any suspects?"

"No. We can't draw a connection. I haven't talked to Fisher about it yet. I just got the call. I thought I'd check on you."

"I'm obviously not fine. My sanity is being tested. I quit my damned newspaper job to get my head back together, and now suddenly I'm confronting . . ."

"You're beginning to take all that stuff seriously?"

Gable got up and walked to the edge of the porch. "It's real, Isaac. I don't know how your murders are tied to it all, but something very wrong is happening."

Arbor raised his hand to his neck, massaging gently. The tension was causing an ache. "I wish I could see it your way, Gable. All I know is I've got a job to do."

"I didn't believe it either, or at least I was skeptical. I'm not crazy, man. It's just that stuff happens, stuff there's no explanation for."

Arbor raised his hands. "I don't think you're crazy," he said. "But I have to go with the tangibles. Maybe I'm an agnostic."

"They're no atheists in the foxholes."

"Right." Arbor smiled.

"We get too tied up to tangibles," Gable said. "We forget about the stories of evil. We think they're fairy tales."

"That's easy to do. I'm sorry, but I've been at this all too long. People murder people, Gable. It happens. They get mad, the weather changes. You know how many people get shot on the first hot day of spring? You wake up on one of those mornings when the humidity is high, and you know you can just settle back and wait because somebody's stack's going to blow. That's not demons."

335

"You're talking about the typical homicides. What about the ones you can't explain? Why is it so hard to believe there's some kind of evil out there? Something that feeds on our foibles?"

"I don't know what to tell you. All I can do, is try to find meaning where I can. Some things I can't answer. You look your way, and I'll look mine. If you find anything, call me."

He left Gable on the porch and walked back to his car. He pushed their conversation from his mind. The supernatural wasn't tied to his case. He knew that.

He guided his car carefully back down Gable's drive and turned down the street, heading back toward his office.

Fisher was going to be hopping now that there'd been another slaying, and he didn't cherish the idea of confronting the big man. Let the young detectives deal with him.

He cruised along, trying to think of anything he knew about the case that might link up with the man named Salem, but nothing came to mind. The pieces should be falling into place by now, but instead, everything was just a big jumble of pieces.

He was half listening to the radio when, for some reason, the movement in the trees beside the road caught his eye.

He wasn't sure what it was, but he pulled over onto the narrow shoulder and got out quickly.

Moving slowly back along the gravel, he began to peer into the grove of small oak trees. Beyond the grove a drainage gutter stretched off into the distance.

Arbor eased his jacket back away from the revolver strapped to his hip and rested his hand on the butt of the gun as he continued toward the trees.

The movement he had detected had stilled, but he sensed there was someone there. Or some*thing*, in light of his recent

336

conversation with Gable. He felt the hair on his neck prickle. No atheists in the foxholes.

He stopped a few feet away from the trees, watching carefully for any sign of movement. There was nothing. Only stillness.

"Hello," he said. "Anybody there?"

No sound.

He flipped back the leather band over his pistol before he took another step. Then he paused, and before he stepped again, he slipped the gun from the holster, readying it in his hand. His fingers curled easily around the grip.

Even the wind was still, and despite the looming clouds the thunder—which had been so constant over the last few days—ceased.

He slowly raised his hand and pushed back the branches in front of him, fluttering away the thick green oak leaves to reveal the contorted, leering face of Walker Vincent.

Arbor jerked backward as if an electrical charge had been shot through him. The face sent a wave of terror down his throat, burning a trail through his abdomen to make his stomach leap.

He pushed the gun forward, leveling it toward the attorney's chest.

Vincent only laughed, his lips peeling back away from his teeth in a grin.

"What's the matter, Isaac? Are you frightened?"

The voice sounded as if it were coming from far away. It was deep and dry, a coarse sound that produced cold sweat on Arbor's forehead.

"What's wrong with you, Walker?"

The lawyer only laughed. "Do you have to ask?"

Arbor felt his legs trembling. He flexed his fingers to tighten his grip on the pistol.

337

"Walker, you need to come with me. It's time to get you some help."

Vincent laughed again, this time so hard that he tilted his head back. A foul stench touched Arbor's nostrils. It reminded him of the smell of decaying flesh, the smell that had turned his stomach one July when they'd pulled a body out of a car trunk where it had been hidden for a week.

The lawyer's clothes were dingy. He looked like he'd been sleeping outside for several days. His face was unshaven and there was something about his eyes that wasn't right. Arbor avoided looking at them.

"Walker, you're sick."

"Fuck you and the horse you rode in on. There's nothing wrong with me."

Arbor started to take a step forward, but Vincent reached out suddenly and seized his wrist, twisting it hard to one side to throw the investigator off balance.

Arbor stumbled and landed on his knees in a puddle of mud. His gun slipped from his fingers and clattered along the drainage canal.

Before he could move to retrieve it, Vincent's hands closed around him, grasping his crotch and neck to lift him into the air.

He struggled but was unable to free himself. He closed his eyes as he felt Vincent's muscles tense. He was hurled suddenly through the air, crashing down into the canal.

Arbor picked himself up slowly and turned around to find Vincent standing only a short distance away, arms folded.

"Go back to your friend Tyler, the writer, and tell him to stay the fuck away from the girl if he values his life." Vincent smiled. "If he values what is dear to him."

Arbor shook his head to clear his thoughts. He couldn't actually believe what was happening, yet the things that Gable had spoken about . . .

338

"Yes," Vincent said. "Frightening, isn't it, that there could be more to the world than is dreamed of in your philosophy. Of course, in your position you can't afford to tell anyone but Gable. Mention it to anyone else and you'd look like a fool. Like a boy who's listened to too many Negro spirituals."

"You bastard."

"Am I?"

Vincent threw a punch, sudden and sharp. It connected with Arbor's solar plexus, doubling the investigator as the wind rushed out of his lungs.

"You'd better run," Vincent said. "If I catch you, I may do terrible things. I'm a spook. If you don't take the message to Gable, you're of no use to me, except perhaps as a plaything."

Arbor tried to straighten himself, but before he could manage, Vincent had suddenly moved behind him. Raising his foot, the lawyer planted the soul of his shoe against Arbor's back, shoving the investigator forward.

Landing with a thud, Arbor wasted no time in scrambling forward, moving away from his attacker. He was in no shape now to retaliate, not considering what Vincent had done to the two uniformed officers.

Finally getting his feet under him, Arbor began to run. He couldn't manage much speed, but he bounced along, clutching the pain in his midsection.

He'd traveled only a few feet before the shot rang out. He heard it whiz past him and strike the concrete a few yards ahead of him, then ricochet once off the canal wall.

He didn't look back. He just kept running.

When the next shot was fired, it ricocheted also, and now Vincent, who was far back along the canal's length, began to laugh heartily.

Arbor ignored him and reached up the wall of the canal,

339

grabbing its edge. It was deeper than he'd realized, and he had to struggle to lift his weight upward.

He lost his grip twice and slid back down before he managed to get his legs over the rim and lift himself out onto the ground.

The trees were thicker here and the area was shrouded in shadow. Arbor dropped down to a sitting position and gasped for breath. There were no more gunshots. He listened, but there was also no sound of anyone moving in the canal.

Slowly he regained his breath and started to get to his feet. He was in mid-motion when he saw Vincent's feet. He heard the laugh.

The blow, sudden and sharp against his skull, sent him quickly into unconsciousness.

Seaview used the rail that stretched the length of the hospital corridor for support as he moved, taking slow steps. The tears in his flesh ached with each step because movement stretched the skin, but he struggled forward.

He tried to smile as the nurses passed, but his face instead formed a grimace.

Other patients looked over at him with sympathy, thankful their own illnesses had not left them in such a state. He ignored the stares as he pressed onward.

Finally he reached the nurses' station, a narrow glass box decorated with silver clipboards and cardiac monitors.

Seaview leaned against the counter at the window and pressed his lips close to the little open circle in the glass.

"When am I going to get out of here?" he asked the nurse. It was a question he could have asked over the intercom in his room, but the struggle to walk had proven he could get himself around. That had been something he'd needed to know.

The nurse smiled. "Not until the doctor determines that it's all right, Mr. Seaview. We've been through this before. You've had a traumatic experience. He wants you here in case there are complications."

"There aren't going to be any damned complications. I want to go home."

"Mr. Seaview, please. It won't do you any good to get upset."

"I have things I have to take care of. Will you please check with the doctor? Tell him it's important."

"I'll see what I can do, but it's still his decision."

Things were about to happen. He couldn't afford to remain confined in the hospital. Gable might need him.

Slowly he made his way back to his room and opened his closet, getting his street clothes ready. He didn't want any delays when the time came.

Without speaking, Fisher pushed past some businessmen in dark suits when he stepped off the elevator into the suite of offices occupied by Doren Terry and Associates.

The receptionist, realizing he had no intention of observing office protocol, was already on her feet when he reached her desk, so he pulled his badge wallet from his jacket and flipped it open at her.

"I need to see Doren Terry."

"I'm sorry, Mr. Terry is in with someone."

"Buzz him. Tell him it's the police." The tone in his voice and the expression he wore prevented further opposition.

She sat down again at the console. Quickly her manicured fingers danced over the keys, and she spoke briefly to

Terry over an intercom, then directed Fisher back to Terry's office.

While they summoned Terry, Fisher strolled over to the window that looked out across the city. The view gave a feeling of looking out over an empire. Perhaps it was Terry's motivation for conquest.

Fisher turned when Terry entered the room. He wore no jacket and his sleeves were rolled up to the elbows. He was trying to look preoccupied. Fisher didn't buy the act.

"What's going on?" the businessman demanded. "I had to leave a conference."

"I'm investigating murders. Several of them. I have something that may interest you. A man they call Salem was found dead."

He rattled out the information quickly, wanting to see how Terry would respond. He didn't have to wait long for a reaction.

A look of shock crossed Terry's features, but he quickly averted his face from the policeman and began to fumble with a folder he was holding. "I don't know anything about it."

"That's funny. I was in front of your house the other day, and he dropped by. I'd run into him before, but I couldn't place him. All I could think about was how bad I wanted a cigarette. Salem, get it? That's why I remember."

Fisher slipped his hands into the pockets of his slacks. "He tried to get in, but you weren't home. Can you explain that, Mr. Terry?"

"I'm afraid I can't."

Raising a hand, Fisher pushed his hat back from his forehead. "You didn't know Salem? His real name being Eldon Reilly?"

"No."

"What about your son?"

"I don't know who all of my son's friends are."

"Well, I guess I'll be asking him. Who knows what we'll turn up when we find where Salem lived and go through his things." Fisher took a deep breath. "I need to talk to your son anyway. It seems he had some knowledge about our investigation that was never released to the media. He could have picked it up somewhere else. You never know. After all, you are friends with the family, but it makes me wonder. Maybe I'll haul his ass in for questioning. It's not firm ground, but it's a reason, and once I start asking questions, who knows what I'll find?"

"I hope that's not a threat," Terry said, but there was no conviction in his voice.

"I'm just doing my job," Fisher said. "I have no vendettas. All I want is the killer."

He headed for the door, taking slower steps than he would have normally, giving Terry time to think.

"Mr. Fisher."

Fisher stopped and pivoted slowly to face Terry.

"I did know Salem."

"And?"

"Mr. Fisher, this is very delicate. There are things I don't want to come out."

"I'm investigating a murder. Several murders. Skeleton closets aren't privileged."

"There are things I . . ."

Fisher's expression softened slightly. He realized Terry was on the brink of talking. "I'll do what I can," the detective promised.

Terry placed his folder on his desktop and folded his hands together. "Mr. Fisher, my son has a weakness. I've known about it for some time, and I've tried to protect him."

"What is it? Does he like to kill priests?"

"Nothing like that. It's women. He has unusual . . . tendencies, and this Salem set him up and photographed it. He's been selling the negatives to me one frame at a time. I've been paying to protect Hamilton. He's to follow in my footsteps. I couldn't allow him to be ruined. Not by a few moments of weakness."

"They have therapy for that sort of thing, Mr. Terry."

"But if word of that leaked out. No. It had to be covered up."

"To what point? At what cost? The loss of lives? How involved were you with Salem?"

"Just in the payoffs."

"But your son? These tendencies? How often has he succumbed to them?"

Terry swallowed, and squirmed in his chair. Rings of perspiration were becoming visible under his arms. There was an expression of anxiety on his face and, in his eyes, an even deeper look of pain.

"I couldn't say. He went to college in New Jersey. There's no telling what went on while he was there, close to New York. It's a difficult knowledge to hold when it's your son. You have to wonder what he's done. I didn't know about any of it before that man Salem appeared."

"He was providing a service your son had gotten used to with New York hookers."

"Mr. Fisher, please. My wife was an alcoholic. She deserted our family. That had a very bad impact on my son."

Fisher stared across the desk, his face twisted into a harsh snarl. He didn't have evidence, but a scenario was forming in his mind. He didn't speak it aloud because he didn't want to set Terry up for filing a lawsuit, but he wondered.

"Your son was a Catholic?"

"Yes."

He nodded. There were some more things to check, but he felt very close to answers now. He raised his fingers to

344

the brim of his hat. "Thank you for your time, Mr. Terry. I may be back. Right now I need to find your son. I'll try to question him in private. I'll be as delicate as I can."

"But Mr. Fisher . . ."

Fisher didn't look back. He walked past the receptionist, out of the office, and back to the elevator.

When he reached his car in the parking lot, the dark clouds seemed to rip open. For a while the rain had subsided, but now it fell heavy and fast, accompanied by croaks of thunder that seemed like the growl of faraway dragons.

The roar of the dragons awakened Gable where he had fallen asleep on his living room couch. It was the first sleep he'd had in days, and in awakening, he realized he'd not really rested. Though he could not remember dreams, there was a lingering sensation of unpleasantness.

He didn't get up right away. The curtains above him were open, so he looked out at the sky. Night was falling, hurried on by the thick clouds and the rain.

The rain was falling in sheets, swept into diagonal patterns by the wind. It looked like the rain that fell in movies, that hurried, concentrated rain produced by machine.

Slowly he sat up, then got to his feet and stood in front of the window. The weather had been kind for so many days, the town was due for the harsh weather, but Gable wondered if there was something more to this. It still seemed to be an ill omen, a portent of some evil.

If it wasn't, he wondered why it had to come now, at the peak of his anxiety, when the horrors were drawing near. Soon the gray would fade into the black of night, and he feared the storm would increase in intensity before it calmed. It would probably not pass before morning.

Finally he left the window and moved into the kitchen, took a Coke from the refrigerator, and sat down at the table.

He could still watch the rain through the narrow windows there. He sipped the soft drink slowly. He couldn't quite understand the feeling of tension in his stomach. It was almost like an expectation.

He couldn't shake it. He wanted to get back to the things Seaview had told him to study, but he felt drawn elsewhere. He needed to check on Dareena. He wasn't sure why, just knew he'd better go to her. It was as if he were being impelled by a hidden force.

That made the short hairs on the back of his neck stand on end. Was there someone in the room with him? He wheeled around, only to find himself staring into empty space.

Was Azarius here somewhere? Had the time come, the moment Seaview had warned about? What would he find at Dareena's? He wasn't ready to face the devil again.

He moved into the bedroom and peered into the mirror. There was nothing there, no flicker of other dimensions or dark angels. Only his own haggard image stared back at him. There were ugly circles under his eyes and thickening stubble on his chin, but he sighed with relief.

It lasted only a second, because the feeling returned, the nagging urge to go to Dareena. He sat on the foot of the bed, trying to reason things out. There was no explanation. At least none that he wanted to accept.

Again he moved into the living room, where he picked up the phone and dialed the hospital. Twice the signal indicating ringing sounded in his ear, then the beeping tone of a malfunction seeped into his ear, followed by a recorded voice that claimed the number had been disconnected.

He looked the number up in the phone book and again

346

reached the recording. Maybe it was the storm. He wouldn't be able to contact Seaview.

And the nagging was getting worse. He wanted to sit down and think, but he couldn't bring himself to get settled. He paced the narrow living room briefly.

His fears was still bubbling along. Perspiration was flowing freely, soaking through his shirt and sending icy drops down his sides.

Finally he got his jacket. There was nothing else to do.

Jennifer heard Gable's car leaving the driveway and looked out her bedroom window. She wondered where he was going. It was unsettling to see him leaving in the rain with so many things expected to happen.

She pulled the curtain closed tightly and moved away from the window, trying to shut out the sounds of the rain. She was frightened, and memories kept threatening to rush in upon her.

Suddenly she was afraid the memories might break through and she would understand what horrible things were buried within her. She didn't want that.

Not knowing was better.

It was easier.

The windshield wipers tried to swat back the rain, but Fisher found it almost impossible to see through the storm as it worsened. He had to drive slowly, and night had begun to take its grip on the sky when he finally reached Hamilton Terry's apartment complex, a full-luxury development with wrought iron ornamentation and a maze of walkways amid the various buildings that were scattered around the acreage, each with English-sounding names like Middlebrook.

The detective pulled into a reserved parking slot near the breezeway of Hamilton's section and ran from the car to the shelter of the building known as Wessex.

There he walked along the breezeway until he found Hamilton's door and knocked on it, three quick thuds. He had to wait a few seconds before the young man showed up in faded jeans and a brightly colored T-shirt.

As he peered out into the hallway, Hamilton adjusted his eyeglasses on the bridge of his nose. "Can I help you?"

"I have some more questions," Fisher said. "May I come in?"

Hamilton stepped back from the doorway and let Fisher walk inside to drip on the carpet.

"Being awfully formal, aren't you, officer?" Hamilton said, closing the door.

Fisher ignored the sarcasm and shook his coat a bit, dispensing raindrops in a quick spray.

"The other night, you mentioned something," he said. "Something you could have picked up from several sources, I suppose, but it struck me odd that you knew it, for some reason. Just a nagging little sensation. I checked the newspaper, and it hasn't shown up in print. It was not released to the media.

"Your father and Jennifer Nelson's father are partners, but you haven't spoken to your old man very much about the murders, have you? I have what you'd call a gut hunch on that. I'm a good judge of people, and looking at your dad and looking at you, I just don't see you conversing on that."

"No. My father and I don't talk that much about that sort of thing. We talk business. That line of conversation. In a lot of ways we aren't emotionally close."

"Do you know he was being blackmailed for your sake?"

"No." Hamilton's mouth dropped open. At first Fisher

348

thought the kid was exaggerating to be smart again but then realized he was genuinely surprised.

The detective decided to keep him off balance. "That's a surprise? Well, how did you know Jennifer Nelson had received threatening phone calls? It wasn't in the paper. I checked that carefully."

Hamilton shrugged. "I heard it somewhere."

"Or did you make them?"

"No. I did not." Nervously he ran his hand through his hair. Most of it fell back into place as it slipped through his fingers.

"Your father told me you have some weaknesses," Fisher said. "Some unusual vices, shall we say? Would threatening an old girlfriend be one of them? That make your dick get hard, boy?"

"No. No."

"What about killing her priest, someone she might have confessed things to. Things you wouldn't want to be repeated, but things that might slip out if he left the priesthood and didn't have to keep confidences anymore?"

"No. Dammit. You have no right to come here and make those accusations. He used to be my priest, too." Hamilton was clenching his fists at his sides now, and the color in his face was rushing to a bright scarlet.

Fisher didn't back off. "If you didn't hear it from your father, how did you know about the threatening calls?"

"I don't remember. You know how people talk. Word gets around."

Fisher changed tracks again to keep the kid on the defensive. "Did you know the waitress who was killed?"

Hamilton clenched his teeth. "Yes. I won't lie. I knew her." His voice was rising. He took a few steps, not going anywhere, just regrouping. He looked down at the floor as if he were trying to reassemble lost thoughts that might have dropped there. Finally he seemed to reach a decision. "We were together," he said slowly, and the words were very soft.

"Ah. When?"

"The other night." Hamilton swallowed hard. Suddenly he seemed like a schoolboy caught in some forbidden act and embarrassed by the confession of the deed. "It wasn't the night she was killed," he stressed.

Beneath the glasses his eyes were wide and nervous. The spectacles were wire-rimmed, probably selected to make him look sensitive and vulnerable. At the moment they only accented nervousness and desperation. He folded his arms around himself and continued to stare at nothing. "It may have gotten a little out of hand, but I didn't kill her. She didn't have complaints when I left her."

With his hands in the pockets of his raincoat, Fisher paced around Terry in a semicircle. It was a calculated move, one that made the detective look like he was ready to pounce. He'd used it many times in interrogations. It didn't always pay off, but it didn't hurt. Sometimes it loosened tongues.

"A little out of hand?" he asked. "What'd you have to do to prevent her complaints? Threaten to take her job away?"

Hamilton folded his arms more tightly and looked away from Fisher. "Maybe I should have a lawyer."

"Why'd you beat her up?"

Hamilton at first seemed reluctant to respond to the remark. It had been a reach on Fisher's part, but again he was acting on a hunch. Physical violence was often a manifestation of anger, especially the kind of emotional anger Hamilton was harboring.

Finally the young man seemed unable to restrain his words. He chewed his lips, then looked into the detective's

350

eyes. He was on the verge of tears. "Something just comes over me.

"Women are so vile. Whores." He removed his glasses and Fisher could see something had clicked somewhere back in his brain, triggering those latent emotions.

"The bitches," he said in almost a whisper. His eyes bulged in their sockets. It was a look of near madness, a look that rattled Fisher a little in spite of all the things he'd seen as a cop. There were tough men and mean men, but none scared him like a crazy man. With madness you never knew what you might be up against.

"Did you kill the waitress?" he asked.

"No. I hurt her, I punished the bitch, but I didn't kill her. I don't know who killed her."

"Maybe you got worried she'd tell people and decided to do away with her."

"No. I don't kill people."

"Did your father know about it?"

"No."

"No one could have told him? So that he might want to shut the girl up? Maybe hire Salem to take care of that for him?"

"No. My father would never have anyone harmed."

Fisher let his words come out harsh and loud, pushing. "Not even women? You don't thing he might have some animosity toward women himself since his wife gave him such a hard time?"

"No."

"You're engaged. Aren't you worried your wife will be a problem, too?"

"No. Julia is different. I've known her a long time. I just didn't discover her until now. She's different. I love her. She's good to me." He snapped his fingers. "She heard

351

about the phone calls. She told me. You see. There's an explanation. I didn't hurt anyone. I didn't kill anyone."

"You didn't know Salem was blackmailing your father? Didn't decide to get rid of him?"

"No. Damn you. You keep coming up with things. I haven't killed anyone. I haven't threatened anyone."

Fisher sighed heavily and shook his head. "I think I'd better take you down to the station. If you'll agree to it. We've got a lot more talking to do, and it might be a good idea for you to call your lawyer. We don't want to violate your rights." He nodded toward the small table against the wall. "May I use your phone?"

Hamilton nodded, then buried his face in his hands. He was sweating badly, perspiration beading across his forehead and on his cheeks.

Fisher lifted the receiver but couldn't get a dial tone. He lowered it back to its cradle.

"I'll have to make a call on the car radio," he said. "The rain must have messed up the phones. Do you want to get a coat?"

"Am I under arrest?"

"Not yet. You don't have to go. We could stay here and talk, but that's not to say we won't wind up downtown later."

Hamilton shrugged, moved to a hall closet, and pulled out a lightweight blue windbreaker which he tugged on.

Then he let Fisher lead him from the apartment.

The rain was coming down even harder when they reached the parking lot. From the edge of the breezeway Fisher couldn't see the car. He tightened his grip on Hamilton's arm and started to lead the young man across the lot, but suddenly there was a slice of lightning and a deafening clap of thunder almost as loud as a howitzer.

When it sounded, Hamilton twisted away from Fisher

and began to run along the sidewalk that stretched in front of the buildings.

"Stop," Fisher demanded, but it did no good. Hamilton quickly disappeared into the darkness.

"Dammit," Fisher cursed, and jogged off down the walk himself. He saw Hamilton dart through an opening that led into the pool area and followed, chasing with as much energy as he could muster. He'd skirted departmental physical exams for some time now, and he rarely exercised.

The kid was young and thin and Fisher wasn't up to this kind of chase, but he didn't want to let him get away. In the state Hamilton was in, there was no telling what kind of damage he might do. If the young man were the killer, there might be another body on the slab by morning if Fisher didn't stop him.

He forced his legs to churn hard, carrying him quickly down the sidewalk. The pool area stretched back to another wall, where gateways opened to a walkway that led toward another part of the complex.

Fisher jogged along the edge of the pool, already short of breath and worried about getting confused. The sidewalks in this place were a labyrinth. Losing Hamilton would mean a real problem. He had to get him before he headed back through the maze of buildings, but the boy was nowhere in sight.

For a moment the detective paused. With no sign of Hamilton he wasn't sure which way to run. He stopped at the end of the pool and peered into the water, thinking for a moment the kid might try to drown himself, but there was no sign of that. The pool light was on, causing a blue-green glow. The rainwater splashed along the pool's surface, but Fisher could see into the depths. They were empty, no sign of a sinking body.

He turned and moved on toward the gateway, exiting onto the narrow walkway beyond.

Again there was no sign of Hamilton. The rain poured down on Fisher's hat brim and ran off the edge in front of his face. He blew air through his mouth, letting his lips sputter in disgust.

Spinning, he hurried along the sidewalk, looking for some sign, some clue. A few feet ahead of him there was another opening—the mouth of another breezeway. It was dimly lit. It could have been a place for Hamilton to duck into.

Reaching under his jacket, Fisher tugged out his pistol, keeping it under the folds of his raincoat as he slowly approached the breezeway.

Even though he rarely used the weapon, he wanted it ready. He let his finger curl around the trigger and tighten slightly. The safety was already off.

The wind swept droplets under his hat brim to sting his eyes. Ignoring the sensation, he stepped forward, placing his feet carefully. He wore heavy shoes with thick soles, but when he had to, he could walk silently.

As he moved he became aware of the rare tension brought on by pursuit. He could almost sense that someone was waiting in the shadows just ahead of him. His heart rumbled in his chest.

He was about to step into the breezeway opening when the figure emerged from the darkness there.

In the rain and the dim light Fisher was unable to make out the countenance at first, but he knew it wasn't Hamilton. The build was wrong, and this figure wore a long black raincoat.

The detective was only a few steps away from the man when recognition struck. He stopped walking. His muscles tightened. He squeezed the grip of the gun to reassure himself it was there.

"Walker. This is important. Did you see a kid run by here?"

Vincent just stared at him. Didn't move, didn't show any expression, just stared. Rain had washed his hair down across his forehead. His face was pale, a white mask.

"Dammit. I'm trying to round up a suspect and he's wiry," Fisher said. "You've screwed up bad, don't make it worse."

Vincent began to laugh. "*We* wouldn't want you messing things up either, Fisher."

"What do you mean?"

"You're getting close. You're getting too warm."

There was no inflection in the voice. It was bland, cold. Yet somewhere there was a flicker, some kind of indication of danger.

The rain poured down on both of them, ripped at their skin. It was beginning to chill the detective and to numb him. Perhaps it slowed his reactions.

He started to yank the gun from beneath his raincoat, but his warning had come too late. The pistol was not clear of the garment before Vincent had his own pistol leveled at the detective's chest.

Even in the rain he was too close to miss. He laughed. Fisher felt the horrible sensation of the laugh's affect first.

Then he felt the bullet. It was a sudden pain, a hot pain.

Then he didn't feel anything at all, not the rain and not the concrete as he toppled to the sidewalk.

CHAPTER 24

The rain on Arbor's face helped revive him. He was able to pull himself into a sitting position on the ground. The encounter with Vincent had left him devastated. He had bruises on top of bruises left over from the first attack in the office.

Slowly he lifted himself to his feet. He had to make his way back to the roadway. It was dark, and he was in pain. His body was a weight he didn't have the strength to carry.

As he tried to move, he searched his pockets, but he discovered his car keys were gone. Also missing was his gun. He could only vaguely remember losing it.

It was a bit unusual for a D.A.'s investigator to carry a weapon at all times, but it was a crossover from his police days. He felt naked without his revolver, but a search through the canal to locate it would be hopeless. In his present condition he needed help more than he needed the security of his pistol.

Also, he felt miserable at the thought of his car being gone. Vincent must have taken it, leaving him stranded.

He started walking anyway, forcing himself to keep taking steps, trying to ignore the pain as he moved.

He followed the canal, wondering what he was going to do if his car wasn't on the street. He'd have to flag someone down. If he couldn't get someone to stop, he would be left on foot, and he didn't have the energy or the strength to cover much distance.

That left only one alternative. He had to find his way to Gable's house.

It would take a while, because each step was a labor and provided a new form of pain.

"It was a dark and stormy night."

Gable stood at the window in Dareena's living room, looking out at the rain.

The dark-haired girl nodded. She was in the corner, arms folded. She wore a simple white dress, and her hair fell soft and long against her shoulders. Without makeup her features looked fresh and innocent.

"What's going on?" she asked.

Gable shrugged.

"I was hoping you might know," he said.

She hadn't seemed surprised to see him, as if she'd been expecting him to appear, yet she had no answers about what seemed to be going on.

"No word from your spirit guide?"

"No." She began to rub her hands along her forearms, caressing her flesh nervously with her thumbs.

Gable ran a hand through his hair. "Well, it sure doesn't look like Kansas," he mumbled.

"What are you going to do?"

"I wish I knew." He looked around the room. "Can I use your phone?"

"Sure."

It was on a small table beside the stairs. He dialed the hospital number again. There was static on the line. It rumbled like someone trying to clear his throat, but finally there was a click and the ring signal sounded.

Someone eventually picked up at the hospital switchboard, and he requested Seaview's room.

After several seconds the professor's voice came on the line with a croak. From the sound of it, he'd been sleeping.

"It's Gable."

"Yeah. What's going on?" the teacher asked.

"I'm at Dareena's house. I had this nagging urge to come here. Nothing's happening so far, but I feel like a missionary at a cannibal buffet."

He heard Seaview draw a quick breath.

"It may be time, Gable. I would have liked more time to prepare you, but Azarius may be planning to strike against you in some way. You'd better take a few minutes of prayer, try to prepare yourself, and don't let him tear away your faith. He'll try to make you worship him. Don't crumble to him. If he gets control of you, he can destroy the girl. He can destroy us all, using you probably."

"Why is that?"

"Because he will have defeated you, turned a good man around. There's a power in that unimagined. Be careful. Please."

When he hung up, Gable didn't feel comforted.

When he returned to the living room, Dareena was sitting in an armchair. Her legs were curled under her, her arms folded even more tightly around her.

"What did he say?"

"That we should get ready for something to happen. Where's your grandmother?"

"She went to bed early."

"Maybe it's best to leave her there."

Walking over to another chair, Gable sat, tilting his head backward to stare at the ceiling. He closed his eyes slowly, almost reluctantly, hoping Azarius wouldn't be able to intrude upon his thoughts as he tried to get ready for whatever happened.

Outside, the rain fell harder. The wind increased, and the thunder was like an explosion as the swords of lightning split the night.

And a lone figure stood across the street—oblivious to the sting of the raindrops—watching the house. Watching and waiting.

The time was at hand.

Hamilton ran through the rain, panting. His lungs and muscles ached, but he could not stop. The fear permeated his being. He wanted to cry, wanted also to curl up somewhere away from the storm, away from the storm and away from everything else.

In his mind he still heard the coarse voice of the detective.

The water ran down off his hair, stinging his eyes. His clothes were soaked to his skin, but he kept moving, forcing his legs to go on in spite of the pain.

The policeman might still be after him, might be following him in a car by now.

He had to get away. He didn't want to go to jail, but most of all he didn't want to disappoint his father.

He had to find somewhere safe. He had to find Julia. She was the only decent woman he'd ever known, and he knew

359

she would help him tonight. She would be whatever he needed her to be.

Julia cared about him. She wouldn't let him down.

Jennifer got ready for bed, slipping on a red and white striped nightshirt that fell to just below her knees. It was her favorite, faded slightly from age but soft and comfortable.

She'd had it since she was a senior in high school. It had been purchased for a slumber party.

On her feet she wore ankle socks, also red. Her toes had a tendency to get chilled if she didn't wear socks, no matter how hot it seemed outside. She tried to ignore the sounds of the rain, even as the storm worsened.

Downstairs she could hear Gardner moving about the living room, probably checking the windows. He was a big man, mostly quiet in his manner, but not sinister as she had first believed. He seemed efficient at his work. Her only wish was that his presence would make her feel more comfortable.

She tried to relax as she sat down on her bed. She wasn't ready to try to sleep, but just the quiet helped.

She still wished Gable were back. She'd checked at the window just before undressing, and his house was still dark. She couldn't imagine where he'd gone on a night like this, unless something terrible was happening. She feared for his safety. She didn't know what to believe, but she knew there was something evil happening, something that went beyond the threats she had received.

She was beginning to sense there was something sinister behind the attempts on her life, some force directing them, a force that was guiding events toward a goal of which her death might be only a small part.

With elements of her upbringing intertwining with the lore Seaview had spouted, she envisioned herself a chess piece, a pawn on the board of some dark angel, a figure of shadows that had no heart.

She closed her eyes only for a moment, because other images tried to form, tried to draw her back into the hallways where she had been before. There were realities lurking in the cobwebs which she did not want to surface.

Opening her eyes again, she slid off the bed and moved to the window. Easing the curtain back, she peered over at the darkened house. No sign of Gable.

There was only the rain, still falling hard. It splattered against the window in sheets. It was like looking through the windshield in a car wash. She let the curtain slip back into place.

She didn't see anyone on the street. If anyone was watching, she didn't notice.

Downstairs Gardner sat on the couch, his feet propped on the coffee table atop a stack of magazines. He watched the smoke from his cigarette curl up toward the ceiling and listened for some sound out of the ordinary. He'd checked all the doors and windows. It was a secure house, but it wasn't a fortress.

He checked the .38 in the holster under his arm, making sure he could pull the weapon free quickly if the need occurred. They'd said there were weird aspects to this case, and he didn't want to make any mistakes. Slipups of any kind could be fatal. He couldn't afford to let his guard down.

He looked up when the girl came down the stairs. She was carrying a rag doll tucked under one arm. In the nightshirt and socks she looked much younger than her years.

Her features bore a saddened expression as she walked across the room from the foot of the stairs.

"Is everything all right?" he asked.

"Fine." Her voice was soft and without inflection.

"You want coffee? I brewed a fresh pot."

She shook her head. Then a moment later she looked over at him, a flicker returning to her face. "I'm sorry," she said. "It's just that I hate storms. And so much is going on."

"Storms can be nasty, but you seem to have a little extra contempt."

"Something bad happened to me on a stormy night. When I was younger. I forgot about it, but now I'm remembering it. A little more at a time, sort of like Gregory Peck in that Hitchcock movie. It's something I've blotted out, but it's coming back. I guess I've been afraid of the rain all these years because I've been afraid something bad would happen again when there's a storm."

"Don't worry," Gardner said. "I'm here."

Hamilton's heart sank when he saw that Julia's car wasn't in her parking space. There were no lights on in her house. He ran to the front door and banged on it with his fist until it rattled in its frame, but he got no answer.

Where was she? She hadn't told him she was going anywhere tonight. She should have been there.

He spun away from the door with his fists clenched at his sides, his shoulders rising and falling as the rain gushed down upon him, washing away the tears that formed in his eyes.

He needed her and she was not there. Just like his mother, who had never been there when he needed her.

Julia was supposed to be different. She loved him. She

told him that time and time again, promising she would always be present when he needed her.

The echoes of her voice sounded in his mind.

"I want to be there for you. I'll do things for you. You don't have anything to worry about."

But where was she? He needed her now. Turning to the door, he banged on it again, hammering his fist against the frame. The door rattled on its hinges, almost giving way.

Hamilton closed his eyes, resting his head against the wall. He had to get out of the rain. He couldn't think with it pounding down on him. Besides, the police might see him standing out front.

Taking a step back, he hurled his weight against the door, sending it crashing into the room.

It was dark inside. He stepped in and pushed the door shut behind him, then sank down to a seat against the front wall. He could still hear the storm, but at least he was free of the crashing water.

I want to be there for you. I'll take care of you.

A puddle formed quickly around him as water dripped from his hair and clothes. It would be a long time before he was dry. He wouldn't be here that long, in fact. He couldn't stay here. The detective might come, or send other policemen.

He allowed only a few minutes to pass before he forced himself to his feet. Tiredness had settled over him now. The resting had let the adrenaline stop pumping. He had to make himself move into the bathroom, where he toweled off his hair and wiped the rain from his face.

The image that met him in the mirror was not a pleasant one. He looked wild, mad. He was like the inbred cousin in a gothic romance, the kind kept locked in a tower somewhere until the final chapters.

But then, perhaps that was true. There was a part of

363

himself he did have to keep locked away. A hidden self. That self was unchained now, no need to continue to sequester it. Not with Julia gone. Not with so much going on.

I want to be there for you.

Where was she? He needed her now, needed her badly, and she was not available. That wasn't what she'd promised. That wasn't the way it was supposed to be.

She wasn't different. Not at all. She was like any of them, like all the bitches.

He went stumbling back into the living room, where he met the gaze of the Madonna on the mantelpiece. It stared down at him, arms open as if beckoning him to come forward.

And he did, moving quickly now, grasping the small statue to hurl it across the room.

The figurine crashed against the wall and shattered into fragments.

Hamilton didn't look back. He was already on his way out the door. He knew where he had to go.

Vincent stood just outside the pool of light cast from the streetlamp, squinting against the rain. The wind tore at his coat, but he ignored it, keeping his hands tucked into his pockets.

Even in the storm he could see the house well, and in the front window he occasionally caught the outlines of the figures moving around inside. The writer was there already. He seemed to be pacing the floor—nervous, uncertain.

Very slowly Vincent turned and moved along the sidewalk a few feet, deeper into the shadows, where the other figure stood waiting.

Its head turned slowly. The face had no expression, but

the gesture was a question. Vincent nodded and remained in the shadows as the figure began to walk across the street toward the front door.

Gable ran his hands through his hair. It was getting long again. In a way he was glad. It helped him feel young, less like he was growing old too quickly, losing himself.

"Are you still sensing something, Gable?"

Dareena had squirmed around in her chair again. There was a lamp behind her so she was silhouetted by light, which made her seem somehow more beautiful. Her hair had a sheen to it tonight; her eyes possessed a brightness.

He nodded in answer to her question. "Aren't you?" he asked.

"It's hard to say."

Finally she got up from her chair and walked across the room. "I have some sort of stirring. I guess you might call it an apprehension."

Gable studied her face. Her features were soft now, her lips quivering gently.

She walked over and looked into his eyes.

"What's going to happen?"

He looked down, shook his head. "I don't know."

"I've been frightened of you, Mr. Tyler. Then unsure, but I've always felt you were a good man. I guess I should tell you that. You haven't shunned me the way other people always have. I appreciate that."

Gable shook his head. "I appreciate the vote of confidence," he said softly.

"Do you really thing Azarius is evil?" she asked. "Even after what's happened so far, I find that hard to believe. He doesn't seem evil."

365

"He wouldn't have been able to captivate you if he revealed his true nature."

"I've loved him for so long. I don't know what I feel."

"It's hard to question something you love. You wind up blaming yourself if you question it too long."

"I suppose that's true. And you?"

"I thought I was over every pain I'd ever felt, but in thinking back there are some regrets. There was a girl I was better off without, but we broke up for all the wrong reasons. I hated myself for a long time after that."

"Are you in love with . . . the other girl?"

"Jennifer? I don't know. I have feelings for her."

"You've been very brave."

"I've been drawn into it. I've had no choice. Don't think I'm a hero. I'm no knight in shining armor."

"Just conscientious."

Gable grinned. "I try."

The knock at the door thundered through the room louder even than the storm.

"It's beginning," Dareena said as she moved to answer it.

Gable rose quickly and grasped her arm, holding her back.

"Don't open too quickly. We need to look out first."

She moved over and flipped on the outer light as Gable pulled back the curtain. He could just make out the shape of the figure on the porch. The man was standing at the door, but he was looking back over his shoulder. Gable could see his back and part of his face.

"It's Vincent," he said.

"More questions," Dareena said as she undid the latch.

Gable shook his head. "Don't open it. He's crazy."

The latch did little good. A second later the door was

kicked off its hinges and Vincent stepped into the room with a smile.

Jennifer returned to her bedroom and lay down on top of the covers, clutching a pillow close to her breasts, resting her chin against the top of it.

Gable was still not home. Downstairs, Gardner was drinking coffee and looking at the newspaper.

He was a big man. He had a gun. She should feel safe.

But there was the rain and the thunder, and she could not help remembering now. All of it was breaking through, everything from the past, everything she had shut from her mind.

It was a hot spring night, sometime in early April before school was out. She was seventeen. She remembered.

She had been dating Hamilton for almost three months. Tonight they had been to see a movie at the new multi-screen cinema.

After the movie they had pizza, and then it began to rain, so Hamilton drove over to the levee. A narrow dirt road curved off at the foot of Aimsley Bridge and ran along the top of the levee back into a wooded area.

She didn't protest. They'd been going out enough that she wasn't frightened to go parking with him. He never tried to go too far and always stopped if she protested.

He finally drew to a stop near a trail that curled off down the levee, and they sat in the car watching the rain on the windshield. The trickles on the glass made funny shadows on their faces, like little dark scars.

"How about a walk in the rain?" Hamilton asked.

She was hesitant, but there was something romantic in the thought of it, hand in hand with the rain in their hair.

"Why not?"

They piled out of the car and met in front of the grill, where he embraced her. They kissed. Then his lips brushed down to her neck, warm against her flesh. She tilted her head back, letting the rain wash over her face as she felt his mouth touch her. His arms were strong around her, holding her close.

She smiled gently, her eyes closed. She almost giggled when her breath quickened, but the muscles of her back tensed when his hands slipped onto the curve of her left breast, fingers tightening softly.

She twisted away from his grasp and took several steps before stopping and whirling around to face him.

"I'm sorry," he said.

She shrugged and shook her head.

"I wish that hadn't happened," she said.

He threw up his hands.

"I said I was sorry. Come on. You're a pretty girl. It's not easy being good."

She bowed her head. "I like you, Hamilton, but sometimes I wonder if that's all you want. If I let you do those things, then you wouldn't want to be around me anymore. I'd just be conquered territory."

"That's not true."

He walked toward her, embracing her again, putting his cheek against her head and swaying gently with her.

"It was a mistake. Okay. I don't want to use you."

"I don't want to be used."

"Come on. We'll walk."

Reluctantly she let him take her hand and together they walked along the pathway as it led through a stand of oak trees.

The trees gave way to a narrow gravel road that ran parallel to the levee. Without speaking they continued along the road.

"Where are we going?"

"We're exploring."

A flash of lightning made the world daylight for a second. The rainfall was soft, but there was a rumble in the clouds that threatened a heavier storm.

"Maybe we should go back to the car," she said.

"No. I saw a house up here in the lightning."

There was another flash, and Jennifer saw it, too—an old two-story house of red brick. It was crumbling now, the porch a sagging stretch of wood.

Shutters dangled from their hinges, and the screens were rusted and torn.

"It looks creepy," she said.

"Spooky."

Still grasping her hand, he moved forward.

"I'm not going in there."

"Come on. It'll be something to tell your grandchildren."

"Ham, please."

"Just for a second. To see what it's like."

"Suppose there's someone in there?"

"Get real. It's deserted."

He tugged her along. They climbed slowly up onto the rickety front porch. The planks were gray and splintering, but he guided her across them carefully and tried the knob on the front door.

It was old, tarnished, and rattled when he touched it. The door opened easily, swinging inward with a creak.

"We can't go in," she protested.

"Sure we can."

They stepped inside, into the dusty front room. It was

almost pitch black in there, but some light did spill in through the windows each time lightning flickered.

"This is too weird," she said.

"Quit whimpering. Don't you feel that fear? It's kind of neat."

"No it's not."

He tightened his grip on her hand and pulled her farther into the room, over to the base of some stairs that led up into even thicker darkness.

She planted her feet.

"Ham, I'm not going up there. Those stairs could give way. Or God knows what could be up there."

"Say a novena and come on." He yanked this time, and there was a note in his voice she didn't like.

"Ham."

"Come on, bitch."

The word was like a knife slicing into her. It was more of a violation than his hands upon her body. It was like a betrayal of their relationship. It was also a warning that something was wrong.

She started to struggle against him, but he was stronger than she was. He got both his arms around her and half dragged her up the stairs. The strength was no longer a comfort. It was a cause for terror.

"What are you doing, Ham? This isn't funny."

"It isn't supposed to be, slut."

He was a different person, someone she didn't know, a stranger who had emerged from within a friend.

"Ham, what's the matter?"

"You are. Whimpering. Slut. Bitch. You fucking whore. All of you are alike."

They reached the top of the stairs and moved along a hallway. The hardwood floor creaked under their weight.

370

Jennifer couldn't see a thing, but Hamilton moved easily, as if he knew the way, had planned it all.

At the end of the hall he threw open a door, and they began to move up a narrow stairwell.

"Ham, no."

He kicked open the attic door and hurled her inside, into the room where the lightning flashed bright through the sky-light.

In the doorway he stood and tugged his belt off, then came toward her and wrapped it quickly around her wrists. She didn't have time to struggle.

Then he threw her back onto the mattress, and before she could try to roll away from him, he was straddling her. The look on his face was like an animal's. He was not the same person; he was insane, bestial. His lips twisted into a smile of almost pure hatred.

Yet he moved slowly, his fingers caressing her for several moments through her clothes before he began to undress her, opening her blouse, pulling her jeans down from around her hips even as she kicked against his weight and thrashed her hands about trying to free them of the bonds.

It was futile. Her head rolled back, and as he attacked her body, all she could see was the rain on the dusty ceiling window, the lightning, and again she noticed the shadows like black scars that reflected on their skin from the pattern of the rain on the window.

A clap of thunder brought her back to her own bedroom, back to the present terrors. Her striped gown clung to her, soaking wet with perspiration.

She sat up on the bed and began to weep. Hamilton. It had been Hamilton. She'd trusted him, and the betrayal had cut into her soul like a saber.

Now she could recall all of it. When it had been over, he had returned to normal, said almost nothing, and for her it had been unreal. As she had straightened her clothes that night, it had been as if none of it had ever happened.

She hadn't known how to react.

She was numb as they sat in the darkness. She could not speak. She put her clothes back on, straightened her hair as well as she could, and followed him back to the car. He drove her home without another word passing between them.

When she walked into her house, she told her parents she'd been caught in the rain, then took a shower. She went to sleep after that, and when she awoke the next morning she remembered nothing.

She just knew she wouldn't see Hamilton anymore, and that she didn't want anyone to touch her.

Now, sliding off the bed, she went back to the window. It wasn't any easier to look at the rain. She fought back tears as she looked over at Gable's house.

He still wasn't there.

She would have to talk to Gardner. This sudden memory must be a key to the threatening calls. She turned from the window and went downstairs, still grasping the doll.

Gardner jumped to his feet when he saw her, tossing his newspaper aside.

"Is anything wrong?"

She shook her head. "I had a dream. Sort of. I know who the calls came from now. I guess we should call the police."

"What happened?"

"I remembered something that happened when I was still in high school. Something terrible. I was raped. By Hamilton Terry. I'd shut it out of my mind, but I remember now.

"He's crazy. He must have decided to do away with me. I don't know why after all this time."

Gardner didn't ask any more questions. He moved to the phone and lifted the receiver. Then he shook his head.

"No dial tone. It's dead. Must be the storm. Don't worry. We can go straight to the station."

She looked around the room, her mouth open slightly as she thought over the proposition. Then she shook her head.

"Not in the storm. It's too bad out."

Gardner took his gun from the holster and gave it a quick check.

"All right, then. We'll wait. It's waited this long. You must have blocked it all out, but that's over. Now all of this is about to be over. Just as soon as we can get to the cops."

She sighed. She didn't know how she felt overall, but somewhere deep down inside there was a relief. Maybe it was over.

The waiting was over now, tonight. The time had come to end it all, to tie up the last loose end. The bitch had been difficult. She'd escaped death, had gained help and protection, but nothing could stand in the way now.

The final hour was here, and the storm had come as proof, to mask the actions, to protect what had to be done.

No one would hear the cries over the thunder. No one would see the horror in the storm, and when the death was finished, the rain would wash away the blood.

Jennifer the bitch, the slut, was inside now, waiting for the taste of death.

"So nice to see you, Mr. Tyler," said the voice inside Vincent's body.

Gable was trembling. Every muscle in his body tense, he had to fight the impulse to charge for the door. When he tried to swallow, the muscles in his throat would not respond.

Dareena moved to his side, gripping his arm for support. He could feel her fingers shaking even through his shirt and jacket.

"What's going on, Gable?" Her words were soft, almost a whisper. It sounded as if she were very far away.

"It's him, or one of his friends," Gable said.

"Yes, Gable," said the demon voice. "A friend. But I will take you to Brother Azarius."

"Where is he?"

"Waiting."

"And if we don't go?"

"Most unpleasant. As you know, Mr. Vincent's form here has been in our service for some time now, occupied by one or another of us. You know the lore. We can move in and out of a person as we wish. You are dealing with great power. Why cause yourself further harm?"

"Then, it's true. Azarius is a leader? A fallen archangel."

"Yes, and many of us are at work here, serving his purpose and his whim."

"What does he want?"

"I'm sure he will tell you that himself. You will learn all of that in time. This is not the place. There are many things he wishes to show you. Many things he will tell you."

Gable tilted his head and gave a grim smile. "If you'll excuse the expression, go to hell."

There was a chuckle. "Defiance. I like that." He raised a clenched fist and slammed it hard into Gable's solar plexus. Gable leaned forward, gasping for breath as the pain

374

burned through his chest and stomach. He thought for a second his lungs had collapsed.

"The pain you've felt thus far is nothing. Think of another verse from your Scriptures, your attempts to explain us and prepare yourselves against us. 'There met him two possessed with devils, coming out of the tombs, exceeding fierce, so that no man might pass by that way.'"

"Matthew."

"You have learned well. So you know the kind of strength you are against. You know of the things that were recorded. You can imagine the horrors not set down."

"But I won't succumb to you."

"You'll have no choice."

Gable staggered forward, uncertain of how to deal with a physical confrontation. The being occupying Vincent was in complete control.

Gable leaned against Dareena for support as she brushed her fingers against the back of his neck, trying to comfort him. He sank to one knee, and she knelt beside him as he drew in air through teeth clenched against the pain.

Through the ruined door wind swirled rainwater into the room.

"Come," said the creature. "Do not fear the night. There are things we will show you, pleasures you can experience. Wouldn't those be preferable to this pain?"

Gable turned his head upward, his expression defiant.

Vincent, or the being that occupied his body, took a step forward, bringing the back of his hand across Gable's face. The force knocked Gable's head to the side, and he felt a warm trickle of blood spilling from the corner of his mouth.

Slowly Gable pulled himself to his feet, locking his gaze on the eyes. Looking into them was like looking into an azure pool. They betrayed what was behind them—the nature and the evil. The eyes portrayed a vast and dark eternity.

He sensed suddenly the need to flee, even stronger than before, but he could not clear his thoughts. His mind fogged. His thoughts were entangled in cobwebs, struggling futilely to free themselves.

Gripping Dareena's arm, he attempted to battle back the onslaught, but he couldn't.

Pain worse than anything he had ever endured swept over him, crumpling him to his knees.

He sensed Dareena at his side, but could not reach out to her. He closed his eyes, sinking into the darkness even as he heard Dareena screaming his name. The sound of her voice followed him down into oblivion. The Abyss.

Jennifer was back in the attic room, wrists bound, struggling against Hamilton's weight on top of her. Her ribs were crushed inward, making it almost impossible to draw breath. She was smothering. Smothering in the darkness. She tried to open her eyes, but there was only blackness, the blackness of total darkness, inescapable. She tried to scream, but there was no breath to push the sound from her throat.

There was only the sound of the rain—raindrops spattering against the window, thunder and wind.

She relived it, a horror that was like witnessing, like living through, her own murder.

She remembered the violation, the pain, the hatred in Hamilton's eyes as he assaulted her. The darkness was suddenly gone, just as it had been that night. She remembered now how her mind swam in and out of consciousness as she tried to endure the torment. Even as the act occurred, her mind was beginning the process of confining the awareness within a tiny box inside her brain, concealing it into no more than a set of unexplained fears.

The relief of rediscovery had faded quickly. Now came all the emotions she had escaped for so long, the humiliation, the shock. She felt dirty, like some discarded piece of refuse.

And suddenly she was awake, finding herself curled up on the end of the couch in her living room, safe and away from that attic but no less tormented. There was a tight ball of pain in her stomach, not real pain, but the ache of emotion and anguish.

She sat up abruptly. Gardner was not in the room. She twisted her head from side to side, but there was no sign of him. He must have gone into the kitchen for more coffee.

She called out to him.

No answer.

Slowly she slipped from the couch, pulling her robe around her more tightly.

"Mr. Gardner?"

There was no answer. She moved into the kitchen. The percolator was plugged in and she could hear the coffee bubbling inside. He was brewing a fresh pot, but he had gone somewhere else while it perked.

The kitchen was empty. Gardner's coffee cup was on the table—the only sign that he'd been there.

Outside, the thunder still roared. Moving to the sink, Jennifer pulled down the shade over the window there, shutting out the sight of the rain against the glass.

Then, turning, she moved back into the living room. Still no sign of the bodyguard. That left the upstairs, where he might have gone to use the bathroom.

She called out again, standing at the foot of the stairs, using the banister for balance as she peered upward expectantly.

No answer.

She looked around the room again. There was no sign of any disturbance, yet she was beginning to feel more and more uneasy. Something was wrong.

She started up the stairs slowly, lifting each step carefully. The calves of her legs were shuddering as she moved, and she continued to clutch the railing for support even as her palms, wet with perspiration, slipped on the wood.

At the top of the stairs she called out again. Only the thunder returned in answer. She wanted to cry now, but she fought back the tears, biting her lower lip as she scanned the upstairs hallway. There was still no sign of Gardner.

She continued along the hallway, trying to listen, trying to detect some sound that was out of the ordinary, but there was nothing. No sound, nothing in view, just the empty hallway.

The carpet was coarse beneath her feet as she moved forward. Perspiration tingled on her legs and back. She wasn't sure what she was going to do now.

She thought about fleeing the house, but there was nowhere to go—not out into the darkness and the storm. There was no one to help. Gable was gone. If she could not find Gardner, she was alone.

And there was something wrong. She could sense it. Suddenly. It was more than just Gardner's disappearance. Someone else was here or nearby.

She stopped at her bedroom door. Had it been closed before? She couldn't remember.

Her fingers trembled as she reached down, slowly clasping the knob and turning it until it clicked open.

She shoved the door in hard and looked forward into the room, ready to flee back toward the stairs if needed.

But the room was empty. With a sigh of relief she hurried into the room, scurrying toward the telephone. She could get the police. They'd come if they thought something was wrong. They knew the situation.

She climbed quickly across the bed to snatch the receiver from the bedside table, but when she pressed it to her ear her heart sank. There was no dial tone. There was no sound at all.

For a moment anyway.

Until she heard something crash downstairs.

CHAPTER 25

Gable's head felt as if he'd had a baseball bat broken over it. The pain throbbed through his temples with waves of agony channeling back through his crown.

He opened his eyes slowly, finding he was staring up at a tiled ceiling, white tile with a pattern of black dots.

He didn't recognize it, so he tried to lift his head from the pillow to look around. The gesture was a mistake. The pain grew worse.

It was like being in a cheap private-eye novel, coming around after being hit from behind and shoved down a flight of stairs, a flight of stairs that might have stretched to the tip of Kilimanjaro.

Through the mist he could hear Dareena's voice. She was speaking his name.

"Gable . . . Gable. Are you all right?"

He rolled onto his side toward the direction of her voice, and he could see her face. She was kneeling there beside the bed, staring into his eyes.

"Auntie Em."

"What?" Her brow wrinkled.

"It sure doesn't look like Kansas, Toto."

"Gable? Are you okay?"

He shut his eyes tightly, bracing himself as he forced his feet over the edge of the bed. The motion jerked him into a sitting position, and he clenched his teeth against the shock wave of pain. The nausea that followed almost turned his stomach over, but he managed to control it.

He sat clutching the covers until he was able to open his eyes again. Dareena touched his hand as he began to look around the room.

It was small with bland furnishings. There was only a dim light shining now, dancing off the drab green walls and splashing across the bed parallel to the one on which Gable sat.

Wherever he was, he'd never been here before. It looked like a hospital of some kind. Then he realized where they must be.

"The mental institution."

Dareena nodded.

"How'd we get here?"

"They had a car. I think it was a police car. It had a radio in it."

"But how'd we get in here?"

"Someone was waiting to open the gate. It looked like a groundskeeper or something."

With her support Gable got to his feet. "It doesn't make sense, though. They just let us walk in here?"

"The people looked strange, Gable. Not just like crazy people. They looked like that man, that lawyer."

"Oh my God. All of them?"

She nodded. "Even the attendants."

Gable walked slowly over to the window, pulling back the curtain to look out at the rain. The night was still violent. The branches of the trees pitched about wildly in the wind.

"That's what's been coming," he said. "He's brought

his minions up out of hell. They can do whatever they want to here tonight. It will just look like the inmates went berserk because of the storm. They don't have to try to conceal what they are. They can just wreak havoc, as the saying goes. Raise hell.'' He didn't smile.

Suddenly the light bulb in the lamp burst, spitting glass in a quick spray across the room. There was not total darkness because the door was ajar and the hall lights cast a glow into the room.

Silhouetted in the light was a figure. At first Gable thought he recognized it. He stepped forward, almost feeling relieved. It was Fisher.

''I never thought I'd be so glad to see a cop,'' he said.

The smell stopped him in his tracks, and then he saw the gaping hole in the policeman's chest.

Gable froze, looking at the face in front of him. The skin slowly began to split open, cracking along the cheeks to reveal globs of coagulated blood.

Azarius was occupying the body, using it as his latest vessel. Gable sensed that. The evil corrupted the flesh. In seconds most resemblance to the detective's features was gone. The skin had turned dark, a greenish color of decay. Pieces of the flesh were peeling away from the bone, revealing portions of the skeleton. The corner of the mouth dangled free, revealing teeth and creating a broad grin. The hair dangled from the scalp, which seemed to have melted down from the top of the skull like a candle.

All sign of symmetry was lost. The shape of the head was twisted from bloated pockets of flesh that had swelled out around the temples.

The lips were peeled back, creating the image of a grim smile, and the flesh dripped away from the hands at his sides. He looked like what he was.

''What do you want here?'' Gable asked.

382

"I have many wants, Mr. Tyler. And there are many things I wish to show you."

"What do you want from me?"

"That will come in time."

"Then tell me who you are."

"Yes, that would be a good place to begin. The name Azarius is a sort of joke I use. You've picked up on that. It was a name used by Raphael. You're familiar with the story?"

Gable rubbed his head. "I've heard it. Azarius leads his friend Tobias to the defeat of a dark spirit."

"I like the irony of using the name myself. My position in the ranks of angels was like his, Mr. Tyler. You've suspected that, I believe, and it's true. I was an archangel."

Gable shook his head, confused.

As if sensing what Gable was thinking, the being shook its head, bits of flesh crumbling away with the movement.

"No, I'm not Satan. Think of me as a lieutenant, a commander of dark forces. I have been known by many names. Azarius I use because of my games, as a further taunt to Raphael since I have returned. My real name has been known to some of your brethren. At least the name I have grown accustomed to lo these thousands of years. A name picked up by some ancient Sumerians. It even took on meaning in their language. I am Alal, the Destroyer. The opposite of the Creator you worship in your futile rituals."

"What destruction are you after here?"

"I sought love. I wanted Dareena for my own, to join me in the depths as my bride. But at 'the same time, my task is always the same. Destruction. I have always sought it. The burning of men's souls."

"What are you trying to prove? Is this the threshold of Armageddon?"

"Hardly. That game is in motion, but the time has not

arrived. I stumbled upon a purpose for you. You came as a threat, but I saw more. You could have been just one more of those I or my brothers used toward our ends. We do that with many people. Often they think they are acting on their own desires when in reality they are being directed by us, marionettes exploited for our purposes, performing things we cannot perform. Often they do not know we are there, but we work through them. Everything is in my control. Now perhaps rather than be a threat to my love you can be convinced to serve me."

"This is all a game?"

The demon's fingers twitched almost imperceptibly, and Gable was struck by a force that came down upon him, driving him to his knees and causing him to crumple onto his side.

He struggled against the pressure, tensing his muscles to resist, trying to fight his way back upward.

It was useless. He relaxed slowly, accepting the weight, giving with it. The pain came suddenly, a shock of agony worse than any he had ever known. It seemed to sear through each nerve ending, throbbing into each molecule of his being, the fingers of pain even raking along the edge of his soul.

Just as suddenly it was gone, leaving him huddled on the floor. His face and hair were now drenched with sweat, his clothes clammy, clinging to his back.

"It is a game," Alal said. "A game of power. A war of infinity. You are a pawn, Mr. Tyler. All of your kind are pawns, manipulated by my master; pawns of a dark angel.

"Often you are wont to ask why there is so much unhappiness in your world. Isn't it obvious?"

"Why? Because of you."

"Because we were banished. Cast out of our rightful place of dominion. Your Creator exiled us, but He did not destroy us. He created the abyss for us, but he did not totally confine us there, and so we carry on our battle. We are beings of torment, and we wage our war against him, against your Jehovah.''

The creature laughed, a long and throaty laugh that echoed down through the ravages of Fisher's body. Gases and fluid bubbled within the standing carcass.

''We strike back at Him. Our purpose is to cause Him pain. To draw you into the abyss with us, so that He can view your torture and your torment. What better way to torture a Creator than to shatter his creations? What better way to hurt a father than to make Him watch the destruction of His children at the hands of His enemies?

''Each one of you that we carry back into the abyss with us is like a thorn driven through His heart.''

Gable pulled himself onto his knees, then managed to get one foot under him. It was going to be a while before he could stand, but it was a start.

''We're your battlefield,'' he said.

''Precisely.''

''I still don't see why you want me so badly.''

''You interfered with me. You intervened with Dareena. I saw it coming, and I made my preparations carefully.''

''Why did I make a difference?''

Alal did not laugh this time. ''We can own your souls unless you turn away from us and reach out for your Creator. Each of you has already joined us in the rebellion in one way or another. You separate yourselves from the Creator with each evil you perform. Yet now you have caused her to turn back to the salvation she was taught, just as you would turn yourself back to the early training you received. In reaching back to the Creator, you attempt to breech the separation. If you find your route to Him, you become His victory. He does not draw you from us. He only offers you

385

a door. What I fear of you, Tyler, is what you might become. You might find that door not only for yourself, but for others also. You might rob me of my pawns as you have done with Dareena.''

"I'm no preacher.''

"You could be much more. Think of the things that can be conveyed through art. You can be of much more benefit if you join me. I can give you power beyond your imagination, writer. Wisdom.

"You can have so many things, and when the time comes you can join us in the Abyss. Join us and reign there at our side. Reign there until we attain our rule here, on this plain.''

"Godhood?''

Gable now managed to push himself to his feet. He wasn't steady on them, but he managed to keep his balance.

"Isn't that what you've always promised? Isn't that what started it all? You sought godhood. Then, when you couldn't get it, you promised it to mankind, drawing the children away from the Creator.''

"You learn well, Mr. Tyler, your lessons of parables.''

"You'd have us believe it was all unreal. That you don't exist. That's how so much of your work is done, isn't it?''

"We use whatever method we must. Many of you don't believe. It's easy in this world to believe that only the tangible is real. When signs of our existence do slip by, there are ways to deal with that. We can always convince you we aren't real, or that we're friendly.''

"Why should the thief tell his victim he has come to steal?'' Gable agreed. "Why not pretend friendship?'' He looked quickly at Dareena. "Or love.''

The head rolled backward. For a moment Gable thought it would topple off the shoulders, but instead a deep and guttural laugh echoed up through the ruined body. Then the demon looked back at him.

"I'm all your legends, all your fears—your worst nightmares and your most pleasant dreams. Vampires, shape shifters, trolls, fairies, and beings of grace—all of those. All your legends are born of the lies my brothers have told to disguise themselves and their purpose."

CHAPTER 26

Jennifer screamed when she reached the top of the stairs, where she could look down into the living room.

There was a pile of shattered glass on the carpet, and the wind swept in through the ruined window, ripping at the curtains.

It was the creature, not the wind, however, that brought the scream up through her throat, the creature and what it was doing. It was on top of Gardner, its jaws tearing open the man's throat.

The bodyguard must have been out on the front porch when she'd awakened, checking out there. The storm had kept him from hearing her call. Then he had come back inside after she was upstairs.

And the creature, the horrible beast, had attacked him, crashed through the window at him.

For several moments she was unable to move, mesmerized by the sight, the carnage below her.

Glaciers were creeping through the veins. The beast was or had been Gable's dog, the playful little white puppy. Some of the features were still recognizable.

But now it was a terror, its fur wet and splattered with

mud, its muscles somehow twisted. It was not a dog any longer, not a dog at all. She could not believe her eyes. The fur had peeled back in some places, and masses of tissue bubbled out, throbbing and expanding. Parts of it were re-forming.

Somehow the front legs had stretched out in length, become like gnarled branches of an old oak tree, yet there was a power in them, visible in the way Gardner attempted to struggle against the onslaught.

The legs kept him pinned to the floor, kept him unable to get up as the jaws ripped at his throat.

She realized there was a reason he couldn't free himself from the beast, more than just the strength in the extended legs. The paws also had metamorphosed, had become, it was unbelievable—hands. There was no fur over there, just bare gray flesh that still pulsed and bubbled from the transformation. Their grip locked on Gardner's shoulders, the razorlike nails piercing his clothes to dig into his flesh. Blood coursed up through the fingers and over the malformed knuckles.

Jennifer started down the stairs, screaming again at the top of her voice.

There was a table at the base of the stairs, and she grabbed a small vase there and hurled it over at the creature. The glass shattered against the beast's shoulder blades without doing apparent harm, but the blow did capture its attention.

The head turned slowly.

It was badly misshapen, the glowing red eyes looking back at her as the jaws gaped open. Saliva dripped from the sides of the mouth, some of it stained pink with Gardner's blood. Bits of the man's torn flesh dangled from the teeth.

Jennifer could not find her breath as she inched backward, being careful not to misplace a step and lose her footing. The thing was worse than nightmares, worse than the monsters she'd seen in horror movies.

"Get out of here," Gardner said. His words were a gurgle through the blood that was spurting up into his mouth, but he jerked his arm violently in a gesture that directed Jennifer back toward the stairs.

She kept moving, trying not to look in the beast's eyes. It was coming slowly, easing its weight away from Gardner and pivoting toward her, crouching low. It was stalking, and she had to look into its eyes, eyes that were piercing, filled with the essence of pure evil. She could feel the evil slicing into her.

Forcing herself to keep going, she reached over and grabbed the table, overturning it to create an obstacle in the creature's path.

Then she did turn and pumped her legs hard, not even thinking of looking back as she charged up the stairs.

Just as quickly the creature was after her. Its breath, surprisingly cold, touched the backs of her legs, but she managed to stay ahead of it, miraculously keeping her balance on the way up the stairs. The claws sank into the tail of her robe, but she let her arms slip quickly free of the garment and moved upward, taking the steps two and three at a time.

Still she felt she was struggling up a peak in Tibet. In slow motion.

She reached the top of the stairs, aimed toward the nearest door, and opened it, slipping quickly into the bedroom and slamming the door shut.

A second later she heard the thud of the beast's weight against the frame.

It was like the day the killer had come after her. She looked around the room for some weapon, finally seizing on a small lamp that had a heavy base.

Pressing her back against the wall beside the door, she cocked the lamp back in her arms, ready to swing it like a club. Images of that dark attic flashed through her brain along with the remembrances of the killer's attack, but she forced the thoughts aside. Terror would not conquer her. She was determined to survive. She wasn't going to let her own mind defeat her.

Through the door she could hear the grotesque sounds of the beast, the harsh growls that rattled in its throat. Worst of all, she could hear its claws begin to splinter the wood of the door.

Just like the knife wielder. She held her breath, trying to fight back the tears. It was useless. They began to flood her eyes.

And the claws ripped through the wood.

She waited, wondering what to do. If she went out the window, what worse horror would be out there?

A piece of the door splintered inward, and a claw shot through the small opening. It was wet, membrane dripping from it as the veins continued to pulse.

Twisting about, the appendage tried to make the opening bigger, then began to stretch upward. The spindly fingers were trying to reach the doorknob.

Slashing the lamp downward, Jennifer struck the limb just above the wrist. It didn't withdraw. It just kept trying to reach the knob.

Lifting the lamp again, she hammered the base down on the arm repeatedly until the bone shattered.

There was a howl of pain and the limb was slowly dragged back through the hole.

Jennifer took a step back to look through the opening. She gasped. One of the eyes was peering through the jagged gash in the wood, and the scratching began again. She could hear the wood on the other side tearing open.

"No."

She screamed and raised the lamp again, ready for the invasion.

But suddenly the onslaught ended. All sound ceased and the creature turned away from the door. Through the crack she watched it depart.

It was moving down the hallway.

Oh, God. It was going back for Gardner.

She opened the door and followed the trail of sticky mucus that stretched along the carpet.

The creature had moved swiftly. It was nowhere in sight. It had already reached the stairs and was started down. Jennifer scurried to the head of the stairs and looked over the railing.

She sighed. Gardner was on his feet. He was pressing a cloth against his throat with one hand, and in the other he'd drawn his gun.

The beast was on the stairs, crouching and eyeing him carefully.

The big man moved slowly, raising the gun inch by inch as the beast's muscles tensed for the pounce. He didn't want it to spring before he was ready, so he was easing the gun into a position for firing.

It was going to be all right, Jennifer thought. He'd be able to shoot the thing, kill it before it could do any more damage, and then she could go down and help him, do something about his throat before he lost too much blood.

The next seconds passed in an instant, and yet they lasted an eternity.

Gardner finally got the gun leveled on the beast and his finger began to tighten on the trigger.

Then he fired, the sound of the shots echoing through the house.

The bullets tore into the monster's chest, ripping through the fur and flesh to draw out three streams of blood.

Yet, already in motion, it continued to travel downward, and Jennifer screamed. The jaws were still open.

The creature's weight struck Gardner hard, knocking him off balance, and he went spinning around the room in a sickening parody of a waltz as the claws closed around his throat again, ripping away the cloth and tearing again at his flayed flesh.

Dropping the gun, Gardner struggled first to push the monster away. When that effort failed he began to pound his fists against its rib cage. That, too, was useless, and his strength was ebbing. He tumbled to the floor, the creature still on top of him.

With its arms it pinned him down again, and in an instant its head jerked backward, the fangs bared. Then the head shot forward, teeth sinking fast and deep into Gardner's neck.

He struggled only a few more seconds. Then he was still.

"No." Jennifer froze again, her hands on her face. She looked out through her fingers. It was like looking through a set of bars.

The creature moved off him, then stumbled. It limped around the room for a moment and lost its footing. As it hit the floor, a rush of wind exploded through the room, bursting up through the center of the house, rattling the pictures on the walls, and turning over tables and plants.

Jennifer dropped to her side and grabbed the railing, holding on as the wind swept through the hallway, rattling the door and tugging at her hair and clothes. It was a cold air, as cold as an Arctic wind must be. She closed her eyes and clenched her teeth against the bitter stench in it.

The house shook, trembled to its very foundation. For a

moment she thought it was going to burst open. She braced herself for the explosion.

But just as suddenly everything was still. On the floor below her the dog lay motionless. In death it looked just as it always had, a soft white puppy.

The storm was still audible, but that was all. Everything had become placid within the walls of the house.

But it wasn't over. Jennifer began to pray because she knew it wasn't over.

And outside, the cold eyes peered through the rain, forced to wait once again. The noise in the house had carried out even over the storm. There had been gunshots and howls, but that was no deterrent. Not tonight.

Whatever was going on in there now was nothing. Not compared to what the bitch could expect. Her worst nightmares, the worst horrors in the world, were nothing compared to what was about to be inflicted.

In the darkness the figure slowly began to walk forward, across the soggy grass of the lawn toward the front door. Tonight would be the night, no matter how long it took.

The halls of the mental institution were filled with bodies in a frenzy. The inmates seemed to be wild. They ran through the corridors, smashing windows and overturning tables.

Barefoot patients tromped aimlessly over the tiles, slicing their feet on broken glass without acknowledging the pain.

A tall thin man in blue pajamas carried a fire ax over his head, slashing it back and forth among the crowd. A few unfortunate victims were sliced open with the blade. They continued to saunter about in spite of the wounds and the geysers of blood that sprayed from them.

Others dashed through the halls, slamming into each other or screaming wildly.

At the end of one hallway an orgy was taking place. People flailed about in a tangle of sweating limbs.

In the kitchen a group had ripped open the cabinets and faces were stuffed with food.

In yet another hallway an old woman carried a butcher knife in front of her, impaling anyone who got in her way.

In the hospital every imaginable desire was being indulged to excess. The minions had rare opportunity to experience human delights with impunity, so until called by their master, Alal, they would indulge.

The most horrible sight was just outside the room where Gable was kept. Two of the inmates were pounding an orderly. He was a young man with dark hair.

Laughing, they slammed their fists into his face and stomach and took turns stabbing him with injections using stolen syringes from the medicine cabinet.

Then finally they grabbed his arms and legs and pulled. The sound was sickening as sockets gave.

His clothing ripped, then his flesh. His arm tore free and one of the men began to belt him aimlessly with it.

The demon-laughter was a horrible echo through the corridor.

"It's terrible out there," Dareena said, peering through the doorway. Tears were running down her cheeks.

"I don't understand what you want now," Tyler said, forcing himself to stare hard at the corpse, looking into the eyes that remained sharp and unaffected by death.

"What I have always wanted," said the fallen angel. "As I have said, to destroy your kind, to draw you away from your Creator. And you, Tyler. You can help me."

"How?"

"You write things. Your words can draw people to us. There are many ways words can deceive. As you've been told, it's what you may become that we desire. Tell them there are many paths to their God. They want to hear that. They don't understand how many paths lead to us, all paths of hatred, lies, all destructions. You can nurture those things with your pen."

"Why would I want to help you?"

"Because of what we can give you. There are so many pleasures, so many riches, and when your time is passed you can join us, reign beside us."

"No thank you."

Gable turned his head away, fighting for each jagged breath. He was drenched in sweat. He closed his eyes.

"No," Gable said. "Not on your terms."

"A man of steel." Alal chuckled. "Then know the threats. If you do not join me, you'll never leave here alive. We will destroy you. You have the choice of accepting the power I can bestow on you, or your own destruction."

"You can try." Gable opened his eyes and stared forward defiantly. "If you kill me, at least you'll know I'm not yours. Better to die here for God than to follow you."

"There's something more you should know. If you die here, there'll be no way you can help your girlfriend."

"What do you mean?"

"If you die here, Jennifer dies also."

"What are you talking about?"

"I do not control everything, Mr. Tyler, but I can manipulate events in my favor. There are those who have used my adopted name. They knew it only because they heard it through Dareena, thinking they were covering their own crimes. They have served my purpose well.

"Tonight my brothers have removed all the obstacles.

Your love can be crushed at any moment. Not by my hand, but by the touch of another. Join me and you can go to her. Oppose me and die here, and her death will be something more horrible than you can ever imagine.''

"She's got a bodyguard," Gable said.

"Dead. Destroyed by one of my brothers. The girl probably thought she was seeing a werewolf. The policeman Fisher was killed because he was close to finding the answers which might have confined one whom I needed."

"You're lying," Gable whispered.

"Am I? Do you dare take that risk." Alal grinned. "This time I do not lie. She will be slaughtered, tortured to the limits of agony."

"Damn you. You're not a god, no matter how much you want to be. You can't control everything."

"I don't presume to. I merely take advantage of the things that occur, of human frailties and sicknesses, of all weaknesses. I let things proceed. The killer would have come after Jennifer anyway, but now it can serve a purpose in my favor. The destruction of the priest was no good to me in and of itself. His soul was not mine to claim. It belonged to your Savior. But the death was part of the design of a mind twisted by lust and hatred. The sort of thing that serves me so well, as I told you. I make the best. So join me, and I will let you go to her, your Jennifer. She doesn't have to die tonight, Gable. She can be protected. Just kneel to me. Bow down and pledge your soul to me."

Gable closed his eyes and shook his head violently. It was all too much to comprehend. He raised his arms to press them against his head. There was a storm inside his brain and his chest was tight.

His body felt suddenly so empty.

"Your time is up," Alal said. Slowly the corpse moved from the center of the hallway. "Crush him." The rasping cry was sudden. It drew the attention of all the creatures in the hallway. They began to shuffle and move forward, merging into a mass of groping limbs.

Dareena screamed and yanked Gable's arm hard, tugging him so that he jerked sideways. He didn't resist as she began to drag him along the hallway, but neither did he respond. He was sweating, half dazed.

"Gable, you've got to run."

He snapped into awareness and followed her, taking her arm and moving with her, running as the bodies behind them began to follow. Alal's laughter echoed off the tiled corridor.

They didn't look back. They hurried along the floor, turning into the next empty hallway with a slight lead on the pursuing mass. Their feet slid on the smoothly waxed floor. Struggling, they maintained balance.

Gable grabbed a fire extinguisher and turned it over, angling the nozzle at the floor.

The foam poured out quickly, and he kept moving backward, hurrying, leaving a trail of the chemicals until reaching a junction with another hallway. There he flipped off the light switch, plunging everything into blackness as he tossed the canister aside. Then he seized Dareena's hand again.

They ran as fast as they could, gasping for breath, ignoring the sound behind them of the bodies slipping and sliding, crashing to the floor.

As he forced his legs to keep pumping, Gable imagined the creatures that were behind him, not in the bodies they now occupied, but in their true form. Thoughts of reptilian scales and claws rushed through his head.

He imagined a horde of dragons and ghouls and other beasts trailing him up the hallway, the monsters of a thousand nightmares.

All your legends. All your fears.

At the end of the corridor there was a pair of doors. Pushing them open, Gable found they led into a water therapy room.

The smell of moisture was in the air. Flipping on the lights, Gable looked through the room. It was all tile with tubs and basins scattered about.

Deciding it was empty, he half dragged Dareena through, looking for another exit.

In the next chamber he was stopped in his tracks. The man with the ax shambled toward him, the bloody weapon raised. In the other hand he was holding a severed head.

It dangled from its hair, and he lifted it for Gable as if it were a prize.

The grin spread across the man's face, his eyes rolling about in their sockets.

"Join us," the voice rasped. The hand opened, and the head dropped to the floor, splattering into a mass of ruined fluid and brain matter.

"Join us," the voice repeated, and the man continued forward, gripping the handle of the ax.

"Join us."

Gable pressed Dareena behind his back and looked around for some sort of defense as the man continued to move in on him.

A cursory glance revealed little. He continued to shield Dareena as he faced the attacker.

The man swung the ax in a broad motion, making an effort to contact Gable's neck.

Gable dodged and the blade brushed a fraction of an inch from his body.

To his left was a whirlpool bath. He inched toward it.

The ax wielder continued to move forward, swinging the

399

weapon wildly now, side to side, up and down, making every effort to plunge it into Gable one way or another.

There was no pattern to the movement. It was erratic and deadly.

"Join us," the voice repeated. "Join us or die."

Gable ducked the blade and caught the ax handle. It was luck that the blade didn't part his ribs before he got a grip on the wood.

His shoes got a better grip on the tile floor than the patient's slippers. Using that advantage over the possessing force's strength, Gable yanked on the handle, tumbling the host into the bath headfirst.

As the man attempted to free himself, Gable and Dareena moved onward.

The next doorway was locked. Gable kicked it open and they walked into a blast of water from a pressure hose.

Tumbling to the floor, both Gable and Dareena were tossed along by the water pressure.

Looking toward the source, Gable could see a huge white-clad attendant. He had the same gaze as the other possession victims, but his hands handled the hose skillfully.

Gable caught Dareena's hand, and together they scrambled out of the path of the water.

The attendant began to adjust the nozzle for another blast.

It sprayed the wall where he had been standing, hitting the tile with a loud clap.

Gable sloshed through the water on the floor, working his way to the tub where Dareena was crouching. He helped her up and they eased back through the doorway from which they had come.

Pulling Dareena between another row of tubes and nozzles, Gable found exit.

Pushing through the doorway, he discovered still another hallway. The place was a labyrinth.

They were halfway down the corridor when they heard the people approaching, a group that came into sight quickly, stumbling forward. They were still human in appearance, not the monsters of legend, but in their eyes the evil within them seemed to glow.

Seaview had told him of their strength. Unreal. Superhuman.

Gable and Dareena started to turn back in the direction they had come, but the doors into the therapy room burst open and another mass of bodies piled out, a unit of unholy soldiers.

The two groups slowly began to inch forward. In moments they would converge, Gable realized, and he and Dareena would be ripped apart.

"Gable, what do we do?"

He closed his eyes and tilted his head back. "They haven't been able to take us, Dareena. In all the time Azarius was trying, he couldn't possess you. There's a shield for us if we claim it."

"What?"

"Faith. It has to be faith. They can't break through it. That's what's kept him from being able to totally possess you."

He entwined his fingers with Dareena's and began to pray, his lips moving as he rattled off the lines of the twenty-third psalm in a brisk whisper.

" 'The Lord is my shepherd, I shall not want. He maketh me to lie down in green pastures,' " he said, speaking the words memorized long before.

'Your God can't help you, Tyler. This is my domain.'

He looked up to see the rotting mass of Fisher's body. Alal/Azarius had made his way to the front of the group pouring from the therapy room.

"You will be destroyed here," Alal said. The two groups

401

stopped—two walls of people on either side of Gable. There was no way to move through them, and they were only pausing, waiting to move forward. At Alal's command they would strike.

"Bow to me," Alal demanded. He was angry now. It had stopped being a game. Gable's defiance was making him furious. "Bow to me you bastard. You little fucking pile of shit. I'll devour you. I'll consume your soul in this instant."

"I won't bow to you," Tyler said.

A burly, dark-haired man in a white attendant's uniform pushed though the crowd and grabbed Dareena, pinning her arms to her sides and holding her with her back against him as two others broke away from the masses and stepped forward. One was a lean blond man also dressed as an attendant, the other, older with gray stubble across his chin. He wore faded blue pajamas, slippers, and a red sweater improperly buttoned. Dried spots of food dappled his clothes. He probably hadn't had a bath in a week. His wiry gray hair shot out from his head in all directions.

"Get away from her," Gable shouted.

He was ignored. The blond attendant moved to Dareena's side, taking one of her arms, while the burly man held the other.

Positioning her between them, they gripped her tightly as she struggled to free herself. Then the old man stepped up to her, running his hands over her body as he buried his face against her neck.

Gable started to move forward, but others pulled from the crowd to grasp him. Hands with iron grips closed on his arms, restraining him.

Someone grabbed a handful of his hair, yanking his head backward so that his gaze aligned with the attack on Dareena. He was forced to watch helplessly as others moved toward her.

"It will take a long time," Alal said. "A very long time until everyone is through. Consider it a preview. Not just of what Jennifer will feel, but of what is coming for you."

Gable wanted to close his eyes but he couldn't. And he couldn't close his ears to Dareena's screams.

Or the demons' laughter. It echoed from their throats, but also from the very depths of hell.

Arbor stumbled up onto Gable's porch, grabbing the chain on the swing for support and then easing himself to a seat. He was on the verge of exhaustion. His clothes were wet with rain and weighed a ton, his limbs, wrought with pain, trembling, almost unresponsive.

It felt good to be under shelter. It seemed to have taken an eternity to walk from the canal to the house, and he'd seen no one along the way to offer him any help.

He let his body relax as the swing creaked slowly back and forth. The house was dark, so Gable wasn't home. No matter. He could sit here and wait. The journey back had been taxing, but he'd managed. The hard part was over. He listened to the loud sounds of the storm and closed his eyes.

Arbor's thoughts drifted in a semidelirium. He didn't worry about anything. Nothing mattered now except rest.

Water ran down his face, but he didn't bother to wipe it away.

All he had to do now was wait until Gable showed up. Gable could call an ambulance. It was only a matter of time.

* * *

Another clap of thunder reverberated through the house, rattling the panes of the windows and jarring small objects on tables.

Jennifer curled on her bed, back pressed against the headboard, legs tucked tightly under her. She had pulled the cover up over her, and in her arms she clutched the lamp base. She had clipped the cord away from the stand and twisted the small shade off as well to make it a less cumbersome weapon.

Sitting here, listening to the storm and quivering with each creak or groan within the house, she began to question her own sanity.

Could any of it be real or was all of it, all of it from the very beginning, just some nightmare from which she couldn't awaken?

She flexed her fingers around the lamp base. Her palm was growing sweaty, but she dared not put the weapon aside. Something could happen at any second. Some other horror.

When she heard the sound of movement downstairs, she wasn't surprised. She'd known something was coming.

She slipped from the bed and moved into the hallway. Maybe she would be able to look over the banister, get an idea of what was coming, and then hide somewhere.

Tiptoeing along the carpet, she paused at the edge of the wall that opened into the stairway area and she peered downward.

He stood in the center of the room, clothes and hair plastered to him. His arms were tense at his sides, fists clenched. He seemed oblivious to the body of Gardner at his feet. And his face was a mask of tortured anger and frustration.

She almost couldn't recognize him as Hamilton. But it was he, the one she'd once loved. He was terrifying to her now, a nightmare, whether this was a dream or not.

She moved back to her bedroom as silently as she could, stuffing the pillow beneath the bedspread to make it look as if she were in bed. It was a lousy trick, but it might buy a few minutes.

Leaving the room, she hurried on down the hallway to the linen closet. Easing the door open, she slipped inside. It was total darkness. She settled into as comfortable a position as she could manage under the shelves, wondering how long she would have to hide here. There would be no way to tell when it was safe.

Her breathing began to grow tense. The darkness was smothering her the way it always had. Perspiration broke out on her forehead and face. She would not be able to stay here indefinitely. She prayed Hamilton would give up quickly.

But she knew he wouldn't. Not until he'd found her.

Images of the night in the old house began to flood into her mind. Her muscles began to tremble. The darkness was taking hold of her. It was as if the darkness were an entity, some incorporeal presence that could embrace her with fear.

She hugged herself, clenching her teeth to keep them from chattering. From time to time she held her breath, listening.

Until she heard Hamilton's footsteps coming up the stairs.

"There are many paths to hell," Alal chided. "All paths away from your Creator, Tyler, lead to my Master. We swallow you, devour your souls."

The people were still swarming around Dareena. Their eyes were vacant, their faces masks—unmoving, waxlike. The groping hands slowly moved over her body.

Gable still couldn't pull free of the those that gripped him, although he continued to struggle. He had little strength left, but he would not submit. There had to be a

405

defense. Alal was evil, was darkness. There had to be some light that would frighten him.

"We haven't spoken of you very much, Mr. Tyler. You think yourself a good man? You think you are righteous? You are a sinner. We can claim you. Why not join me? Accept the power you can command. There are so many things I can promise you. You can be a clairvoyant, a visionary, you can be whatever your whim. Just serve me."

Gable still shook his head, his lips beginning to move slowly in prayer to the God he had been taught in childhood. " 'Blessed Jesus, meek and mild, will you bless a little child?' "

"It's futile, Tyler. Invoking prayers? Where do you think a cry will get you now? Do you expect your Jehovah to reach down and pluck you out of this? You are free, a man of free will. Bask in your freedom. You are free to choose us. Take the power. I offer you the strength of eternal evil. Take it."

One of the attendants twisted Dareena's arm behind her and shoved her to her knees, causing her to cry out as she thudded to the floor.

"You'll watch her ripped apart," Alal said. "And Jennifer will feel the same pain, and perhaps, Tyler, if it suits my mood, I will let you live awhile longer. Five or ten minutes. Just so you can suffer the agony of their deaths."

"Do whatever you want," Gable said.

He wanted to close his eyes and make it all go away, but he didn't struggle now. He just kept his expression defiant.

"Have it your way," Alal said.

And they twisted Dareena's arm tighter and forced her to bend forward. Someone grabbed her hair and yanked it upward and someone else's fist struck her in her stomach. The pain made her cry out.

406

Gable had to close his eyes then. He couldn't stand to look at the expression of pain on her face.

He kept his eyes closed, but he couldn't shut out her cries. They rang out through the hallway, echoing off the ceiling and the tile walls, vacant and hollow cries of torment.

"Think of what hell will taste like," Alal said.

There was another scream. Gable forced himself to raise his eyelids. They still had her arms twisted behind her, and trickles of blood were spilling out both corners of her mouth to run down her chin.

They twisted her again, forcing her down onto her back. One of the attendants stepped forward, putting one foot on each of her shoulders to pin her down while the other man grasped her ankles, splaying them apart.

She began to cry helplessly as hands began to tear at her clothes, ripping the cloth and peeling off her stockings.

"Please. No." She jerked about, trying to dislodge herself from the captors and escape the probing hands that were upon her body.

"Stop it," Gable shouted.

They continued to swarm over her.

"Stop it," she screamed. "Please don't." Some of them were kissing her face and neck now, slobbering on her skin.

Gable tensed his muscles and tried to break free again. It was a futile effort, and for good measure someone slammed a fist into his stomach. He tasted acid bile in his throat as the wind rushed up through his chest.

And there was more laughter, the laughter of a thousand demons feeding on the suffering. There were perhaps thirty or forty people in the hallway, but he realized each body might be serving as the vessel for many demons. That was what the Scripture writer had sought to convey in the account of Christ's encounter with the possessed man—many of them could live in a man. " *'My name is Legion; for we are many.'* "

The gray-haired man was standing over Dareena now, looking down at her with a grin on his face.

"Stop it," Gable demanded. "Azarius. Alal. Stop this. Leave her alone."

Fisher's rotting body pushed through the people and walked over to stand at Gable's side.

"Or what?"

"I'm not the one you have to reckon with," Gable said. "You know what you'll have to face from God."

"He's waited so long to take action, perhaps He never will."

"He will," Gable said. "If you exist, then He exists, and He won't let this last forever."

"Keep going. You'll sound like what your people like to call a Holy Roller. If you can work yourself up enough, we'll get you a revival tent. Tell people how the world is going to come to an end. They love to hear that, too. It gives them something to look forward to."

The old man bent over Dareena, his hands beginning to tear at her skirt and brush along her thighs as the flesh became exposed. She tried to kick at him, but hands closed around her ankles to stay her legs.

She cried out again, her voice shrill with terror.

"Get your fucking hands off of her," Gable shouted.

"So temperamental, Mr. Tyler."

"If I give in to you, will you let her go? Will you get that bastard away from her?"

Dareena opened her eyes. She was choking and sobbing but she shook her head.

"Gable, you can't."

Gable drew several quick, deep breaths. "I can't let them

do that to you. Whatever they do to me, you can go back and warn people."

"Yes," Alal said. "They'll listen well to a half-mad spinster who talks to angels."

"Don't submit to him." Even through her own fear she resisted. She had more courage than Gable had imagined. "They won't listen to me, but you're a writer. There are ways you can warn people."

"He's told me too many things," Gable said. "He never intended to let me walk out of here. Not unless he had control of me."

"Don't do what he wants."

"I don't have a choice."

The hands slipped away from Gable and he straightened and stood facing the corpse.

Slowly the molten hands raised, dripping pus and decayed flesh. One was laid on each of Gable shoulders, and the rotted lips parted. The face began to move toward Gable's.

"The rite of necromancy used to be performed this way," Alal said. "Men believed that if the necromancer bit the tongue from the mouth of a corpse that he had summoned back to life, he would be able to tell the future. Join me, Tyler. Become one with me. Accept this kiss of power and of light."

Tyler wanted to vomit and weep at the same time. Instead, he closed his eyes, awaiting the touch of the morbid flesh. He'd prayed for some alternative, but there had been no answer.

The contact of the pulpy flesh of one hand against his face was cold and wet. The stench touched his nostrils and almost made him wretch as his lips slowly parted.

There was almost total silence in the hallway. None of the other creatures uttered a sound. This moment was something they all seemed to be awaiting, as if with reverence. Only Dareena's quiet sobs broke the stillness.

A soft draft of air began to pass through the corpse's lips. It was icy, like the air from a freezer. It began to move over Gable's lips, tickling his nostrils. He could smell death.

Slowly the corpse's mouth opened wider, letting the tongue move slowly over the blackened teeth. It was swollen, bloated to a purple shade, and a shower of writhing maggots tumbled from it as it extended. Some of the twisting larva remained embedded in the organ. Inching closer to Gable's lips, it began to twitch about as if it had a life of its own. It was like a bloated snake moving toward its prey.

Gable was frozen. At his sides he clenched and unclenched his fists, trying to prepare himself for the ordeal as Alal pressed closer.

When the voice cried out, Gable jumped, startled, but he recognized it. He didn't know where it was coming from or how it got there, but he knew it.

"In the name of God, Father of our Lord Jesus Christ, I command you to depart."

It was Leonard Seaview's deep southern drawl.

Jerking backward, Gable slipped from the corpse's grasp and raised his arm, slamming his forearm against the thing's chin.

The decay had progressed so far that the force tore the head from the shoulders. Rotted flesh and tissue ripped loose as it toppled down to the floor, splattering open like a melon.

Gable didn't look at it. He moved through the bodies to Dareena's side. There was no effort to stop him as he helped her to her feet and draped his jacket around her shoulders.

He put his arm around her to support her as the crowd began to part.

The bedraggled figure of Leonard Seaview passed through the opening. He was unshaven. His clothes were wrinkled

410

and torn. They must have been the ones he had been wearing the night he was taken to the hospital. They'd been wadded in a drawer somewhere, and he'd retrieved them.

His hair was uncombed and it sprouted from his head in oily tangles.

He looked like a crazed holy man, some demented Moses parting a new sea. In his hands, raised above his head, he was carrying a large wooden cross.

Gable moved toward him, but the corpse righted itself and stood between them.

"You think some symbol will stay my minions, preacher?" Since the head was gone, the voice rattled up out of the jagged throat like a growl.

"We are protected by the shield of faith," Seaview said. "You can't claim anything here. Go back to the place you belong. The place that was created for you. This is not your hour. These souls do not belong to you."

"I am here to destroy. I will take you, too."

"You'll take nothing. Not Tyler. Not the girl. You have no right to them. They are a part of the body of Christ, and in his name I command you to be gone."

"Do you think you are some exorcist? You think you can rebuke me with a wooden cross and the dogma of a dead prophet?"

Seaview jerked his head, motioning Gable behind him. Gable obeyed, dragging Dareena with him.

Together they began to inch backward, through the wake of the crowd.

"You cannot stop me," Alal called out.

"Maybe not tonight," Seaview said. "But there will come a time."

"Not before my hour is known."

"But your hour is not now. In the name of God and His only Son Jesus Christ who died for us I rebuke you."

411

"You can't stop me."

"Then come on," Seaview said. "Come and get me." He stopped moving, planting his feet wide apart. He kept the cross raised, gripping it with both hands.

The corpse had been clopping forward one step at a time. It stopped. It hesitated, began to quiver. The ruined muscles twitched and trembled, slowly at first, and then more violently. Seaview continued to move backward along with Gable and Dareena, but they couldn't stop looking forward.

The vibrations of the cadaver increased, rumbling and gushing. Black blood began to spill out through cracks in the darkened skin. Other liquids began to bubble through the chest cavity as it split open. A gurgling sound issued from the mass, continuing until the body burst apart, shattering like a statue being blown into pieces. Masses of flesh and bone spewed about in all directions, splattering onto the floor and walls and some of the people. Moments later a gust of wind that seemed to have the force of a tornado swept down the hallway.

"Down," Seaview shouted, and they dropped together, hitting the floor just as the wind whipped over them at gale force. It tugged at their clothes and hair and chilled them. It felt like the breath of eternity and cut to the bone.

Ripping on down the hallway, it tore extinguishers from the walls, chopped away doorknobs, and shattered glass. The sound was deafening, and it sent the people in the crowd spinning. They toppled into each other, and one by one they began to drop to the floor.

The wind picked up speed, howling as it rushed through the narrow corridor. Seaview, Gable, and Dareena were slowly pushed along the floor, scraps of paper on a vast plane.

They tried to dig their fingers into the tile, fumbling for

handholds of some kind as the force continued to increase. In a few seconds it would be powerful enough to lift them.

It was like being on the face of a sheer cliff, Gable thought, like trying to climb against a hurricane.

He and Seaview gripped each other's arms, pressing Dareena between them. Then they extended their feet to the walls on their respective sides of the hallway, pressing against the wind with as much strength as they could muster, wedging themselves between the walls as a mass.

It was just enough to keep them from being hurled down the corridor and slammed into the wall as the rush continued to pass over them. Gable gritted his teeth. His muscles began to ache, but he couldn't let himself relax. He didn't have much power left, but he tried to blot the pain from his mind as he shoved his feet against the tile, the tread of his sneakers digging in with a slight suction.

If they were picked up, they would be killed, smashed to death. The other people were safe. They were not in its path now. They were the wind's source. That was why they had been dropping, Gable realized. They collapsed as their demonic visitors departed.

The force of the blast was directed at Gable, a final onslaught as Alal abandoned his effort. Or perhaps it was a warning of just how much power he commanded.

The pressure of the blast began to weigh down upon them. Gable could feel the force against his shoulders. It was like having a giant standing on his back.

Pressing his face against the floor, he tried to draw breath. It was almost impossible to fill his lungs. He fought for breath. If he passed out, his grip would relax and the wind would take him.

He willed himself to remain conscious and to dig his feet even harder against the wall. He could feel himself slipping, could feel Dareena being pulled from between him and Seaview. Quickly he readjusted his grip.

Seaview had to adjust also. They turned their faces away from the wind.

"It can't go on forever," he shouted. "Just keep holding."

"I'm trying," Gable yelled back.

And they held, enduring the storm, clinging to each other and praying for the surge of demonic power to stream over.

Finally it ended. There was silence. Gable and Seaview relaxed, rolling onto their backs to draw deep breaths. Dareena rested her head against Gable's shoulder, coughing.

Down the hallway the people in the crowd began to cry, and, pulling themselves to their feet, they began to run up and down the corridor. Some of the attendants tried to corral them, but it was hopeless. It was going to be a while before things settled down. They collided with one another and laughed loudly. No longer possessed of the demons, they still shouted out in madness. The ordeal had touched off a frenzy.

The dark-haired attendant came along the corridor just as Gable was helping Seaview to his feet.

The attendant was confused, shaking his head and rubbing his neck with one arm. "What the hell's going on here? Who are you people?"

"There's no time to explain," Gable said.

"Why not?" Seaview demanded. "What's the problem."

"You've got transportation?"

"Yeah."

"I'll explain on the way."

Seaview led them quickly down the corridor and out into a covered parking area. There were only a few cars, parked in two rows, but he hurried on past them.

414

Near the exit an ambulance was parked, a van-style vehicle with bright orange stripes.

Gable flashed him an inquisitive look.

"Well, it was all I could find," Seaview grumbled. "Where do we have to go?"

"Jennifer is in danger. Azarius wasn't the source of her phone calls. He just let those events take their course and he was using them to his advantage. Somebody else may be trying to harm her right now. He hinted that something has already happened to her."

Seaview handed him the keys. The three of them climbed into the vehicle and Gable fired the engine to life, then looked up at the switches on the ceiling.

"You know how to handle this thing?" Seaview asked.

"I'm a fast learner."

Gable began flicking switches, turning on the flashing lights and the siren.

"We've got them, we might as well take advantage of them," he said.

Gable eased out of the parking place, burning rubber as he started toward the exit.

Walker Vincent appeared out of nowhere. He stood with his feet set wide apart. He was raising the pistol that was clutched in both his hands.

The first shot ripped through the glass just above the rearview mirror on Gable's side of the windshield.

Gable jerked to one side, and the slug thudded into the seat, exited, and plowed into a stretcher in the rear of the vehicle.

Dareena ducked to the floor.

Seaview went down behind the dash.

Gable hit the brake and twisted the wheel, spinning the vehicle around. It skidded sideways for a few feet, the tires smoking as rubber striped along the garage's concrete floor.

The vehicle stopped only a few inches before slamming into Vincent.

Gable twisted the wheel again and headed the van back up the aisle, wheeling around the last car on the row and starting down the second aisle. Another shot rang out. He could hear the blast even over the whine of the siren. It flew wild, shattering one of the flashers on top of the ambulance. The pink glass cascaded down briefly in front of the windshield.

As Gable sped along the aisle, Vincent moved through a space between cars and continued firing. A shot tore through the side of the van near the rear, shattering a case of medical supplies.

Then Vincent was in front of them again, the gun leveled at the windshield.

Gable swerved around him, keeping his head low as he moved past.

Another shot.

This one shattered the mirror on Seaview's door. They had to get out of the garage, Gable thought. In a second something vital was going to get hit.

There was a yellow guardrail over the opening at the end of the second aisle. Ignoring it, he pressed the pedal to the floor and the ambulance tore through the wood, sending splinters in all directions. Vincent was left behind.

The rain hit like a blanket when the van cleared the building. Gable flicked the wipers on quickly for visibility, but a shower of water began to spew in through the hole torn by the bullet. It spattered into his face like the spray over the bow of a ship.

Dareena tore a strip from a sheet in the back and reached forward over Gable's shoulder to stuff the cloth into the opening.

Gable wheeled the vehicle around the outside of the building and along the narrow street. He almost lost control as he spun out onto the highway, but when he straightened the vehicle, he didn't let up on the gas. The rain continued to fall in sheets and the road was slippery. He shoved the pedal down even farther. He was praying he'd get to Jennifer in time.

He was praying he'd be some help against whomever she was up against. The being called Azarius had been vanquished for the moment, but he wasn't beaten.

He was coming up the stairs. She heard him moving, one step at a time. There was a creak when his weight touched the fourth step from the bottom. She knew the sound because that step always creaked.

She heard the footsteps continue on up the stairs, moving slowly until he reached the top. Then he turned down the hallway. She listened to the footfalls progressing along the carpet until finally he stopped just outside the closet. Did he somehow sense that she was inside?

Jennifer closed her eyes to force the images out of her head. Using her sleeve, she wiped some of the perspiration from her face. The closet was stuffy. There was no ventilation and the thin line of light that shone in under the door wasn't much comfort. Even if the room hadn't been stuffy she would have been smothering. She tried to force herself to breathe slowly.

She sat in the corner with her back pressed against the wall and her knees drawn up to her chin. The hems of her old dresses and the coats she wouldn't need until late autumn brushed against her.

Maybe now she wouldn't need them at all. She closed her eyes and began to whisper a prayer to Mary, mother of God. "Pray for us sinners now and the hour of our deaths."

Would this be that hour? Her fingers entwined tightly as she continued to pray.

What a place to die, a closet. So dark, so musty. There was a poem that said the grave was a fine and private place, but it was a lie. This was an anteroom at the mouth of hell.

She jumped when she heard the door opening. The tingling sensation of fear flared through the cells of her skin, and it took several seconds for that feeling to pass after she realized it was not the closet door but the door of the bedroom she'd heard.

She forced her lungs to draw a breath and expel it slowly. He would be making his way down the hallway, opening every door until he found her. It was just a matter of time now.

Unclasping her hands, she returned them to the lamp where it rested against her leg. Gripping it, she held it at the ready.

Straining her ears, she tried to detect Hamilton's footsteps. Perhaps she could crack the door just an inch, peer out, and get an idea of what he was doing.

She dispelled that thought when she heard the latch flip on the next door in the hallway—the bathroom. It wouldn't take any time for him to go through there. Just a glance, then time enough to throw back the shower curtain, and he would know she wasn't there. He'd be on his way to the next door, the last one on the hall before the closet, a sitting room. He'd search that in a few seconds.

She heard the sitting room door open. The latch clicked, and the knob bounced against the wall as the door was thrown open. He must be angry. The search was probably increasing his rage.

Jennifer closed her eyes. She tried to prepare herself, tightening her grip once more, readying the makeshift weapon and hoping that there was a slim possibility he wouldn't see her behind the clothes.

Yet she was ready for him to appear at any second. The doorknob was about to turn. Any tick of the clock might be the last before the door burst open.

But it didn't. She listened for footsteps but she couldn't detect any. She began to pant. Where could he have gone? Was it possible he had missed the door, overlooked the closet at the end of the hall?

More seconds ticked by, more labored breaths, more fluttering heartbeats.

Perhaps he had gone away.

She waited a few more seconds. Or were they minutes? In the darkness, in this cell, there was no way to judge. She forced herself to remain in the corner, poised as still more seconds ticked by.

Still nothing.

He must have gone away. Must have figured she'd left the house. She pushed some of the clothing aside and looked through the darkness at the narrow line of light under the door. It was a straight golden line, not disturbed by any sign of movement or shadow.

Slowly she eased forward.

Nothing happened. The door didn't move. The knob didn't rattle.

She adjusted her weight, rising to a crouch, balancing on the balls of her feet, the lamp over her shoulder.

No sound.

No movement.

The darkness in the closet was like a blanket over her, heavy and thick. Beads of sweat dripped down from her forehead into her eyes, stinging.

She had to get out of there. Surely he was gone. She forced herself to take another breath, another slow one. That eased the tension in her chest briefly, giving her a few more seconds to wait.

But just as quickly the weight of the darkness returned. Trembling, she reached up for the knob. The metal was cool to her touch. Shutting her eyes for a moment, she braced herself, then threw the latch and eased the door open just a crack.

There was just enough space to let her peer into the hallway. All of the doors were open, but Hamilton wasn't in sight. Had he gone back downstairs or was he still looking around in one of the rooms?

It didn't matter, she decided. She'd have an element of surprise either way. She could run past the rooms, pause at the top of the stairs to see if he was in sight below her, and then she could make another decision—either hide up here or make a beeline for the front door. Outside she could lose herself in the darkness and the storm. It wasn't the most appealing thought in the world, but it was the best one available. Staying here was death. The storm was terrible, but she wasn't going to let her phobia cost her her life.

She pushed the door open a little farther, rising slightly, letting her legs straighten out a bit. That eased some of the tension in her muscles.

She continued to look down the hall. He wasn't at the top of the stairs, wasn't visible in the doorways of the rooms.

She shoved the door completely open and spun around to face Hamilton standing at the end of the hall. She wasn't quick enough.

His fist slammed into the side of her face before she could react. The blow jerked her head to the side. The pain was worse than she could have imagined. Tears filled her eyes and she lost her balance.

She stumbled about but somehow maintained her footing, and she still had the lamp ready.

She swung it in a broad arc in front of her, missing Hamilton by several inches but at least keeping him at bay.

He moved all the way to the end of the hallway, pressing his back against the wall. He carried no weapon, but he clenched his fists at his sides, and in his eyes there was an intense anger.

Jennifer kept swinging the lamp in front of her, trying to prevent him from moving forward, but he watched the movement and managed to calculate the pattern.

Dodging past the weapon, he grabbed for her, missing her only by inches as she pulled back. She managed to strike a glancing blow across his shoulder. He twisted away from her next swing and balanced himself for a pounce. It was now Jennifer whose back was to the hallway's end, but she didn't back up.

She stood facing him, the lamp again drawn back over her shoulder like a baseball bat.

"You bitch," he muttered. "You were a bitch then and you're still a bitch."

"What do you want, Ham?"

"Bitches have to be punished."

"That's so long in the past."

"Nothing is ever over. I have to punish you again. And then Julia. I thought she was different, but she's like all of you. I had to come back to you first because it's your fault."

"What's my fault?"

"The policeman came after me because of you. They said you were being threatened. They were going to take me in. That's your fault. And Julia wasn't there when I needed her. All your fault."

He wasn't making sense. He seemed to be rambling. "If you hadn't come back after me, the police would never have been called," Jennifer said.

"I had to come here tonight."

"But before. Why did you make those calls?"

"I never called you."

He lunged, again managing to duck under the swing of the lamp. He struck Jennifer hard with the force of his weight, his arms encircling her waist as they thudded back to the wall and then tumbled to the floor.

The lamp slipped from her fingers and went rolling down the hall, out of her reach.

She started to kick her legs violently as he grabbed her wrists. His weight was on top of her and she couldn't struggle free.

She screamed as he pinned her hands down and bucked her weight upward at a moment when he was trying to adjust himself. He was off guard and he lost his hold, enabling Jennifer to scramble away. She lunged for the lamp, but he caught her ankle. He was starting to get a grip on her calf when she slammed her foot into his face. She felt his nose flatten under her sole. Glancing back, she saw a crimson spray coming through his nostrils.

His hands released her and reached to his face, fumbling to stop the bleeding.

Jennifer made it to the spot where the lamp rested. Lifting it, she turned and swung it hard, catching Hamilton in the ribs.

The sound of the contact was empty and sickening, and he crumpled to his knees.

Jumping back to avoid his grasp, Jennifer kept the lamp ready. But he didn't look at her. One hand pressed against his nose and the other gripped his side where the lamp had struck.

He whimpered slightly.

Then, without warning, he was on his feet and charging her. She tried to connect with another blow, but he hit too quickly, throwing his weight into her again, this time with even more force than before. Her breath rushed out of her.

She'd been hit like a football quarterback being sacked. She rolled to the floor, unable to breathe. Involuntarily her legs curled up against her. Her eyes closed. She was going to pass out; she could feel it coming. There were black spots in front of her, and they started to get bigger, merging into one.

And he was standing there, standing over her, she could just make that out, could see him bending toward her, bending slowly. Sweat poured off his face. Blood dripped from his nose and down his chin. He drew closer, reached forward. . . .

And she rolled again, toward him. With all the strength she had left she slammed the base of the lamp into his face, catching him just above his left cheek.

He cried out and staggered away from her. His face was covered in blood now, a bright red mask. He had to put one hand against the wall to steady himself, and when he moved, a bloody palm print remained.

Jennifer dragged herself to her feet. She couldn't stand without wobbling, but she planted her feet and tried to keep her balance.

Hamilton half turned toward her, and she shoved the lamp forward like a bayonet into his stomach. He doubled over, but she shoved it forward again, driving it deep into his muscles.

He twisted about on his feet, trying to place them properly without success. He moved several feet away from her before he righted himself.

The next step was back in her direction, his left hand stretched out in front of him, and he got a handful of her hair, yanking it downward so that her face was tugged toward the floor.

In the same instant he brought his knee up, catching her on the chin. The shock waves rumbled through her head and neck. She tasted blood, then realized her nose was bleeding and there was a warm trickle from her lips.

He tried to get her with his fist, but she ducked it, staggering into him. That moved them back against the wall, entangled again. He couldn't get his hands to her throat, so he wrapped one arm around her neck. It didn't close over her windpipe, but he started twisting. The lamp slipped from her fingers.

It was going to end. It was going to be over, but she wouldn't survive. She sagged slightly, her weight supported by his grasp.

He began to chuckle, preparing to tense the muscles in his arm across her throat.

She sagged a little farther, her weight dangling from his arm now. He relaxed just slightly.

She took a quick breath and shot her weight upward again, driving her knee up into his groin.

He released her, whirling backward.

Jennifer started for the stairway. She couldn't move fast now, had to have the wall for support, but she pushed forward, dragging her feet along.

She'd taken only a few steps when he lunged after her, trying to get some kind of grip on her. She moved into him, pressing against him. There was no force in the motion, but he wasn't prepared for it. She grabbed handfuls of his shirt, pulling him toward her.

They spun around twice, building momentum, and then she let go, pushing him backward.

They were at the top of the stairs now, and he crashed into the railing. It remained standing, but his weight pushed him over. The sound of his body shattering when it hit the floor was horrible.

Jennifer didn't look at anything. She just pressed her back against the wall and sank down to a sitting position on the floor.

The spots clouded not only her vision now but her brain. The pain throbbed through her nervous system. She breathed slowly, preparing to collapse. She couldn't do any more.

She barely managed to maintain consciousness, and was about to drift off into oblivion when she heard the stair creak.

When she shook her head to clear her brain, the spots parted just enough for her to see Julia standing at the top of the stairs.

She didn't know Julia very well, and remembered her only slightly.

She couldn't imagine why Julia would be carrying a knife, especially such a big one.

Stalled cars were scattered along the shoulder of the road. The constant rain had formed pools across the highway in several low spots. In other places the standing water made the roadway slippery and dangerous.

When the van sped through the puddles, the spray from the tires splashed up against the sides of the vehicle, sometimes even reaching to the windows.

Gable was hunched over, peering out into the darkness as he drove, his fingers curled tightly around the ridges in the steering wheel.

He was conscious of the ticking of his watch. He wished there were some way to stop the seconds from dying, but they were continuously slaughtered by the Timex second hand, giving themselves up willingly to its blade.

"We're getting closer," Seaview said.

"I don't know if we can be there in time," Gable said. "That wind, it was the demons leaving the bodies. Does that mean they went to Jennifer's place?"

"Maybe not. Not if Alal was just manipulating events. If he'd set something into motion, it was probably capable of flowing on its own. I don't know what we're going to be up against, but it's probably something that will go on whether or not Alal is there to oversee it."

The tires hit a slick spot on the road and began to skid, sloshing the ambulance about.

The vehicle hydroplaned along for several feet with Gable fighting the wheel more than he knew he should. Finally he managed to steady it just as he came upon the rear of a pickup truck.

It was an old International, and only one taillight was aglow. The driver was puttering along, moving slowly to compensate for the rain.

They were on their way into a curve, so it wasn't safe to pass. As soon as the two vehicles moved around the turn, Gable realized there was still another twist in the road that would prevent passing.

The truck's driver seemed reluctant to pull off onto the shoulder even though the ambulance lights were still flashing. Gable started to pass, then saw oncoming headlights.

He eased up on the gas and flexed his fingers impatiently around the steering wheel.

"This is an ambulance," he said. "Don't people know the traffic laws in this town?"

Gable focused his attention on the road just in time to see the International turn slightly to the left and then jerk to a stop, blocking the lane.

"What is this?" Gable muttered.

Seaview grabbed his arm.

"Don't stop. Something's wrong."

The headlights from the oncoming car were in sight, but Gable swerved into the other lane. For a split second he was on a collision course with the approaching lights, but he shoved the wheel hard to take him back into the right lane in front of the pickup.

The grille of the ambulance avoided the front of the oncoming care only by inches. It was a white sedan, and it skidded, but it didn't seem that the driver was making any effort to avoid an accident.

Gable moved into the curve, pressing the gas to pick up speed. Behind them, the white car spun around and started to pursue.

"They're trying to stop us," he said.

"Now you know where the demons went," Seaview said. "In this weather traffic accidents can be explained away. They'll do what they have to."

"Gremlins," Gable said. "A way of explaining mechanical malfunctions. He said all our legends were tied to his kind. A devil by any other name."

"They can manipulate many forces. We've got to hurry," the professor said. "If Alal is trying to stop you, that means he doesn't want you to get to Jennifer. There's still time to help her."

"Grab something and hang on," Gable said.

He slammed the brakes on, steadying himself against the wheel. The ambulance skidded slightly before coming to a complete stop.

"What are you doing?" Dareena screamed. She was looking out the rear window and could see the headlights barreling forward.

"Just hold on," Gable shouted.

The white car crashed into the van's rear bumper, jolting the vehicle forward.

Gable bounced forward, but his grip on the wheel pre-

427

vented him from going through the windshield. Seaview and Dareena were tossed about the van's interior but escaped injury. The rear doors crumpled inward but didn't collapse.

Gable hit the gas, leaving the sedan stalled behind them. The van fishtailed across the slick highway, but he kept it between the ditches and headed on into the night.

Tears rolled down Julia's cheeks, discernible even though her face was spattered with rain and her hair hung in limp strands, dripping about her face.

She stood frozen at the top of the stairs, dressed all in black, the eldritch hatred in her eyes gleaming through the tears.

Jennifer was on the verge of collapse, too feeble to run anymore. She stood, breathing heavily, one hand against the wall to steady herself and keep from falling.

"What do you want?" she asked, drawing heavy breaths through her mouth.

Julia tilted her head forward slightly. "You. Your life."

"Why?" Her heart was raging. The blood was pounding in her ears.

"Because after the priest, you're next." It was the coarse voice, the voice on the telephone that night, that horrible gravel sound.

"I don't understand," Jennifer said.

"It was for him. Hamilton. I loved him, and he was going to be mine. Just mine. I wasn't going to let anything take him away from me."

"But why kill people?"

"He had his weaknesses. He did things. If people knew about him, we might have been separated."

"You're responsible for all the killings?"

"You are!" Julia shouted. "It started with you when he was just becoming a man. You were there when he was vulnerable, and he succumbed to the temptation. I've been watching you. You're so beautiful, so slender and perfect." Her tone was mocking. "You were there, enticing him." She took in brisk, short breaths, her brow furrowed into a frown.

"But why kill Father Conzenza?" Jennifer's own tears were beginning to spill for her eyes and trickle down her cheeks.

"He was your priest. You would have confessed to him back then. He would have known about what happened between you and Hamilton, and he was about to leave the priesthood. It wouldn't have been a secret anymore to him. He could have told people what happened. Conzenza had to die. He had to be silenced."

"No." Jennifer began to weep. "I never told anyone what happened. I didn't even remember it until tonight. I had shut it all out of my mind. I never confessed it. It was so horrible I blacked it out." She put her hands on her face, fighting the sobs.

"That doesn't matter now, does it?" Julia screeched. "He's dead. After all I did to protect him." Her voice continued to rise, losing all vestiges of the gravel sound. Jennifer had never heard a banshee, but the sound Julia was making fit her mental image of what such a cry must be like.

"I'll make you pay. You little whore. You dirty little whore."

Julia started to move forward in slow, deliberate steps, the knife raised, The blade quivering slightly in her grasp. Her eyes narrowed to slits.

"You killed others?" Jennifer asked, trying to delay an

429

attack until she could think of some way to escape. She couldn't fight again. There was no way her body would endure another battle.

"The slut at the hotel, because he broke down with her, too. His weakness, his one weakness," Julia screamed. "She shouldn't have led him on."

"The other man?"

"Salem. He was blackmailing Hamilton's father. He wanted to blackmail me. He came to me and told me things Hamilton had done. I wouldn't let him push me. I couldn't. I had to protect Hamilton. He was the only thing that mattered to me. We were going to be together. It was going to be so perfect."

She turned her face away from Jennifer, and her voice softened as her thoughts drifted. She stared into nothingness, her eyes seeing some faraway dream.

"Our wedding was going to be so wonderful. I had the most beautiful dress picked out. We would have been so happy." She looked up again, suddenly searching Jennifer's eyes for understanding. "I couldn't let anything stand in the way of that. It's all I've ever wanted."

Jennifer looked at her without changing expression, staring coldly. "You're as sick as he was."

"No."

"What led to this? Was it finding out someone you loved had such dark secrets?"

"No. Just protecting him. Protecting myself." She'd convinced herself of that.

She moved forward, lashing out with the knife. Jennifer swung her arm up in reflex as the weapon arched toward her. The blade sliced through the sleeve of her gown, the metal splitting the skin of her arm. It was not a deep wound, but it stung, and blood began to soak through her sleeve.

Jennifer dropped back against the wall. Everything was spinning.

Julia came after her, slashing the knife out in front of her in a wide arc.

Gable bounced the van around the corner of the street in front of his house and sped along, no longer trying to keep control of the vehicle. The rear wheels skidded from side to side as the ambulance proceeded up the pavement. The passengers inside were tossed about even as they gripped whatever they could for support.

With the pedal pressed almost to the floor, Gable urged the vehicle forward. When he reached Jennifer's place he jerked the wheel hard, plowing the ambulance across the sidewalk and through the soggy lawn until the tires sank into the wet ground. Then he flung open the door and jumped from the vehicle to run across the grass without looking back. The siren continued to whine, and the flashing lights splattered erratic patterns of color onto the house.

He was up the front steps in a few seconds and tearing through the front door.

The carnage in the front room struck him like a blow to his heart. The sight of death was hideous and frightening— the mangled bodies like an opaque scene from a long-ago nightmare.

For a heartbeat he did nothing.

"Jennifer," he screamed when he could react.

Her reply was a cry of terror from the second floor. He looked up to see her struggling against Julia. The dark woman was clutching a handful of Jennifer's hair and slashing at her with the blade. Jennifer was on the floor near the wall, kicking and dodging the knife as well as she could. Her clothes were bloody from where the knife had already slashed her several times. Because of the struggle the strikes hadn't been deep enough to kill.

Gable jumped over Gardner's body and headed up the stairs. He reached the top just in time to see Julia raise the knife, preparing to plunge it down into Jennifer's body.

Jennifer was still struggling, but she was battered and exhausted.

Gable shouted, causing them both to freeze in mid-motion. Julia spun toward him. She let Jennifer's hair slide from her grasp and took a step away from the girl.

Gable steadied himself, planting his feet slightly apart for balance. She was going to rush him, and the blade looked nasty, crimson on silver.

He wasn't sure he could keep her from driving it into him. He had visions of it plunging into his abdomen up to the shaft.

"You can put that down," he suggested, extending his hand toward Julia. "We can work this out."

Julia's lips peeled back, revealing her teeth. "Everything is going wrong."

"Right. It's all going wrong. We'll settle it. Nobody else has to get hurt."

"Someone has to pay." Her whole body was trembling, and fresh tears were pouring down her cheeks.

He drew a quick breath just as she launched forward, screaming as she ran toward him. Light flashed off the knife blade as she lunged, raising it into the air.

Gable's arms shot out in front of him as he attempted to get a grip on her wrists. He missed and she slashed the knife down onto his left shoulder, cutting through his shirt and dragging the blade point down through his skin.

The gash opened muscle and blood vessels. Blood began to pulse down his arm, painting his hand scarlet.

He staggered, and her weight crashed into him. She was

trying to lift the knife again when he caught her arm. Trying to twist free, she shifted her weight, dragging them over the top stair.

Gable tried to find a footing, but it was futile. They tumbled down the stairs, the blade waving about as they rolled over the steps. When they finally hit the floor, the weapon bounced from her hand, and she went scrambling for it.

Gable caught her ankle with his right hand and yanked her backward, then he threw himself on top of her, using his weight to hold her down. His injured arm flopped uselessly at his side.

She kicked and screamed, and he continued to press down on her, but she was too strong for him. She had the knife again. She turned on him. He was on his feet but not ready. He moved backward, tugging his belt off.

As she raised the knife, he began to swing the belt around in a circle. If she came toward him, she risked being struck by the buckle. It wouldn't do that much damage, but it made her hesitate and flinch, and when she did, Gable launched himself, dodging the blade and crashing into her. He drove his right shoulder into her breastbone.

She went down hard, and he hit her on the chin with his fist. It jarred his arm and slammed her head back against the floor. He lifted the belt, preparing to use it to bind her hands, but she drove her knee suddenly up into his side, slamming him hard just above a kidney. A wave of nausea hit him, and he rolled off her, landing on his side and then plopping onto his back. He was still losing blood, and his head began to swim.

Rising, she started toward him, holding the knife high over her head. With the last of his strength he raised his foot and stomped it into her stomach. When she doubled over he hopped up onto one knee and drove his right fist up into her face once again. It was as hard a blow as he could deliver. It sent her reeling, and he got to his feet, ready to hit her again if necessary.

But she went down, falling onto her face. She didn't move.

He picked up his belt and headed toward her, preparing to use it to bind her hands.

Just as he reached her a blow struck him between his shoulder blades. He fell to the floor, gasping for air as he looked for his attacker. There was nothing there.

Still on the floor, he turned his face back toward Julia's form.

There was a blaze, brighter than lightning. It seared his eyes, burning bright colors that clouded his vision.

He blinked several times until he could see Julia again.

For a moment she lay unmoving, but then her eyes fluttered open, and the lips suddenly curled into a hideous grin.

Her face contorted, taking on a shape that stretched the skin and remolded the muscles. The veins in her temples and across her forehead began to bulge. The eyes rolled back in the sockets, glaring white.

Unbelievably the canine teeth began to grow, becoming more pointed. The fingers twisted into claws.

"Welcome, Tyler." The voice was distorted, deep and slow. It was an inhuman tone.

The girl's body rose into a crouching position, as if preparing to pounce.

Gable froze.

"You thought you had won?" Alal asked. "Did you forget that I could come and go at will? Or that I could occupy any person not resisting me? You rushed to get here, only to die. This child has never resisted. My minions have used her frequently for our purposes, given her strength to act. I can use this body now to rip you apart, like a vampire

434

from another of your legends." The fingernails grew even longer, daggers.

"Leave here," Gable said as he pulled himself up. "You've caused enough pain."

"Not for you. Not yet."

Julia's body pulled itself from the floor, but looking into the eyes, Gable could detect no vestige of her consciousness. Alal was totally in control.

The eyes began to glow. A small orange dot in her pupils blossomed outward.

"I can finish you," Alal said. "Amid all this madness no one would ever know. They would just think your murder was the product of the girl's twisted mind."

"Someone will know something isn't right."

Alal laughed. "What will they find if they investigate? There will be no trace of me. It will all look like the madness of individuals. Hamilton has a history of antisocial behavior. He and the girl have been acting the last few days at my direction without being aware of it. He has done his deeds with a little encouragement from my brothers, and she has followed behind him, trying to clean up what he has done in order to protect their relationship. At my brothers' urging, of course. Since Jennifer was in Hamilton's past, we directed Julia toward her. We could see far enough into the future to determine that you would be drawn to Dareena.

"As fate would have it, Jennifer's trouble was what sent you to Dareena. It seems even demons cannot master fate. Our first plan to interest you in Jennifer because she was in danger and thus avert your meeting with Dareena did not work, but it was successful in a way. It gave a tool to use against you. You care about the one called Jennifer. Perhaps you will enjoy watching her die."

Gable looked around the room. There were no weapons

435

visible. He was too far from the door or the window to escape.

"I can take you as well," Alal said. "I can drag you into the pits of flame that I showed you. There you will watch the flesh ripped from her bones. You have one choice. Join me willingly. I can take your soul now, or you can bow to me and I will allow you to reign beside me with my master. Turn to me. This world will be ours."

"It's a lie," Seaview said from the doorway, where he had just entered.

"He is in sin," Alal said. "I can destroy him."

"You cannot," Seaview said, shaking his head. "There is grace to redeem him."

"You speak of myth and legend. You have no savior. We killed your redeemer once."

"It was not final," Seaview said. "You have no power here. Leave us."

"You have not the faith to force me away again."

"You fled earlier."

"Only to implement the remainder of my plan."

"Or because you are bound, your power limited?" Seaview asked.

"No. That is not true."

"We're not alone," Seaview said. He stepped into the room, followed by Dareena and Arbor, who was leaning against her for support.

Arbor peered into the glowing eyes of Alal. His weariness was visible in his face, but he did not flinch.

"He is an unbeliever," Alal said.

"Until your actions convince him otherwise. New faith, Alal, Azarius, or whoever you want to be. Faith and desire for goodness. You cannot defeat that. All your evils, all your hatreds, cannot defeat that. Man is the image of God. All your attempts to corrupt that have failed. You thought you

436

succeeded with the first corruption. You thought you succeeded when you saw the death of Christ and a thousand other times. Yet all your bombs and false doctrines and lies do not succeed. You take skirmishes and claim you are winning the war. Instead, you're already defeated.''

"I'll see your grave, Seaview, purveyor of lost faith. I'll claim your soul as well.''

"You'll claim nothing," Gable said. "We command you to be gone. Your place is in the abyss. With your master.''

Both of the body's arms lifted. The knife was still poised in the air in preparation for striking, but the body was trembling.

"You can harm no one here," Seaview whispered.

The eyes darted from face to face, studying the expressions.

Gable's: Defiant.

Seaview's: Stoic.

Arbor's: Unafraid.

The strength found in fear and confusion was not available.

The demon turned to Dareena. The glow in the eyes was fading.

"My love, I need you," the voice whispered. "Join with me.''

"You're not love," Dareena said. "You're hatred. You can't own me. I'm free of you.''

"Flee," Seaview said. "You have nothing here." He moved closer to Dareena and Arbor, and they edged over to stand beside Gable.

"We are the children of God. Wherever two or more are gathered in His name, He will be there also," Seaview said. "You are lost. Be gone. In the name of one you say is dead, I command it. In the name of faith and goodness, I command it. In the name of Our Father I command it.''

437

The body charged, raising the knife and slashing wildly.

Arbor stepped forward, sidestepping the charge and grabbing the body from behind. Even though he had been on the edge of exhaustion, he found a new surge of energy which let him face the monster.

The demon's strength began to twist the muscles about in Julia's arm in an attempt to gain freedom.

Adjusting his footing, Arbor flung the possessed form onto the floor.

The mouth opened widely, and a sound of utter rage that came from the pits of hell rumbled into the air. Then the girl rolled silently onto the floor.

The windows that were not yet broken shattered.

Items on tables began to fly through the air.

Furniture overturned.

A whirlwind with a force greater than they had endured earlier swept through the room. The furniture was lifted upward, spinning to the ceiling, where it slammed into the plaster and crumbled it.

Heavy chunks crashed downward. The group had to dodge and duck to avoid the bombs.

Gable and Arbor did their best to shelter the others. Jennifer had run down the stairs and joined them at the center of the room.

They clung to each other, intertwining their arms and holding on.

As the whirlwind continued, Gable felt razorlike slashes cut into his back. His injured arm was throbbing. He gritted his teeth against the new pain.

"What the hell is that?" Arbor called. He was apparently feeling the same thing.

"The same sort of attack that was launched on the professor," Gable said. "He's not in a physical form any longer, but he's still making swipes at us."

More furniture was hurled about. Something hit a beam in the ceiling a short distance from the huddle of bodies. When the beam snapped, a large portion of the ceiling collapsed, raining down more plaster and fragments of support braces.

"We've got to get out of here," Arbor said. "I'll get the girl."

Gable nodded, and while Arbor was lifting Julia into his arms, Gable led Jennifer and Dareena toward the door with Seaview just behind him. More plaster fell, then more beams. Insulation showered down.

Inches from the door, Gable felt a slashing claw bite into his side. He jumped back a few inches, avoiding the cut.

"Faith, Gable. Faith," Seaview shouted.

Gable looped his arms around his charges. Together they staggered onto the lawn and collapsed. The touch of the dew was cool against their flesh.

Seconds ticked away with no sign of Arbor. The crash of debris continued inside.

"I've got to go back in," Gable said.

"You'll be killed," Jennifer said.

"I've got to chance it."

He moved back through the doorway and found Arbor with Julia in his arms trying to dodge his way through falling rubble. A piece of wood had cut a gash across the detective's forehead, causing blood to run down into his eyes, half blinding him.

Charging toward him, Gable grabbed his sleeve and led him through the mess. More things hammered down on them, and the creaking of the upper floor reached a crescendo.

"It's coming down," Arbor called.

They ran through the doorway, rolling across the porch

z
439

and tumbling onto the grass just as the entire ceiling gave, dumping everything downward.

The crash was like an explosion, and dust and other particles gusted out through the windows and doorways.

The frame and the roof of the structure remained, but it was only an empty hull.

The wind passed in a few seconds, leaving them standing quietly on the lawn.

They looked at each other in silence, unable to speak.

Motionless, Julia rested on the ground.

Jennifer curled against Gable's side. "Is it over?" she asked.

"For now," he whispered. "Yes."

"Get me out of here. I'm going insane."

"No. It'll be all right."

Seaview had helped Arbor over to a seat under a tree.

"Glad you could make it," Gable said. "I think your case is solved."

Jennifer rested against Gable's side. "I can tell you what happened with Hamilton," she murmured. "Later. Just get me away from here. There's been too much. It's all too much."

Arbor nodded. "Get us all the hell away from here. We'll take statements in the morning. If anybody really knows what's happening, I'll listen. But don't expect me to believe it."

"You'll believe it all in time," Seaview said. "You've already begun. Where do you think you found the strength to do what you just did?"

"I couldn't tell you."

Seaview got a length of bandage from the ambulance and pressed it against Gable's wound.

The investigator and the writer looked at each other for a moment.

EPILOGUE

The day was one of sunshine and blue skies, the only clouds white tufts of cotton billowing across the horizon.

Gable steered with his good arm, tooling along the highway to Penn's Ferry as he listened to soft tunes on the radio.

He was clean shaven, and except for the circles under his eyes, he looked fresh and alert.

He found Seaview in his office. A couple of assistants were helping the professor pile his books into cardboard boxes.

When Gable entered, Seaview shooed the girls away. He nodded toward one of the boxes and Gable had a seat, careful not to move his left arm too much. It was in a sling, and he didn't want to pull out the stitches.

"Where are you going?" he asked.

Seaview shrugged. "I don't know yet. All I know is that there are things I have to do."

"What? You going to start seeking out brush arbor revivals?" Gable asked, referring to old style Pentecostal meetings which were held under arbors woven from tree branches.

"They don't have revivals under brush arbors anymore. They have air-conditioned churches now. I'm not looking for anything that severe, but I need to do something for the Lord."

"Is it that cut and dried?"

"What else can we do? Does anything else matter?"

"If Jesus rose from the dead like he said he did, there's nothing for you to do but drop everything and follow him. Isn't that how the quote goes? If you don't, then you might as well do the best with the time you got left. Do some meanness to somebody or whatever."

"What's that from again?"

"*A Good Man Is Hard to Find.* Flannery O'Conner."

"I guess it's true. Azarius isn't dead, Tyler. He'll be back. And others like him. You'd do well to remember that and prepare yourself. They're looking for something. Chaos, but also more. They wanted you, Gable. They wanted to use you."

"For what?"

"More earthly power. Ways to strike back at God. They'll keep looking."

"For power?"

Seaview shook his head, and one corner of his mouth curled up in a grim smile. "Someone who'll say yes. They found plenty of help. Hamilton, Julia. Walker Vincent. What a mess, all engineered in differing degrees for the purpose of evil. Vincent was the most completely controlled. Hamilton and Julia were not aware that something was controlling their actions, but from what I can tell, the fallen ones did the same thing with Vincent, utilized his own desire to impel him."

Gable nodded.

"It'll come for you," the professor said. "What you're beginning to feel intellectually will grow deeper. Faith, my boy." He smiled.

Gable nodded again, watching Seaview turn to pick up a few more books.

"What I wonder about," Gable said, "is where the other angels were. The good angels. In the Apocrypha Raphael helped Tobias."

"Gable, Azarius intended to manipulate your path so that you would never free Dareena from his influence. Yet you were drawn to her anyway. Did you ever stop to think something might have directed your path? By the grace of God we defeated the effort of destruction."

"Oh," Gable said.

"How is Jennifer?" the professor asked.

"She's home. Her folks want her to stay, but she's bucking to get out. I think a lot of things cleared up for her. Things she'd been bottling up. I really thing she can straighten herself now."

Seaview nodded. "Emancipation from her past."

"They have Julia in the institution for evaluation. Things have settled down over there now. They're saying there was hysteria the night of the storm."

Seaview piled some paperbacks into a box and closed the lid. He showed no surprise.

"The girl, what triggered her?"

"Salem, the man who was killed on the street. She had her whole life planned out—big wedding, Junior League activities, the country club. And she really loved Hamilton, I believe. She wanted to protect him. I guess she couldn't accept his being sick, so she turned the emotion inside out, blamed everyone else—Jennifer for what happened years ago, Salem, the priest, the waitress. All that worked perfectly for Azarius. Once she started, it got easier and easier. She wrote Azarius on the wall of the church because she thought she would avert blame from herself. She never knew what she was really doing, playing another part of Azarius's game."

"Why did he let her write the name? I thought everything he did was secret."

"It was just a touch of her own. Remember, she acted at his urging, but the seeds for it all were in her personality to begin

445

with. Just like with Hamilton. They were disturbed people at the outset. The fallen angels just pushed them over the edge.

"Julia followed Jennifer for days. She was waiting outside the house for an opportunity to kill Jennifer when Hamilton went in. Azarius had his bases covered. It all started before the first phone call was made. He wanted me to become concerned with protecting Jennifer so I would never meet Dareena."

"Fallen angels aren't omnipotent. They can't see everything."

"It will take us all a while to forget it."

Seaview picked up a few more books. "Have you spoken to Dareena?"

"She's working. Waiting tables for now, but she's applying for a job at the library. Her grandmother broke down and let her out of the house. I think Dareena stood her ground a little more firmly this time."

"What about the lawyer?"

Gable rubbed his forehead. "They found him. He was in his apartment."

"How was he?"

"They called it an accidental hanging."

"I see." Seaview placed another book in one of the boxes. "You're going to write about all this?"

Gable looked at the floor, nodding slowly. "I guess that's why Azarius was afraid of me."

"I'll keep you in my prayers."

"You take care, too," the writer said.

They shook hands, and Gable walked from the office, heading downstairs with uncertainty. He didn't really know where he was going.

CRITICALLY ACCLAIMED MYSTERIES
FROM ED MCBAIN AND PINNACLE BOOKS!

BEAUTY AND THE BEAST   (17-134, $3.95)
When a voluptuous beauty is found dead, her body bound with
coat hangers and burned to a crisp, it is up to lawyer Matthew
Hope to wade through the morass of lies, corruption and sexual
perversion to get to the shocking truth! The world-renowned author of over fifty acclaimed mystery novels is back—with a
vengeance.

"A REAL CORKER . . . A DEFINITE PAGE-TURNER."
— USA TODAY
"HIS BEST YET."
— THE DETROIT NEWS
"A TIGHTLY STRUCTURED, ABSORBING MYSTERY"
— THE NEW YORK TIMES

JACK & THE BEANSTALK   (17-083, $3.95)
Jack McKinney is dead, stabbed fourteen times, and thirty-six
thousand dollars in cash is missing. West Florida attorney Matthew Hope's questions are unearthing some long-buried pasts, a
second dead body, and some gorgeous suspects. Florida's getting
hotter by deadly degrees—as Hope bets it all against a scared
killer with nothing left to lose!

"ED MCBAIN HAS ANOTHER WINNER."
— THE SAN DIEGO UNION
"A CRACKING GOOD READ . . . SOLID, SUSPENSEFUL,
SWIFTLY-PACED"
— PITTSBURGH POST-GAZETTE

*Available wherever paperbacks are sold, or order direct from the
Publisher. Send cover price plus 50¢ per copy for mailing and
handling to Pinnacle Books, Dept.17-229, 475 Park Avenue
South, New York, N.Y. 10016. Residents of New York, New Jer-
sey and Pennsylvania must include sales tax. DO NOT SEND
CASH.*